EROTICA EXOTICA

TALES OF SEX, MAGIC, AND THE SUPERNATURAL

Visit us at www.boldstrokesbooks.com

EROTICA EXOTICA

TALES OF SEX, MAGIC, AND THE SUPERNATURAL

edited by

Richard Labonté

A Division of Bold Strokes Books

2011

EROTICA EXOTICA: TALES OF SEX, MAGIC, AND
THE SUPERNATURAL
© 2011 BY BOLD STROKES BOOKS. ALL RIGHTS RESERVED.

ISBN 13: 978-1-60282-570-3

THIS TRADE PAPERBACK ORIGINAL IS PUBLISHED BY
BOLD STROKES BOOKS, INC.
P.O. BOX 249
VALLEY FALLS, NY 12185

FIRST EDITION: OCTOBER 2011

CREDITS
EDITORS: RICHARD LABONTÉ AND STACIA SEAMAN
PRODUCTION DESIGN: STACIA SEAMAN
COVER DESIGN BY SHERI (GRAPHICARTIST2020@HOTMAIL.COM)

For Asa, for twenty years…
of dogs, trucks, love, and magic

CONTENTS

INTRODUCTION: MAGIC UNDER THE SHEETS

Vampires and voodoo, bodybuilders and werewolves, magicians and the walking dead, shape-shifters and priests, ghosts and nightmares, lovers resurrected from the afterlife, beautiful men lured to a haunted death—even monsters slithering from the bottom of the toilet bowl: the supernatural and the sexual come together horrifically and terrifically in this collection of the eerie and the erotic.

The fourteen stories here are linked less by thematic type—jock, bear, daddy, twink, hustler, frat boy, muscle man, beautiful boy, S/M master, porn star, whatever—and more by the wide-ranging, otherwordly imaginations of their authors. The anthology was inspired by a slew of short stories submitted my way for assorted other collections—stories that, despite their quality, weren't quite thematically right for the sexually defined collections I was then assembling.

Don't get me wrong: editing an anthology focusing on one look, one fetish, one sexual act, even one body part, has its thrills. We readers—and editors—choose to be turned on by print rather than by pictures, and two-hundred-plus pages of the kind of sex that pushes the best of our buttons, be they buff boys or tickled toes or rough sex or first dates, can be everything from a welcome diversion to a functional companion.

But challenging the universe of writers of queer erotica to incorporate settings and elements of myth, magic, horror, and the supernatural—of the "other"—into their arousing storytelling resulted in a collection that is certainly exotic, unquestionably erotic, and exuberantly eclectic. Some of the characters may be muscle men—but they're muscle men whose bulging biceps have a sinister source. Some of the characters may be men in love—but they're men in love whose idyllic lives are going to be overturned by supernatural forces. Some of the characters may be homophobic street hustlers—but happy homos are destined to take over their chiseled, youthful bodies. And some of the characters may be new lovers reveling in an outdoor adventure—until old-world apparitions change their sexual ways.

There is magic under the sheets in these stories, myths walking the world, passion that transcends life, potions that right wrongs—and, in one searing story, tragic panic about who we are, fear about being who we need to be. And isn't that dread of the unknown a part of what we were before we grew into our queer selves?

The stories in *Erotica Exotica* aren't rooted in horror; they're not particularly scary, overall. But they do spring from a dimension of the queer imagination that broadens the erotic. Queer sex, meet the supernatural.

Richard Labonté
Bowen Island, British Columbia

POSSESSION
'NATHAN BURGOINE

To be fair, binding myself to a vampire and a demon seemed like a good idea at the time. I'd found myself in a crappy position with zero options and had found a loophole, so I took a shot and risked pissing off everyone—including the vampire and the demon. Now the three of us were a coven.

Sort of.

Sitting in a church and looking at the four men and one woman surrounding me in the pews, however, it occurred to me that as decisions went, the triad I'd formed with Luc and Anders might not have been in my top-ten best decisions of the decade.

"Let's be clear," Malcolm said. Like all of them, Malcolm Stirling looked like he was a high-powered CEO, not the head of a coven. He wore a very expensive suit, a burgundy silk tie, and a glower that told me my chinos and T-shirt weren't passing muster. He cleared his throat, peering at me over his glasses. "You conjured a storm. From an otherwise clear sky."

"Yes." There was no use denying it—it was the truth. "In self-defense."

The lone woman offered a smile that—though perhaps not quite amused, at least wasn't malicious—and said, "Oh, this'll be good."

"Katrina, please." Malcolm frowned.

She raised her hand to acknowledge that her interruption broke protocol.

I tried not to smirk. The covens of Ottawa, Canada's capital, are huge on etiquette. What can I say? Government town.

"Explain," Malcolm said.

Between us, sitting on the pew, was a single white feather, impossibly balanced on its tip. It had barely stirred as I spoke. The feather would fall if a lie was spoken. So far, so good.

❖

I took a breath. "Someone sent a pack of demons to assault me in my home." Truth. "The demons battered down the wards I had in place, and didn't care that they'd be weakened by a lack of invitation into my residency." Also true. "I used sorcery to defeat one, but there were nine. I was overwhelmed." I paused, remembering. "Overwhelmed" in this case meant having a big blond demon with his hands down my underwear, sucking on my soul. "My coven couldn't deal with the surprise assault, but my use of sorcery provided a distraction. That tipped the balance." True, but dodgy on the details. I resisted the urge to look at the feather.

The men exchanged glances. Katrina regarded me, mouth twitching in what I hoped was her attempt to hide a supportive smile.

"How so?" Malcolm asked.

Crap.

"I made it dark," I said. "They didn't see the attack coming from my coven in time." This was also true, but even dodgier. The storm had made it possible for Luc—the vampire in my triad—to get out of the basement and join the fray. He shouldn't have been awake at all; it was the middle of the day. I didn't want the coven heads to know about that.

The older men—most were around triple my age, I was sure—shared long looks. Malcolm began to frown again. I decided to plow ahead.

"The last thing I want is to anger the coven heads," I said. That was one hundred percent true. "I did it because I saw no other choice that would defeat nine demons." I let that hang a moment. My trio, I wanted to remind them, had indeed clobbered *nine* demons. "As we agreed before—I just want to be left alone."

"But someone doesn't want to leave you alone," Katrina said.

I locked eyes with her. "My thought exactly." I looked at the feather, suddenly inspired. "Since you've worked so hard on the truth spell, perhaps you could all take turns saying you had nothing to do with the attack?" I pointed at the feather.

Malcolm plucked it from the bench. "This meeting is adjourned."

"Thanks for having me," I said. It might not have sounded sincere.

❖

I remained seated while they left and tried to gather my thoughts. The church was quiet. I had no illusions why the small church was the meeting place of choice. Neither Luc nor Anders could enter consecrated ground, and no matter your path of magic all practitioners considered holy places to be neutral territory. The coven heads had invited me somewhere I'd be alone and, bound by very old magical laws, not able to assault them.

Then they'd made me take the magical equivalent of a lie detector test.

I sighed, then made my way among the pews. Outside, the sun was setting on a bright autumn Ottawa day, and I blinked as it caught my eyes. There was a lovely stone-bordered park beside the church, a typical bit of pretty green space in the Glebe. Maybe I'd go sit there for a while.

"No fun being the new kid, eh?"

I turned. Leaning against the church wall was a tall, fair-haired man in his early thirties. He was dressed less formally than the coven heads had been, in a crisp white dress shirt and navy pants, no tie, and no jacket. Between his scruffy goatee and his cigarette, I wasn't sure if he was part of the covens or not.

"I'm sorry?" I said. I pulled my glasses from the neck of my shirt and put them on. I don't need glasses, and they don't have a prescription. What they do have is a particularly good enchantment on them—if I do say so myself. The tall man glowed with a pale silver light through my lenses.

Mage.

"The old boys' club," he said, taking a drag. He nodded. I noticed that the coven heads, except for Katrina, were all having a rather animated discussion in the parking lot.

"Ah," I said. It seemed safest.

"I'm Ben," he said, offering his free hand.

"Curtis." We shook.

We watched the old men in their suits. "You've got them talking."

I was the topic? Crap.

"I think they'd all adopt you," he said, tossing the cigarette into the grass. "You don't have to worry. If you're not sure which family to join—"

"No."

He frowned. "I'm sorry. I thought you were an orphan."

He meant it in the magical sense—a wizard born to a nonmagical bloodline—and he was right. He probably didn't know that he'd be just as right in the more traditional use of the word, or that one or more of those wizards were responsible.

"I have my own coven," I said.

That gave him pause. "A new coven?"

I nodded.

"Then you're petitioning to be a coven head?" This came out uncertainly. I was throwing Ben for a loop. I felt bad. He was cute, in a tall and scruffy way.

"No," I said. "I just want to be left alone."

"If you're not petitioning, why are you here?" He looked genuinely confused. Maybe even worried.

"Someone tried to kill my coven," I said. It rolled off my tongue blandly, but inside I felt a cold lump in my chest. Technically, it was more like someone had tried to kill *me*.

"Why would someone do that?" He didn't seem ruffled by what I'd said. Anders—my demon companion—compared the magical bloodlines to the mafia. I was starting to think he had a point.

"I have a few ideas," I said. "Either someone hates me, or someone hates vampires, or someone hates demons." I paused. "I guess it could be all three."

He stared. "What?"

"My coven," I said. "It's me, a vampire, and a demon."

"That's…" Ben struggled for a word. He didn't find one, and just kept looking at me.

Screw it. I wanted a cup of tea. "Well," I said, with false cheer, "thanks for your time."

"Wait," he said. "I'd like to talk to you again."

I frowned. "Why?"

"It wasn't so long ago I was the new kid." He smiled. "Besides, you're cute."

"Oh." I felt my face heat up. I've always been an easy blush.

"Benedict," a voice called. Malcolm. It looked like the old boys' club was breaking up.

"Time to be a chauffeur," Ben said. "I'll pick you up tomorrow night? At eight?" He was walking backward, watching me. It made him seem younger somehow, though he probably had a decade on me.

It occurred to me that Anders looked to be about forty, and I'd found a flyer from the 1967 centennial celebration of Confederation in one of Luc's dressers when he'd moved in. Hell, for all I knew, Luc could have been present for Confederation itself. So what if Ben had a decade on me? When was the last time I'd had a normal date that hadn't been with a demon or a vampire? I couldn't remember.

"Okay?" he asked again, yelling louder now. He pressed his hands together like he was begging.

"Sure," I called.

❖

Luc was up when I got home, the sun having set on my way back from the church. He rose when I walked into my living room. I'd inherited my parents' Riverside home, and Luc and Anders had moved in after we'd formed our triad. The room looked different with Luc's beautiful period piece furniture. I hadn't changed the house at all since my parents had died, until Luc and Anders had moved in. A part of me felt almost guilty about letting him redecorate even this much.

At least Anders had agreed to keep his seventies gay porn posters in his bedroom.

"How did it go?" Luc asked. The vampire took my shoulders and squeezed gently. He always took my breath away. He's taller than me—though that's not a challenge—and handsome in a dark French Canadian way. He's got beautiful cheekbones and a lean, muscular build that he doesn't have to maintain at the gym, owing to his undead nature. Some mornings when I go running, I think about his perfect physique and hate him a little.

But then he does something like this and I forgive him. Having someone wait for you, to ask how your day went—it's just so…normal. I haven't had much normal in the last couple of years. I felt a pang of guilt about flirting with Ben.

"Well," I said, "they didn't change the status quo. I measured my heart against a feather and came out okay."

Luc blinked. "You are the only one of us capable of that, I'd say."

"Aw." To my total humiliation, my eyes teared up.

"Don't, *lapin*." The shoulder squeeze became a hug. I nestled into his chest—one of the rare benefits of being a short man—and let him hold me.

"Sorry," I said. "Some all-powerful wizard, eh?" I wiped my eyes and stepped back. Then I looked at him. He was impeccably dressed, as always. He'd obviously already showered, dried his hair… I glanced at my watch. "What time did you get up?"

"Almost a full hour before sunset."

We regarded each other. That should have been impossible. Vampire and all that. Our triad was having an effect on all of us. My magic had always been strong but exhausting. Now I could go a lot longer and perform more powerful magic. Even sorcery, magic's answer to the shotgun, was coming to me now.

I sat down, and he joined me on the couch. I leaned into him and felt him force air into his lungs.

"You smell magnificent."

I smiled. "You sound like Anders."

"No, he doesn't," Anders said, stepping out of the hallway. "I'd tell you you smelled fuckable."

Such a charmer. I sat up. "Any luck?"

Anders shook his head. While I'd been at my interrogation, Anders had decided to have a chat with the demons on the street.

In every way that I find Luc attractive, Anders is his opposite— and yet somehow just as hot. Anders is an incubus, which means sexy is just part of the package, but it's a package he delivers well. Anders is taller, wider, more muscular, and has the most amazing hairy chest. He's uncouth, loud, abrasive, and always looks like he hasn't shaved in a few days. His face is masculine, not beautiful, with a deep brow, strong chin, a nose that looks like it has been smashed once or twice, and dark eyes that have a way of looking at you like you're edible.

Which he was doing. I shivered.

"Even with our rep," he said, "the other demons won't say who sent the pack after us."

"Or they aren't aware who did," Luc said.

Anders shrugged. "Maybe."

I sighed and rose. "Well, I want to get cracking on new wards for the house."

"Don't exhaust yourself," Luc said.

❖

If you've never leaned on an incubus's hairy chest while a vampire rubs you with a hot lathered sponge, I tell you, you're missing out.

My relaxing bath before bed was rapidly turning into anything but. Not that I was complaining. Mostly I was groaning. And maybe purring.

"I adore your legs," Luc was saying, lifting my ankle onto his shoulder and rubbing the sponge along my calf. He was at the other end of the tub, naked, wet, and looking fine. He let go of the sponge and started to rub my leg with his strong fingers. It felt amazing.

"You did too much magic today," he said. "You are very tense."

"Needed better wards," I mumbled. I closed my eyes. Anders shifted in the tub behind me, and his hardness pressed against my back. He scooped up some more hot water in his hands and let it pour down my chest. I rolled my head to one side.

"Let's just live in here," I said.

"No," Anders said, rubbing his rough hands up and down my chest. "Let's go *live* in your bed."

I smiled. To say I was fond of *living* in my bed with Anders would be an understatement.

"Non," Luc said. "You will go and find some of your usual trash upon which to sate yourself."

"What?" Anders said.

"He's exhausted," Luc said. "He needs rest."

I opened my eyes. Luc was looking over my shoulder. Anders's chest tensed under me. Wow. Were they actually fighting over me? It's not like we didn't all get together every full moon to renew our bond. And quite a few nights in between.

Hey, they're both really hot, and I'm a healthy young man. Don't judge.

"Fine," Anders said, surprising me. He gently rolled me forward when he got out of the bath, and I sank back into the bubbles. Hot water and soap slid down Anders's muscular back, revealing the stylized tattoo across one shoulder that reminded me of a feathered wing. His ass was all muscle, as were his thighs. Damn, it was a good view.

He wrapped a towel around his waist and left without another word. I couldn't tell if his feelings were hurt. I wasn't even sure what his feelings were, most of the time. Other than horny.

"Come," Luc said, gently lowering my leg from his shoulder. "We dry off, and then to bed."

❖

Luc climbed into my bed, and his arms encircled me. He was still warm from the hot bath, which was a nice change from his usually slightly cool touch. We spooned.

"You need to slow down," he said, kissing the back of my head.

I snuggled. "I know. I just don't understand how they broke through so easily." The demons, all nine of them, had pretty much sauntered in. The Law of Residency, one of the oldest magical rules, should have at least slowed them down. My fuzzy brain wasn't giving me a hint, though, and I couldn't stop worrying the subject.

"Relax," Luc said. "You need to sleep."

"I know." I shifted again. His cock hardened behind me, and I couldn't help but smile. "I thought you chased Anders off so I could sleep."

"You are rubbing that runner's ass against me on purpose, *lapin*."

I wriggled. "Maybe."

"You are teasing me," he said, but his voice was playful. His hand stroked me lightly and I stretched against him.

"Maybe I just need to really exhaust myself. Then I could sleep," I said.

"If that's what it takes," he said, amused. He pulled away, rolling me onto my back, and slid down my body until his lips brushed my dick. I curled my hands in the sheets when he took me into his mouth—that almost coolness was always a shock at first—and swallowed me in one long motion. He didn't have to breathe. There are benefits in bed to that ability.

He sucked me while I lay back and enjoyed everything he was doing. His fingers seemed to be everywhere, teasing one nipple, then the other, scratching my thighs lightly, gently tugging my balls in his hands. I was soon writhing and gasping, and the air was crackling with accidental magic. Static sparked on my lamp, and Luc increased his pace until I was almost over the edge. He released my cock, and as his sharp fangs bit into my thigh I shot hot cum onto my stomach. He swallowed once, then licked at the two small holes. I gasped, my entire body lurching. There was something about a vampire's bite... I shivered again. By morning, there would barely be a mark.

"I will clean you up again," Luc said, his accent heavy. "And then you will sleep."

I was already drifting.

❖

I woke up with my face pressed into a hard, hairy chest. I lifted my eyes to see Anders looking down at me.

"I'm pretty sure I fell asleep with a vampire," I said, blinking.

Anders grunted. "You traded up."

I laughed, and he groped my ass. "How you feeling?" he asked.

"Better," I said. I stretched, and Anders's hands were soon all over me, rubbing my stomach and chest. He rolled on top of me, his morning intentions perfectly clear. I chuckled, and he went for my neck with his rough scratchy beard.

"Good," he said.

"Though I still"—I gasped as he flicked my neck with his tongue—"have no idea who tried to kill us."

Anders paused in his assault on my neck, though one of his hands was sliding down my side. "Maybe the pack had a grudge against me for hooking up with you and Luc." His fingers tugged at my waist, rolling us over until I was on top of him. I pressed against his hairy chest. His hands grabbed my ass tightly.

"It would have to have been a coven," I said, then bit my lip as one of his fingers started to rub at me. It was hard to think. "I can't think of anyone else…with enough power…to make demons attack…from weaker ground…" He pulled his finger away long enough to make me lick it, but then paused, frowning at me.

"Weaker ground?"

"Residency," I said. "You know, the whole 'I invite you in' thing. Vampires can't get across a threshold at all. If a demon does it without permission—or a mage, for that matter—it knocks down their power quite a lot. It's like fighting with a handicap."

Anders shook his head. "I know. But they weren't weaker. They were fighting at full strength. Trust me. I figured they'd tricked you into getting an invite."

"No. They broke in." I blinked. "That doesn't make sense. Crap."

"It's not like we can ask them," Anders sighed. His hands resumed their probing. "Too bad we don't have cameras. Then we could play it back and see…"

I slid off the bed, barely dodging his hands. "You're a genius." I thought I knew what to do. It wasn't something I was particularly good at, but I was sure I could make it work.

Anders regarded me as I opened my chest of drawers. "If I'm a genius," he grumbled, "why am I here with a hard-on, and you're over there getting dressed?"

❖

"You're going to ask the house?" Anders asked, skeptical. Luc stood beside him. We were at the back door, which had been repaired after the demon assault.

"Sort of. I'm going to ask the whole area for a replay. *Memento Loci*, I think it's called. Everything holds a kind of trace of everything that's ever happened there. I'm not very good at illusions—that's a fire magic, and my fire magic has always been crap—but you both have that whole predator sight thing. If I craft the illusion maybe you'll see what's going on." I took a deep breath, steadying myself. The magic welled up inside me as always, eager to be used and so much stronger than it had been before we formed the triad.

"Okay. Here goes." I closed my eyes.

I held my hands in front of me, picturing the area around the door enclosed within a circle of light. Next I imagined the sun moving across the sky in the wrong direction, mentally walking back through time until I was at the moment the demons had arrived. Holding that image, I drew the magic up through my core.

"Memor," I said. I caught the sharp scent of brimstone, and my skin shivered. *"Ostendo."* I spread my hands. The magic burned on my fingertips, then left me in a rush. I heard Anders gasp.

"The sun," Luc said. I opened my eyes and gaped.

It was the best illusion I'd ever seen. I felt a kind of pull between myself and Anders, and realized with a start that his ability to draw on allure to shift how he looked to seduce men was in every way an illusion. He was a being of fire. Was I borrowing his ability, and channelling it through my own magic?

My backyard appeared exactly as before, with the original door. It was a sunny morning, as Luc had said. I hadn't thought of that, and glanced at him, worried. But Luc was looking around with wonder in his eyes—the illusion of sunlight wasn't bothering him. Every detail was perfect. As we stood there, demons started stepping out of the shadows cast by the trees along my backyard. The largest one, blond and muscular, approached the door with something in his hand. I physically took a step back from the image, before it could walk through me. Holding the spell together was a constant heat on my skin, but it wasn't especially tiring—I could keep this up for a while. I glanced at Anders, who met my gaze and gave me a brief nod. Whatever I was doing, he sensed it was involving him somehow.

The blond demon—who would later nearly kill me—walked up to the back door and held out a small metal object.

"Is that a pocket watch?" Luc asked.

I went cold.

"Yeah," I said. "It is." It was an antique. Silver and, I knew, inscribed with one word: "Baird."

"Is it magic?" Anders asked. As we watched, the demon touched the door and the wards I'd set in place crumpled like tissue paper, the door twisting, igniting, and collapsing all at once as the spells went off with no one to target. The demon carelessly tossed the watch aside, where it fell into the shadow of the trees and vanished without a trace, back to wherever the demon had willed it to go.

"No," I said. "It was my father's. I had him buried with it." I waved a hand, and the illusion collapsed into wisps of light and heat, then faded into nothing. The night returned.

❖

I didn't hear the doorbell. I was on my bed, staring at the ceiling, trying to think of my next move. I was furious. I couldn't think of anything that didn't involve going to the gravesite, and I couldn't use the same memory illusion spell because I didn't know exactly when the watch had been stolen.

Stolen from my father's grave.

I closed my eyes, jaw clenched. The air crackled with static electricity. If I didn't rein it in, I was going to ruin something.

Luc knocked at my door. "Curtis?"

"Yes?"

"There's a gentleman to see you." His voice was muffled. He paused for a moment. "He is under the impression that you have a date."

I sat up. Ben. Crap! I looked at the clock. It was just before eight. I groaned.

"Curtis?"

"I'll be right there," I called, and slid off my bed. "Just give me a second." I should change my shirt at least.

"Of course," Luc sounded amused. He added, "He's with Anders right now, at the front door."

I decided I didn't need the second.

I rushed into the hallway and passed Luc—who showed me a hint of fang—and hit the stairs.

I came down the steps as fast as I could manage. Ben stood waiting just outside the front door, which was open. Anders stood watching Ben, arms crossed. The demon looked furious.

"Sorry," I said. "I forgot."

Ben winced. "Ouch."

"No," I said, realizing how it sounded. "It's not...uh..." I was blushing. "Something came up, and I lost track of time." Ben looked good, even with the scruffy goatee. I'd forgotten how tall he was, and he definitely rocked the blue T-shirt he had on. It set off his eyes, which I hadn't noticed before were gray. Also, it was quite a bit tighter than his dress shirt. He was definitely fit.

"If you need a rain check—" Ben began.

"That'd be good," Anders said.

I frowned at the demon, but he didn't even look at me. "No, tonight is fine," I said. I thought I heard Anders growl, but decided to ignore him. "I could use a distraction."

I stepped out into the night.

❖

"So a vampire, a demon, and a wizard walk into a bar," Ben said.

"I've heard that one before," I said, pushing the pasta around my plate.

"Curtis?"

I looked up, my face burning. "I'm sorry. I'm horrible company tonight. And you made a lovely pasta, and I'm barely eating it." I sighed. "The first normal date I've had in years, and I'm completely ruining it."

Ben leaned forward. We were seated on opposite sides of his small kitchen table. "Normal? Damn. I was aiming for spectacular."

I grinned. "I meant normal more in a..." I paused. "I'm not sure what I meant."

He smiled, which did nice things to his eyes. I've always liked smile lines. "You're not ruining it. You're brooding, but it's a good look on you."

I felt myself blushing again. "I'm sorry."

"You apologize too much."

"Do I? I'm—" I caught myself just before I apologized again. "I'm like that."

"What's bothering you?"

I looked at Ben. Maybe what I needed was another magical opinion. "Residency laws."

He looked wary. "You mean the magical sort."

I nodded. "When we arrived, you invited me in."

"I didn't want to feed you pasta through the mail slot."

"Kind of you. But by inviting me in, you allowed all of me— my power—in through the door. I thought that was the entirety of the residency laws, but apparently there's more to it than that. I'm feeling ignorant." I scowled. "It's leaving me a little grumpy."

"And brooding." Ben nodded.

I laughed. "And brooding."

"So what's confusing you?" Ben asked.

"Something that belonged to an occupant of a house. Can that be used to break residency?" The thought of the blond demon with my father's watch made me angry. The air tingled on my skin. I tried to calm down.

Ben frowned. "What do you mean?"

"The demons that were sent after me had my father's pocket watch." My fork sparked with a random static discharge, so I balled the magic into the palm of my hand and said, *"Ostendo."* An image of my father's watch appeared, pale and watery. I could see right through it. I blinked. I was back to being crap at illusions.

Ben peered at it. "A possession of the owner of a home…" He frowned, rubbing his scruffy goatee. "It could work. I think."

I sighed. "It did work." I closed my hand. The image washed away with a warm pulse.

"Have you considered that you're going at this problem the wrong way?" Ben asked.

I looked at him. His gray eyes were soft, but still a little wary. "How so?"

"You're living with a vampire and a demon," he said. "You're stepping on the toes of the other covens, and they're not going to put up with it."

I frowned. "Is that a warning?"

"Damn." He leaned back. "Curtis, I like you. But I think we both know what you meant when you said this was the first normal thing you've done in a while." He reached across the table and took my hand. "I asked Malcolm about you. I'm sorry about your parents. I wish things were different. Your…solution…isn't going to hold."

His hand was warm. I looked at it. He squeezed. I looked up at him, miserable. Was he right? Luc and Anders and me… Was it only a matter of time?

"Hey," he said, and pulled my hand to his face. He kissed my palm. "You're okay."

My eyes teared up. Crap. Worst date ever.

He rose, letting go of my hand. "Come here." I stood and he hugged me. He was even taller than Anders, I realized, pressing my face into his shirt while he held me. There's just something about being held.

He tipped my head and kissed me. Someone else could make my decisions for a while. I needed a break. His goatee was softer than I thought it would be.

In his room, we undressed slowly. He was indeed fit, with a smooth tanned chest and a series of runes tattooed around his left biceps. We continued to kiss me as we shed our clothes and he nudged me onto his bed, his lips shifting to my chin, and then my throat. I held on to him, rolling onto my back and pulling him on top of me, and we lay together, rubbing against each other, kissing and touching, teasing each other, until the kisses became more earnest and his hard cock rubbed against mine. He broke off a particularly long kiss, and, breathing heavily, asked, "This okay?"

"Yes. Oh, yes."

He grinned, then reached past me to his dresser, digging out a condom, and we broke apart long enough for him to get ready. When he'd gotten it on, I rolled over, and his hand brushed my ass.

"Gribouiller," he said. A warm liquid spilled onto me from his fingertips. Magic flickered in the room.

"French?" I said, turning my neck to look at him.

He grinned. "I suck at Latin." He lowered himself on top of me. "Besides, French is the language of love." I felt his hardness against me, pushing. I tilted my head back, and pulled my own magic before saying *"tenebrae."* All the lights went out.

After that, we didn't talk at all. He entered me gently, wrapping strong arms around me and kissing the back of my neck. I pushed back against him, revelling at the feel of him inside me—not on the edge of being too hot, like Anders, and not cool, like Luc. Our pace built slowly, and when he came, he tugged me over onto my side, keeping himself inside me while his hand stroked my own climax out of me. We cleaned up by the dim light of the street lamps, before he pulled the blanket over us both.

I fell asleep.

❖

Breakfast was toast, with coffee for Ben and tea—which he scrounged from the back of a cupboard—for me. He kept looking at me while I ate. Finally, after I was sure my face was very red, I said, "What?"

"Nothing." He grinned. "You're cute."

I blushed more.

"Last night was…magic," he said, and wagged his eyebrows when I groaned. "I hope it wasn't just a one-time deal for you."

I took a deep breath. "I don't normally just throw myself into a guy's bed on a first date, if that's what you mean."

"Good," he said. "Because although I've got a long day of being Malcolm's errand boy ahead of me, I would like to see you again."

I nodded. "I think I'd like that." I hoped I wasn't leading Ben on too much. I liked his company, and the sex had definitely been good, but... "I'd like to take it slow."

He raised an eyebrow, but said nothing. I went back to my toast.

"I could talk to Malcolm about having you join our coven," Ben said, after a while.

"That would be taking things fast, not slow."

He grinned. "Can't blame a guy for trying. Let me put my number into your cell phone."

I handed it to him. We finished breakfast, and when I got up, he gave me a tight hug. Stepping into the morning air, I took a deep breath. I wasn't sure what I felt.

I'd not gone more than ten steps before I saw Anders leaning against the side of a tree. His jaw was tightly clenched and his arms were fists at his side.

"Anders?" I said. His eyes flickered with pale white flame. His stiff body emanated heat.

"Good morning," he said. His salutation didn't sound particularly pleasant. I could sense his anger, like an echo at the back of my head. And something else. Maybe he was...hurt? I rubbed my eyes. I didn't want to deal with the strangeness of the triad this morning.

I walked past him. He fell into step.

"Curtis," he said. It was more a growl than a word.

"Look," I said, turning suddenly and poking him in the chest. "You're like a rutting pig. You've fucked half the gay men in the city. And I get it—you're an incubus. You have to. But don't play the slut card with me, Anders, because it's not okay."

"That's not why I'm here," he said. "You shouldn't trust him."

Damn it. I wasn't going to let him get to me. I'd known damned well that we weren't...what? Boyfriends? He was a demon! I sighed. "Why not?"

He held out his hand. In his palm was my father's pocket watch.

❖

It was almost ten at night when Ben parked at the curb, still driving Malcolm's car and wearing the white shirt I assumed was his driver uniform. When he came around the front of the car, he tripped and had to right himself for a moment, one hand on the car's hood. I bit my lip, tensing.

"What's wrong?" he said, recovering and coming up onto the church's yard. "I got your message. Why did you want to meet me here?"

I looked at him. Blond, tall, scruffy goatee. Hard body, gentle in bed. I took a deep breath, and kept my voice even.

"Consecrated ground. It seemed safest," I said. "I figured out who took the pocket watch from my father's grave."

He stared at me for a long moment. "And?" His gray eyes showed nothing.

"I was hoping for a reason," I said. I pulled the watch out of my pocket.

He sighed. He didn't bother to dissemble. "When did you find it?"

I shook my head. "Anders found it. In your basement. Pretty much right under where you were fucking me." I glared at him. "What the hell was the point of that, Ben? Why seduce me?"

"I like you," he said, and the matter-of-factness in his voice was infuriating. "Whatever else, I think you're better than the situation you're in, Curtis. I'd like to be with you."

I stared, incredulous. "You stole from my father's grave and sent demons after me. For all I know, you're the one who killed my parents!"

He shook his head. "No. I got the watch from your father's grave, and I worked the spell on it to break your wards. That's all. I had no part in anything else."

He didn't fire the gun, he just loaded it and handed it to a killer. I shook my head. "I can't believe I was dumb enough to trust you."

"You need to be with your own kind," Ben said. "What you call a coven…"

"Luc and Anders have never lied to me," I snapped. "In fact, all they've ever done is protect me."

"The bonds you build during worship are supposed to be sacred, Curtis." His voice was imploring. "They're not just magical, they're holy."

"My bond with Luc and Anders *is* holy," I said. "It's just, y'know, holy in a gay threesome sort of way."

"The covens won't put up with it," Ben said. The jerk even sounded genuinely sad. "You could have a normal life. I can save you."

"Wow," I said, and shook my head. "What makes you think I need saving?"

"Look around. You're scared enough that you brought me to a churchyard to talk," Ben said.

I smiled. "Actually, that's not true. This," I said, and raised my hands, "is a trap." I released the illusion, and the churchyard melted away with a palpable wash of heat. The small park—complete with the stones along the curb that Ben had nearly tripped over—appeared around us. The churchyard was about twenty feet to the left.

Ben jerked and turned to face the churchyard, but Anders stepped out of the shadows the moon cast under the maples, and Luc approached from the opposite side. Anders nodded at me. If he'd been tired by supplying all the oomph for my illusion, he didn't show it. I felt only the slightest drain. Ben turned his face back to me, his hands raised.

"Crépuscule," he snapped, and the light fled the park. My eyes became gritty and smudgy. I heard him move, and gathered power from within. This close to Luc and Anders, the magic leapt to my call, coiling and strong inside me.

"Necto," I said. My spell pulsed out, lightning quick. It grazed him and mostly deflected by some sort of ward. Too late I remembered the runes around his biceps.

"Get him," I said, and a moment later I heard Ben fall to the ground with a startled grunt. My vision cleared. Ben lay prone just at the edge of the park, Anders leaning heavily across him. I could smell burned cloth.

"Necto," I said again, and this time the spell took hold. Anders looked at me. I nodded, and the demon rose. Ben stayed down, arms heavy and pressed into the earth. Two ashy handprints had burned into his white shirt. The power of the binding was strong. I was drawing

entirely on my own power, but maintaining the spell was nowhere near as exhausting as it once had been.

Ben shivered as the three of us gathered above him, fighting against the weight of the spell but not succeeding.

"You're a freak," he managed, through lips mostly numbed by magic.

Luc moved with vampire grace, so fast he was a blur. His hand was at Ben's neck, holding him with casual menace. Ben grew pale as Luc leaned over him. "Be polite."

"If you kill me," Ben was nearly choking in Luc's grasp, "they'll destroy you!"

I shook my head. "We're not going to kill you."

"It was a close vote," Anders said.

"We're not going to kill you," I repeated, louder. "But you're going to pass on a message to Malcolm." I waited until Ben met my gaze. "Here it is: leave us alone."

"Or else," Anders added.

"Yeah." I nodded. "That, too. Anything that happens to any of us, we're going to hold you responsible, Ben."

Luc let go of Ben's throat, and the three of us stepped back. I released the binding, and Ben scrambled to his feet, obviously shaken. He raised a hand to his chest, wincing. Blood seeped through his shirt. I wondered how badly Anders had burned him.

"You're crazy if you think they'll put up with you three," Ben said, but his words lacked conviction, given how much he was shaking.

"*Détente* will do," Anders said. Luc glanced at him and smiled. Then he hissed at Ben with his fangs fully extended. Ben scrambled back to his car.

As he drove away, I couldn't help myself.

I waved.

❖

I was still wide awake when the bed shifted as Anders slid in beside me. Without speaking, I curled against his hairy chest. His strong arms wrapped around me. He was so warm—warmer than a normal human being.

"Luc out feeding?" I asked.

"Yeah." Anders gave my ass a quick squeeze. "You okay?"

Concern always sounded awkward coming from him.

"Yes."

"He was full of shit," Anders said. "About you. You're not a freak."

I laughed. "Yes, I am. But it's okay. I'm starting to think normal is highly overrated. Maybe I don't get a normal life, but I get you, and Luc, and the magic." I smiled.

"You do," he agreed. He started to rub my back, and his dick stiffened against me. I reached down for it, and he let out a little rumble in his chest when my fingers wrapped around him.

"How'd you get the watch?" I asked.

"What?" Anders said. Clearly I was distracting him. It was a nice change.

"You got the pocket watch from inside Ben's house. But you weren't invited in. How'd you get in without breaking down the door?" I stroked him.

Anders moaned, and his hand moved further down my back. "Same way you said he got the demons in here, except the other way around. I didn't have to break the door. There was a big enough shadow to walk through."

He'd shadow-walked in without an invitation? I blinked. "I don't get it. Did you steal something from him?"

Anders rolled me onto my back, and then lifted himself over me until we were looking eye to eye. He took my hands, first one, then the other, and pressed them above my head, holding my wrists in one strong hand. "No. He brought something of mine into his house." He smiled. "That let me in."

I frowned. I still didn't get it. "What?"

"He had *you* in there," Anders said, and moved his hips to grind us together. His free hand took my chin. "And you're *mine*."

"I'm..." My breath caught. Above me, the demon held my gaze, waiting for me to say something. Crap. Sometimes, I can be really dumb.

"Mine," he repeated.

He was waiting for me to speak. The demon that…what? Claimed me? Cared about me?

Loved me?

I swallowed.

"Prove it," I said, and a smile tugged at the corners of his mouth.

He proved it twice before midnight.

GHOST TOWN
DALE CHASE

It is said a man was killed every day in Bodie, and I do not doubt this, for I was one. A California mining town born of gold, it flourished from 1878 to 1882, at one time boasting thousands of inhabitants, miners mostly but also gunfighters, robbers, gamblers, and prostitutes. It was during this period that I came prematurely to my end, but unlike most, I was condemned to neither heaven nor hell. Left behind, I continued as spirit and watched the great town's demise, population fleeing when the gold played out. Now empty and much burned in a great fire during the last century, what remains is kept in little more than arrested decay as a state historical park. I reside here with a few others who likewise met an early end and who also failed to reach the great beyond. We are an odd band, not knowing our purpose or if we shall ever move on.

Few come here now. Those who do must traverse a rough thirteen-mile road, and when they step out of their tin contraptions, they spend the first moments remarking on the difficult trip before they allow the step back in time. Of course, they never truly know it, no more than I know their time. Progress for me is measured by their appearance and the horseless wagons they drive. Having traveled on horseback mostly, I appreciate the quickness of travel afforded the living, but I also think they have lost something along the way, as too many seem impatient. Eager to arrive, they become eager to leave, and I watch the great tin beasts roar away, leaving dusty clouds in their wake.

The horseless wagon this particular day is a beast of a thing, tall as a prairie schooner and possibly as long. It is wide, white, and shiny, and brings not the expected family with children to scamper about but two men clad in Stetsons. The rest of their attire is not what one would expect of a cowboy, although both wear rough-laced boots. Bare legs, short pants, and undershirts tell me they are city folk done up for amusement.

The men are young and playful, alighting to gawk at what remains of our town. "What's this?" one asks the other as he stands before the Central Market.

"Bodie Store," the other declares, referring to a paper in hand. I alone know he is wrong, but this is no matter as the two enjoy thoughts of what once was. After a minute or so, they venture up the street and correctly identify the Palace Laurel Saloon alongside the Mono County Bank. I find this knowledge welcome, as most visitors are little educated about the town.

As the two men meander here and there, I follow along unseen, which is my usual state. although I can, if I choose, materialize into the man I was at my demise. That man was no older than these two, twenty-two on the fateful day. As the newcomers reach the Methodist church, one turns to his friend to inquire, "Hey, Frank, was Oren a churchgoing man?"

"I doubt it," says Frank, who is striking in appearance. "Being a gambler, I'd say he's more heathen."

They share a laugh and peer into the church, which withstands time better than the other dwellings, as if perhaps more favorably looked upon by the man above. As I move in close, I encounter an unmistakable heat that both surprises and pleases me. Though the men exhibit no outward sexual overture, desire burns in them that sets my own alight after long years dormant. I feel the stir below, and when the two move from the church, I follow.

They work their way up the street, exploring every inch of what remains, then move out into the graveyard, where they spend some time examining the markers. When Frank slides his arm around his friend's waist, I am seized by recall of my own man, Ty Wilson, who left Bodie soon after my unfortunate end.

The two men talk more intimately now, and Frank plants a kiss upon the other's cheek, at which my disembodied cock gains new life. I inhale their powerful notions as if I might take them as my own.

The unnamed man presses himself to Frank, then knocks off their hats to reveal thick blond curls upon Frank's head and short dark hair upon his own. "Christ, Wade, not here," Frank says as his friend grinds against him.

"Why not?" says Wade. "Who in hell is going to see? Snakes?"

"Later," Frank cajoles, unsticking his man. "I want to find Oren."

Wade does as asked and the two resume their search, which I know is futile if they are looking for Oren Hart's grave. He is indeed buried hereabouts, but his marker, like most, is long asunder. So many killed and put to ground.

"He's not here," says Wade after some time.

Frank becomes downcast. "He's here. He's just not marked. Look at all the rotted wood." He points to a scrap that bears "Mac" and lights up. "Look at this. It might be Hugh MacKenzie, the one who shot Oren."

"Yup," Wade says. "Or MacDougal or MacDonald. Hey, maybe the burger franchise started out here. Golden arches made of real gold."

"That's McDonald's."

"Oh, yeah, right."

Wade is silent now as Frank fingers the scrap, which is likely Hugh's. He's out here along with Oren and Lucas Lathrop, friend of Oren, who shot Hugh to avenge his friend and took a bullet in the neck in Hugh's final act as a dying man. They're all three buried here, but then so am I, yet none of us rests.

As Frank lingers at the scrap, Wade again comes to him and slips an arm around his waist. "My own cowboy," he coos.

"Don't I wish. C'mon, let's get something to eat."

They return to their wagon and drop the back gate to reveal a chest from which they take their grub and bottled drinks. As the sun is high, they scoot back into their manmade shade to enjoy their meal, after which Wade stretches out. "Come here," he says to Frank, who remains elusive and hops out of the wagon. Wade laughs, jumps down, and grabs his friend. "Don't you want to?" he asks.

"It's hot in there."

"Okay, out here. Like your cowboys did."

"Like they fucked on Main Street."

"Hey, I'd do you in the saloon if the buildings weren't padlocked." Here Wade exhibits such manly desire that I see why Frank is taken with him. "I want to figure out the gunfight," Frank says as he is pulled into Wade's arms.

"Absolutely. We can pace off and kill each other, but right now it's just the two of us and this heat makes me want to do things."

Wade begins to kiss Frank, and I am swept into their river of desire. In my disembodied state I am able to slither better than a snake, and as their lips and tongues meet, I join in, feeling my tongue come alive in Frank's. And when the two men grind below, I am between them, cock urgent upon Wade's and just as eager. When he pulls off his friend, he strips away his shirt and Frank does the same.

I have not seen a bare chest these many years and am much taken with the thick fur spread across Wade's. It reminds me of Ty, who also bore a dark pelt. Frank is smooth but well developed, as if he might indeed do ranch work. Wade's hands slide over Frank's chest and I join him in fingering tit nubbins while again kissing. Then Wade again pulls off, drops his short pants. He is now full naked, fat prick hard out.

Frank is reluctant, looking around, and it amuses me that he will indeed be seen even as he is led to believe not. Perhaps he can sense my presence. This I consider as Wade urges him to strip, and I find I am pleasantly unsettled with the idea that a living man might feel me near. How much else might he feel? I draw close, wrap my arms around him, blow my breath upon his neck, and see him shudder, then look about. "I don't know, Wade," he offers. "I'm just not comfortable in the open."

"Well, babe, all we have is open, unless you want the SUV. C'mon, a little adventure. Think of Uncle Oren. All those men drinking and gambling. You gotta know they were hot to fuck."

When Frank at last relents, I suffer an ecstasy I cannot justify with words. He throws his clothes onto the pile and stands bare, prick but partway up, as if it is no more convinced than its owner of the rightness of what is about to take place. I, meanwhile, am aquiver with anticipation and holding back from leaping upon Frank to fuck him myself, which I now believe I could do, such is the fire these men have stoked.

Wade takes Frank's cock in hand, works him, then drops down to suck the thing into his mouth, and I am unable to restrain myself. I slip around to Frank's backside and run my prick up his crack, humping him like some dog until he cries out to Wade, "Fuck me!"

Wade flips his friend around, positions him standing bent at the wagon's gate. When he drives his prick into the bottom, I engulf the two with my non-being, taking them both at this point, feeling the rod driving into me while also thrusting into the welcoming passage. As they fuck I am reborn, alive though I know it cannot be. But I am as close as a spirit may get to knowing flesh and desire, and when Wade cries out that he is coming, I feel his cock fire its load and feel also Frank's hole welcome the issue. For the time they are in the throes, I am likewise. Gone to glory, so to speak. Through them I am viable.

It is not a climax as I knew while living, but I refuse to quibble at particulars. While the men part and mop up, I remain close by. Once settled, they open bottles to drink and I allow some distance to think on what we have accomplished. It is as I watch them that I begin to contemplate what may yet take place. If I can get inside them as I have just done, what is to keep me from pressing further and attaining full release? They seem to have broken my limits. Thus I shall not settle for anything less than what every man desires.

I think back to going at Ty that last time until sweat flew and we stank of cum. Then next day he was called to Sacramento, where his pa lay dying, and he was gone a full week, the end of which saw the end of me. How I ached for him while he was away. As we'd done one another every day before that, fucking until we could barely stand, it was pure agony to be without him, but I couldn't leave my claim. Nights I abused my dick something awful, but a hand is poor substitute for a man's bottom hole.

The week was all but gone when a dispute rose over my claim and words were exchanged, then bullets. I killed one of the tormentors but the other killed me, and when Ty returned two days later, I was gone to him. That I lingered was little consequence as I, being new to my undead state, had no idea I could call to him or show myself. Ty left town brokenhearted while I remained filled with longing that remains to this day.

Now Frank and Wade drink their drinks, then lie back inside their wagon, where they have bedrolls and such. They remain naked, dozing, hands entwined, and I envy their connection to one another. But I must leave them because I am drawn elsewhere. There is no need to consult the sun. Two o'clock is nigh.

My place is out front of the Central Market, which I had just exited on that fateful day. I take up my position to the right of the door and from there see Oren Hart come out of the saloon opposite. I know now, as I did not then, that Oren had lost at cards and accused Hugh MacKenzie of cheating. Why Hugh chose not to draw when challenged but to follow Oren outside is unknown, though many thought Hugh attempted restraint only to be overcome by taunts from those at his table. Whatever his reasons, he followed Oren, and I see him now come through the door and pause to take in the scene. Oren has spotted his friend Lucas Lathrop and starts over until Hugh calls him out.

The present now succumbs to the past as I see the town thriving, buildings returned and peopled, and for a few minutes I enjoy what once was. Then Hugh and Oren fire at one another, and Oren, being the lesser shot, falls dead, which causes Lucas, who is a good shot, to shoot Hugh. Hugh, dying with gun in hand, staggers back and in his last act of life gets off a shot that hits Lucas in the neck. Within minutes all three lie dead.

Others crowded around on that day, but none do so now. I am compelled to remain by the store until the players disappear into the netherworld from whence they came. This causes no sense of loss, as they will resurrect themselves tomorrow at two o'clock and do it again, as they have every day these many years. The dead men often take some time to disappear, and thus I am captive at the store when I see Frank and Wade coming up the street.

How I wish to call out to Frank that his kin lies dead before him. Unable to assist, I think instead on what odds the house would give on such unlikely circumstance as Oren's kin coming to find him. I also cannot help but wonder what Frank's paper says. He consults it often as he looks for Oren. A letter from the past telling how things went? Many witnessed the gunplay and Oren was well known, thus someone likely sent word to his family and they kept the letter, which has now come down to Frank.

"Cheated at cards," Frank tells Wade as they stand in the street not ten feet from where Oren lies.

"Oren cheated?" Wade asks.

"No, MacKenzie did, or so Oren believed. Called him out, threw down his cards, and left, but MacKenzie followed and they drew." Here Frank pauses to consider his kin. "And Oren lost," he adds.

The killing, be it present or past, gives off a hard energy that lingers in the air like smoke from a pistol. It will remain until the dead men depart. Frank, being close to where the men have fallen, shrugs like he is attempting to unshoulder some burden. "It's weird, being here," he declares.

"No shit," Wade replies. He seems unaffected by the carnage and starts to display some of the impatience I see in most who come to gawk. But he allows Frank room and presses no further. And then Frank turns and looks to me.

Behind him the dead are fading, and I feel myself unleashed though I do not move. Frank's gaze is stern, as if he's onto something, and he takes a step toward me. Then another.

It is in my power to show myself, though I've done it only twice: once when it was new to me and resulted in frightening several people who had known me in life, and again more recently when a wagonload of heathen children roared in and set to desecration. I long to take on my body, as Frank is most appealing, but I know to exercise caution in such pursuit.

"Frank," Wade calls as his friend comes up beside me. Frank waves him off.

"What are you doing?" Wade asks, coming over.

"Quiet," says Frank.

Wade cocks his head to listen and when he hears nothing, he turns playful. "C'mon, you're creeping me out."

"He's here," Frank says. "I can feel his presence."

Wade's roll of the eyes is unseen by his friend.

"It's Oren," Frank says. "He's here."

That he is mistaken in who he senses is of no consequence. I study him as his eyes fire with awareness and he stands to new attention. When Wade questions the certainty of Frank's declaration, he is told again to be quiet.

"Stop saying that," Wade demands. "How much fucking quiet do you need in a ghost town?" He strides away, then reconsiders and comes back. "You know, guys who want to impress a man with a weekend getaway usually opt for Palm Springs or Monterey, but I get a fucking ghost town, and now I'm not quiet enough?" He stomps toward the wagon, where I see him perch on the gate and open a bottle to drink.

I slide around Frank and feel his welcome. I do my best to feed this, slipping beneath his skin to take up with him. He is erect in body, flexing fingers and toes, buttocks and shoulders to such extent he is compelled to stretch and bend backward a bit, as if he needs to make use of what is set upon him. His prick is on the rise, and while the cause is uncertain to him, he welcomes the arousal.

I choose not to enter him fully but rather to keep to his surface, enjoying his awakening while priding myself on such accomplishment. In all my century here, I have never done this, which I put down to never having had a visitor as receptive as Frank. He brought himself here to search for the past, and I mean to be an able guide.

The temptation to show myself throbs my innards. In body I could get at him as would a living man. A battle occurs in me as the practical spirit reminds me Wade is not far off and would see us, but the urge in me, the ache I've known so long, is of such force that I am set reeling and thus take a step back, which allows my desire to break from Frank's. I am sorry for this, but much as I want him, I cannot let my prick decide the when and where.

His mouth falls open. He exhales deeply, as if he can expel what has come upon him. His hand reaches down to adjust his privates, and he moves out into the street while still gazing at the store.

Not knowing if I can reach him otherwise, I attempt such by sliding over to him and telling him without speaking words that we will indeed fuck. His head whips around at this, body following to turn in place, and I know he has heard me in some manner. His desire flares, as does mine, and we remain entwined for long seconds before I again break away. He slumps, shakes his head, and starts toward the wagon where Wade sits watching.

Of course I follow, because it is twilight and most folks leave about now. If Frank leaves, I'll be lost again. "Let's stay the night," Frank says to Wade. "We've got plenty of food, the weather is good, and we can sleep under the stars."

"You have to be kidding," replies Wade.

Frank pauses and I see he gathers patience. "This means a lot to me, Wade. We've come a long way and I don't want to hurry back."

"You've seen the place. What else is there to do?"

"Experience it. The gunfight. You said we could pace it off and reenact it."

Wade makes his finger point like a gun. "Stand out in the street, bang, bang," he says as he shoots Frank.

"Why did you agree to come out here if you didn't like the idea?"

"Because I like you."

"It's one night."

"All our stuff is back at the hotel. I don't even have a toothbrush."

"So we rough it. Seems appropriate. C'mon, I'll make it worth your while." Here Frank nuzzles Wade, kisses his cheek.

"Promise you won't go all Rooster Cogburn on me?"

Another kiss. "Promise."

My relief is such that I give the men room for a while. At a distance I see them make a supper, drink their drinks, and when night falls lay a blanket upon the front of their wagon. They climb up there and lie back to watch the stars. I also look skyward where we are taught resides the Maker and I ask him as I have a thousand times why I have been left behind. He surely took my man Ty when his time came, and I wish to join him in heaven yet am denied such for no reason I can see. So I ask again, and when I am not lifted up, I think on Ty and how we'd spread our bedrolls out under the stars and fuck the night away. I can still feel my dick inside him, never mind our time apart. The ache for him has never left me, and while Frank is not my man, he is in some way as willing, which compels me to want him as much as I do Ty.

The night fails to cool, which leads the men to shed their clothes and play with one another until Wade raises up, puts Frank over the wagon's cab window, and mounts him. The wagon creaks as it rocks beneath. I move closer as I can smell the sex.

It is late when they get inside the wagon and lie naked atop their bedrolls to sleep. Sliding in with them, I hear Wade's heavy snore but see Frank still awake. He gazes out a side window where the town basks in the light of a full moon.

I move over Frank and ease my mouth onto his soft cock, at which he issues a start, then lies back in welcome. I fall to serious sucking as he stiffens. He thrusts up at me to tell me he approves, and soon I hear his soft grunts and heavy breathing. Then he bucks and lets go a load that will appear a mess upon his stomach but which I still swallow. When he quiets I slip away to wait nearby and sure enough, here comes Frank. Clad in boots and short pants, he eases from the wagon and starts toward me.

I move up the street until I am at the saloon because I want to fuck him in the middle of things, both as they are now and were long ago. The men of the daily gunplay make themselves scarce beyond that appearance, so I do not know if they are about. I think on the town that was and, as a remnant, I wish to claim it this night, much as I mean to claim this living man.

When Frank is at the saloon, I allow my ache its full weight. Holding back nothing, it wells up and overflows my banks, spilling out to wash Frank into the deep, and I see him draw a breath and know he can feel my presence. It is then I come to body.

His eyes widen at the sight of me, but he does not flee. "You're what I've been feeling," he says. "You sucked my dick."

I nod.

"Oren?" he asks.

"'Fraid not. I am Ben Darby, but I knew Oren."

A smile flashes across Frank's lips. "This is…" He shakes his head. "Totally unreal."

"You drew me out," I explain. "You accompany your search with powerful feelings and I am led to believe you can feel mine."

"Yes. I kept feeling a presence."

"Your man doesn't feel it," I tell him.

"Oh, Wade, yeah. He's not really into this whole thing. We've only known each other a month. It was a mistake to bring him here."

"But now he sleeps."

"What do you want?" Frank asks.

"I once had a man as you do and much loved him. And fucked him regular. Then I was killed and he left Bodie and I never got past the ache for him. I am denied heaven or hell, condemned to reside here while not knowing why. Then you bring such feeling that I am all but reborn. And I watch you and Wade when you fuck, and my longing is unbearable. I am in great need."

He reaches a hand to my cheek. "You're warm."

"In body I am as any man."

Here he undoes his pants, drops them, and it comes to me that I have not been unclothed all the years here. I strip all away, hard cock pointed at him.

"Where?" he asks.

"Right here."

I do not attempt to kiss him. The instinct that guides me through my non-life tells me to leave off that, but I do pull him into my arms and grind my dick against his as my hands clutch his buttocks.

"Oh, man," he moans.

I then turn him toward the saloon wall, hands upon it, and I spread his legs and get in behind. I look down to see my fingers part him and watch my dick push in. "Oh, man," he says again.

The fuck is a fury, as if all my years alive and dead are risen up to power my cock. I pump in and out, and where youth always made me quick, I now enjoy Frank at length, doing him well into the night as he moans and begs and twice tells me he's coming. At this I look over his shoulder to see his stuff white upon the ancient wood as all the while I keep to the fucking.

At last he begins to tremble and I see his legs weaken from the long assault. The time has arrived for what I seek, and I think of fucking Ty, coming in Ty, and the rise begins. It is as glorious as anything heaven might provide and dirty as something risen from the bowels of hell, the two forces joined in my privates. The come is a gusher and sets me pounding poor Frank, who nearly buckles, but I hold him fast at the hips as I gain release. It goes for some minutes, which I take the result of a century's worth of stored-up spunk. I ram into him again and again until I am empty, then withdraw. When I let go of Frank, he falls into a heap.

We both labor to breathe, and I savor taking air as a living man. I squat down to Frank who assures me he is fine. "Jeez," he manages at last. "Some fuck."

"I am grateful," I tell him. "You bring me completion."

"You bring a hot dick," he counters. I help him to stand, and we dress. When I gaze into his eyes, I feel satisfaction rather than ache. "I would stay longer, but I cannot," I tell him.

"That's okay. I should get back to Wade."

We are reluctant to part, having shared such intimacy. "Oren is here," I offer. "He was indeed killed by Hugh MacKenzie. They and Lucas Lathrop who shot Hugh are condemned to replay the gunfight each afternoon at two. Stand here at the saloon and Oren will pass by, as will Hugh. As you possess a sense for lingering souls, you may feel their smoke."

"Will I feel your presence again?" he asks.

"I witnessed the killing and am compelled to attend it every day since. I will be in front of the store."

He holds out his hand and I shake it. "Much obliged," I tell him.

"Likewise."

We part, and as I watch him enter his wagon, I note again that I am absent the ache. Then a shudder runs through me, as if a wind has come up the plain, and I turn to see a man approaching. The walk is known to me, as is the battered Stetson. It is Ty Wilson.

WOLF MOON/HUNGER MOON
JEFF MANN

I

"He won Best Butt at the Roanoke Bear Run," Matt whispers. We're watching our waiter's ass with avid fascination as he crosses the café to place an order. I can smell the boy from here—my vampire senses are almost always an advantage, unless I'm around garlic or that Appalachian equivalent, the wild onions called ramps that folks hereabouts love to feast on in the spring. Something about his aroma is abnormal; there's a feral whiff I find both arousing and worrisome. I can smell animal in the musks of most men, which is why I like my prey unwashed—no damned colognes for me—but this boy's scent is wild in a way I haven't smelled in a very long time.

"Woof!" Matt says, grinning. "I'd sure like us to make a sandwich out of that cub! You didn't see the Butt Contest, since it was held in the afternoon and you were sleeping, but, man, I did. They had the contestants strip down to underwear and then doused 'em with water and had 'em bend over, and, Lord, that waiter. Big ole chunky rear! Through the wet boxers you could see the hair all over his cheeks and in his ass crack." Matt smacks his lips. "No wonder the lil' bastard won."

My husbear's as horned up as ever, and I love it, whether the object of his lust is me or other men. We've been together for ten years; his age is finally showing a bit. He's forty-five, as muscular as ever but thicker around the middle. His shaggy hair's stippled with gray, as is his bushy goatee. When he grins, there are faint lines around his hazel eyes. He's never been handsomer, more desirable, but still I recognize the signs, the slow way he's leaving me. I too age when I haven't fed for a while—tonight my black beard and ponytail are silver-streaked as well—but after several deep draughts of blood, I'm young again, I look like I'm thirty again, the age I was when I was turned.

"I know what you're thinking," Matt says, flashing me the fur-framed grin that made me fall in love with him. "You're thinking how damned black that hot little waiter's beard is, compared to my grizzled-geezer look, and how much you'd like to tie him to our bed and pump that plumpcious rear of his."

"'Plumpcious'? Great! Actually, I'm thinking that I'd like to have you two roped down side by side so I could take turns riding your butts. He looks like a younger version of you." I sip my wine and look out the café window: January flurries dusting the streets of Monterey, Virginia.

"Yeeow! That would be a hot scene!" Matt rubs his hands together. "Might try to arrange that. Let me lay on my hillbilly charm. Hasn't failed me yet!"

Matt's enthusiasm is adorable. His earthy, untrammeled sensuality is one of many reasons I cherish him. "Or I could mesmerize him," I say, "if you want him that bad." My knee bumps his. It's always been fun being Matt's conspirator in seduction. Four-fifths of the time, his good looks and aggressive appeal are enough. "Though I doubt we'll need my powers of glamour. You're a long damn way from being a geezer, and you know it. With your charisma, you can still land any stud you want."

"Hmm." Matt strokes his beard and chuckles. "Such flattery. I love it! Well, don't know about charisma, but I will say I look a little younger every time you bareback me. I'm thinking that…the human lovers you had before, did you notice that—?"

"Yep." I sip my red wine and grin, flashing a split second of bared fang. "Regular assloads of vampire semen do seem to prolong a mortal's youth."

"Well, then, how 'bout later tonight you inject me with a little of that fountain of youth, Daddy?" Matt's whisper is husky. Beneath the table, his Carhartt boot rubs mine. "Get us a fire going in the bedroom. Cuff me and cuddle with me. Work my nips some. Stuff a jock in my mouth and—"

I savor listening to Matt's hoarse butch-bottom requests as much as he savors composing them, but his lusty whisper's interrupted by our waiter, who reappears with a solemn look and a heaped tray. There's something tense about him, an anxious aloofness.

"Here we go," he says flatly, doling out a plate of cat's head biscuits and a bowl of beef stew for Matt, plus more wine for me. "Hope y'all enjoy." His bass voice is almost absurdly deep. The cub half turns to leave, giving me a meaty profile of pec- and belly-flesh filling out the front of his black T-shirt.

Matt's not about to let this shy find get away so easily. "Donnie, right?" he says, breaking open a biscuit. "I saw you at last summer's run. The one the Virginia Mountain Bears put on."

The boy turns back to us, running a nervous hand over his buzz cut. He's short—several inches less than Matt's five foot eight—with broad shoulders and a burly frame. Not more than twenty-five, I'd wager. Can't recall the last time I saw skin that pale, eyes that dark, a beard so black. Or arms so hairy. The fur starts at the wrists, coats his forearms, and continues on up to beefy biceps before disappearing beneath the sleeves of his T-shirt.

"The run? Really?"

"Really. I saw you win that contest too. You deserved it." Matt stares at him. "Finest butt in the New River Valley, I'd say."

I may be a preternaturally powerful member of the undead, but Matt's infinitely bolder when it comes to flirtation. The boy blushes furiously, the stern look breaking into a sheepish grin, a glint of white teeth, before returning to tense solemnity.

"W-Whoa, man. Thanks, thanks," he stammers, dark brown eyes sidling sideways. For a guy so handsome, he seems painfully shy. "That run was fun."

"I'll bet you had a slew of admirers," Matt says. "Not much in the way of queer nightlife around here, I'll bet."

"In Monterey?" Donnie snorts. "Hell, no. Nearest, uh, nearest bar's Roanoke."

"Yeah, we get it," Matt replies. "We're small-town boys too. I'm Matt Taylor," he adds, offering his hand.

They shake. The contact continues about two seconds longer than it would have if they were straight.

"Strong grip," Donnie says with a wince. "Now that you mention it, I remember you too. And you too, sir. Are y'all partners?"

Sir. I love it. "Yes indeed. I'm Derek Maclaine." I offer my hand. Donnie's grip is firm and warm. His feral-scented musk washes over me. It seems familiar; my cock hardens and the hair on the back of my neck prickles with unease. "Have a seat." I pat the booth beside me. "If you have time."

Donnie looks back at the kitchen. "Well…" he murmurs, then half reluctantly scoots in. "Thanks, bud, uh, Mr. Maclaine. I, uh, I got, uh, a few minutes. So what y'all doing here? Do y'all live around here?"

The booth's narrow; Donnie's denimed thigh is a warm pressure along mine. "We live up in West Virginia," I say, "in German Valley. About half an hour away. Big mountaintop farmhouse we call Mount Storm. I telecommute—I'm in publishing—and Matt here works for the Forest Service."

"Yep," exclaims Matt. "And I'm a damn good cook, if I do say so myself. Y'ought to come up for dinner sometime. We got a fireplace and a hot tub. Bring your boyfriend if you'd like."

"Uh, I'm single as of, of yet," Donnie mutters, an admission that causes Matt to break into a pleased grin. Donnie drops his gaze and brushes a crumb off the tablecloth. "But, well, uh, sure, man. Sometime. Do you like, do you like our little café?"

"Derek here, he works days, so he don't make it down much, but, hell, I'm here at least once a week gobbling up y'all's pintos, chowchow, and cornbread. Plus I can't get enough of these cat's head biscuits! How come I ain't ever seen you in here before? Good-looking cub like you I wouldn't have missed."

Donnie musters another blush and clears his throat. "Thanks for the compliment, bud. You all are, you all are a handsome couple, for sure." He looks intently, first at Matt, then at me before yet again dropping his eyes. "Uh, well, I'm new 'round here. Just moved to the area. I rent me a little trailer near Head Waters."

Matt takes a deep breath—I can feel him gathering his energies, preparing to make an even bolder move—when Donnie abruptly rises. "Well, look, Mr. Taylor, Mr. Maclaine. It was real nice, it was, uh, real nice to meet ya. Y'all seem like real cool dudes, but, um, I better be getting back to work."

"Whoa! Hold on! Here!" Matt fumbles out a business card and pushes it into Donnie's hand. "E-mail's on the back. And there's my cell phone number. What's your number?"

"Thanks, man. Gotta go." He hurries off, our gazes once again affixed to his butt.

Matt's stew and biscuits are soon scarfed, my wine soon done. We rise, tugging on our coats. Donnie's avoided us the remainder of the evening, save for shyly leaving our bill, then taking our money with a stuttered thanks and averted eyes. I leave a big tip nonetheless.

We step out into falling snow and head down the street to Matt's 4x4. "Shit," Matt says, cocking his WVU cap over his eyes. "I thought for sure he was into us. So much for my hillbilly charm, huh? Next time, Derek, use your glamour. Man, we gotta get us some of that!"

❖

A week later. Matt's got a wood fire going when I enter the den, refreshed from my day's sleep in the cellar. Long used to my undead rhythms, he gives me a hard hug and a wet kiss on the cheek. "Here ya go, honey," he says, handing me a tumbler of Tobermory, my favorite single malt, from the Isle of Mull, home during my mortal life so long ago.

I can smell bread baking. "Making me some pumpernickel to go with sausages and sauerkraut," Matt says, rubbing his belly. "My Germanic ancestors have bequeathed me certain appetites. Wish you could eat some. But I guess I feed you in other ways." He gives me a salacious wink and rubs his butt against my crotch.

"Vulgar redneck!" I say, squeezing a pec.

"Damn right! Ain't that why you love me?"

I sit back on the big leather couch; Matt sits at my feet, stein full of beer, his head resting against my knee. The music of Loreena

McKennitt's new CD fills the room. Beyond the windows, the flurries continue; a full moon rises, breaking every now and then through clouds to silver the snow-pale lawn. Unspeaking, we watch the fire flicker and leap. Ten years together have made our companionship as much comfort as passion; it's a precious balance, something that, before Matt, I hadn't had for over half a century. I still miss him, my last human lover, Gerard McGraw, that sweet, cocky boy who died in World War Two.

Matt rises. In the kitchen, he stirs kraut, sets out the bread to cool on a rack, and pours another beer. "Look here now," he says, tossing me the newspaper as he settles once more at my feet. "Today's *Pendleton Times*. Ain't this odd?" He points at the headline.

I skim it fast. Over the last two nights, a bunch of dogs have been killed in the southern end of our county, Pendleton, and down in Virginia too, in Highland County, around Monterey. A few dead deer as well. All maimed by something sharp-toothed and savage. A rabid coyote, they surmise, an especially large one.

I fold up the paper and run my fingers through Matt's hair. Finishing my Scotch, I stand. "I'm going out for a bit."

"Honey? What's wrong? I know you. What's up?" Matt rises and grabs my shoulders. "Do you need to feed? You don't need to go out for that. Here." He unbuttons his flannel shirt, shucks it off, and peels his thermal undershirt over his head. He stands before me, naked to the waist.

I can't resist him—his rich smell, his fur-matted chest, his rounded redneck belly, his prominent, very hard nipples—and he knows it. My little mission can wait. Matt laughs, softly, triumphantly, as I hoist his burliness over my shoulder, carry him into the bedroom, and lower him onto the big four-poster. He winces and sighs, clinging to me as I sink my teeth into his breast and begin a long, slow, carefully measured supping. He's weakening by the time I pull out and begin lapping his neck. He looks up at me, sleepy, with a lopsided grin. When I sink my fangs into his carotid, he emits a tiny gasp and a soft sigh before going limp.

❖

Matt's still passed out, after my cautious blood-feast, tucked beneath the quilts. He'll sleep till morning, giving me time to enjoy a little reconnoitering around the Potomac Highlands. I brush tangled hair from his face, kiss his nose, and leave him. Perfectly safe, slightly drained, and snuggled in, that's how I like my husbear to slumber.

I step out onto the porch, then down onto the snowy lawn. Mountaintop winds slam me; above the stand of spruce trees back of the house, the full moon breaks free from cloud. I break free from human form, spreading membranous wings, and take flight.

Exhilarating, to cruise over these sparsely populated mountains and the great valleys in between, to dip over snow-heavy boughs and ice-edged creeks. I move southwest, veering in and out of cloud-shadow and moonlight. The Wolf Moon, that's January's. Apropos for tonight's jaunt, for, reading those headlines, I was able to remember where I'd smelled a scent like Donnie's before.

The lights of Monterey. Of course he won't be on duty tonight. Not if I'm right. It takes me exactly five minutes to shift form in an alley, glamour the hostess at the Allegheny Café, get Donnie's address, and once more take flight. Up over another mountain range, the winds fierce up here, battering me, then over the tiny hamlet of McDowell, across the black bulk of Bullpasture Mountain, and there's the white church at Head Waters, the moon-shimmering creek, the holler, the tight cove, and the trailer in a stand of pines, a ramshackle car parked beside it.

Shifting again, I stride onto the stoop. The place is dark, but, yes, I was right, here in the snow are tracks—misshapen amalgam of human foot and wolf paw—and more of that animalistic scent.

I mist-sift under the door. Convenient to have outgrown, after my first couple of centuries, that pesky need for an invitation to enter. I explore. Heaps of dirty clothes. A banjo with a broken string. A couple of pizza boxes. Piles of books on the kitchen counter and on the floor: *Leaves of Grass, Oedipus, The Consolation of Philosophy*. CDs: Led Zeppelin, Old Crow Medicine Show, Alison Krauss. If it weren't for that wild smell filling the trailer's stuffy space, it could be any literate country boy's messy man-cave. I pick up a pair of dirty underwear, take a long sniff, and lick my lips.

It's when I mist-sift back outside and re-congeal in human shape on the stoop that I hear growling. Ah, good. Let's see how this were-cub fights.

There he is, on the edge of the woods, a short, stocky silhouette. He moves closer, stepping into the moonlight, hunched, the snarls growing deeper and louder. Pretty much the shape of the boy in the café—threateningly muscular—except he's bare to the waist and covered, as many a legend would lead one to expect, with shaggy black fur. And he sports dangerously large fangs, much more prominent than mine. He bares them at me and rumbles with rage.

"Donnie," I say, moving toward him a step, staring into his wide golden eyes, deep-set beneath bushy brows. Might as well try a little mesmerism. It didn't work the last time I encountered one of these beings, but that one was much larger and much older. "Donnie. It's Derek. Remember me? Calm down, were-cub."

My mind reaches out, fingering for a way in. Human minds are full of little creases, inconsistencies, internal conflicts, self-doubts, and confused desires, more than enough room to wedge in my will. But, shit, just like that older lycanthrope, in this one too the mind is solid and hot, like charred, smoldering wood. When I try to manipulate it, it burns me.

No time for further attempts at mind control. Now the were-cub leaps. Very fast, but I'm faster, sidestepping. He crashes into a snow bank. Snarling, he scrambles to his feet, crouches, and leaps once more. Again I step aside. This time he smashes into the side of the trailer and falls to his knees.

Predictable critters. Their rage addles them, making them less than graceful in their attacks. I stride forward, grip the unkempt beast's head in my right hand, and make ready to slam him into the trailer wall again.

As if to prove me wrong in my assessment of his agility, the furry fiend turns and sinks his teeth into my left forearm. "Cur," I hiss, trying to shake him off. Damn, I'd forgotten how strong they were, how much their saliva stings. Now the little monster's beginning to gnaw, and it fucking hurts. Teeth that sharp, he's about down to undead bone.

I punch him in the right eye, then the left. His jaw goes slack; his teeth release me; he staggers back.

"Troublesome brute," I spit, shifting into mist. "I'll be back for you."

He leaps again, lunging through my smoky wake, sinking wolf-teeth into vapor.

From mist I move to dark wings. The eastern horizon has that warning flush. I'm on my way home, flapping fast to beat yet another dawn. My flight's crooked, slowing my course. That damned werewolf saliva throbs through my left limb. If I were human, such a bite might eventually transform me. As it is, I'm going to be sore for days, and surly too.

I reach home just in time to check on my sweet Matt and his stentorian snores before taking to my cellar coffin. I fall asleep plotting my revenge. I'll taste that bad dog's blood yet.

❖

"You were right," Matt whispers. A few days later, moon waning, we're sitting in our favorite booth at the Allegheny Café. "He's gotta be that wolfie-beast. The boy has a helluva set of shiners."

Donnie's more sheepish and aloof than usual. "Howdy, guys. What y'all want?" He flips open his order pad.

"Other than your phone number? So where'd you get those black eyes?"

"I'm, uh, I was boxing. With my cousin," Donnie mumbles, exhibiting his customary blush.

"Boxing, huh? Sorry, man, don't mean to be nosy. Well, you're still sexy as hell. Makes you look dangerous. Wild, y'know?" Matt gives Donnie's shoulder a soft punch. "Downright ferocious."

Now that we know the cub's secret, Matt seems even more interested in bedding him. "You like it rough? We can give it to you rough," Matt says with a wicked grin. "When you going to come to dinner, bad boy?"

Donnie's pale face grades into flustered amusement. He ruffles his order-pad.

"One of these days. Uh, I cain't, uh, talk now. So what y'all, what y'all want to eat?"

"Wow. Ain't you a tease? And here I thought I was irresistible." Matt shakes his head and emits an exaggerated sigh. "Derek just wants some Merlot. I want macaroni and cheese and the pulled pork sandwich. And how's about a slice of that coconut cream pie in the pastry case?"

Donnie scribbles without looking up. "Slaw on your sandwich?"

"Slaw? God, yes. What Southern boy don't want slaw with barbeque?"

"Thanks, bud." Donnie turns and trundles off. Again we watch his broad rear-end recede.

"Wow," Matt repeats. "First time I've ever wanted up a werewolf's butt. Ten years cohabitating with a vampire, and now this. So how did you know?"

"His smell." I chuckle. "And keep your voice down."

"*Really*? He just smells like a hot lil' guy I'd like to fuck. What do you smell?"

"Animal. Wolf. I met one of these before. The scent's very distinctive."

"Yeah? Where? When?" Matt bends toward me, eyes gleaming. Years cuddling with the undead have made him more fascinated than fearful when it comes to the supernatural.

"Russian steppes. I encountered him during one of my nightly wanderings. He'd killed a goodly number of cattle in a village and a couple of villagers too. He was a mite stronger than I was, though not as fast. We fought pretty much to a standstill. It was his territory, though, and I was just passing through, so I let him be after that. This boy, he's not as strong as that one, but he bites deep. My arm still burns."

"So whatta we do? He's dangerous, right?" Matt rubs his forehead; his eyes range over the unaware inhabitants of Monterey enjoying their meals. "We don't want him prowling around our neck of the woods. What if he hurts folks we care about? What if he comes after us? He's gotta be pissed that you blacked his eyes."

"I doubt that he remembers what happened. Probably doesn't even know how his eyes were blackened or that it was me he encountered while he was in wolf form. Lycanthropic memories are spotty that way, or so the esoteric literature indicates. Wait till the next full moon, sexpot. I'm going to conduct a little experiment, and, with luck, you might end up with an unusual Valentine's Day present. We have a farmer's almanac at home, don't we? I need to consult the schedules for sunset and moonrise."

II

February's Hunger Moon rises like an enormous opal over the eastern ridge. The sky above Donnie's trailer is cloudless. The wind's still bitter and strong; evergreens sough around me; old snow below me gleams with a hard crust of ice. I claw-cling to a spruce bough, wings folded about me, and wait. Tonight, I intend simply to watch, just to be sure beyond a shadow of a doubt that our hot waiter-cub is indeed what we think he is.

The moon rises higher; its light slants through the forest, creeping across the snow, and soon it's bathing the little trailer. Inside, the lights go off; something shatters. There's a mounting series of whimpers that rise to an agonized crescendo. Then silence. Then a low growling. The door flies open; the hunched black shape lopes out, sniffs the night air, and darts off.

I follow him for hours, watching from above. His movement is leisurely and mindless. He zigzags over pastures empty of everything but blue snow and broom sedge; he circles a pond; he skirts houses, snuffles around a barn, causing many a terrified whinny from the horses housed inside; he tracks, chases, and brings down a deer; he inspires hysterical barking from a farmyard bluetick hound and makes a quick messy end of it, bounding off with a bloodstained gnashing of teeth when the dog's owner comes to the back door and releases a round of buckshot.

I've seen enough. He is what we thought. When my stocky were-beast sprints into a deep stand of pines, I veer off over a nearby ridge. Been a while since I've visited my favorite redheaded weight-lifter/historian Kent in McDowell. I'll need the full complement of my powers tomorrow night, and that calls for a hearty meal this evening.

❖

Last of the three nights of transformation the moon's fullness allows. I have to move fast. Talk about cutting it close: sunset's at 6:05; moonrise is 6:51. I leap from my coffin and rush up the basement stairs. "Careful," Matt shouts as I tear past him onto the porch and take flight.

As rapidly as I sky-speed toward Donnie's trailer, I have to sacrifice a good minute on his porch to catch my breath before knocking. Panting would, after all, compromise my vampiric dignity.

"Who is it?" Donnie shouts through the door, customary bass rumble turned anxious tenor.

"Derek Maclaine," I say.

Clicking of locks; the door opens a crack; overheated air pours over my face. Donnie's face appears, dark eyes wide with fear, his beard-black jaw set. "What are you, what are you...doing here, Mr. Maclaine? You got to go, bud. I, uh, I got, uh, a crisis I got to deal with, so you got to go, okay? Don't mean to be rude, but"—he chews his lip, stealing a quick look over my shoulder at the eastern horizon—"you really, *really* got to go."

"We don't have time for this," I say, staring into his eyes. "Look at me."

He may be impossible to manipulate in lupine form, but right now he's just a terrified young man. It takes me exactly five seconds to swallow up his will in the maw of mine. "Open the door, Donnie boy."

He obeys instantly. "Why, sure." Smiling blankly up at me, he steps aside, and I enter.

The boy's wearing nothing but boxer shorts; I take in the black mat of hair coating his thickset chest and belly and lick my lips. His feral smell is even stronger tonight.

"I've come to help you." I grip his bare shoulders. "I know what you are. Will you trust me? Will you come with me?"

He tenses beneath my touch. Glamoured he may be, but waves of fear, shock, and doubt contort his face nonetheless. "You know? How?"

I rub a palm over his buzz cut. "I've encountered your kind before. Is the change deliberate or uncontrollable?"

Donnie bursts into tears. "Deliberate? God, no! I never chose this!"

"Ah, kid," I say, pulling him to me and wrapping my arms around his wide shoulders. He clings to me, sobbing.

"Okay, I guess that's my answer. Family curse it is. Look, boy," I say, tipping his wet face up to mine, "we can talk later. We've got to go. The moon's due to rise soon."

Donnie pushes me away. From beneath the trailer's sunken couch, he pulls a pair of handcuffs. "Here!" he says, tossing them to me. "Please? I don't want to wake up covered with blood again! Please!"

I toss them back. "Cuff yourself," I whisper, "and I'll take care of you till dawn."

"You promise?" he says. "You'll keep me from killing?"

I nod. Donnie takes a deep breath. "Thank God," he says, clicking the metal around his right wrist.

"Behind your back," I order. "Then I'll take you somewhere where you'll be secure."

A second clicking of ratchets, and now he's sweetly caught, thick arms locked behind him. "Damn, don't you look pretty? Come here, cub," I murmur, beckoning.

Donnie steps forward, leans against me, and presses his face against my chest. I embrace him for a full minute—the boy's clearly in powerful need of comfort—before sinking my teeth into his neck.

He gives a little cry and a moment of weak fight before he faints. I gulp and growl, savoring him for the few seconds I can spare. His blood's rich with manliness and youth, downright delicious, but I can taste a musty under-tang to match his aberrant scent. Retracting my fangs, I lift his limp body into my arms and step out into the snow. Along the eastern ridge-top's a pale glow. The moon will rise within the half hour.

❖

First, my hasty return to Mount Storm, captive clutched in my great claws—somewhat of a workout, for between cub-fat and cub-muscle, the boy must weigh nearly two hundred pounds. Next, dashing down to the basement dungeon, a windowless play-space equipped with assorted pieces of BDSM furniture and toy-filled cabinets. Next, locking the great steel door behind us, so that Matt will be safe no matter what happens. Finally, applying the many yards of chain in dim candlelight.

I finish with only minutes till moonrise. Donnie lies on his side at my feet. He's still out cold, hands still snugly cuffed behind him. A thick section of chain stuffs his mouth, pulled between his white teeth and locked around his head, the silver links glinting against his black beard. Since there's only Matt in the house to hear his inevitable protests, it's an aesthetic touch, I admit: I most enjoy a captive gagged. Longer, thicker lengths of chain are padlocked around his furry torso and arms, around his thick thighs, around his knees. A chain fastened around his neck is secured to a ring in the wall; further chain fastens his ankles to the opposite wall. He's stretched taut, like a spider's snack. I never thought, when I built this underground room, that it might serve to detain a werewolf, but, as it is, this is the perfect space.

Bending over my plump prisoner, I stroke the hard curve of his belly and sigh with lecherous delight, relishing my complex link-and-lock handiwork. Few things are more beautiful than a masculine, muscled man in tight, thoroughly inescapable restraint. Well, no human being could escape all this chain, but an angry werewolf, we'll see. That might be another matter. I could have a ferocious fight on my hands if the monster breaks loose.

The boy-not-yet-quite-brute whimpers; his eyes flicker open. When he tries to move, he finds himself nearly immobile. He tenses against the tight circles of chain, then gives a deep groan: discomfort, I'd guess, mingled with relief. The panic in his face softens.

I kiss his cheek. "I said you could trust me."

He nods. He stares up at me, gaze aglow with gratitude, body relaxing into precious helplessness.

"You're not going to hurt anyone tonight. We're underground, in a locked room. Even if you break all this chain, which I seriously doubt, the door behind me—"

No time to finish. His face distorts; his eyes widen. Teeth gnashing the chain, he gives a series of sharp sobs before beginning to thrash.

I watch it all, the weird, panting devolution. It's fascinating, horrible, exhilarating, as I'd expected, to see a boy so desirable shed his humanity and return to our communal source in savagery, re-achieving tooth and claw. A slower process than I'd thought, the black hair already plastering his human form growing thicker, coarser; the dull fingernails curving into spiky weapons; the jaw metamorphosing, lengthening; the nose darkening and moistening; the beard bushing out to join new hair around the eyes and across the brow; those blunt human teeth that gritted the chain sharpening into a dangerous animal's. The eyes, the brown-eyed human terror fading, replaced by glaring golden malice. And the smell, that savage scent, so adulterated in Donnie's human form, so pure and distilled in this trammeled being before me. The reek's rolling off him, stink of dens inside the earth.

I keep my distance for a while, watching the beast writhe, listening to him snarl. Blood-foam builds up between his teeth as he champs the chain; he rolls, jerks, kicks, squirms, batters the floor with hairy heels. I let him exhaust himself. That Russian wolf-prince of the steppes might have had the strength to tear himself free of these fetters, but my were-cub Donnie seems to be fair and squarely caught, just as I'd hoped.

He lies limp at last, clearly exhausted, emitting a deep, continuous growl. The growl grows louder as I approach. He begins thrashing again; I seize his shoulders and hold him down. Scarlet drool mats his chin.

"Risky, yes. But I can't resist this," I say. I breathe in his scent, extend my fangs, and puncture his throat.

Crazing syrup hits the back of my gullet, a flood rush, a black smolder. I close my eyes, sucking hard. Red flickers across my eyelids; manic shakes seize me; my chest tightens. It's intoxicating and sickening all at once. I could drink him dry, or I could vomit it all up now.

I'm about to take another draining draught when the dim memory of that handsome boy in the café flits across my consciousness. Sweet, awkward, scared. His present monstrous state is not his fault. If I don't pull out now, I might kill him.

I retract my fangs. Part of me curses, aching for more. I lap his bleeding neck, and then I stand, swaying. The creature beneath me shudders, jerks, and falls still. I wipe my mouth, lean against the wall, close my eyes, and pass out.

❖

I wake to a pounding. A dual pounding: my head and the locked dungeon-room door. The sun, I can sense, has set.

I'm lying on my side. I sit up. The room's a mess: St. Andrew's cross splintered, paddle bench torn to pieces, candelabra smashed, toy cabinets tipped over. There's Donnie, only a few feet away. He's naked, his bonds still in place, his boxer shorts torn to shreds. He's staring at me, brow creased with anguish, face frantic and tear-stained, teeth clenching the chain. His chest heaves. Against the stifling links of steel, he moans my name. He's lying in a smelly puddle of his own piss and weakly tugging at his chains.

I right myself. Unsteady yet. *Ufff.* I unlock the door.

Matt rushes in, giving me a bear hug. "Oh, God, I thought he'd killed you! Damn it, Derek! How fucking stupid—?"

"Oh, shit!" He releases me, hurrying over to my prisoner. "Oh, damn, poor kid! Help me let him loose! Where are the goddamn keys? He's been chained up for twenty-four hours! Derek, what the hell happened in here? Who the fuck wrecked this room?"

"Uh, I guess I did. I don't remember doing it. Maybe his blood, uh, maddened me?" Head bent beneath my husbear's righteous harangues, I unlock our captive. Beneath the long-applied metal of cuffs and chains, his neck, mouth, wrists, and ankles are rubbed raw. His limbs are so sore he can't walk, so I carry him upstairs to the bedroom. I'm nauseous with both guilt and were-blood by now, and—no fucking help at all— Matt won't stop cussing me. When I try to make a joke of it—"Sorry I left you chained up so long, but it serves you right for biting me last month"—Donnie sniffles, again on the verge of tears.

"Hey, hey! Easy, easy," I mutter, tucking him into our bed. "You sleep, and Matt will fix you some food." The boy's out by the time I close the bedroom door behind me.

I straighten the dungeon room and trash-bag the wreckage. Shit. Drinking were-blood equals mindless destruction and blackouts. Nice to know. I believe I'll limit my future Donnie-feeding to times other than the full moon. Matt whips up a salad with blue cheese dressing and some spaghetti carbonara. We wake our guest, who takes a shower before shuffling stiffly into the den clad in one of Matt's robes. Matt bandages the cub's chain-chafed wounds. They eat and drink in silence by the fire; I watch them, sipping wine. By the time they're through with supper, both men are buzzed, talkative, and in better moods. They're also touching one another—casually, briefly, but frequently, the way guys who are flirting do. Here a pat on a shoulder, there the rub of a thigh or the nudge of knee against knee. This evening might end far more happily than it began.

"I'm truly sorry," I say, adding a log to the fire before lighting candles around the room. "I never meant to leave you bound all day. I meant to free you when the moon set. But I drank from you and, uh, well, kind of—"

"Ran amok and passed out. Like a goddamned frat boy." Matt rolls his eyes, scoots closer to Donnie, and wraps a protective arm around him.

"Drank from me, you said. So you're...sort of like me? Not exactly normal?"

"Well, let's just say that bondage and blood sports are among my favorite enthusiasms. Let's just say that the good folks of Highland and Pendleton counties would approve of me about as much as they'd approve of you...if they knew the truth."

Donnie smiles weakly. "Pitchforks and torches, huh?"

Matt pats Donnie's knee. "Derek was turned in 1730. He's a vampire."

Our guest's dark eyes widen. "Uh, well, so, so—" He stares into the fire, silent.

"Derek and I have been partners since 2002," Matt says. "He can, well, he can be dangerous, but mainly just to assholes, people who hurt folks he cares about. He fucking hates fundamentalists!"

"Hell, me too!" Donnie grins. "Y'ought to kill off as many of them as y'can!"

Matt snickers. "Yeah, I get that! Several nasty homophobes have, shall we say, gone missing. With other folks, well, when he feeds, he's learned to be real careful." Pulling his shirt collar back, Matt displays the red mark on his throat.

"You fed on me in my trailer, right? When, uh, after you had me cuff myself?"

"Yes," I say. "And you tasted mighty fine. I'd be grateful for another abstemious sip if you're willing."

"Speaking of feeding." Matt slips a hand inside Donnie's robe and rubs his belly. "Mmm, *mmm*, love all this hair. Hell, even hairier than me! Did you have enough to eat?"

"Yep, yep, you bet!" Donnie smacks his lips. "I'm single, bud; I'm used to fast food or canned pork and beans! That meal was a fucking, a fucking, uh—was much 'preciated, thanks!"

"You want some deeeeeees-sert? I got some apple crisp needs eating."

"Uh, that sounds great. But first, I just wanna know... Uh, say, buddy, can I, uh, can..."

"Spit it out, cubster." Matt hooks an arm around him. "God, just spit it out!"

"I, uh. I'm sorry I was so standoffish at the café. I've just been so afraid of getting close to people. 'Cause, well, with a secret big as mine, but, well, now, so...now you know, and y'all have a big secret too, so, look, you all are so...I ain't never met...look, you're *hot*! So can I spend the night? Between you two? Will, uh, y'all hold me all night?"

Matt and I exchange big grins. We all finish our wine; we all rise.

"Got a goodly number of hours yet till dawn," Matt says, taking Donnie's hand. They head for the bedroom while I blow out candles and close up the fireplace.

❖

Wind shakes the farmhouse, muttering in the chimney. The bedroom's lit only by the wood-fire my husbear's started on the hearth. We're all three naked now, lying on our sides. Donnie's cuddled between us, facing Matt, a leather dog collar buckled around his sturdy neck; Matt's whispering in Donnie's ear, caressing his beard, lavishing him with deep kisses; I'm kissing Donnie's back, nibbling his shoulders, pinching his prominent nipples, fingering his moist butt crack.

Donnie trembles and sighs, his face pressed against Matt's. "Please, won't y'all, won't y'all both fuck me? Please? Please? I need a plowing awful, awful bad."

"With pleasure," I say, rolling Donnie onto his belly and spreading his thighs. His butt bare is just as beautiful as we'd imagined: beefy and broad, firm cheeks plastered with black fur. I feast on his ass for a long time, my face buried in that wild crack-fuzz forest, easing him open with my tongue, fang-nipping and kissing his buttocks. He's opened up a bit, but he's still tight, hurting some when I stretch out atop him, lube us up, and start working my cockhead up his hole.

"Yeah? *Yeah*? Like that?" Matt murmurs, stroking his face. "That dick can really fill you up, cain't it?"

"Yeah, but, *hhhhuhh*! Hurts some. Uh! Wow. Big!" Donnie winces, pressing his face into the flannel sheets as I slide farther inside.

"Slower, Derek! And Donnie, easy now, just relax!" Matt takes the boy's head in his hands and silences his pained whimpers by pushing his tongue into his mouth. I ride Donnie slowly, starting with shallow strokes before fucking him harder.

"Yeah, yeah. Take it, boy!" Matt growls. "You're so damned hot, you hairy little bastard."

"Oh, yeah, that's feeling real, real good now, Derek!" Donnie gasps. "Uh, Matt, man? Fuck my face, bud. Please, bud?" Donnie begs, fumbling for Matt's cock. "I want you guys to spit-roast me, okay?"

"*Hell*, yes!" Matt rearranges us: Donnie on his hands and knees, me giving it to the cub from behind doggy-style—appropriate for a werewolf, I guess—and Matt stuffing Donnie's bearded mouth with dick. My husbear and I bend together over our guest, kissing one another while filling him at both ends. Donnie groans and slobbers around Matt's cock, nodding with happiness, and bucks back onto my cock.

The boy's asshole is so tight it doesn't take long. With a shudder, a grateful groan, and a final thrust, I finish deep inside him. Matt's turn now. He takes his place behind Donnie, applies lube, and pushes into him.

"Oh, my *God*, you're tight!" Matt pants with wonder. "Superlative hole!"

He gives Donnie's buttocks a series of sharp slaps before commencing a vigorous in-and-out. I slip in beneath our were-boy, lapping his fleshy chest, finding a nipple in that wilderness of midnight-black fur, slipping in my fangs, and nursing from him, lush mouthfuls of blood.

Donnie doesn't resist; the pain my teeth inflict seems to excite him. He rocks back and forth above me, hissing with pleasure as Matt slams him.

"Man, oh man, you two sure know how to fuck a hole," Donnie sighs.

I feast on his other nipple, then slip lower, first to nip that luscious overhang of a belly, next to take his fireplug cock in my mouth.

"Oh, man!" Donnie groans.

Matt plows him harder. I nibble Donnie's cockhead, then slip in a fang.

"*Oh!* I love, uh! I'm gonna—*Oh!*"

Donnie bucks against my face. Semen mingles with blood, filling my mouth with blended sweet and bitter, like the elderflower. Matt finishes immediately thereafter, plunging to the hilt inside Donnie, climaxing with a blissful yell.

❖

"Can I, uh, can—?"

Donnie's voice is tight and low, almost a whisper. "I really love it here. And you guys are great. Can I, can I, uh. Can I come back?"

The room's dim with ebbing firelight. I lie between my hefty boys, arms around both, Matt's head on my right shoulder, Donnie's on my left, quilts pulled over us. We are, this combination is, I realize, both irony and miracle: a long-dead man sandwiched between the doubled treasure of fleeting human warmth.

"'Course you can come back. Right, Derek?"

"God, yes," I say, kissing the top of Donnie's head. "You're adorable."

"How 'bout next weekend?" Matt says sleepily. "Bring that banjo Derek told me about, and I'll git out my guitar…w'can work up a few songs. I'll cook us up some bourbon-barb'que ribs. And some tater salad. Some braised kale, maybe some deviled eggs. Y'like all that?"

"Mmm, oh, yeah."

Their fingers fumble over my belly, meet, squeeze, and interlock.

"You hillbilly boys are always hungry, aren't you?" I run my fingers through Matt's unkempt locks and fondle the whorl of Donnie's ear. "You're welcome here anytime, Donnie-boy. You can keep Matt company during the day. And maybe, next full moon, since I've drunk from you, I can control you in your other form. If not, we can keep you in the dungeon room."

"Yeah," Donnie mumbles drowsily. Matt's already snoring. "Don't wanna hurt anyone…"

Now Donnie's snoring into my armpit.

"Always wanted me a pup," I say to no one. "Yep, a pup. A husbear and a were-pup. Goddamn, I must have done something right. You two are a plethora of riches. Couldn't ask for anything better than this."

I lie there for hours, watching them sleep, my two burly, insensible mountain men, their arms flung over my undead body. Sleet spatters the windows; hard wind grumbles down the chimney; the fire slowly dies. There's something calm inside my chest tonight, something sated, a warm swelling, like a snowdrop, an apple bud in spring, as if my heart had never known rage or loss, as if the regretful gods had decided to give back some of what they'd robbed over the centuries.

When dawn approaches, I slip out of bed, doing my best not to disturb their slumbers. Donnie rolls onto his side; Matt pulls the smaller man into the circle of his arms. Donnie grunts, Matt mumbles, both smile in their sleep, sigh, and start up snoring again. I rearrange the blankets over them before heading downstairs toward the cold room where my coffin waits.

When in Rome…
Anthony McDonald

Dominic awoke in terror, alone in the darkness of the small hours. Darkness but not silence. He had been woken by the smash—smash sound of an ax raining violent blows on a piece of furniture—he guessed the chest of drawers—less than two meters from where he lay. He fumbled for a light switch. He seemed to remember a bedside table-lamp with a switch some way along the cable. The smash—smash of the ax continued. It must surely wake the whole *pensione*, Dominic thought, his panicked brain clutching at straws just as his panicked fingers made contact with the lamp cable and felt their way along it like someone fumbling with rosary beads. *Ave Maria, gratia plena…*

His fingers found the switch. He pressed…and there was light. And sudden silence. Dominic looked around him uncomprehendingly. There was the plain little room: the rug on the tiled floor, the old-fashioned washbasin in the corner, the bare table and the wooden chair, the hanging-cupboard…and the chest of drawers, intact, as he had last seen it a few hours ago, just before turning the light out and going to sleep. The door was shut, the windows closed. Dominic's heart was pounding, his forehead clammy with sweat. Slowly he got out of bed. Checked the door—firmly locked. The window—latched. With trepidation he opened the hanging-cupboard. No-one hung there. He ran his hand over the surfaces of the chest of drawers. He had expected to see it halfway towards the condition of firewood. But there were no ax-marks, no more scratches than were consistent with normal wear and tear. He stood still, naked, in the middle of the floor, for a full minute. At last his pounding heart began to slow. He found that he badly needed to piss. He still felt too frightened to leave the room to make use of the communal facility along the dark corridor. Instead he took two strides toward the washbasin, pulled back his foreskin, and emptied his bladder down the plughole, chasing the torrent down with a hygienic dispensation of cold water from the tap. Viewed in the mirror above the taps, his cock appeared larger and heavier than it did when seen directly from above, and he felt reassured and curiously comforted by the idea that that was how it must appear to others, and in particular to John, who would be joining him in a little over twenty-four hours. In fact, he thought, the whole of his mirrored top half—the smooth lean chest, the flat stomach, the faintly visible but not ostentatious muscles of his arms—looked pretty good, and that thought gave him succor as he climbed back into bed, still quite frightened, alone on his first night in Rome. He was nearly twenty-one. Nevertheless, he kept the light on while he drifted, none too quickly and with some apprehension, back to sleep.

And it was only the fact that the light was still on when he awoke again into bright autumn sunshine that convinced him that the whole nocturnal disturbance had not been a dream. Even so, he began to think that though his waking terror had been real enough, the violent sounds that had occasioned it were mere products of his imagination. He dressed and prepared to go out in search of breakfast in the sun. On his way downstairs, and rounding a bend in the corridor on the floor below his, he passed a young man in the act of locking the door of his own bedroom. He was someone of his own age and very nice looking, not to say beautiful, with dark hair and eyes, but he stood out mainly because of the clothes he was wearing: he was draped from collarbone to ankles in a black, button-fronted *soutane* or cassock—the street garb of a Roman Catholic priest. Dominic said *buon giorno* and the priest, if that was what he was, said *buon giorno* back. Something about the way he said it made Dominic guess that the young man was no more Italian than he was, but he didn't give himself the chance to find out, continuing instead around the angles of the corridor and down the last flight of stairs. Then he hung his key on the hook on the board behind the untenanted reception desk and stepped out into the bright sunshine.

Pity about the cassock, Dominic thought. The young man had looked both sexy and nice. Much too young to be a priest... Unless they caught them in their teens here, like the *castrati* of times past. A silly line of thought, Dominic told himself. He wasn't here to ogle the young men of Rome; John would be here tomorrow. And even if that were not the case and he were looking for fun in the Eternal City, to start his search among the priestly classes would have been exceptionally perverse.

He found a café, sat at a pavement table, ordered a cappuccino and a brioche, and sipped and munched contentedly in the warm sun. He took his phone from his pocket and dialled John's number. But John must have switched his mobile off, because the machine invited him to leave a message. He was alive and well, he said. Would talk later. "Love you," he finished. Had John answered, Dominic might have told him about his night-time terrors or he might not have done, but it was not a piece of news he was going to leave by way of a phone message.

By the end of the morning Dominic had explored a substantial part of the old city. He was surprised by its compactness. He had seen the Piazza Barberini, the Spanish Steps, and the Mausoleo de Augusto, had stood beside the Tiber and looked across the water toward Castel S. Angelo and the Vatican. He did not cross the river. In-depth exploration of the city's treasures would wait till John joined him the next morning, after arriving by overnight train from Brindisi. This afternoon he would be on a ferry, coming to him from Greece.

How bright the sun was here—and by contrast, how deep and black the shadows. Together, sun and shadow turned the whole cityscape into a pattern of jet and bright ochre. Indeed the window and door recesses of the sunlit buildings around him seemed so fathomlessly black that Dominic found himself thinking of the sockets and orifices of skulls.

More cheerfully, his other principal impression of the city was the sheer physical beauty of its young males. They swaggered through the streets and piazzas with a breezy sexual self-confidence that seemed to say, *I'm up for it, just say the word.* Dominic had to remind himself that nearly all of them would be straight and would not welcome any kind of come-on from him—and also that he wasn't supposed to be up for it himself. John was coming tomorrow. All the same, he thought he might check out one or two spots in the Trastevere district that night and see if Rome's gay youth came up to the standards set by their heterosexual counterparts.

By way of exception to the general rule of male peacockery were the priests, walking black shadows themselves, who streamed in both directions across the bridges between the old city and the Vatican, heads downcast as if to avoid sight of the temptations all around them. But even here it was as if beauty could not be completely quelled; it triumphed here and there and shone out, beacon-like, from a good number of youthful faces, and Dominic remembered the young man he had said good morning to in his *pensione*.

After a mid-day pizza and a beer had rounded off his morning's exploration, Dominic returned to his room. He felt surprisingly tired and thought that perhaps a siesta was in order. First, though, he went to his window, opened the shutters and casements to the autumn warmth, and leaned out. It was a room without much of a view. The *pensione* was built round four sides of a courtyard and his window gave onto that. There was no sign of life here—until a movement inside a window opposite caught his attention and he focused his gaze on that. The window was on the floor below his, and through it he could see the bottom half of a bed and, stretched on top of it, a pair of jeans-clad legs and bare feet that looked as if they belonged to a boy or young man. It was the legs that were doing the moving. Dominic couldn't see the whole of them: his view was cut off about halfway up the thighs by the top of the window. But they were twitching about in such an extravagant way that Dominic could only conclude that their owner was either having some sort of a fit, or else… The feet suddenly lifted off the bed and were drawn rapidly back, up and apart, almost following the knees out of sight. A few seconds later and they were back in their original position, but this time they lay relaxed and still. Dominic was aware that inside his own jeans his cock was thickening. There was not much doubt left about what he had just witnessed—or rather, tantalizingly—not quite witnessed. He watched from his window for a half minute more, but there was no further movement of any kind. The show was clearly over. He turned away from the window, towards his own bed. An idea of what he might do next was stirring, not so much in his mind as in his pants.

He stopped, rooted to the floor with shock and fear. His bedside light was on. It hadn't been when he had entered the room a few minutes ago. But it was worse than that. No longer did the lamp sit demurely on his bedside locker; it was on the floor, on the far side of the room toward the door. The flex—how extraordinarily, unnecessarily long the flex was—stretched all the way from the wall socket, past the end of his bed…and…and this was the worst thing…the flex was being pulled, straight and taut.

For the second time in twelve hours Dominic found himself terrified into immobility in the middle of his *pensione* bedroom. And, if anything, this time was even worse. For the implication of this second manifestation had quickly flashed upon his mind. The bedside light had been his ally last night. Switching it on had caused the shattering noise of the ax to stop, had returned the room to normality. But the light was no longer at his command. *It had gone over to the other side.*

After what felt like an eternity Dominic approached the shining light. After all, he had to do something. Step by step he crept toward it. Equally cautiously he bent down, reached out a hand—and was thrown back across the room like someone who has attempted to repair an electric cooker without first switching it off. Whatever had dragged the lamp across the floor was not about to let go.

Back at the window again, Dominic glanced quickly out of it and down at the window he had been watching just a minute ago. The bed was now unoccupied; the legs had gone. There was no other sign of the room's occupant. Not brave enough to attempt to switch the light off (the switch on the cable was rather too near the lamp itself for comfort), Dominic had a new idea. He made his way gingerly toward the wall socket and, with the quickest movement he was capable of, unplugged it. The plug jerked away from him, the bulb went dark, the lamp appeared almost to jump a foot or so toward the door, then fell over with an anticlimactic bump.

Dominic had never felt less like a siesta, with or without an autoerotic prelude, in his life.

Gingerly skirting the now inert lamp on the floor, Dominic left the room and locked it behind him. Was it possible, he asked at reception, to change rooms? No, he was told, the *pensione* was full. It was a Saturday, after all. Why did he want to change? Dominic's Italian was not up to this challenge, nor, he supposed would the receptionist be able to make much of his answer supposing he decided to give an account of events in English. "It's okay," he said. "It doesn't matter."

He went out into the street. He tried to phone John again but couldn't make contact. He'd never before tried phoning someone on board a ferry in the middle of the Ionian Sea; perhaps it wasn't as easy as all that. He looked for another nearby *pensione*, even though he had arranged to meet John at the one where he'd spent last night. He found two and enquired at both. They too were full. Did he not know it was Saturday night?

He sat at a pavement café and ordered a coffee and a grappa in the hope that a plan of action would occur to him while he drank them. Still the sun blazed on the ochre walls, still the shadows ran black through the alleys, still the windows and doorways had for Dominic the sinister aspect of the portals to the inner recesses of human skulls.

And then the obvious struck him. If his room was spooked or haunted in some way (the word *poltergeist* had already come into his mind some time ago) then the solution lay close at hand. There was a young priest in his *pensione*; they had said good morning right outside his room. He'd go to him and ask him to carry out an exorcism or whatever might be required. The young priest would know what to do. When in Rome…

As Dominic made his way up the stairs he realised that the priest's room must be on the same corridor, on the same side of it even, as the room in which he'd seen… The thought made him smile. Then, supposing it was the very room? In spite of his very real state of anxiety, by the time he was knocking at the young man's door there was a grin on his face which he could not remove.

Until, that is, the door opened and he was confronted by the attractive face he'd seen that morning but without the black *soutane*. Instead, the young man was naked to the waist, barefoot, and dressed only in the faded blue jeans that Dominic had seen from the window.

He looked just great. Polite Italian formulae deserted Dominic. "I think I need your help," he said in English.

"Come in," said the other.

Ten minutes later they were drinking an incautious quantity of grappa out of toothpaste-y glasses. The young man was not yet a priest (if he ever would be) but a student for the priesthood at the Luca College. A few of the student rooms had not been ready at the start of term, and he and a dozen others had been farmed out to various *pensiones* for the first week or so. His name was Alex. He explained all this in faultless English, though he was in fact from Luxembourg and had an Italian mother. (That explained the raven hair and deep brown eyes, thought Dominic.) Alex listened attentively while Dominic told his story and was silent and thoughtful for a moment after he'd finished it. Then he said, "I'm not sure if I can help you as much as you would like me to, or deserve. As I said, I'm not a priest. But even if I were, the responsibilities of exorcism are not undertaken lightly. Usually, each diocese has one priest appointed as official exorcist and specially trained, though obviously it's not their sole responsibility. And they don't shout from the rooftop about that aspect of their work either. I've no idea who the official exorcist for Rome might be. And if any other priest wants to carry out the rite, they need special permission from the bishop."

"Don't you know a priest that you could get hold of quickly and then ask the bishop yourselves?" asked Dominic.

Alex paused and smiled. "I think even you know who the Bishop of Rome is."

Dominic thought for a moment. Then, "Yes, I see what you mean. It wouldn't be all that easy to get hold of the Pope."

"So, as you see, I can't be much help from a sacramental point of view," finished Alex. "But I could try to be a friend. Would you like us to go and take a look at your room together?"

Dominic was touched by the fact that, in his concern for his welfare, Alex didn't stop to put on shirt or shoes but walked up the stairs with him, bare-chested as he was. He wasn't a big fellow but lithe and slim, and Dominic, having spent some time enjoying the sight of Alex's naked top half, couldn't help wondering about the rest. He unlocked his door and the two of them walked in together. All was as he had left it, including the bedside lamp, which was still in its capsized state on the floor at their feet. "Shall I?" offered Alex, and bent down, picked the lamp up, and placed it in its usual spot on the bedside locker.

"Thank you for that," said Dominic. "But do you mind if we don't plug it in just yet?"

They strayed towards the window together and looked out.

"You can see your bed from here," said Dominic. Perhaps it was the grappa making him flirtatious.

"Oh yes," said the other. "So you can."

"In fact..."

"In fact what?"

Dominic's next question was meant quite seriously.

"What's celibacy supposed to include—for you people—and what not?"

"Celibacy just means not getting married," said Alex. "But we're supposed to be chaste as well." He smiled—a bit teasingly, Dominic thought. "That's a whole lot harder. It's something we're supposed to be aiming at, but not everyone gets there all at once."

"What about wanking, then?"

"What's wanking?" asked Alex.

Dominic gaped at him in astonishment. Then he realized that though his new friend's English was pretty faultless, he might not know all the colloquial words to do with sex. Rather than wade embarrassingly into a verbal explanation Dominic did a high-speed mime with hand and wrist.

"Oh no!" said Alex, laughing, but blushing furiously at the same time. "How much did you see?"

"Only from there down." Dominic drew a line with his finger across his own thigh, halfway between crotch and knee.

"Well, that's a relief at least." Then Alex reached forward with one of his hands and gently took hold of one of Dominic's. He looked into his eyes diffidently and said, "Now you've embarrassed me."

Dominic returned Alex's gaze steadily and then there occurred that seismic moment when two people of the same sexual orientation look into each other's eyes and learn from them *He's like me*, and, a second later, the message's perfect anagram *He likes me, too.*

There was an unmistakeable outline now in Alex's jeans, straining against the fabric. With his free hand, which trembled, Dominic reached forward and undid studs to give the pent-up form release. He was not surprised now to find Alex's cock unencumbered by any underwear as it came popping smartly out, framed only by a small neat triangle of shiny black pubic hair, while his jeans slid down his legs. Alex was cute-cocked rather than well-hung, something Dominic found reassuring—he was not such a very big boy himself. He watched as a clear droplet began to form at the tip of Alex's foreskinned penis like a dewdrop on a budding rose.

Within a minute they were both stripped naked and all over each other on the floor, busy with hands, wet tongues, and wet and glistening cocks. Then, before they'd even negotiated who would do what to whom, they'd done it anyway, coming simultaneously in floods, pressed hard and pulsating against each other's bellies.

They lay still together for a while. Then Dominic got up to get a towel.

"I'll have to go in a minute," Alex said, sounding suddenly flustered as he mopped himself down. "College supper."

"Couldn't you skip it just for once? I was rather thinking of checking out Trastevere, do a few clubs or bars. It would be nice if you came too."

Dominic could see prudence struggling with desire in Alex's eyes, but only for a second. Desire quickly won. "Okay, I'll come. To hell with the consequences." Then his face fell. "I don't think I've got the right clothes."

"Come as you are," suggested Dominic to his still-naked friend. "You'll be a sensation. No, but seriously. Your jeans'll do just great. And I'll find you a nice shirt. We're about the same size." He tweaked Alex's waning erection playfully, to point up the double entendre.

❖

They explored the bars, they wandered the streets, they saw the city's lights reflected in the Tiber like stars, they drank and danced, they exchanged the stories of their lives. Alex told Dominic the tales he had heard about exorcists and demons and possessions. "Even the very experienced exorcists have to be careful. The spirits are full of tricks." He told one story about a priest who had successfully carried out the exorcism rite, as he thought, then found himself breaking into a sweat. Reaching in his pocket for his handkerchief, his fingers had encountered… *"not a handkerchief but a lump of human shit."*

Alex knew the shortcuts home. They threaded their way through narrow ways lit halfheartedly by lamps on the walls of the ancient houses. Occasionally their path brightened as they turned a corner where the beam of the three-quarter moon had managed to pry a way in, between the crowding eaves. "I need to pee," said Dominic suddenly, and Alex said, "So do I."

Relaxed and comfortable now in each other's company, they both pulled down their jeans a little way. A little farther than was strictly required for their immediate purpose, actually, but gay boys will be gay boys. Turned halfway toward the wall, halfway toward each other, they enjoyed seeing their slender streams sparkle in the moonlight, and turned a little more toward each other to make their silver swords cross, like kids do.

But, in the places where their attentions were really focused, they were beginning to look less and less like kids. Both their cocks had started to swell, bulge and lengthen, to stretch out and up. They had to turn apart, toward the wall again, to avoid hosing each other with their now upward-founting springs. Eventually—though the final spurts were difficult to accomplish, as in this situation they always are—their urgent task was done, and they were left to face each other with large exposed erections that would be difficult to put away.

They didn't try. "Can I?" Dominic asked. His voice was breathy with sex and nerves, but he didn't take the risk of waiting for an answer. He reached forward and took Alex's now fat penis in his hand. It was wet with something. Pee or pre-cum. He didn't care. Probably both. Alex's hand curled tentatively round his own full-stretched dick. Alex hadn't said anything, either to answer his *Can I?* or to ask his own. It was as though he knew he shouldn't be doing this, but he had already done it—more or less—with Dominic earlier that day, so might as well be unfrocked for a sheep as for a lamb. In any case, the fewer words were offered as hostages to the situation, the better.

They kissed as they began to work on each other's hard-ons. Deep kisses like an exchange of friendly snakes between their mouths. Dominic wondered if Alex the student for the priesthood had ever done this before. He seemed to have no trouble with the exercise. Perhaps it was one of those things you didn't need to learn…Like what they were doing with their hands.

Their hands caressed each other's nape and hair, ran down the outside of shirts, then scaled the warmer, yielding heights inside. Like the hands of blind people they explored the melon contours of the other's buttock cheeks—a little crop of short hairs, a very few, over Alex's tailbone; Dominic's all smooth. Made daring darts beneath the arse, from behind, to engage with hot, tight, furry balls.

And with the other hand? That too was something neither had needed to learn. Though there was room for a little variation even here. Alex pumped Dominic's cock—as he presumably pumped his own—in short speedy bursts that lasted a couple of seconds or so. Then a one second's pause, and then repeat. Dominic applied himself to Alex's dick with the steady, slower, rhythmic stroke he'd used all his life, on himself, on John, and on pretty well everybody else who'd come his way. But the novelty of Alex's attack produced a result more quickly than Dominic expected or had grown used to. "Oh hell, man, I'm coming," he said.

Alex didn't falter in his stroke. Just pulled his chest back a little, to get a better view, while Dominic's bulging prick let flow his semen like an offering into, and overflowing, Alex's cupping hand.

Alex spoke now. "Me too," were all the words that left his mouth. But he was not so frugal in what he delivered through a smaller—smallest—orifice. Dominic felt his friend's penis swell like a time-lapse mushroom, and then from its hooded tip his liquid lance of sperm clove the dark space between them, arcing from Alex's body to Dominic's, moonlit white: as sudden, powerful and brilliant as a lightning streak across the face of heaven. Dominic felt its sudden heat sear the undercurve of his balls, then trickle, cooler now, down the inner, private regions of his thighs.

They stuffed themselves away after that, too high on each other's company to bother about wiping up, or worry which bits of their clothing all that liquid magic had found its way to—and whether it would show. Only now did they realise their luck in not being spotted, sharing themselves in an alley in this blatant way. "Come on, we'd better get out of here," Alex said, and taking Dominic by the hand for the first few yards, led him towards the exit of the passageway.

As they finished their journey, Dominic asked Alex if he'd ever fucked a man, been fucked by one, had his cock sucked, sucked another's cock? Alex answered a bashful no to all those four. They were answers that could be changed before daybreak, Dominic thought. Well, some of them at any rate. Perhaps not all four. Dawn wasn't all that far away…

It was after three o'clock when Dominic and Alex returned, sharing a special kind of cloud-nine high, to the *pensione*. The duty receptionist gave them a discreet nod and they made their way up the dimly lit stairs. "We'll check your room out first," said Alex in a businesslike tone. Dominic had almost forgotten there was a problem with it.

They didn't need to turn the light on when they opened the door. They stood in the doorway and gazed, appalled, at the scene before them. The bed, Dominic's bed, was illuminated from within like something in a religious painting. The table-lamp was inside the bed, mounding the bedclothes and shining, glowing, through them. In the very place where Dominic should have been. Would soon be? With Alex? Not on his life. For the light was not the only sight they saw. Dominic's clothes were strewn across the floor. "Jesus Christ," he murmured, almost without breath. The chest of drawers was a substantial pile of firewood, of jagged, broken planks that leaned at awkward angles against each other and against the wall. Involuntarily Dominic and Alex clutched at each other.

"You're not sleeping in here tonight," Alex said firmly. "You're coming to bed with me." They kissed each other fiercely as soon as they left the room, and Dominic locked the door on whatever had taken control within.

❖

John got the room number from reception and went up to find his friend. Although it was ten o'clock, Dominic had not been out yet, they told him at reception, or even been seen. Still, it was a Sunday morning.

John knocked and waited. He knocked again. Waited some more. Knocked harder the next time, and louder. After five minutes he gave up; people would be coming to complain. He went back to reception. A handsome young man was talking earnestly to the receptionist. He was tall and muscular, as was John himself, with a healthy tan and the strawberry-blond hair and blue eyes of northern Italy. What a waste, thought John, noticing—you could hardly help noticing—that he was clad from shoulder to shoe in priestly black. Only then did he begin to register what the new arrival was saying.

"...didn't appear at supper...breakfast...morning Mass...not answering his door..."

"He returned very late last night," the receptionist said. He looked up and caught sight of John. "With the young man that our friend here is looking for."

A minute later, escorted by the duty manager, John and the blond young man in black were climbing the stairs together. They reached Alex's room first. After a quick courtesy knock, the manager opened the door with a master key. They walked in. And froze. They were unable to utter a word, any of them, though their gasps of shock and distress were as audible as cries. John's fingers sought and clutched spontaneously at the other young man's hand.

The bedside light was on. Its improbably long, strong flex was hideously tangled around the necks of the two young naked bodies that lay—limbs caught by death in desperate flailing motion, their two heads drawn together by the wire—among the dishevelled and thrown-back sheets. Somehow their two heads were raised a little above the pillows and the light projected their two shadows—so black they were, it seemed to John that they made two real holes, like the pair of eye sockets in a human skull—against the bright ochre wall.

It was many hours later, as the two of them waited in an arid waiting-room to be seen by yet another police official, that John and the blond young man—whose name was Antonio, he said, and who wasn't a priest yet (if he ever would be) but only a student for the priesthood—found their fingers interlocking, almost involuntarily, for the second time that day. John and Antonio looked into each other's eyes, and through the pain and hurt there John saw something else. He thought, *He's like me. And he likes me, too.*

HOT DAY AT MIDNIGHT
JONATHAN ASCHE

I didn't know how many miles I'd been walking before I reached Midnight. Probably only three or four, but it felt like twenty.

"Of fucking course," I groaned, shaking my head incredulously at what a rusted sign identified as Midnight Gas & Oil, now a crumbling shell baking in the harsh afternoon sun. Capped-off, rusted pipes that once supported pumps rose from a concrete island.

The cowboy was on the north side of the building, one foot braced against the wall, muscular legs straining the seams of his Levi's, a generous package straining the buttons on his fly. Melon-sized biceps bulged out of the rolled-up sleeves of his western shirt. From beneath the shadow of his cowboy hat peeked a mustache-topped smile.

Neither the smile nor that basket could soothe my frazzled nerves. "Is this the only gas station around here?" I asked.

The cowboy said nothing.

"Do you know anyplace that has a pay phone, maybe? I had an accident a few miles back. I can't even get a goddamned signal out here."

The cowboy none-too-subtly adjusted his package.

"Hello? Can you speak?"

The hunky cowboy gave his bulging crotch a squeeze and jerked his head toward the abandoned gas station. His smile deepened into a suggestive leer.

I ignored the silent invitation. Being stranded in a desert hellscape had put me in a less-than-sexy mood. Still, it took a lot of effort to pull my eyes out of his crotch and continue walking down the street. He followed me with his eyes.

The rest of the town didn't look much better than Midnight Gas & Oil, and my plight was looking worse. Then I saw a man sweeping the front entrance of a small, ramshackle grocery. He was rugged looking, with silver hair and an ageless body. As I neared him he stopped sweeping, and I asked if I could use his phone. Like the cowboy he said nothing, just stared, a lecherous smile on his lips. A tickly unease vibrated in my stomach.

"Never mind," I squeaked, hurrying on my way.

Across the street a shirtless black guy painting a storefront stopped what he was doing to watch me. I looked at him long enough to appreciate the sweat shimmering on his ripped torso before looking away, conscious that his eyes were still on me. Ahead of me, leaning against a splintery wood column, a handsome blond enjoyed a cigarette. Though his physique made his khaki pants and white button-down look like fetish wear, I kept my eyes level with his. Regardless, he made sure I noticed his hand slide to his pronounced package.

There were other people in Midnight. I could sense them watching me from their windows, but when I looked their way I only saw were rustling curtains. In a second-floor window a young man with curly hair stared back at me, his nude torso framed behind cracked glass.

The roar of an engine shattered the town's eerie quiet. I turned to see a motorcycle, its rider's head covered by a helmet and his thick arms covered with tattoos, heading right for me. I froze, the proverbial deer in headlights, then, adrenaline surging, dove out of the way just ahead of the bike, landing on the gritty pavement.

The bike spun around me, kicking up clouds of dust as it skidded to a stop.

The town's spooky silence had returned by the time the biker took off his black helmet, exposing a shaved head and an unshaven face. He nodded, resting a fingerless gloved hand in his crotch. His smile was as seductive as it was menacing, but I was too angry to be seduced or intimidated.

I got up on my feet, dusting myself off and shouting: "Are you a fucking psy—"

From the corner of my eye I saw them, and the words stuck in my throat. Walking toward me, at a slow, deliberate pace, were the men I'd passed—the cowboy, the shopkeeper, the painter, the blond guy—and many others I hadn't seen earlier. Their expressions made me wonder if they planned to kill me or fuck me. I didn't want to stick around to find out.

A pair of tattooed arms circled my chest. "You were sayin'?" hissed the biker, his hot breath on my neck, his gloved hand pinching one of my nipples through my T-shirt.

"W-what's going on here?"

His laughter was a razor slicing along my spine. The other men had reached us now, forming a semicircle around us, still wearing those peculiar expressions that made my blood rush and my cock twitch.

"Don't get much new blood here," the biker said. He touched his hot tongue to the base of my sweaty neck. I shivered like he'd dropped an ice cube down my back.

"Maybe you all should get a new welcoming committee."

More razor-edged laughter stung my ears. "You'll change your mind once you open our gift baskets." The biker ground his well-packed crotch against my ass, driving his point home.

With his one arm across my chest holding me in place, his other hand slid down my flat stomach, down between my legs, and cupped my junk.

"Please, I just want to use a phone," I pleaded.

But my cock made a liar of me. The biker undid my shorts with such alacrity I barely realized he'd done so until he reached into my boxers and curled his gloved hand around my stiff cock. His fingers played along my swollen shaft, his touch surprisingly gentle.

"Got a real meaty one on 'im," the biker told the crowd. "Feels like a real mouthful."

Murmurs of appreciation buzzed through the crowd. The cowboy from the gas station, standing front and center, lazily stroked the hard ridge his swollen cock created in his jeans.

The biker ripped open my shirt with one quick, sharp pull, then sent me back to the ground with a sudden, violent shove. A bone-cracking pain tore through my body. Gasping, I tried to stand up, rising up on all fours before I felt the biker's heavy boot resting on my butt. "Got a nice ass, too," he said.

My shorts were around my knees with one jerk.

Hands pried apart my butt cheeks; fingers toyed with my ass lips. "All hot 'n sweaty," whooped the biker. "Looks like I'm gonna have to cool you down."

A silence followed. I looked up at my audience, some watching the biker, some watching me. They all looked like they were in on the joke and relished my discovery of the punchline.

The warm stream hit my ass. Seconds later, the familiar, sour odor hit my nose. "Oh, Jesus, no," I whimpered.

My cock belied my protests, throbbing as the biker's piss sluiced between my splayed ass cheeks.

"C'mon, show me that hole," the biker ordered. "Raise that ass up."

I obeyed, and took a direct hit of piss against my asshole—bull's eye. My dick quivered.

One of the guys—the blond I saw earlier smoking a cigarette— stepped out of the crowd, the toes of his shoes coming to a stop just inches from my fingertips. I looked up at his smirking face, watched him slowly unbuckle his belt. He said: "Think it's 'bout time to take him to the hitchin' post."

"The hitchin' post!" seconded another guy. Others chimed in, until the crowd was chanting. *The hitchin' post! The hitchin' post!* I was no longer afraid; I was terrified.

The blond reached down and grabbed one of my arms, pulling me roughly—painfully—to my feet. A sinister smile was the only warning I got before he pulled his belt from his pants and quickly wrapped it around my wrists, threading the leather through the buckle and cinching my wrists tight.

I was led down the street, a pathetic spectacle as I stumbled behind the blond, smelling of piss and sweat, my T-shirt now a rag hanging from my shoulders, my shorts tangled up around my ankles. Weak as I felt, my cock remained strong, still stiff and trembling.

"The hitchin' post" was in the center of town and not really a post at all but two posts, about four feet apart, from which chains descended, and at the end of the chains leather cuffs. A couple feet in front of the two posts was a small, wooden parallel bar, about waist high. The blond pushed me against the bar, then handed the belt to the biker, who pulled me forward and with practiced skill fitted my hands in the leather cuffs, adjusting the buckles so they fit tightly around my wrists. Someone else reached between my legs and lassoed my cock and balls with a thin leather cord, possibly a shoelace, and trussed me up tight until I could feel my dick pulsating.

I was bent over the parallel bar, ass out, my arms outstretched and fastened above my head. The perfect position for what they had in mind.

Filthy words of admiration stained the desert air as anonymous fingers assaulted my asshole, worming past my contracting ass ring and making me quiver. The fingers inched deeper into me while another hand curled around my cock, forcing out a sharp cry—a cry that was promptly stifled by a blunt, veiny dick. I tried to look up at the possessor of the cock, but his hands held my head in place as he fucked my mouth, not allowing any clues to his identity beyond bushy black pubes, plump balls in a tight nutsack, and stocky legs in equally tight jeans.

The hot shock of a tongue stabbing into my pliant asshole sent a shudder through my body. The tongue made a quick retreat, the tip twirling gently around my pulsing sphincter, then it plunged back into me, forcefully, like a cock. My arms jerked, rattling the chains as that mystery man's tongue—hard, wet, relentless—snaked up my chute. Then he chomped down on my knotted sphincter, bringing tears to my eyes.

Just as relentless was the anonymous cock stabbing into my mouth, hitting the back of my throat. I was aware of, but did not see, other men gathered around us, watching, cheering and waiting their turn. The man stuffing my mouth drowned out the crowd with his groans, growing louder and louder until his cock erupted, his tart cum washing over my tongue. He was still coming when he pulled out, leaving a final splat on my lips and chin while the other guys told me to eat that hot load.

Another man, this one nude, presented his fleshy, uncut club of a cock to my face. He made sure he wasn't anonymous, cupping a hand under my chin and directing my eyes up, over his tight, sinewy torso until I reached his face. A man about my age—early thirties—looked back at me with cold blue eyes. His lips curled into a smirk as he batted that clublike cock against my gasping mouth.

And then: the tense pressure of a cockhead pushing against my ass lips, working its way past my winking hole. I gnashed my teeth, enduring the tug-of-war between pleasure and pain as the dick burrowed into me, with pleasure quickly winning out as the unidentified cock nudged my prostate, making my dick jump and my body quiver.

Cold Blue ordered me to stick out my tongue, resting his uncut monster on it like it was a pillow. He squeezed his foreskin, milking out a salty drop of pre-cum, a taste of what was to come.

The man at my ass began ramming me ass in full, deep thrusts. The man at my mouth heaved his cock forward, sinking it into my gullet. I gagged, coughing as Cold Blue withdrew. His prick popped from my mouth, slinging thick ropes of my bubbly spit. Someone sneered: "Too much for ya?"

I barely caught my breath before I was again gagging on Cold Blue's cock. The anonymous stud pounding my ass picked up speed, grunting loudly each time he sank his cock up my chute, until his grunts became one long, guttural groan. I could feel his dong throbbing inside me, his copious load filling my insides. I was filled from both ends: Blue Eyes came, feeding me his creamy jism. When he was done, he smacked my face with his slimy wet cock.

The man fucking me withdrew, immediately replaced by another unseen cock. I tried to look over my shoulder at the man, only getting a glimpse of a long, narrow face surrounded by unruly black hair before my head was twisted back around to face two other men demanding use of my mouth. One man looked to be in his mid-forties, his beefy body covered with hair but bald on top of his head. The other guy was younger, very tan, his hair a tousle of sun-bleached locks—he looked like a surfer. But the men only wanted me to appreciate one feature of their anatomies, and were quick to redirect my attention, hitting either side of my face with their stiff rods.

My body tensed and I closed my eyes, whimpering as the man invading my ass hit home, his cock buried to the hilt. He withdrew, then dove back in, hitting my ass so hard he nearly knocked the wind out of me.

Both the beefy guy and his surfer sidekick stabbed their dicks at my mouth, but only the older man made it past my blubbering lips. He let out a satisfied groan and raked his fingers through my sweaty hair as I swallowed his cock. The surfer tried to crowd his way into my mouth as well, but only succeed in smearing pre-cum across my cheek. The beefy guy unloaded quickly, his body pressed against my face, my nose digging into the base of his cock as he coated my throat. The surfer, unable to wait his turn, jacked off furiously, his load raining down on me in heavy, sticky drops. Through it all, the guy at my ass kept pounding away, grunting furiously as he edged closer and closer to his big finish.

A big, black cock throbbed before my eyes. It was the painter I'd seen earlier, his white overalls rolled down to the tops of his thighs. Under different circumstances I might have made a joke—*glad to see some stereotypes are true*—but not now. Not when I was bent over a wood bar, my hands chained, covered in piss, sweat, and cum, my neglected hard-on strangled in leather, painful with need.

The painter's full lips stretched into a smile. He grabbed the base of his cock and rubbed his dong up the side of my face, scooping up the viscous cream left behind by the surfer. When he was done he presented his stiff rod for my inspection, the deep chocolate-colored head frosted with pearly white gobs of jizz. He said, "Go on an' get it all slick for that sweet white ass." And then my mouth was full of his meat.

A whiny moan sounded behind me, the anticlimactic signal of a climax. The persistent pounding ceased, the unseen man frozen atop me as he fired his load into my guts.

The painter pulled his cock from my mouth. It was dripping wet, lubricated with spit and sperm. He chuckled softly as he walked behind me. The cock occupying my chute was withdrawn. My asshole got only a moment's reprieve before the painful entry of the painter's mammoth tool, stretching my sphincter even wider than it had been already, the strain boring through my body and exiting my mouth in an anguished moan.

As usual, someone stepped in to muffle my cries. This time it was the blond, the one who instigated tying me to "the hitching post," who appeared before me, out of his clothes now, his spectacular body glistening beneath the bright desert sun. His dick was bowed and listing to his left, the shaft thicker than the head. I opened my mouth, inviting the blond's cock inside, thinking: the quicker they get off, the sooner *I* get off.

The blond surprised me with a sudden about-face, presenting his well-formed ass. Soft blond down covered his shapely globes, with darker, coarser hairs lining the crack. He bent at the waist and spread his legs, opening his cheeks to expose his tawny bud. In two backwards steps his ass was pressed against my face and my tongue was pressed against his butthole.

"C'mon, shove it up there," the blond stud ordered.

I struggled to comply, my tongue piercing his ass ring, slithering into his chute. But it was difficult to luxuriate in this perfect ass when the painter was punishing my butt with his unremitting ramming. My engorged cock pulsed each time that fat black rod plowed into my chute, and I wondered if I might come without any direct stimulation—a waking wet dream.

Both the painter and the blond beat me to orgasm. The painter's bass groan announced his release, his body quaking with the same thunderous intensity. The blond spun around, ordered me to open wide, and jerked his metallic-tasting load onto my tongue. Satiated, they stepped away, freeing my orifices for the next round.

Instead, the restraints came off. Strong hands came down on my shoulders, pulling me to my feet. My legs were wobbly, my arms were rubber, and my wrists were raw and burning. My leather-choked cock was a purplish red, swollen and dripping. I reached for it, but the man who had pulled me to my feet grabbed my arms, pulling them back until a knot of pain twitched between my shoulder blades. "Not till we say," he said, grinding his hard-on into my ass crack.

The silent cowboy from the gas station stepped forward. The way he licked his lips made me feel like prey. He unbuttoned his shirt, exposing a broad chest covered by a thicket of black hair. Once the shirt was off, he started on the jeans, unbuttoning them slowly, keeping his dark eyes on me. My eyes fell below his waist, and stayed there.

He moved closer, until the brim of his hat nearly touched my forehead. His hand went to my vibrating hard-on, his fingers caressing the drooling head and his mouth curling into a smile as he watched me tremble and moan. Those same fingers, wet with my juice, were at my lips, sliding into my mouth. A moment later, the hands holding my arms relaxed their grip and I was sliding down his furry chest, to my knees.

I slowly took his cock into my mouth, relishing every inch that slid over my tongue. He was impatient, thrusting forward until his dick was deep in my throat and my nose was deep in his musky pubes. I gagged, but quickly recovered. The gravel on the street cut into my knees, but I didn't care. The cowboy's moans rumbled deep in his chest. He raked up a handful of my hair, plunging his dick into my mouth while guys in the crowd urged him to "fuck that mouth" and "choke 'im with cum."

He pulled his cock from my mouth. I looked up at his face. He'd lost his hat, and I could see he had black, curly hair, flattened where the hat had rested. His jaw was clenched, his lower lip trembling. His eyes seemed unfocused as he pulled on his cock, stroking it faster and faster. A gruff voice whispered in my ear: "Stick out yer tongue."

I obeyed. The cowboy's shallow breaths turned into sharp, stuttering grunts and groans. Thick, curling jets of cum landed on my face and tongue. The crowd made noises of approval and admiration. The cowboy stood over me, shaking the last drops of jizz from his cockhead, and then stuffed his pulsing rod into my mouth, just to make sure I got every last drop.

Heads turned in the direction of a distant rumbling. The noise grew louder and the crowd parted. The motorcycle was heading right for me—again. *And this is how I die*, I thought a split second before the biker cut the wheel, making another one of his theatrical stops that enveloped us all in clouds of dust and exhaust.

The biker hopped off the motorcycle with dancerlike grace. He had stripped since I'd seen him last, now only wearing his fingerless gloves and scuffed combat boots. He swaggered before me, showing off a body covered with knotty muscles, scars, and tattoos.

"Ain't you a picture," he said, caressing his cock like it was an AK-47. "A dirty, dirty picture."

He stood over me, grinning like a class bully about to steal a kid's lunch money. Everyone was silent. All I could hear were the harsh calls of vultures overhead and the thunderous pounding of my heart.

"What, my dick's not good enough for you?" he taunted, pushing his hard-on toward my face. "You gonna suck everyone else's cock but not mine?"

I opened my mouth, and in went the biker's dick. My hands went to his thighs, bracing myself against his thrust. I took his pole down my throat in quick, furious gulps, eager to get my creamy rich reward.

Fluid filled my mouth, bitter and vaguely salty.

I jerked my head away, spitting out the biker's piss. Everyone laughed, but I only heard the biker's nasty cackling. He went on peeing, a high, wide arc streaming from his hard cock. The biker wiggled his hips, making his piss zigzag through the air. I tried to move out of the way, but two anonymous hands—possibly the same ones that lifted me off the hitching post, possibly a new pair—came down hard on my shoulders, holding me in place as the biker's piss splashed down on me, soaking my hair, my face, my torso. A few warm, ammoniac drops landed on my cock, and I almost came.

His bladder emptied, the biker ordered me to stand up. The same unidentified hands that held me to the ground helped me to my feet. I kept my head down, not wanting to look any of the men in the eye. I was a mess—a sweaty, dirty, cum-splattered, piss-soaked mess. I was totally demoralized, and yet I was desperately horny.

I was pulled forward. I raised my head just enough to see I was being lead to the biker, now leaning against his Harley, looking like a modern day satyr. The anonymous hands pushed me toward him, and he received me in a rough embrace, surprising me with a deep, sloppy kiss that made me melt against his rocklike body. His fingers slipped into my ass, hooking into my chute, priming me for his hot cock.

"Feels like they got you more than ready," he said, jabbing at my prostate and making me whimper. "Got that ass all broken in and lubed up with spit and cum."

The biker spun me around. As I faced a crowd of crazed, lusty stares, the biker's cockhead pushed against my slick asshole, popping into my chute with ease. I closed my eyes, sighing as the biker's thick tool filled my ass. I rolled my hips in a slow grind, urged on by the biker.

"That's it, that's it," he grunted, thrusting into my hole, working his cock against my swaying ass. "You know what I want."

He pinched one of my nipples, twisting it until I begged him to stop. The biker chuckled and then sucked in his breath as I squeezed my butt muscles against his throbbing tool. He made a hard thrust into me, making me shudder and the motorcycle rock. Undaunted, the biker reached between my legs and cupped my balls. I guided his hand to my anguished dick. "Please," I hissed.

The biker pulled his hand away. One more cruel denial, I thought. But the biker raised his hand to my mouth, commanding me to spit into his palm. When he had a handful of my saliva, he returned to my aching prick, pressing down on my hard-on. I pushed my cock against that spit-slick, leather-encased hand, gasping as the hot, tingling pleasure shot through me.

I came, practically weeping as I gushed all over the biker's hand.

The biker abruptly pushed me off his cock. Just as suddenly he was standing in front of me, a merciless smile across his face. He stepped forward, pinning me against his bike. He raised the hand that had been on my cock, showing off the gooey mess I left on his glove, and then surprised me by licking the glove clean, his tongue lapping up my cum up in long, savoring strokes.

He seized me, grabbing my thighs and lifting until my shoulders rested against the motorcycle's sticky seat and my ankles rested on his shoulders. The biker rammed me in swift, angry thrusts, snarling like an animal each time he sank his cock into me. The crowd's cheering grew louder, yet it sounded more and more distant the harder the biker fucked me, until all I heard was the biker's final, deep-chested cry as he pumped my chute full of spooge.

And then…

❖

"Dude, you okay? C'mon, open up."

I opened my eyes, wincing from the light. My head was resting on a plastic pillow. It felt like I'd been hit across the shoulders with a baseball bat, and when I inhaled through my nose I tasted blood.

"Can you sit up?" a male voice asked.

I slowly peeled my face from the airbag, my body protesting every movement. Through the cracked windshield I saw crumpled steel and smoke, and beyond that a red, sandy desert stretching into infinity.

A hand covered with a fingerless leather glove pressed against my chest. "Let me help you up."

I looked out the open driver's door, horrified.

"You're a little banged up, but I think you'll be okay," the biker said. "Your car's fucked, though. Can you stand?"

I rose unsteadily out of the car. Once I was on my feet I was aware of the telltale protuberance in my shorts. My underwear was sticky. The biker noticed my hard-on. He smiled but said nothing.

"Guess I fell asleep at the wheel," I said, pulling my cell phone from the front pocket of my shorts.

"Forget calling anyone out here," the biker said. "Tried. No signal. I can give you a ride to the next town, though."

We sped down the highway, headed west. I was seated behind the bike, my hands on his waist, acutely aware of my boner pressing against his butt. I looked over his shoulder for some sign of civilization. All I saw was a weather-beaten sign on the side of the road: Midnight, 5 miles.

THE PRESCIENT
MARK WILDYR

From a park bench cloaked in the deep shadow of night, I observed the progress of the quasi-organized brawl these people called baseball, a neighborhood game of frequent bawdy disputes, usually resolved just short of mayhem. Despite the throbbing pain occasioned by bright, glaring pole lamps, only marginally eased by heavily smoked glasses, the raucous vigor and raw emotions of the rowdy participants were ambrosia, feeding my vortex, easing the gnawing of a voracious hunger and restoring my pranic energy sufficiently to dull the edge of my depression, a condition I often suffer.

Yet even the massed force of those straining, sweating, cursing young men on the field would not sate my appetite—not completely. For that, I required an intimate confrontation with the tall, wiry young man with the broad Magyar brow generations of New World blood had not significantly altered. This youth, whose towering aura occasionally flickered in my direction, surpassed the collective beauty of all who cavorted on the field.

My name is Tancready, although that is not the appellation bestowed at my birth in 1047 *Anno Domini*. While not my first alias, Tancready is the one that has served for the last two hundred years. I am an Eternal, or if you prefer, a Vampire; not the idiotic caricature of fiction or the loathsome, bloody fiend of legend who stalks the unwary with deadly intent, but one of a miniscule elite who escape the usual constraints of humanity. I exercise an eccentric lifestyle and develop unorthodox relationships, such as that I seek from the most uncommonly beautiful human I have encountered since the Italian Renaissance, the youth I patiently stalk.

Over virtually a millennium, I have endured many lifetimes, embracing death often over the centuries, but true to my ilk, I endlessly return from the earth to assume another name, another persona. I endured Vlad the Impaler's tortured reign and witnessed his assassination. I died at Hastings with the Conqueror's army and attended Henry's knights as they slew Thomas à Becket at Canterbury, fought with the Mongols on the steppes when Temujin became Genghis Khan. I battled the Emperor in Russia and again at Waterloo. I died at the hands of German Nazis at Stalingrad. I have seen...lived...momentous history!

The game on the sports grounds ended in a pungent burst of sweaty enthusiasm as redolent as a potent Russian brew. The field began to clear and the terrible lights slowly died, allowing my photosensitive eyesight to regain its sharpness. Body vibrating, nimbus soaring, the boy approached on the paved walkway, his corded arm riding the shoulders of a young lady. The easy, comfortable companionship between the two elicited an instant and unintended burst of energy from me. The boy's rich luminescence, yellow with affection and friendship for the creature under his arm, suddenly flashed red as he crossed the path in front of my sheltered bench. Tentacles reached toward me uncertainly. I quickly reined in my raging jealousy and sent a more benign form of kinetic energy toward him, seeking to block his unconscious curiosity. I overdid it, as was frequently the case; he visibly staggered, but recovered and continued across the park, his aura drawn close against his body. His flesh, I knew, would be puckered in a case of "heebie-jeebies," in today's pedestrian vernacular.

The boy was aware of me now, too much so at this point, although he had no real understanding of that fact. Nonetheless, I would need to proceed carefully. His name was Boris Balint, a good Hungarian name miraculously not yet Anglicized into Valentine. Born in the mountains of northern New Mexico twenty years past, he now attended classes at the university in Albuquerque. His passions were chess and photography. All this and more, I knew from clandestine midnight visits to the university records room. Chess, I decided, would be my gateway into his life.

As my quarry passed from sight, my energy level dropped precipitously. Edginess and irritability, frequent companions, returned until I focused on a distant figure on the field. My need honed to a keen edge, I moved toward the sleek young Hispanic responsible for securing the game equipment. Anticipating the touch of his smooth, dark flesh, I salivated. He was at that brief age when adolescent *mestizos* were as pretty as girls, yet exuded the budding *machismo* of their elders. Delicious!

Although he had not yet seen me, the youth demonstrated a sharp alertness as he slowly turned from the equipment shed to nervously scan the darkened pathway. I flooded his slender form in tentacles of friendship, yellow and purple desire, overpowering the fearful red of his suspicion. His resolve faltered, and enveloped in my powerful sexuality, the boy obediently trailed me into the deep shadows behind the equipment shed. Without physically touching him, I pulled him to a halt before me. He swallowed hard.

"What is your name, my beautiful young friend?"

"Car...Carlos."

"Ah, Carlos. You bear a noble name."

He flinched at my hand on his cheek; no sign of a beard. Beautiful. The boy stood hypnotized while I stripped him naked in the cool, high-desert air. My sensitive fingers traced the broad, bony shoulders, the curve of the thin chest. His heart raced at my touch. I inhaled the push of air from his diaphragm as I slid my hand down a gently bowed belly. He awakened at my touch. Well endowed for one so young and slight, the boy responded readily.

Young Carlos moaned, torn between fright and desire. I wrapped my physical arms around his waist and pulled him to me, allowing the salt of recent sweat, the aroma of strenuous exercise and sexual arousal to tease my nostrils pleasantly. His hands closed on my head; his hips twitched. He was lost, and I was greedy for his fresh young semen.

The youth's thin frame jerked in the throes of an orgasm he would fruitlessly strive to match for the remainder of his days. Shuddering, this fledgling Carlos, this namesake of powerful kings and emperors, would have fallen had I not eased his weight to the ground. I contemplated arousing him again, but he was drained beyond quick recovery. Satisfied for the moment, I disappeared into the night, leaving the boy naked and spent. I smiled to myself. The boy's seed, while sweet, had yet to reach the peak of its potency. The lad was an immature eighteen; in a year or two, his sperm would ripen.

❖

Born the seventh son of an *Upir*, a Russian Vampire Prince, on the feast day of my sire's patron saint to a mother who was also an Eternal, I came squalling into this world with my head hidden by a caul. Thus was my fate sealed; I was given the kinetic challenge of all Vampires, inverted circadian rhythms and odd body cycles that bring temperature peaks and sleep hormones at unusual times, thus dictating that we Eternals are night creatures on a biochemical level. Even so, I can function in daylight, although with difficulty. Sunlight is painful, whether or not it reaches my skin. My eyes are extraordinarily photosensitive, which gives me marvelous night vision, yet renders me myopic in normal light. Although shaded eyewear lessens that condition, I am most comfortable during sunlit hours in repose, not in some draconian coffin, but comfortably abed in a well-shrouded room.

Amassing huge amounts of wealth during an endless series of lives presented no difficult challenge; however, reclaiming it upon each new emergence was trickier. Even so, wherever my fates took me, I was careful that adequate assets remained available to me regardless of where they were concealed at the time. Most of my many lifetimes were spent ranging from Russia to Europe, with long periods in the Hungarian Carpathians and Transylvania. The persistent, amorous pursuit of a Romanian *strigoivii*, a live witch who became a Vampire upon her death, hounded me out of the Old World and into the New. I had been in the Western Hemisphere for the past century and in this unassuming place called New Mexico for twenty. Why this place? Why not? Except for some of the more remote northern mountains where Penitentes held sway, Vampires, even pranics, were merely the stuff of novels and films.

Now, as I prepared for the ordeal of a daytime pursuit of the fair

Boris, I examined one of my more exotic treasures, an ornate Arabic chess set, observing its intricate carvings with renewed pleasure. Then, moving through a secret dimension denied to ordinary mortals, I arrived instantly on the university campus in a sheltered spot near what is quaintly called the Duck Pond. Recovering my equilibrium, one of the effects of my unorthodox mode of transportation, I scanned the area near the near the path Boris Balint would shortly tread if the past was any true measure.

Troubled by our near encounter last night, I puzzled over the possible reasons for my disquiet as I placed the inlaid board on a backless concrete bench shaded by an evergreen bower. Carefully arranging pawns and pieces, all fashioned of ivory, ebony, silver, gold, and Persian turquoise, I grew irritable over the unwelcome attention of passing students drawn by the marvelous old set. I discouraged most with subtle tendrils of hostility and put off the boldest with a display of cold curtness. Anticipation always brought out the unpleasant side of my nature…unless, of course, it is narrowly focused on a particular target. At last, a long, manly stride bore the beautiful Boris into view.

As he came within eyesight, his calm aura flickered. At fifty feet, I washed the boy in an aura of friendship and congeniality, seeking to smother the orange of his alarm. Gradually, his emanations subsided, and he slowed as he spotted the set. My bait was as irresistible as planned. Appearing reluctant, he nevertheless approached across the horribly bright green grass.

"That's a gorgeous set. Unusual," he observed in a voice that came up out of his belly like a mature man's. His slate gray eyes examined my present persona, a slender, aristocratic man of approximately thirty, possessed of dark good looks.

"I acquired it years ago at a New York auction," I lied smoothly. In truth, I took it as booty from a slain Moorish emir when Ferdinand and Isabella's troops, of which I was one, sacked a castle in Leon. "You may examine it, if you wish," I added graciously.

Instantly, he laid the camera he carried on the bench and slid his long legs astride the concrete slab. Rather than touching the board, he examined the positioning of the pieces and looked up at me with a question in his eyes. Regretting my need for the dark glasses that prevented me from directly engaging his beautiful orbs, I satisfied his curiosity.

"Capablanca versus Corzo, 1901, Havana. End game. Ninth match game."

"Capablanca was just a kid, wasn't he? A prodigy."

"Twelve at the time. He won."

Only then did Boris carefully cradle an exquisite ebony knight trimmed in gold and silver in his strong, brown hand. Gypsy blood likely coursed with the Hungarian in those pulsing veins.

"Beautiful. How old is it?"

"It is likely Arabic, but possibly Persian, dating from circa 1100."

"Geez, almost a thousand years old!" he breathed, husky voice full of awe.

"Do you play?"

"Love it!" he enthused. "But I'm not very good."

"Black or white?" I asked by way of invitation. He hesitated only a moment before claiming the white.

The boy was an instinctive player, and with tutoring could become quite good. I beat him readily the first game, and then critiqued his handling of the pieces. His enthusiasm fired, we undertook another game while I nearly swooned from the effort of refraining from draining his energy. Eventually, onlookers gathered, and I sent my thirsting quests toward them, sopping up their energy while refracted sunlight bled away my own.

By the end of the third game, I was sweating and weakened, but by the effort of pure will, I held onto the self-possession needed to advance to the second phase of my plan. "You carry a camera, I see." I pointed to the instrument between his exciting legs. "Canon Z155 thirty-five millimeter. Nice."

"I'm sort of a shutterbug," he said with a deprecating grin that sent blood rushing to my head.

"I have some equipment that might be of interest. I own some Leicas. An M7 Rangefinder, for example."

"Wow! That's worth a couple of grand."

"And a Hasselblad 205. Also some Japanese equipment, but I prefer the German lenses."

"Man, I'd give my eyeteeth for a Leica. I found a Minilux Point and Shoot for five hundred the other day, but my budget doesn't stretch that far."

"Perhaps you would like to go shooting some afternoon. I will be happy to allow you the use of some of my cameras."

Uncertainty scrolled across his fine features. His aura flared in warning. He ran an agitated hand through his shaggy brown locks. He was fighting a furious battle without knowing or understanding it.

I quickly extended my arm. "My name is Tancready," I announced, exuding all the magnetic charm I possessed, which was considerable. His hand closed around mine firmly. Washed in the yellows and golds of my will, he relented.

"Sure. I'd like that. My name's Boris. Boris Balint."

"Ah, Hungarian," I noted.

"Way back, maybe." He grinned engagingly. "Well, my great-grandfather, I guess. I probably know more about my mother's people."

"Spanish?" I ventured. "No, let me guess. Pyrenees Gypsies."

He laughed. "Right. Mountain people all the way." He began to look uncomfortable, so I reluctantly released his manly grip.

"Tomorrow is Saturday, and I am free," I ventured.

"I guess I could," he said hesitantly. "No classes. Can I try the Leica?"

"Of course. I have a Minilux such as you described that I will bring along."

"Great!" He allowed his enthusiasm to surface, costing me my control. I drew energy from him before I could stop myself. He wilted visibly, but quickly drew on reserves. After we made arrangements, he walked away with vivid, warning blues among the more pacific hues of his halo. I watched him hungrily.

In years past, I was a bloody Vampire, although my donors were voluntary and survived my feeding without lasting harm. None, for example succumbed to that ridiculous old wives' tale that the bite of a Vampire created a Vampire. Preposterous! Were it so, the preponderance of the global population would be Eternal after all this time, undoubtedly overwhelming the world's resources and dooming us all...Eternal or not.

It took half a millennium, but I discovered another powerful source of pranic energy and rarely opened human veins thereafter. That source was semen, the distillation of the essence of a man...his cum. Since then, I prefer the company of men, young men, mature men, seniors. But the most powerful and intoxicating elixir is the seed of a youth in his sexual prime. And this I needed from Boris Balint. But there was also a strange, long-dormant stirring deep within me that I recognized as a yearning for the taste of his rich, ruby blood. Only a Vampire can directly absorb the life energy of blood. After all, as the Bible correctly states, the blood is the life!

Harvesting a man's semen for the maintenance of my life force exposed me to yet another danger. The human's irrational terror of Vampires is matched only by his homophobic fear of deviants. The pursuit of a man's seed resulted more than once in the hasty use of my other dimension to escape the wrath of closed minds.

Returning to my home, I ate voracious amounts of fresh fruits and vegetables, another source of energy, and then retired to my bedchamber. I slept soundly, but awoke after sundown, hungry and restless again.

I returned to the university and prowled the night until I found young Boris beneath the blinding lights of the campus tennis courts doing battle with the young woman who had accompanied him last night. They played at playing, obviously enjoying one another's company, which sent me into a sudden fit of unbridled jealousy. My halo flared dangerously. Worse, his aura blazed in unconscious response. He sensed a presence...my presence.

In the grip of a deep melancholy, I withdrew and chanced upon a blond student retiring from the courts. Embroiling this hapless substitute in reds and yellows, I overpowered the youth quickly and pulled him into a darkened recess. After licking the sweat of recent exercise from his exposed belly, I quickly coaxed the seed from him. Barely in control of my senses because of hunger and lust and jaundiced envy, I entered the towhead and fucked him brutally while watching the distant, manly grace of Boris Balint. When I came, I bent to the whimpering boy again and replaced my spent seed with fresh cum.

❖

I roused myself the following morning with difficulty. Despite the excitement of my coming time with Boris, I was reluctant to expose myself to the dreadful sunburn and excruciating headaches an all-day excursion necessarily entailed. Nonetheless, it was necessary. The prospect depressed me so deeply that I was able to function only by concentrating on my approaching proximity to the delectable Boris. Briefly, I wondered why I did not simply overwhelm the boy and take what I wanted, as with the Hispanic and the towhead and countless others, but something within me cautioned against rashness. This prize was unique in both physical sensuality and an innate sensitivity to the unusual.

And that brought me face-to-face with a potential problem I had sought unsuccessfully to ignore. As I gathered the equipment and awaited the boy's arrival, I considered the unease that was twin to my pleasure in his exciting presence. The youth was extraordinarily aware of me. For all the studied casualness of one of his age, his halo betrayed his true, perhaps unconscious feelings. There were, of course, individuals who were quite perceptive when it came to Eternals, although they would be rare in this part of the Western Hemisphere, given its lack of such lore. Dhampires, sons of Vampires, existed, of course, and were attuned to our rhythms. That would present no particular problem, but there was a sensitive of another sort, presenting another problem.

Was it possible Boris was a Prescient? Mortals with an uncanny sensitivity to Eternals, Prescients are sometimes dangerous since many are Betrayers, or worse, Slayers. Over the ages, I have known many Prescients, some of whom, the ignorant, fled in terror. Others, more enlightened, provided many hours of pleasant company. One, a delightful woman of lush body and bright mind, was a constant companion in a long-ago lifetime. She occupied my mind and body as few have done over the centuries…a role I envisioned for Boris in this one. Those were my blood days, and Sara willingly presented her veins to me when my hunger became truly demanding…without ill effect, I might add. Accustomed to disastrous relationships because of my inverted systems, internal clock, and desires, I was constantly astonished over the fifty years of our relationship that she was so steadfast. Even today, I speculate on her given name, Sara, who was the black goddess Kali to her Gypsy people.

A few Prescients have betrayed me into the hands of enraged, terrified mortals, who are the deadliest and most bloodthirsty of all creatures, and a small number have sought my doom. These I dealt with as brutally as Vlad dispatched his enemies.

Boris's bloodlines allowed for this possibility, but his family had been in the New World for generations with no exposure to my kind. Yet his aura clearly showed he was unusually receptive to my mere presence. That did not necessarily mean he knew the *why* or the *what* of his apprehension. Shrugging away my usual caution, I completed preparations for our outing, thereby laying bare the depth of my need. My hunger for the boy was both natural and unnatural; natural in craving his pranic energy, his semen, and unnatural in a lust that was overwhelmingly sensual, a different thing altogether.

At the appointed hour, his white Jeep appeared before my closed gate, and I threw the lever to admit him. Carefully placing our equipment atop an old tent he carried in the back, I was pleased to note he drove an enclosed vehicle, which would ease my exposure to the sun. I had agreed to allow him to provide the conveyance, suspecting this would satisfy his masculine code of etiquette.

We elected to explore the Bosque, a unique hundred-mile swath of cottonwoods lining both sides of the Rio Grande, an ecological treasure sentenced to a slow death once a system of dams put an end to the annual flooding of the river that was required to nurture seedlings. The once mighty Rio Grande now trickled through a narrow channel that wandered willy-nilly in its wide, sandy bed.

Boris took to the Leica Minilux like a born photographer. It fit his hand and eye perfectly. He shot images of driftwood on white sand, river birds in flight, an ancient turtle sunning on a semi-submerged log, and even a reclusive red fox. He rolled up his pant legs to reveal strong calves lightly brushed with fine brown hair and waded in the river, cavorting like a boy. His aura ran wild with joy and budding friendship. He grew so comfortable that he dared tease me about the abundance of clothing covering me from head to foot on this warm autumn day. I explained it for what it was, the protection of sensitive skin against the brutal sun. He had no such constraints. He tore off his shirt, baring his broad, muscled chest to my famished gaze. I briefly lost control and sopped up his radiations, but recovered before any damage occurred.

My desirable young companion had a commitment that night, so we made arrangements to meet the following morning for a quick trip to the mountains before developing our film in my darkroom. Once he was gone, I applied ointments and unguents to my poor flesh and retired.

In the dark of night, I rose and prowled the alleyways behind the bars on East Central, locating a man whose aura showed no trace of disease. I took his cum while he swore and sang drunkenly until the shock of his extraordinary climax silenced him.

❖

The lush conifer forest on the east side of Sandia Mountain, a ten-thousand-foot peak directly east of Albuquerque that the local Indians called Sleeping Turtle, was less harsh on my system, and the boy's growing amity made the effort worthwhile. He was an odd combination of venturesome youth, childish juvenile, and mature man. His company delighted me even as it aggravated my lust. It was not merely his physical presence that kindled me, but his mind and spirit as well. We discussed the great photographers. He was much taken with Ansel Adams and Ernst Haas, but agreed that Dmitri Kessel's powerful plates of the ornate Benedictine church at Zwiefalten, Germany, placed him among the elite. With difficulty, I stopped short of boasting that I had served as a seminarian at that magnificent structure in another lifetime.

We stood for long intervals and listened to the forest speak while I fought a raging battle to control my impatience for him. Boris blundered upon a black bear rooting for acorns, disturbed grazing mule deer, and photographed a magnificent golden eagle. We ascended Sandia Crest, named for the hue the autumn sun gave its western face at sunset, turning it a watermelon pink, to cast our eyes west over the broad Rio Grande Valley to Mount Taylor, one of the Navajo's four sacred peaks. At a turnout lower on the mountainside, we gazed north to Santa Fe, hidden in the foothills of the towering Sangre de Cristos…a beautiful name, Blood of Christ! With that thought, I hungrily observed the vein pulsing in the boy's neck as he snapped a picture. I wanted him so badly that I achieved an erection, something I rarely do until it is required. Sexual energy escaped my control, lapping against him in mauve waves of desire.

He dropped the camera from his eye and faced me. From the sudden flare of warning red, I saw he was alarmed. His mood changed dramatically; Boris was more thoughtful and less gregarious on our return trip despite my attempt to keep a conversation going.

The boy was quite skilled in the darkroom. Devoting our attention to this task, we labored into the night. Prolonged proximity to his sculpted body taxed my control to the limit. Waiting for our prints to dry, I hovered near him and carelessly sent a wave of desire up his back, retreating when his aura flared. But the damage was done. Boris turned to me, his color heightened by the crimson of the developing lamp. He licked his lips nervously.

"You…you're a homosexual, aren't you?" The tone was wary.

"I have lain with men," I answered rather pompously.

"That's what you want with me, isn't it?" he rasped, his energy flaring alarmingly. "You want in my pants!"

"That is crude, Boris."

"Oh, hell! You do! You want to…do things to me. No way, Tancready! I don't go for that stuff. I like my girl. We make love. Oh, man, I knew something wasn't right about this. Shit!" he cursed, tearing off the protective apron I had given him for working with the darkroom chemicals. Without another word, he slammed out of the room. I caught up with him in the hallway.

"I gotta go now. Early class tomorrow," he babbled.

"Your prints, Boris! Your photographs?"

"I don't know." He waved a hand in the air. "Maybe I'll come get them later."

The boy fled into the night. I sadly opened the gate by remote control as his vehicle raced down the long drive. The house was lonely and oppressive once he was gone. My black mood turned into rage. They made love, did they? He and that…that girl! A bottomless jealousy tinted the room an iridescent green, overpowering even my anger. Straightening things in the darkroom and pulling prints from the dryer, I considered removing my competition. It would be easy enough. I could sate my newly awakened blood lust, turning it into a deadly feast. By a narrow margin, reason prevailed over impetuosity. The female creature's demise, especially in such a manner, would excite unwelcome attention, not only from Boris, but also from the authorities. Such a disastrous end to a magnificent, albeit a taxing day! Abruptly, I abandoned the house.

Using that other dimension, I easily reached the campus ahead of Boris. From a place of concealment, I observed him pull into a parking spot and crawl out of the Jeep. Slowly, as if totally exhausted, he trudged toward the buildings, passing his dormitory and making for the Duck Pond to claim the bench where we had played chess. He sat down heavily.

Cautiously, I drew near, but his psychic energy flared. He glanced around warily as I eased back into the shadows. Even from afar, I observed the erection trapped between his leg and the denim of his trousers. He sat with his chin on his chest while his blood subsided and the goose bumps that puckered his flesh faded away. He was as frightened as he had ever been in his short lifetime, but he had not yet divined his true fear. He perceived his present agitation as merely a challenge to his manhood by a pervert. I wondered when he would truly understand. Finally, he rose and walked directly to his dorm.

Craving Boris more desperately than ever, I found a rowdy bar and fed my ravenous appetite by absorbing the frantic energy flooding the place. When the tavern closed, I roamed the night until I chanced upon a youth hurrying through an alley. My dark psychic energy brought him to a halt. He was an Indian in his late teens, good-looking, innocent. I sucked the seed from his long, pulsing cock while he stood frozen against an adobe wall in the darkness. Then, ignoring his terrified, soulful eyes, I threw him to the ground and shoved my swollen prick between his buns, penetrating him the way I so ardently desired to ravish Boris. Still not sated, I licked the smooth, pulsing neck and drew blood for the first time in a century. I left him lying half-naked and weakened but alive in that silent alleyway. His body would heal; I closed my mind to any other damage that may have been inflicted.

❖

Boris showed up Friday evening. Expecting such an event, I had not closed my gate against the world for the past few nights. I opened the door and expressed false surprise.

"Tancready," he said, nervously shifting from one foot to the other. "I came to apologize for the other night."

"That is kind of you, Boris. Won't you put the incident from your mind and come in?" His internal struggle was obvious as he stepped over the sill. I snapped on a small, weak lamp for his convenience.

"That's the problem. I can't."

"Because you are curious?" I suggested gently, releasing the tight rein I held on my energy. He nodded uncertainly as an orange tendril caressed his handsome face. "Have you had any experience with a man?" He shook his head, his torso now engulfed. "But you wonder what it would be like." I made it a statement.

"I don't know. Maybe." He licked his lips nervously. I recognized his urge to flee...and his inability. "How did the prints come out?"

"Boris," I said, releasing my sexual energy to go where it would. "Forget the prints, at least for the moment. This needs to be dealt with."

"H...how?" he stammered, even as he reluctantly submitted to my will and slowly approached. "Damn, Tancready! What am I doing? What are *we* doing? Why can't I stop myself? Why—"

I cut off his words with a kiss. He resisted momentarily, and then surrendered those rosy lips. His reluctant tongue entwined with mine.

With that kiss, I fed my pranic energy, indulging my long-suppressed desire for this young Leandro.

I took a moment to drink in his masculinity. The boy's curly hair had a fetching, careless look, flowing down into sideburns that ended in a point, like a child's that had never felt the bite of a razor. Huge, magnetic eyes; wide, expressive mouth; skin without blemish, glowing with health and the vitality of youth—these dominated his features.

He stood rooted to the spot as I slowly removed his shirt. With wry amusement, I noted a thin chain around his neck, a tiny gold cross he had instinctively worn as protection. I concluded that perhaps he was consciously or unconsciously edging toward an understanding of the situation. When I touched the small Christian symbol without alarm, his defenses shattered.

I stroked his broad shoulders and ran my hands across his smooth hairless chest. Gently drawing him into my arms, I smoothed his horripilated flesh with my palms. His belly fluttered from excitement or fear, probably a bit of both. I traced the vee of his back to his belt line. Holding him helpless in my aura, I freed him of his clothing. The sight of his naked loins deprived me of the last of my control. He was as perfect as I had imagined, masculine, physically powerful, yet totally vulnerable; frightened of a carnal encounter with a man, yet anticipating it. His psychic energy flared with every color in the spectrum. Fear, loathing, desire, anticipation, disgust, lust. Wild with my need, I lifted his long, uncircumcised cock, which was already filling with blood. I skinned back his foreskin and tasted his throbbing flesh. Boris writhed at my hot touch on his cool flesh, doing battle with his carnal desire and his panic. Each was an aphrodisiac to me. When his time neared, he lost the will to resist and moved his hips, slowly at first and then with all the power of those sturdy thighs. He placed a hand behind my head and threw his erection into me. Then, abruptly, he came and gifted me with great gouts of his essence. It was as potent as I knew it would be. My energy level soared! My strength surged! My awareness became so hyper it was almost unendurable. I shared the ecstasy of his ejaculation, knowing he had experienced what few ever achieve...the love of a Vampire.

He lay exhausted on the thick carpet while I rested my head on his breast, glorying in his soft breath against my cheek. Rising to his side, I explored his features to fully understand the beauty of this extraordinary young man. I covered him with the cloak of my love, the aura of my friendship, the whole of my devotion!

A mistake! Too much, too soon. He scrambled to his feet and, without pausing to dress, clutched his clothes to his breast and ran naked to his Jeep. Sated and overloaded with energy, I turned sullen and morose.

❖

As before, the boy kept his distance for a few days before appearing unannounced on my doorstep. Neither of us spoke when I opened the door. Faint bruises beneath his eyes bespoke hours of worry and lost sleep. His aura was wild, fretful, fearful. Yet he was here. He moved into my living room and turned on me accusingly.

"What have you done to me? What is this hold you have over me? It...it's *ungodly*! Why don't you leave me alone?"

"Is that what you wish?" I asked quietly.

He fought and lost his battle standing in the middle of a darkened room in my home. "No!" he moaned, clutching me to his breast and kissing me with a passion that took me by surprise.

Ripping off his clothing, Boris took my head in his strong hands to guide me down his smooth torso. I followed his lead, and soon he was feeding my energy with magnificent, hungry cock.

"God! It's as good as the first time!" he gasped in dismay as his flesh bruised the depths of my throat. Young Boris's manly flesh filled me to capacity. "Who...are you? How do you make me do these things?"

I paused to answer. "I make you do nothing you do not already crave."

"No. Yes. No! Please...don't stop." A moment later, his hard tool swelled in my mouth as cum shot through it. He staggered backward, and I saw his eyes widen with the shock of understanding. "You're going to make me do it to you, aren't you? You're going to make me fuck you?" He gave me no time to reply. "Are you going to do it to me, too?"

I flinched at the anguish in that question. "Only when you want me to, Boris. And you will...eventually."

"Who are you?" he cried. Are you who I think you are?"

"And who is that?"

"One of those creatures Grandpa Balint used to talk about." His moved away from me, his dilated eyes full of doubt. "That can't be! Those are nothing but old wives' tales. Folklore. Oh, Lord," he exclaimed, pacing restlessly around the darkened room, oblivious to his naked beauty. "What am I saying? This is the twenty-first century. This is the good old US of A. I...I'm a modern guy." He halted and indulged in a sour grimace, which turned him absolutely fetching. "I'm just all messed up over getting it on with a guy. That's all; that's all it is."

"Do your sexual regrets usually span days?" I asked quietly.

"No, but this was with a *man*!"

"Boris, at a guess, I'd say that half the male student body at the university has had an experience with another male, and they do not appear so agitated."

"Yeah, but...but I came back for seconds." He resumed pacing again. "Something's not right. I gotta figure this out. Gimme my prints, Tancready. I'm not coming back. Not ever!"

I gave him a doleful smile and handed over an envelope from the coffee table. "Yes, you will. Here are your film and the prints. But be warned. Every time you view them, you will remember this magnificent experience."

"Never!" he breathed, and once again headed out the door naked.

"You are welcome in my home any time, Boris Balint." I sent a tentacle toward him and viciously drew on his energy. He reeled against the door frame and stumbled outside.

❖

He was back within a fortnight, wild, disheveled, and at the edge of his sanity. As I opened the door, shading my sight against the sudden light, he pushed his way inside. Immediately, he turned fretful.

"Why am I here? I've got no control anymore, Tancready. My life's gone to hell in a handbasket. I broke up with my girl. My grades have taken a nosedive. I can't sleep. Eat. Do anything. And it's all your fault!"

He stopped directly in front of me, his eyes flickering as his suspicions fell into place. "You're one of them. A Vampire! God, I can't believe I'm saying it out loud! But nothing else makes sense! How you make me do what I don't want to do! How you got me to talk to you in the first place even though I knew I shouldn't." That sent a look of surprise across his handsome face. "How did I even *know* it was wrong to talk to you?"

"You are a Prescient," I replied. "A human who is sensitive to Eternals."

"Eternals," he laughed harshly. "*Vampires*, you mean. That explains so much. You can't stand the light; you wear those damned shades all the time. You live in the dark! But..." He hesitated. "I thought you burned to a crisp in sunlight."

"False folklore," I scoffed. "I have difficulty, but I can function by day."

"That's why you cover up with clothing." He seized on the point. "And another thing...I drove like a madman the other night, but you beat me back to campus. I sensed you. How did you get there so fast?"

"I have other means of travel," I answered vaguely. I saw his look. "No, I do not fly around like a bat." I stroked his smooth cheek; he looked panicked but suffered my touch.

"Maybe not, but you can see in the dark like one, pick a flying insect out of the air with your radar. And you feed off people, Tancready. I've seen it! You draw from them...drain them. You've done it to me."

"Yes," I admitted. "I feed my energy by drawing from others. But I always sought to spare you, Boris. *Your* power is your cum, your seed." I rubbed my thumb across his mouth.

His eyes became saucers, and his aura flared. He feebly batted my hand away. "I'm a fucking meal to you?"

"What I take from you, I am willing to give to you." I parted his lips with my finger, raked a nail over his teeth.

He struggled a moment, and then his broad shoulders slumped. He licked the end of my finger. "You want me to blow you, don't you?" The spirit was gone from his voice.

"Yes, I want you to taste me, as I have tasted you. I want to imbue you with my power."

Tremulously, he opened the robe I wore and ran his hands down my chest. "I didn't know Vampires were handsome, like men," he mumbled, moving to lick my sternum. His moist lips were electrifying; his touch set off sparks. I was so swollen I thought it might burst. He was awkward and inexperienced, but ultimately quite successful. Afterward, I knelt to embrace him, cooing in his ear as he fought his emotions.

"Giving pleasure begets pleasure," I philosophized inanely.

The boy rose to his full height, every inch a man. "I can't believe it! You made me do it!" Alarm flooded his halo. "Will I be all right?"

"You will be fine. As much as I would like you to stay the night, my beautiful Boris, I think you should return to your dorm. Try not to fret. Get some rest, and return to me this weekend. There is much for me to teach you."

He dropped his head into his hands for a moment and then looked at me again. "You want us to do it, don't you? I mean really do it! You're going to make me fuck you! And you're going to do it to me!" His hand suddenly went to his neck. "You want my blood, too, don't you?"

I responded quietly. "You must trust me not to harm you."

"Trust you?" he demanded. "Yeah, Tancready. First you take away my power to resist. Then we do this. Now you want my fucking blood! Will it turn me into...a creature like you?"

I shook my head slowly. "No, that is another lie told over the generations." I brushed his hand away and fingered the pulsing vein in his throat. He shuddered. "Go now, Boris, with the certain knowledge that I love you beyond all things. And when you return, you will understand my meaning."

I was sated when he left me and had no need to prowl for partners, willing or unwilling. Nonetheless, I went to the campus to see that he arrived safely. As he entered the dormitory, I could tell my handsome young Prescient was aware that I hovered near.

❖

When he arrived Saturday night, Boris seemed resigned, albeit nervous and agitated, even though the marks of distress had disappeared from his handsome features. The big, soulful eyes were clear again. He had accepted his fate, perhaps even worked up some enthusiasm over the experience I promised.

"Do we have to do this?" he asked quietly.

"We must, Boris, in order to fully express our mutual love."

He walked into the room and stripped, taking the unconscious stance of an ancient Greek marble, hip sprung, a jacket clutched in his right hand. This night, I led him into my bedroom and observed his curious examination of the dreaded Vampire's den. Feigning unconcern, he tossed his jacket on the bed and fell on his back across the mattress, waiting expectantly as I shrugged out of my clothing. I draped myself over his long frame, my groin kissing his. His body was warm beneath mine. His chest heaved against my breast in excitement and nervousness.

He opened his mouth to accept my kiss and entwined his tongue with mine. It had been five hundred years since I felt a kiss like this one…with a husky young Bulgar cavalryman, as I recall. I expected Boris to be timid, inexperienced, but twisted his body so that he was atop me. I fingered his cock, and it rose expectantly. He got between my legs, and I opened to him. Once mounted, he grew in confidence, thrusting boldly, rutting so vigorously that I feared he would injure himself. Then I let go of my worry and wholly engaged myself in this magnificent act of love.

Cataclysmic I had promised, and cataclysmic it was. His orgasm sent his aura soaring, creating new colors, brighter hues! He shuddered above me as if in the grip of a cerebral stroke. When it was finally over, he loomed above me, ecstasy slowly fading from his countenance. He opened his tortured eyes.

"You will find it difficult to match the power of what you just experienced," I boasted. "And it was more awesome because of our love."

He was silent while absorbing this. "Do you really love me? If you do, you won't do this to me. Don't fuck me, Tancready," he begged.

"It is the only way to consummate our love. You are the object of my intellectual desire, my spiritual desire, my carnal desire. You are as close to perfect as I shall ever find, and I must experience you every way possible," I babbled, my vortex rising, my aura probing him with increasingly red tentacles. My energy level peaked and absorbed his vibrations.

His handsome countenance took on a look of quiet desperation. "If we can leave it this way, I'll come back to you. As many times as you want. But don't fuck me, all right? Please!"

"I will not enter your body unless you agree to it," I said quietly.

"That doesn't mean anything," he reasoned aloud. "I won't be able to help myself, will I?" Abruptly, he leaned forward so that our noses almost touched. "Why, Tancready? Why me?"

"Boris, I have loved you from the moment I laid eyes on you in Zimmerman Library the semester you first arrived."

He closed his eyes briefly. When he opened them again, they were filled with tears. They ran down his face. A look of utter anguish crossed his handsome face. "And you're going to take my blood afterward. I won't be able to deny you anything, will I?"

"You will suffer no harm, I promise. But only then will we truly be one," I answered carelessly, reaching to caress a cheek still damp with his tears.

"Then so be it," he whispered. Sighing deeply, he fumbled with his jacket at my shoulder and then straightened his torso above me. My aura flaring in sudden alarm, I was aware of several things at once. He grew rampant inside me. His strong, corded arms rose, revealing clumps of dark, damp hair deep in his armpits. The muscles in his upper chest rolled. I glimpsed the sharpened tent peg in his hands. Fear and total devastation twisted his features.

"I'm so sorry, Tancready," he moaned from the depths of his soul. The dark magenta of loss and despair swept his halo as he brought down those powerful arms in a mighty blow.

THE RAIDERS
EVAN GILBERT

Times were tough.

Kentrell Lewison had less than twenty bucks to his name when he stepped off the bus in New Orleans. Much of the city still lay in Katrina-wrought ruin, and the economy overall just plain sucked. Jobs here, as in the rest of the country, were hard to come by.

Kentrell was smiling.

He stowed his backpack in a locker, feeding enough coins into the meter to cover forty-eight hours' rental. He shouldn't need any more time than that. It was 11:15 p.m. The summer night was hot and clear. Perfect business conditions. He left the station and went straight to Bourbon Street.

He had been just a kid the first time he came to the French Quarter, three years before the infamous hurricane that would all but drown the city. Apparently, an ocean wasn't enough to wash out the perpetual smell of upchuck and pee. Or to keep the party people away. Kentrell slipped his way through the Friday night crowd, making eye contact with men and women alike. Maybe he'd get lucky. There were a lot of females out and about. Women seemed to feel safer playing in numbers. In places like this, groups of girlfriends had taken him on eagerly, multiplying his pleasure and, more importantly, his pay.

But luck wasn't with him tonight. Plenty of the ladies—and even some men—looked into his eyes, intrigued, smiling, but easing away before he could strike up a conversation. No problem. He parked himself outside the main entrance of Frenched, the city's biggest fag bar. Within, music was pumping so hard the beats were shaking the wall at his back. Men of all ages, sizes, creeds, and colors flowed back and forth through the gaping double doorway.

Kentrell presented an enticing product. A dark-skinned African American, his slender, five-foot-ten body was chiseled, muscles honed through daily workouts. He was twenty-four, but his cute, hairless face made him look innocent and barely eighteen. Yet the outfit he wore—a size XX jersey, baggy jeans sagging off his narrow waist, scuffed black work boots—gave him the look of a gangbanger. "Rough trade," as the fags put it.

And he had actually been a gangbanger once, back in his mid-teens. That career had been violent but, thanks to his mom, brief. He ran up a string of arrests for everything from truancy to assault with a deadly weapon before *mater* decided she'd had enough and kicked him out. He'd thought of his gang as his "real" family, but none of them would do him the favor of taking in his homeless ass. With plenty of rival thugs gunning for him, he left Detroit and hitched his way to New Orleans, where he discovered being young and cute could pay big-time.

He got into doing the ladies, of course. Unfortunately, it was mostly men who wanted his services. Fags disgusted him, but they were bigger, bolder spenders than women and, if he closed his eyes, their mouths on his dick felt no different than a female's. His terms with men were simple: cash up front, you suck me, keep your hands off my ass. He could live with that and so, apparently, could the fags.

He unbuttoned his jersey, displaying the white wifebeater that clung like paint to his pumped pecs and six-pack. A grin tugged at his mouth but he kept it off his face because thug sold better in this venue, and everyone knows thugs don't smile. Not even five minutes passed before the first prospects started circling.

He decided on a tall, skinny, middle-aged white man, simply because he offered two hundred bucks, far more than anyone else present was willing to shell out. That would be enough cash to get him back to Nashville, where he currently made his home, and keep him solvent for a few days. Which was all he needed. Two years ago, he'd stumbled into another profession that was just as lucrative as pimping himself out to men, and far less disgusting. It was to further that second profession that he had come back to New Orleans.

The white man led him down the block and into an alley. They found a shadowed doorway. Kentrell leaned back against the door and held out his palm. The white man handed over two crisp hundred dollar bills and got to his knees. Kentrell tugged down his drooping jeans until his dick popped into view. The man actually licked his lips. Kentrell grinned and shook his head.

Fags never ceased to amaze him.

This fag's mouth was cold from too many daiquiris, which didn't help Kentrell's reluctant cock come to life. Tough shit. He only agreed the man could suck his stick, and he was fulfilling his part of the bargain. There'd be no refund if he couldn't get it up.

Kentrell closed his eyes and turned his thoughts to more important things. He could start his real work when this freaky shit was done. Much as he hated to do it (he was exceedingly cheap), he'd have to spend money on a cab.

The tomb he planned to rob was outside the city.

❖

Kentrell thought the Internet was the best thing since God made women. Any knowledge, any bit of information you needed, was just a few keystrokes away. Obituaries, for example. You could pull them from anywhere in the country. And they included such helpful data. What the decedent's profession had been. The charities the decedent supported. Where the decedent would be buried. That kind of stuff told you whether the poor dead sap was worth digging up.

Well-to-do folk buried their loved ones with all kinds of bling. If you were clever enough, and had balls enough, you could make a decent living plundering graves. Along with watches, rings, and other expensive jewelry, Kentrell had recovered items that simply astounded him. In one coffin, he found gold coins stuffed in the corpse's pockets that turned out to be more than a hundred years old. A collector paid him ten thousand dollars for the lot. A paltry sum, perhaps, compared to what he could have gotten if he'd been able to sell them legitimately on the open market, but it was still the most money he'd ever gotten from his enterprise.

Kentrell preferred to go in within a day or two of the burial, while the soil was still freshly turned. That way, no one would be the wiser, and he wouldn't have to pick his way over a rotted body. But in New Orleans, disposal of the dead was a bit different. Being somewhat below sea level, the city was begging to be flooded. Floods could bring coffins buried underground bobbing to the surface like boats. To avoid that ghoulish mess, and in keeping with practices their ancestors brought from France and Spain, the good citizens of New Orleans buried their dead above ground.

Kentrell loved the cemeteries here, which looked more like small towns with their rows of tombs lining narrow streets (and the streets actually had names!), the dead resting comfortably inside imposing stone structures. He had to break open the tombs here, of course, which made it rather hard to fully disguise the breach. But that, together with the fact that the city's hot climate caused entombed bodies to bake away to bones in just about a year, meant that he didn't have to limit himself to the recently deceased.

Benoit Bonner died a multimillionaire in 1950, made rich by wineries he owned in California and France. He'd been born in Boston, where his former slave parents had established a successful tailoring shop. He had fallen in love with New Orleans on a childhood visit with his father, and he'd made his home there as an adult. His tomb was in Lafitte Cemetery, on the western outskirts of the city. His love of jewelry was legendary, and it was common knowledge that he'd been buried with enough to choke a hog. Rumor had it, however, that his tomb had never been so much as touched because of some curse laid on the place by a voodoo queen in return for a hundred thousand bucks, a deal made just before he'd expired at the ripe age of eighty-nine. Rumor also had it that Bonner left the bulk of his money in trust, to be dispersed by the venerable law firm of Judd and Garland to any person who could recite verbatim the elaborate set of codes he'd hidden in his will.

The second rumor implied that Bonner had descendants, to whom the codes would somehow be magically passed down. According to every website that Kentrell found with information about the man, Bonner never married or had children, so he thought the stuff about curses and mystic codes was just so much bullshit. The stuff about the bling, however, he felt was quite real.

Kentrell met Rashawn Gaffney on the years-ago night he first prowled the Big Easy. They were both turning teenaged tricks on the same notorious corner. Rashawn had a sharp, bony face, but he was tall and strapping, which got him a fair amount of attention. He, too, had been a homeless adolescent, with a stubbornly violent temper that got him into a good deal of trouble. Taking exception to his father slapping him for backtalk, he kicked the shit out of the man and ran off when he realized his mother had called the police.

He was as straight as Kentrell and absolutely hated gays. He needed the money they paid for the privilege of blowing him, however, so he tolerated their touch, if just barely. He got through the sex by slapping the johns around. In the early days of his hustling, he would often wait until he was alone with a john, then beat the crap out of him and take his wallet. He soon realized he had to cut that out. Gays weren't stupid. Word would get around, and the punks would avoid him as if he were a two-headed Christian conservative.

Kentrell and Rashawn had stayed in touch over the years, even after Kentrell moved to Nashville. Kentrell preferred to work alone when it came to robbing graves, but he'd need help to crack open the Bonner tomb. And that's where Rashawn came in.

Once the white guy was done, Kentrell slipped his wet, cold dick (it never got more than semi-erect, even with the fag's best efforts) back into his jeans and hurried out to the street. He pulled out his cell phone and dialed a number as he walked.

After seven rings, the line picked up. "Yeah?"

"Ray. What's up? It's Trell."

"Trell, man. You in town?"

"Yeah. I'm on Bourbon Street. Where you?"

"Headed that way. Wish I didn't have to do it, but I gotta pay the rent."

"If you hate it so much, get your ass a job."

"Fuck you. You show me somebody around here with a job to offer, and I'll take it. Till then, shut the fuck up."

Kentrell grunted out a short, choppy laugh. "Maybe I got a job to offer."

"Yeah? What?"

"Don't go sounding all hopeful, fool. It's just a one-night thing."

"Okay, so what is it?"

Kentrell told him.

The line went completely silent.

"Rashawn? You there?"

"Stay away from that Bonner grave, man. I heard stories about that place. People go in there and never come out."

"They just stories, man."

"I'm telling you, Trell. Don't go in there."

"I'm telling *you*, there's gold and all kinds of shit in old boy's casket. Now, you gonna help me get it out and take half for yourself, or you gonna sell dick to the punks all night?"

There was another stretch of silence on the line, but only half as long. "Meet you at Frenched in five," said Rashawn.

"Cool."

❖

The cab dropped them off a block from the cemetery's main entrance. They walked the remaining distance in silence. The towering metal gates were closed and locked, as expected, so they hauled themselves over the brick wall. The tombs spread before them in endless, rolling waves, shining white monoliths in the moonlight.

"Hope you know where we're going," Rashawn whispered. He

believed the dead listened in on the living, especially when the living had the gall to walk among them in the night.

Kentrell did know. He led the way straight down the main street, which divided the cemetery into its North and South sections.

The street was two miles long.

"Shit," Rashawn huffed. "Are we there yet?"

"Shut the hell up."

The night was warm and deep around them, with only the distant rush of traffic and the scratching of crickets to break the silence. A short time later, they arrived at the end, where the main street met its final cross street in a T. On the other side of the cross street, directly in front of them, was a white granite mausoleum larger than the five-room shack Rashawn called home. Above the entrance, *Bonner* was etched in elaborate Roman script. Below that, in the same script but slightly smaller, was a directive: *Do Not Disturb Us.*

The door itself stood open.

"This is gonna be easier than I thought." Kentrell grinned as they stepped up to the entrance.

Rashawn hitched up his pants, which promptly slid back down his hips. His black denim jeans were cut off below the knee, and he wore a yellow muscle shirt that displayed the ropy sinew of his brown arms. He looked up again at the words over the door. "Let's just hurry up and do this," he whispered.

They walked in. It was obvious that the marble door had been forced; Kentrell saw the large chinks along the edges where someone had long ago broken the seal. It was just as obvious that no one had bothered to restore it. Maybe they were too late. Maybe what they were after was long gone. Still, they had come this far. Might as well see for themselves.

They entered a large antechamber. There was enough moonlight that they could see fairly well. The antechamber was empty except for a single pedestal in the center of the room that bore a Carrara marble bust of a hugely smiling, handsome black man. The blank stone eyes somehow managed to sparkle with delight. Kentrell recognized the countenance of Benoit Bonner.

Rashawn didn't like the way the bust was looking at him. "Shit," he hissed.

"Stay there at the door, keep a lookout," Kentrell said. "I'll call if I need ya." He now regretted bringing Rashawn along. He had thought he would need the brother's help breaking in, but that deed had already been done, and the fool was starting to shake like Scooby-Doo.

Kentrell crossed the room to the door that led deeper into the tomb. Above that door was another inscription: *You Were Warned.*

He passed through without hesitation.

He walked down a wide corridor, switching on the flashlight he carried. The corridor opened into another chamber. Above the opening to that chamber was yet another inscription: *What's The Matter? Can't You Read?*

He grinned as he entered.

The walls of this chamber were lined with vaults, all apparently unoccupied. There wasn't a single name or date on any of the smooth slate coverings. Kentrell indulged himself in a moment of smugness. If old boy Benoit had left any descendants, surely some of them would have joined him here by now. There was no "us." Just the old boy himself.

Kentrell crossed to the door and the corridor that led to the final chamber. And above that door, a final inscription: *I'd Turn Back If I Were You. Really.*

Kentrell laughed. Old boy had one fucking sense of humor.

He plunged on, down the corridor.

The final chamber was sealed with a finely polished green limestone casing. There was no sign it had been disturbed, which gave Kentrell hope. Maybe he'd get what he came for after all. From his belt, he unclipped a nylon pouch, which he'd retrieved from his backpack at the bus station before hailing a cab. He bent down and stood the flashlight on its end, the beam blazing up to illuminate the immediate area. He unzipped the pouch and hauled out a hammer and chisel. Wedging the chisel firmly against one edge of the casing, he raised the hammer.

Don't even THINK about it.

Kentrell froze. The thought was in his head, but it was not his voice.

He looked back up the corridor. It was empty. But the hair standing up on the back of his neck indicated that he was not alone here.

"You just punking out, man," he quietly chided himself. He turned back to the casing.

Well. You're determined; I'll give you that. Tell me, is that stubbornness, or are you simply dense?

Kentrell shook his head, as if that would dislodge the unwelcome guest. "You imagining stuff, fool, that's all."

Delude yourself if you wish. But you can't say that you weren't given fair warning. In case it isn't glaringly obvious to you by now, my resting place is indelibly cursed. Those who violate it do so to their lifelong regret. If they live at all, that is.

"This is crazy. I ain't trying to hear this shit," Kentrell snapped at himself.

That much has been plain from the start. But if you are bound to break through that seal, then by all means, go right ahead.

Kentrell raised the hammer again.

And hesitated.

Having second thoughts?

"Would you shut the fuck up?"

Oh, never. I'm quite enjoying our little conversation. Please, go on with your breaking and entering. I'd love to have you hang around for a while.

"SHUT UP!"

"Kentrell?" Rashawn's voice called shakily from the darkness. "What the fuck you doing down there? You talking to yourself?"

"Ray, get your punk ass back to the door and watch out!" Kentrell shouted back.

My. What a lively little thing you are. And how convenient that you brought a friend.

In a fit of rage, Kentrell slammed the hammer against the chisel. The cement seal cracked down to the floor. Air hissed through like a sigh from within.

Ahhh. You have no idea how good that was for me. Thank you.

"Fuck you."

In due time.

The implication escaped Kentrell, so angry was he as he pounded away, breaking the rest of the cement around the casing.

Really, I do so appreciate you. Others have gotten this far and, when I began speaking to them, they somehow lost their nerve. The only good thing to come from those encounters, at least as far as I'm concerned, is that they brought me knowledge, kept me up to speed on current events. My speaking drove them quite insane, I'm afraid, and they all ran off to do who knows what with themselves. Pity. Many of them were very pleasing to the eye. But you're of a different mettle, thankfully. You're the first one stupid enough... Oh. I beg forgiveness. That was ungracious of me. I meant to say that you're the first one with a big enough pair of nuts to actually break the final seal.

The casing fell inward, slamming to the floor of the chamber beyond with a loud crash, splitting into pieces and sending up a cloud of dust. Kentrell dropped his tools and lifted the hem of his wifebeater to cover his mouth and nose. He picked up the flashlight and stepped through into Benoit Bonner's burial chamber.

He shone the beam around. Dust. Cobwebs. A stone bier bearing two identical ornate mahogany caskets.

Two caskets?

The darkness swam before Kentrell. He staggered back, leaning against the edge of the door.

It was some time before the dizziness passed.

Kentrell's eyes opened. His arms pushed him upright, away from the door. His hands began probing at his chest, his stomach. His lungs inhaled deeply.

What? What happened? The voice in his head was his own.

"My God. This is marvelous—" The voice that issued from his mouth was not.

Benoit Bonner, in the body of Kentrell Lewison, spun around drunkenly, laughing with absolute delight. "Finally! Finally!"

Wait—

"I'm done waiting." Benoit, released after long decades, rushed back along the corridor in Kentrell's body, reveling in the feel of strong young muscles bunching and releasing, of a heart beating faster with each step, of the anxious tingle spreading up from warm, snug, and suddenly engorging genitalia. "Jesse! Jesse, are you there?"

Ahead, a tall silhouette appeared in the doorway of the moonlit antechamber. It opened its arms. "My love," it said breathlessly. "My sweet, I'm here."

Kentrell's body rushed into the waiting arms of Rashawn's body. They met with all the passion of lovers separated for far too long a time. At once, Rashawn's hands were everywhere, sliding over Kentrell's back, clutching at his ass.

Shit! Shit! Get the fuck away from me, Rashawn! What the fuck's wrong with you?

"No, no," said Benoit. He took Jesse by the shoulders and pushed him firmly back. "Let me look at you for a moment. Let me look into your eyes."

The deceased lovers stared at each other in awed silence.

"I like your body, my sweet," Jesse said at length. "It's nicely built. And your face is so pretty."

"Your body isn't bad either, baby," said Benoit, grinning lasciviously. "Although this is a bit of a reversal. I'm used to being the tall one."

"God, come here!" Jesse reached out, grabbing Benoit around the waist and pulling him in. "I've missed touching you. I've missed holding you—" Jesse lifted a hand and gently, lovingly caressed the smooth face before him. "I can't believe how beautiful you are." Jesse closed his eyes, leaning his face down.

Fuck! Rashawn, don't fucking KISS m—

Benoit surged forward, pressing his mouth to Jesse's parted lips. Tongues met hungrily, arms locked their bodies in a writhing embrace. Thick hands grabbed at muscular asses, clutched hard chests, caressed powerful thighs. Moans filled the chamber, not the whining of lost souls but the urgent growls of two men insane with need for each other. Jesse's cock bulged beneath the loose black denim, pressing against the equally straining hot mass of Benoit's dick.

This ain't happening, Kentrell! This just fucking ain't happening!

Benoit's hands grabbed the hem of Jesse's shirt, yanking it over his head and off his body. He leaned in and kissed his way down Jesse's supple neck. He nipped playfully at Jesse's flat brown nipples, eliciting surprised, delighted gasps.

"Remember how much you used to like it when I did that?" Benoit said between bites. He slid his hands down the Jesse's slender torso, marveling at the warmth of firm, living flesh. He undid the belt, shoving the black denim shorts and the white cotton boxers beneath to the dusty floor. He took in the long, dark cock that speared at him from a thick tangle of pubic hair. Kneeling, he kissed his way from the button of a navel to the base of the cock.

No way am I doing that!

Benoit gently kissed the tip of Jesse's dick, ignoring the frantic voice that cursed up a storm in his head. He looked into his lover's new face. "Not as big as the original, but I love it," he said. "I love *you*." He peeked around Jesse's side. "Hm. Butt's a little on the narrow side, but by Fod, it will do!" He smacked the narrow rump for emphasis.

"Now let me see what you've got," Jesse said eagerly, stepping out of his jeans and boxers. He stripped off the jersey and wifebeater worn by the body Benoit now possessed. The well-turned chest and rippled belly were hairless, but there was a nice patch of black fuzz peeking over the elastic band of the tighty-whities under the low-hanging jeans. Jesse peeled away the jeans and shorts. He gasped when a rigid cock sprang out at him. After drinking in the sight, he gripped Benoit's shoulders, slowly turned him around, and gasped again.

"Well, damn," Jesse said with a pout. "It seems you got all the dick *and* the ass. That's hardly fair."

"Ooh, love, no worries," Benoit cooed. He shook his round apple of a butt. *"Mi culo es su culo—"*

Jesse growled and grabbed Benoit from behind. "I *love* it when you talk dirty in a foreign language."

The hot, satiny length of the cock pressed against the trough of Benoit's butt. Tremors of pleasure rippled along his nerves—as an appalled screech from the essence of Kentrell tore through his mind so virulently that his eyes twitched. Sensations steadily built within him, and he loved every one—the enveloping warmth of the hard, naked body behind him, the caress of hot summer air on his skin, even the smell of cheap liquor on his own breath. He wondered, idly and fleetingly, just what the hell kind of swill this Rashawn character had imbibed.

Sweet Lord, it was just so damn wonderful to be alive again!

He turned suddenly and, locking his arms around his old lover's new body, rushed them both headlong through the mausoleum door. They stumbled backward and, naked except for boots and sneakers, fell in a tangle of young, manly limbs on the soft, sweet carpet of green grass.

"Are you insane?" Jesse gasped. "We can't be out here like this. Someone may see us."

"Let them," Benoit barked. "I've got to have you, here, now. Better to do it on the lawn than scrape ourselves raw on that concrete floor. Besides, this is a freer age than we knew, when it would have been scandalous just to have you openly buried beside me after you died. I say we make the most of it!"

Oh, shit. Kentrell's silent wail echoed Rashawn's anguish.

They kissed, crushing their mouths together. Their lips brushed and nuzzled, their teeth bit tantalizingly. Soon Benoit's fingers were probing at Jesse's backside with an urgency that Jesse remembered all too well.

Jesse pulled his lover's demanding hands away from his rump. "Please, baby. You have such a pretty ass there. Let me get some of that first."

WHAT?

Benoit smiled. "We have a bit of a problem. There's the matter of that little four-letter disease. This Kentrell fellow has never been tested for it."

"Neither has Rashawn," said Jesse.

"Well, until we know their status, we can't indulge ourselves the way we did back in our day. At least not without the proper precautions. And unfortunately, Kentrell brought no condoms."

Now Jesse smiled, roguishly. "Ah, but Rashawn was a bit more cautious in his dealings than his friend was." He reached into his right sneaker and produced four foil packs.

Benoit squeaked with delight. "And they're already lubricated. What a marvelous age this is!" He turned over, presenting his dimpled ass to Jesse.

Jesus Christ! Don't do this! Please!

Benoit looked over his shoulder and winked at Jesse, chortling at the panicked voice screaming hysterically in his head. "Be gentle. I haven't done this in sixty-seven years."

❖

More than an hour later, they lay together on the grass in front of the mausoleum. Sweaty. Out of breath. Deliciously tired.

And utterly in love.

"We should get moving," Jesse said.

Benoit pulled Jesse's long, brown arms tighter around him. "Mmm. In a moment."

"My sweet, this grass is making my ass itch something fierce."

"Oh, all right. Kentrell has a couple of hundred dollars in his pocket. We'll get ourselves a hotel room somewhere, have a nice, long soak together in a tub, and we'll snuggle up in a proper bed. In the morning, I'll go to Judd and Garland, give the codes, and take back my estate." Benoit rolled over and planted a long, luscious kiss on his lover's neck. Then he pulled back and smiled. "Amazing what a silly rumor and greed can accomplish. As if I would actually stick my precious jewelry in a musty old tomb."

Jesse laughed, stood up, reached down and pulled Benoit to his feet. "It took more than sixty years, but it was worth the wait."

"Indeed," Benoit agreed. "We'll have to go to Massachusetts, buy a nice house. We can get married there. I can finally make an honest man of you."

The two men stood facing each other. A tear swelled in Jesse's eye.

"Jesse? What's wrong?"

"I'm just…happy. I thought I'd never get to touch you again."

"Oh, ye of little faith. Come. We have another long life ahead of us." Benoit turned toward the mausoleum.

Jesse delivered a sharp swat across Benoit's bare butt. "And I'm looking forward to more of you. Every day, every night. For years… decades to come."

Benoit laughed, reached out to return the favor…and froze. "Hear that?" he asked.

Jesse listened. "I don't hear anything."

"Neither do I. Kentrell seems to have gone mute in my head."

"Same here with Rashawn. I wonder what shut them up."

"I think the poor fellows are traumatized at having breached each other's posteriors."

"Too bad for them. Who knows? In a year or two, they may come to love it as much as we do."

Smiling, the couple returned to the mausoleum and dressed. Then they headed up the main street of the cemetery, hand in hand, dead men walking into life.

SIREN SONG
JAMIE FREEMAN

The Craigslist ad, titled Wet Dream for an Artist, turns out to be an ad for a rental house. The long narrative that accompanies the single, blurry photograph seems unrelated to the house itself, being instead a rambling fragment from the libretto of Wagner's *Gotterdammerung* in which three Rhine nymphs implore Siegfried to return a golden ring they feel is rightfully theirs. Siegfried makes fun of the nymphs, taunting them and sending them away empty-handed into the river. An addendum, which seems to have been written by someone else, describes the house as "a fully furnished dream mansion perfect for artist or writer type available for a two-year lease." When Gabriel calls the rental agency, the girl who answers the phone says, "Yeah, what?"

"I'm calling about the ad—"

"Which one?"

"The ad about the Lorelei Springs house?"

There is a long silence and then he hears her muffled voice screaming, "Karen, somebody's on the phone about that place...you know? *That* place."

There is a scuffle and some heavy breathing on the line and then he hears another voice, this one as deep and gravelly as Kathleen Turner on a bender.

"You're calling about Lorelei Springs?" she says.

"Yes, the house is—"

"Very expensive," she says.

He tells her his name.

"The artist?"

"The same."

"When would you like to see it?" she asks.

❖

The house is a marvel, a sprawling, serpentine heap of bricks and stone; wood beams and pine floorboards; vaulted ceilings, oak beams, and expansive windows. He can't pinpoint a single overarching architectural style, but from the seething turbulence of design elements emerges a comforting feeling of continuity, cohesion, and fluidity.

The foyer, dominated by a twisting staircase and an enormous crystal chandelier, is larger than his New York apartment.

Karen watches him staring at the chandelier for a while, arms folded across her red Anne Klein suit jacket, Mercedes keys clutched conspicuously between her perfectly manicured fingers.

"You can look at the other rooms if you want to," she says.

She trails him through the house, pointing out features in a bored voice. He wanders from room to room, counting sitting rooms and fireplaces until he loses track.

"The fish tanks are maintained by the owner, of course," she says when he stops in front of an enormous freshwater tank built into the dining room wall.

"Why is the house so inexpensive?" he asks.

"It's not."

"For a house this size, it's a steal," he says. "Even as a rental."

"Do you want me to raise the price?" she asks. She glances at her watch. "I have other clients," she says. "Do you want it or not?"

"You don't have other clients," he says, stepping down into a broad empty room with a row of French doors leading out to the back terrace, the swimming pool, and beyond that, the gently sloping pine forest that runs along the edge of a wide, slow-moving river. He walks along the row of doors, unbolting them and flinging them wide to let in the sun and the gentle spring breeze.

Gabriel hears Karen's heels clacking across the immaculate pine flooring. "It would make a beautiful studio," she says. "You could paint more masterpieces here."

"Yeah." He inhales the mix of pine trees and flowers, water and rotting leaves.

"Just don't let your dog go down by the river alone," she says.

"What? Why?"

"Alligators."

"You're kidding," he says.

She pivots on her heel, arms still crossed in front of her. "I think dogs taste like chicken," she says.

"Jesus, Karen—"

"I'm just saying—"

"Fine. I'll watch out for the alligators," he says. "So, when can I move in?"

❖

Gabriel had spent the past four years traveling, showing and selling his work, but creating nothing new. Weeks spent in sterile hotel suites surrounded by flowered bedspreads, bland furniture, cable television, and facile landscapes slowly sucked the life out of him. He became headachy and anxious, arguing with Jason—his boyfriend and eventually his business manager, and later still, his melancholy ex— and the gallery owners about details that in truth, he didn't care about at all. He grimaced his way through business dinners and drank his way through meet-and-greets with the press and local buyers. True, he sold a hell of a lot of paintings for a hell of a lot of money, but he felt himself drifting further and further away from himself. And so, six months earlier, he had started saying no. He said no to the proposals for a series of elaborate shows that would have run through 2011 and into the spring of 2012. He said no to a coffee table book because of the obligatory book tour. He said no to Ellen and Oprah and finally, he said no to Jason.

They had loved each other for a while—for years actually—but the shows and the schedule of the road had driven them apart. In the last year they had argued and reconciled and argued and reconciled, but in the end Jason's passion for the gallery circuit eclipsed his passion for Gabriel. Gabriel had seen glimmers of it before the end, like heat lightning streaking the horizon to herald a summer storm, but he had ignored the signs until the night he said no to Oprah.

"Don't you understand what this will do for you, Gabriel?" Jason had asked, his voice nearly pleading.

Gabriel watched him and felt his spine turn cold. He let the silence stretch out between them until there was no turning back.

"Don't you mean what it will do for *you*, darling?" he said finally.

And there, written across Jason's face as clearly as if the letters had been formed with black marker, was the answer. And Jason had seen it too, his eyes tearing up and his mouth opening and then closing in silent, confused confirmation.

After that it had been easier, amicable even. They knew where they stood. Jason would continue to represent Gabriel's work; he would sell individual paintings and book small shows like the one in London in September; and he would continue to love Gabriel, only silently now, and from a distance.

Jason had found his own apartment in New York and Gabriel had moved as far away from his big-city roots as he could manage, driving south to rural north Florida based on photos and an article he'd found in an in-flight travel magazine. He lived in a hotel for a while and then stumbled upon the ad for Lorelei Springs as he trolled Craigslist for hook-ups.

It is not until he has moved his meager belongings into one of the upstairs guest bedrooms and begun a methodical exploration of the house that the true eccentricities of the property come to light. Fox—an old Labrador with a graying muzzle and a missing eye—follows Gabriel, padding from room to room, sniffing the furniture and poking his nose behind draperies and statuary. He is an ornery old dog, prone to growling and backtalk, but he is smart and loyal and he seems to like the house, wagging his tail lazily as they explore.

There are stairways that lead to locked doors, bedroom windows that open into hallways or adjoining bedrooms, and closets that lead to interior balconies, as if the whole house is looping in on itself like a giant nautilus shell.

But the most unusual thing about the house is the water. There are at least two dozen enormous aquariums containing pump-driven river rapids, each labeled with a small engraved plaque that bears the name of a German river: Danube, Rhine, Elbe, Weser, Oder. In some rooms, the windows are tinted and textured to warp the light, creating the illusion that the rooms are underwater. Portholes rather than windows line the walls of the downstairs hallways. Intricate fountains have been retrofitted into fireplaces and the sound of running, dripping water is omnipresent. Nothing is wet, though; the air is crisp and clean and the humming air handlers seem to be keeping the humidity in check.

In addition to the architectural water features, the river motif swirls through rooms overflowing with lush curtains, throw pillows, and upholstery in shifting blues and greens. The walls are lined with paintings and prints of sailing vessels, river fortresses, waterfalls, sport fishermen, and rambling riverscapes.

On the wall over the fireplace in the largest of the sitting rooms, the one adjacent to the room Gabriel has chosen as his studio, there is a portrait of a pair of beautiful, muscular men with billowing hair and perfect torsos emerging from a torrent of rushing water. One is tall, dark and lean; the other is stockier and blond with the muscles of a Viking warrior. The two men, despite their differences, share a remarkable, almost familial similarity. They are reclining on opposite sides of the canvas, like two halves of an oyster. Their heads are thrown back in frankly erotic poses, eyes closed in ecstasy, bodies stretched out to accentuate their slab-like pecs, swollen nipples, and the thick V-shaped racks of muscles that descend modestly beneath the frothing water that obscures their crotches. The gilt-framed painting is enormous—larger than life-sized—and a small plaque has been tacked to the base of the frame identifying the subjects as "River Gods, Rhenus."

When Gabriel calls her to ask about the painting, Karen tells him she is not a historian, she is a realtor. She reads him her state license number aloud, pauses, sighs, and then tells him the painting was purchased at auction in Germany and shipped back to the house by the owner. No, she didn't know how old it is or who the hunky guys are, but she does have a friend named Chad she thinks Gabriel might like to meet. "He's a fantastic hairdresser," she croons. "An artist, really—you'd *love* each other." He thanks her, begs off on the date—even when she assures him it would be a "sure thing"—and hangs up the phone.

The phone rings almost immediately. Karen is calling back.

He leaves the phone ringing on the table and pushes out through the French doors in the studio to explore the patio, the pool, and the grounds beyond.

❖

On the afternoon of his third day in the house, he hears the music for the first time.

He is napping on an overstuffed sofa in the library—Fox curled at his feet—when he hears what sounds like a hunting horn in the distance, a repeating pattern of seven notes in the round brassy tones of a cornet. He sits up and looks around the room. Fox leaps off the sofa, instantly wild-eyed and awake, his hackles bristling along his spine, his head cocked to one side as he triangulates the source of the sound.

As they listen, the music becomes more complex. French horns repeat the opening tones, calling back and forth to the cornets. Strings join them, starting low and growing to surround the brass like the rising tide. Gabriel remembers the libretto in the Craigslist ad and thinks of Siegfried confronting the Rhine nymphs. The music sounds broad and orchestral enough to be Wagner, but he doesn't recognize it or know enough about Wagner to pinpoint the melody.

Fox scrambles out of the room and runs down the hallway. Gabriel follows him, listening to the music and looking for speakers. He can feel the melodies surrounding him, pushing against his body like waves as the music accelerates, urging him forward not with the syncopated percussive sounds of modern motion—not trains or automobiles or starships—but with an older, fuller sound he associates with the unfurling of giant sails and the rush of water against wooden hulls. Violins leap and canter through the melody like dolphins or otters frolicking in the ship's bow waves. And then a pair of male voices rise out of the symphonic river, a tenor and a baritone, their voices intertwined in an intricate, beguiling song.

He follows the music from room to room.

When he finally finds Fox, the dog is standing beneath the painting of the river gods watching a black disc spinning on an ancient Victrola.

There is such a disconnect between the booming clarity of the music and Gabriel's expectations of the Victrola's sound quality that it takes him a moment to identify the device. His mind is still grappling with the problem as he kneels next to the dog and removes the needle from the spinning disc. It scrapes against the grooves and the music abruptly ends. In the ringing silence, Fox lets out a mournful howl that makes the hair on the back of Gabriel's neck stand on end.

The music haunts Gabriel, invading his dreams and occupying the perimeter of his waking life. He hears the seven-tone melody repeated in the song of the mockingbirds outside his bedroom, in the melodramatic soundtrack of midnight movies, or in the creaking of the cypress trees at the river's edge.

Gabriel has come to Lorelei Springs to escape from his career, and from the smoldering remains of his life with Jason. He has come seeking a quiet place to heal and revive himself, and most importantly, to paint.

But the music leaves him restless and inarticulate.

By the time he celebrates his two-week anniversary at Lorelei Springs, he has not committed a single new idea to paper or canvas, has not produced a sketch or a watercolor or a doodle. Sometimes when he can't stand the pressure of his artistic silence any longer, he stands in the studio, listening to the eerily disembodied music from the ancient Victrola and holding the brushes between his fingers. He prays silently to himself or to God or to anyone who will listen, praying to restore the spark in his aching fingers, but inspiration never comes.

Today he leaves the house altogether, changing into running shorts, tugging on his Nikes and taking off into the woods in search of something to quiet his anxious body.

Alternating waves of cool shade and hot sunshine flash across his shoulders as he runs from dense woods to broad clearings and back again. Fox paces him for a while and then disappears into the undergrowth in pursuit of a rabbit.

Gabriel's feet lead him along a well-worn path through the woods in the direction of the river. The light grows brighter and the foliage begins to thin as he approaches the final turn before he reaches the lookout, a giant natural outcropping of stone that overlooks the slow-moving water.

As he rounds the far turn, Gabriel launches himself forward into a searing sprint and then leaps up onto the broad flat lookout rock. Fox has returned from his rabbit chasing and runs around the far side of the rock to climb the steps carved into stone. Gabriel's Nikes hit the edge of the rock at the same moment that Fox's surprised bark pierces the air.

Gabriel stops short, lungs heaving, sweat pouring down his face and chest, and stares into the amber eyes of a stranger. His heart leaps in his chest.

"This is private property," Gabriel says, and then to Fox, "Back off, little man."

On the far side of the rock, Fox stops barking and sits silently at attention, head tilted, good eye locked on the stranger between them.

"I'm sorry, I didn't realize," the stranger says after a moment, a half smile flickering across his lush downturned lips. He is tall with a tumult of dark unkempt hair that flutters in the breeze. He wears a pair of blue board shorts but no shirt, and he is barefoot. His body is tightly muscled with a riot of hair playing up across his long legs, thick curls tufting over the waistband of his low-slung shorts. A trail of black curls climbs up across his ridged abdomen and branches onto the broad furred plain of his chest. He has the bearing of a man of strength, but his limbs are willowy, the muscles somehow understated.

Gabriel's cheeks flush with desire.

"What are you doing here?" he says, his voice suddenly filling the awkward silence.

"We're just walking, maybe going for a swim."

"We?" Gabriel asks.

They stand in silence for a moment, Gabriel's eyes locked on the stranger's startling amber irises.

A second pale luminescent form steps around the edge of the rock, coalescing and appearing suddenly as if he has drawn corporeality from the loose molecules floating in the air around them. Fox literally jumps off the ground in surprise, paws scrabbling at the sandy earth to regain his footing, hackles rising in a black ridge along his spine. He barks furiously, head pivoting back and forth from Gabriel to the pair of confounding strangers.

Gabriel looks at the new arrival. He is short and thick, heavy with compact muscles. His blond hair is close cropped in a military cut, his body hairless except for a cluster of copper wisps that ring his broad tan nipples and a line of fine hairs that drop down from his navel into his shorts. He too wears blue board shorts. The two men could not look more different, but their physical opposition seems to reinforce an underlying similarity of bearing and manner that makes Gabriel think they are connected somehow.

They look familiar, but Gabriel cannot decide where he could possibly have met them before.

"Where did you come from?" he asks.

The two men stare silently at him, the sun beating down on their shoulders and hair. The light glistens across them, swirling around them like a visible aura. Gabriel imagines delicate brush strokes and indistinct lines surrounding them, blurring the separation between their bodies and the lush greenery around them.

The blond points vaguely upriver, but doesn't say anything.

"Men of few words, then?"

The dark-haired man shrugs. "What's to say?"

"You could try answering my questions. Or maybe you could say: I'm sorry for trespassing; please don't let your guard dog tear me to pieces."

The man laughs, white teeth flashing. He glances at his blond companion, who nods once, but says nothing.

Gabriel watches them, standing still and quiet in the breezy sunlight. He glances at the blond, then back at the dark-haired man, finally realizing why his mind has registered a startling similarity between them despite their very different looks and body types. Their faces are similar enough in contour and shape to imply a close genetic relationship—cousins perhaps, or even brothers—but their startlingly beautiful eyes are identical. Two sets of fiery amber irises stare at him with unnatural intensity.

"Are you okay?" the blond asks, his voice higher, more lyrical than his companion's. "We can't tell if you're for real."

Gabriel arches an eyebrow. "What does that mean?"

He shrugs.

They look at each other, then the blond says, "What we mean is: do you really want us to go? Or do you want what we have to offer?"

"What do you have to offer?" Gabriel asks.

"Inspiration," the blond says.

"And a swim," the dark-haired man says.

"That's kinda presumptuous," Gabriel says.

The men laugh, the blond's tenor and the dark-haired man's baritone full, almost harmonic in the hot summer air.

"You like that," the blond says. "Don't you?"

Gabriel grins. "Maybe," he whispers.

"I'm Jaeger," the blond says, holding out his hand. "This is my brother Kurt."

"Gabriel." He shakes hands with each of them in turn, Jaeger's grip firm and abrupt, Kurt's softer, lingering. "And that's Fox." Gabriel nods in the direction of the anxious dog, who is pacing back and forth at Gabriel's side, sniffing the air and snorting contemptuously, still unsure of the two visitors.

"He's a fox?"

Gabriel laughs, realizing that he is still holding Kurt's hand. Gabriel blushes and finally withdraws his hand. "No, he's a dog named Fox," he says.

"He is a warrior?" Jaeger asks.

"Who? Fox? No. He's—why do you ask that?"

"He is missing an eye."

Gabriel puts his hand down and tousles the fur between Fox's ears. "He's had a tough life," he says.

"He goes where you go?" Kurt asks.

"Yes."

"But he is not a fox?"

"No." Gabriel watches them processing something, but he's not sure what it is. Fox growls and snaps his jaws in annoyance. "Easy, boy," Gabriel whispers, massaging the tips of the dog's ears between his fingers.

Kurt looks nonplussed, but he smiles. "So is this your..." He falters.

"Gehöft?" he says to his companion.

"This is your home? Your land?" Jaeger says.

"Yes," he says, then, "Well, no."

"Which is it?" Jaeger looks at him curiously.

"I'm renting the house for a couple of years."

Jaeger nods, but his face is blank.

"So you live here?" Kurt says.

"Yes."

"In the house with the blue pool and the deep winter sky?"

"Yes." Gabriel notes the odd modifiers, brow wrinkling in curiosity. Obviously Kurt has seen the pool with its cobalt tiles and the mural of the winter sky painted across its depths. They have been here before.

"And you used to paint?" Jaeger says.

"How did you know that?"

"You are famous, are you not?" Kurt asks.

Gabriel shrugs, but he feels the hair on the back of his neck standing at attention. Fox whines and nudges Gabriel's leg.

"But you have no paint on you now," Jaeger says. He kneels and takes Gabriel's right hand in his. He turns it over, running his fingertips along the palm, rubbing the calluses and tracing the length of Gabriel's lifeline with his thick forefinger.

Gabriel's cock stiffens inside his flimsy running shorts. He tries to will the erection away, but he can't focus on anything but the feel of Jaeger's hands caressing his.

The brothers look at him, waiting for a response.

"I haven't been painting lately," he says, looking away, feeling the enthusiasm in his shorts waning.

"You need inspiration," Jaeger says. He gently kisses the palm of Gabriel's hand.

"And a swim," Kurt says.

Gabriel looks into Jaeger's amber eyes and feels a flash of vertigo. "What do we do now?" he asks finally.

"You must accept what we have to offer," Jaeger says.

"Inspiration," Gabriel says, nodding slowly. "Yes."

"And a swim."

❖

As they make their way back to the house, Kurt and Jaeger become more talkative, asking questions about the yard, the plants, and the history of the house. They laugh and talk over one another, walking on either side of Gabriel, vying for his verbal attention. Gabriel finds himself laughing and enjoying their attention. Fox trots along behind them, tail wagging, his initial suspicions fading as he spends more time with the strangers. Yellow butterflies dance along the edges of the trail, landing gently on the brothers' shoulders, flying circles around the panting dog, and flashing in the occasional shafts of sunlight that pierce the dense hammock above them.

Jaeger grins as one of the butterflies lands on his outstretched finger. "And pluck the wings from painted butterflies to fan the moonbeams from his eyes," he says, laughing and urging the butterfly again into flight.

Kurt glances at Jaeger, then at Gabriel, and laughs.

Gabriel smiles, but says nothing.

As they crest the final hill, the house comes into view, its serpentine structure clinging to the hillside, wrapping gently around the broad slate terrace and the cobalt-blue tiled swimming pool. Jaeger and Kurt stop suddenly and stare at the house.

"It has changed a lot over the years," Kurt says.

Jaeger glances at him, then smiles at Gabriel.

"You've been here before?" Gabriel asks.

Jaeger squints in the harsh sunlight, pauses, and then says, "We once knew a man who lived here."

"The painting," Gabriel says. "Oh, my God. You're the ones in the painting over the fireplace."

"Perhaps," Jaeger says.

"What does that mean?" Gabriel asks, but neither of the men responds.

"And the music?" he says. "What about the music?"

Gabriel watches Jaeger's eyes roving the contours of the house, the steep slope falling from the pool to the lower patio. He starts to ask another question, but is startled when Jaeger and Kurt simultaneously whoop with joy and lope off across the lawn in the direction of the pool.

Gabriel glances at Fox, who stares after the two brothers, tail wagging, tongue lolling in the heat.

"What do you think, boy?" he asks.

Fox barks once, then takes off at a run in the direction of the pool, tail wagging fiercely.

The brothers drop their shorts on the lawn and run naked in the direction of the pool. They hit the slate terrace at a run and leap up into the air, beautiful bodies suspended for an instant in flight, dark and light in stunning contrast under the bright scrutiny of the sun. Gabriel sees them frozen there over the water, a beautiful painting come to life. Something awakens inside him.

After what seems an unnaturally long moment, the two men drop with giant twin splashes into the pool. Before the water can settle, Fox comes careening across the terrace, paws scrabbling against the slate. He twists and slides into the water backwards, front paws scrabbling vainly along the edge of the pool, his upturned face gleaming with canine jubilation. Gabriel tugs off his running shoes, peels off his socks and shorts, and runs after them across the lawn.

In the distance he hears the sound of cornets and French horns, calling out to each other across the rising tide of strings and woodwinds, as he plunges feet first into the cool water, letting himself slide down toward the cobalt tiles below, bubbles settling lightly on his skin. He glances around and sees two pairs of legs moving lazily, treading water: a long dark pair to his right, a shorter muscular pair to his left. Between Kurt's long legs, a slender pale cock floats gently at half mast, dark curls rippling slightly around its base. Jaeger's cock, on the other hand, is short, thick, and almost fully erect. Tiny ginger hairs curl close against his skin. Gabriel leans back and settles deeper into the pool, letting his back lead the way, his limbs trailing upward in the direction of the surface.

Above him, Fox swims in happy circles, propelled by his front legs, his snout dipping into the water periodically, probably flicking water droplets excitedly into the air above him as he does when he is happy.

Gabriel closes his eyes and drifts downward.

He thinks of the two men treading water above him, imagines the possibility of lying naked between them, of being sandwiched between the long slender cock and the smaller thick one. He imagines Jaeger's arms crossing over his shoulders from behind, hands sliding down Gabriel's chest, his hard cock probing Gabriel's buttocks, seeking entrance while Gabriel, in turn, slides himself inside Kurt, the three of them bent over the lawn furniture or clustered on soft cotton sheets upstairs in Gabriel's bedroom. He wonders if he will allow these things to happen, if it is not a bad idea to give these odd men access to the house, or, indeed, to allow them access to his own body.

His mind is tumbling through these thoughts, images of sex eclipsing common sense and caution when he feels a hand wrapping itself around his right arm. He opens his eyes and finds himself staring into Jaeger's bright, smiling eyes.

Jaeger leans toward him, his lips touching Gabriel's, his hands pulling Gabriel close. Jaeger kisses Gabriel and for a moment, Gabriel senses his lungs filling with fresh oxygen. The pulse of energy lifts him forward, and he meets Jaeger's kiss with a vigor that surprises him. Gabriel pushes their mouths together, his tongue sliding between Jaeger's lips and running behind the upper row of perfect white teeth. Jaeger pulls him closer, his erection poking Gabriel gently. His own cock grows thicker and harder. His body begins to use its oxygen faster and he feels the need to rise up out of the water. He lets his feet drop against the bottom of the pool and bends his legs at the knees, preparing to launch himself up to the surface.

But Jaeger curls around him, his mouth never leaving Gabriel's. Their hungry kiss continues as Jaeger's left hand slides down Gabriel's hairy chest and stomach to stroke his cock. Gabriel starts to kick off against the bottom again, but Jaeger's right hand lights on his shoulder, holding him in place. A burst of adrenaline courses through Gabriel, but as he starts to pull away, Jaeger's lips part again and another gust of oxygen pulses down into his lungs. Gabriel pulls back, startled, and looks at Jaeger for a long moment. Jaeger is silent, but he winks an amber eye and leans forward again, taking Gabriel's cock in his hand and resuming their kiss.

Gabriel relaxes, realizing that each time his body needs oxygen, Jaeger's kiss somehow supplies it. He knows this should disturb him, but the growing excitement between his legs, the gentle swirl in the pit of his stomach, and the soft feathers of desire that tickle him behind the eyes all encourage him to discard his recent celibacy and let the current take him.

He pulls back from the kiss, reaches out and runs his hands down Jaeger's muscled chest. He moves forward, his decision propelling him as much as the muscles of his arms or legs. Gabriel wraps his legs around Jaeger's hips, pulling Jaeger roughly toward him. Jaeger laughs soundlessly, tiny bubbles of light slipping out of his mouth and rising around them. Gabriel pulls Jaeger close until their bodies are aligned, Gabriel's thick runner's legs wrapped around Jaeger's waist. Gabriel can feel Jaeger's erect cock sliding along the ridge between his balls and his ass. Jaeger's arms wrap around Gabriel and their lips meet again.

As the oxygen pours into Gabriel's lungs, another set of hands slides between his body and Jaeger's, long thin fingers, their touch tentative, almost flighty. Kurt moves behind Gabriel, his hairy chest rubbing slowly against Gabriel's back until his long cock slides between Gabriel's buttocks. Curving along his crack, the thick head of the cock surely encounters the tip of Jaeger's cock sliding between Gabriel's legs from the other direction. The two brothers pull him close until the three of them are lost in the sensations of smooth hands and probing fingers, coarse hair and muscled skin all gently muted by the water that surrounds them. Gabriel kisses Jaeger again and feels Kurt's mouth against the back of his neck, stubble scraping his skin, teeth nipping softly.

Gabriel feels four hands moving him gently, pushing him up slightly then pulling him back down. His ass glides across Kurt's stomach. He repositions himself slightly, and then slides down until Kurt's cockhead pushes gently against his hole. Jaeger kisses him again, pushing oxygen into his lungs and pushing him onto Kurt's long cock. Gabriel gasps, unused to the length of the man, ejecting a turbulent stream of bubbles from his mouth and nose, but Jaeger's lips are close, breathing life and calm sweetness into his lungs. The cool feel of Jaeger's kiss and the reassuring hands on his chest and his hips comfort and relax him. He feels himself glide down the length of Kurt's cock until his ass rests gently against Kurt's pelvic bone. He lets out a sigh of bubbles that waft upward in a lazy spiral.

In front of him, he feels Jaeger dislodging himself and sliding his cock up along Gabriel's chest, the round pink head pushing against his lips. Gabriel opens his mouth and engulfs the cock, oxygen once again rushing into his lungs. Kurt starts to move slowly beneath him, his rhythm gentle as a breeze. Gabriel feels the two cocks inside him pulsing in opposition, Jaeger pushing into his mouth, then Kurt pushing into his ass, and then Jaeger again. He falls into their rhythm, reaching down to stroke his own cock in a third-party contrapuntal rhythm that sends an electric shiver through him.

Kurt begins to move incrementally faster, his lips becoming more insistent against the back of Gabriel's neck. Jaeger too increases his rhythm, his cock sliding deep into Gabriel's throat, Gabriel's muscles flexing around the cock to increase the sensation. Jaeger slides his legs around Gabriel's shoulders, one on each side of Gabriel's head, feet crossed behind Kurt, pulling the three of them closer, tighter, the point where Gabriel's lips meet Jaeger's curly ginger public hair forming the center of an erotic equation of sexual force and potential. Jaeger's rhythm increases; Gabriel can feel Jaeger's thighs begin to quiver and shake and then, in a blinding moment, Jaeger shoots a long string of cum down Gabriel's throat, his body constricting, then relaxing, and then constricting again.

Jaeger pulls back for a moment, his body growing momentarily pale, almost translucent as he disentangles himself from Kurt and Gabriel. Kurt continues to slide in and out of Gabriel, his movements achingly slow and rhythmic. Gabriel gasps for a moment, but finds that he does not need air.

Jaeger swims in a lazy circle around their still-fused bodies, fingers playing across Gabriel's skin, then Kurt's, and then Gabriel's again before he swims close to kiss Gabriel's lips. Gabriel shivers as Kurt's cock slides against his prostate. Jaeger does not break the kiss, but slides close again, rubbing his cock against Gabriel's chest. His erection, which had seemed to be departing as he swam around them, has now clearly returned. Gabriel breaks the kiss and looks down between them at his own hairy chest and Jaeger's smooth chest, stomach, and cock.

Jaeger slides down Gabriel's chest and stomach, wrapping his muscular thighs around Gabriel and positioning himself over Gabriel's raging erection. The moment of contact is like a spaceship docking with a space station, an exact movement surrounded by the silence of the water. Gabriel feels the heat as Jaeger's ass engulfs his cock. His eyes meet Jaeger's and a smile drifts across Jaeger's sensuous lips. "Yes," he mouths, and then kisses Gabriel again.

As Jaeger settles onto Gabriel, Kurt steps up his rhythm, taking control of the trio as he thrusts his long cock into Gabriel, then pulls out slowly, almost to the end before thrusting back inside, each time a little faster, a little harder. Jaeger pulls back from his kiss and matches his movements to his brother's, sliding to the end of Gabriel's cock just as Kurt reaches the far point of his own extraction. Gabriel shudders between the two men.

Jaeger leans past Gabriel's face to kiss his brother's lips. Gabriel feels their bodies tense, muscles straining together as the three of them fuck in bewildering, watery unison.

Kurt and Jaeger increase their speed, Jaeger leaning back to kiss Gabriel again, infusing him with so much oxygen that Gabriel feels dizzy, disembodied. The first click of orgasmic activity sounds deep inside Gabriel as Kurt thrusts to his deepest penetration yet, Jaeger simultaneously slamming himself hard against Gabriel's pubic bone. Gabriel feels crushed, pinioned between these two startling beauties. He feels the second click an instant later and the locks begin opening before the relentless flood of his release.

He feels Kurt burst first, flooding Gabriel's insides with heat. Gabriel comes an instant later and looks down to see Jaeger's cock bobbing between them, shooting burst after burst of hot glittering semen into the water around them. Kurt pulls Gabriel close and Gabriel in turn pulls Jaeger to him, mashing their lips together and breathing deeply from his lungs, their kiss becoming almost desperate in the heat of their watery dénouement. Gabriel feels the three of them fuse for a long moment. They drop, hearts beating, hands and legs grasping each other, holding each other close, bubbles and sparkling streams of semen drifting upward as they settle on the cobalt tiles of the pool floor, their bodies sliding to a halt against the field of white tiled constellations.

Gabriel wakes to Fox's fretful ministrations. The worried old dog is licking his face and pawing gently at Gabriel's shoulder, trying to alert him to the fact that the sun is falling slowly through the western sky and the stars are rising with equal implacability in the east.

Gabriel sits up and hugs the dog, looking out over the broad, slow-moving river from his perch on the flat lookout rock where he had earlier met the brothers. He feels achy and hungover from the adrenaline and the physical exertion of their encounter. He looks down at himself, realizing that he has been sleeping here naked. In the first blurry moments of wakefulness, it seemed right that he should be lying here, unclothed, in the waning evening sunlight, but now, as he sits up, he realizes he cannot remember anything after he sank with Kurt and Jaeger to the bottom of the pool.

He looks around, but there is nobody in sight.

He rises and walks down the stone steps to the path, looking around the base of the rock for his clothes, but not finding them.

He looks at Fox, whistles him home, and heads up the steep path in the direction of the house.

Where the forest trail gives way to manicured grass lawn, Gabriel spots his clothes and two pairs of blue board shorts, but sees no other sign of the brothers. He picks up his shorts and slips them on to cover his nakedness, then wanders across the lawn, picking up his socks, his running shoes, and two pairs of blue board shorts.

He drops them all on a lawn chair and pads across the stone patio to the edge of the pool.

He looks down into the dark water, shimmering points of light forming the patterns of winter constellations across the bottom. He searches the pool for evidence of his afternoon.

He spots something floating on the water near the far edge. Whatever it is, it is glowing gently, flashing in the gathering darkness as the summer breeze gently ripples the water. He walks around the pool, Fox following excitedly at his heels. When he reaches the far side, he kneels down and cups his hands in the water, lifting the glowing remnant and staring at it.

The water flows through his fingers, leaving in the palm of his hands a viscous streak that glows amber and pulses in the darkening evening.

❖

That night Gabriel begins to paint.

He paints for a month without coming up for air. He is submerged in his work, phoning in orders for food and painting supplies and stalking the moon across the nighttime sky, painting all day and long into the summer nights, accompanied by the voices of the river gods emanating from the ancient Victrola. He begins to experiment with textures and colors, shutting the door on his signature styles and seeking new languages of light and texture and meaning.

He runs by moonlight with Fox, pounding out the rhythm of his days along the sandy paths. He feels full and excited, reveling in the call of his canvases, feeling the warm pulse of their siren song dancing behind his eyes.

Some nights he and his canine companion stop to howl at the moon from the flat expanse of the lookout rock, their voices mingled in a cacophony that makes Gabriel bubble over with joyful laughter. The world around them is crisp and clear and beautiful and it sends Gabriel running back to his brushes and his canvases.

One month stretches into two and then three.

By early September, just days before his departure for the London show, he has produced a series of twenty-seven large canvases and sixteen smaller ones. The night before he leaves for the airport, he paces barefoot in front of the arrayed paintings, scrutinizing them in the evening light. The doors to the patio are open, a warm breeze sweeping in from the river and gently rustling the papers on his desk and the mail that has piled up on the hall table. He paces, staring intently at the paintings, searching them for flaws, mentally editing the lush romantic canvases. His eyes slide along the contours of his summer idylls: touching here the plane of a muscular thigh or a curved pectoral, tracing there a long straight shaft of summer sunshine. He scans the proportions of the black dog running along the foreground of one piece, howling on the lookout rock in another. He counts the stars in the shimmering winter constellations, consciously distorted by the water through which they shine. He paces long into the night, bare feet against thick carpets, his wineglass smeared with paint, his eyes red, manic, engrossed.

As the clock in the hall strikes three, Fox looks up, tail thumping gently against his hearth rug. Gabriel is crouched in front of the largest of the paintings, tracing the lines of a small yellow butterfly with his paint-smeared finger. He never looks up from his work as the two figures appear behind him, materializing out of the darkness.

They watch him for a long time with startling amber eyes. The taller one runs his hand down the furred contours of his muscled chest and grins at his blond companion. The blond reaches out as if to touch

Gabriel's bare shoulders, but before his fingers meet the warm flesh, the two of them fade into the darkness.

❖

When Gabriel doesn't arrive in London, Jason calls the house and then Gabriel's cell, leaving a series of increasingly frantic messages. He calls and calls, but gets no answer. When he phones the limo service, the manager tells him the driver arrived on time but nobody ever came out of the house or answered the doorbell or the phone.

Jason drives from the airport in a rental car and finds Fox lying delirious and dehydrated in the gravel driveway of Gabriel's house. He strokes his glossy black coat, talking to him in soothing tones, but the old dog's remaining eye is glassy and distant, his paws scrabbling ineffectually as he tries to stand.

The front door is unlocked and there is music coming from the studio. Jason isn't sure what it is, something heavy and orchestral, like a vast, raging river dotted with cataracts and engorged by the spring thaw.

He walks through the foyer, calling Gabriel's name.

At the studio door, the smell slams into him like a wall, stagnant water and the earthy smell of decay, not the sickly sweet stench of rotting flesh he had half expected, but something dark and lush and malignant.

He looks down and sees Gabriel lying on the floor at the base of an enormous painted canvas. He kneels beside Gabriel, but his eyes are drawn against his will to the painting. It's a sprawling green forest scene dominated by a trio of nude men cavorting in and around a bubbling cobalt spring. A tall dark-haired man stands waist-deep in the water, his broad, muscular back glistening wetly, his hands flinging droplets of water like glittering constellations into the air above his head. A muscular blond man and a thin man with a hairy chest wrestle playfully at the edge of the pool. Yellow butterflies dance in the air above the trio.

Music pours from an ancient Victrola, enchanting Jason, dulling his reactions like those of a drowning man.

Later when he tries to describe the scene to the police, he will not be able to rationally explain how he failed to notice the water.

His eyes explore the painting, following the long shafts of sunlight that drop from the leafy canopy to the forest floor, tracing the muscular planes and curves of the trio of men, and becoming lost in the dark glossy coat of the black dog half-hidden between a pair of slowly waving palmetto fronds. And then he sees the water. Bubbling up out of the cobalt spring and streaming down the front of the painting onto the floor. When he looks down he realizes he is kneeling in several inches of water. Water is streaming into the hallway and tricking down the steps toward the open French doors. Gabriel's body is white and cold beneath Jason's hands, and from between his lips bubbles an endless stream of cold, shimmering water.

Jason collapses over Gabriel's body, his shoulders convulsing wildly as the first racking sob tears its way up through his chest.

GAY ORPHEUS
GREGORY L. NORRIS

I wish we had more time," Tom says from the bedroom door.
Looking back, those words seem eerily prophetic. The image
of this scene from our life comes clearly: me, on the bed, plucking a
lazy, melancholy riff on the guitar, dressed in cotton shirt perfect for the
season, summer transitioning to autumn, boxer-briefs, wool socks; him,
his policeman's uniform only half-on, belt unbuckled, unzipped black
pants showing the best part of the tight-whites beneath, basic white
T-shirt hugging a magnificent chest, black socks on huge feet, uniform
shirt and tear-away clip-on tie, badge and gun belt over the easy chair,
shiny black shoes waiting to be filled.

The memory is like a succession of snapshots or a short film
archived inside my head, imprinted forever. I stop plucking the guitar,
laying down a few awkward notes at the end, and glance at the clock.
If only I had the power to knock those digital numbers into reverse.
Twenty minutes more. Hell, fifteen. I'd even take five now, to quote
Dave Brubeck. I'd be grateful for mere seconds.

Turning back to Tom, I see the disappointment on his face.

"That song," he says.

"That old thing?"

"It's really good."

"It's just some old ballad from the 1960s that no one remembers.
Except me and a handful of people on YouTube."

"I love it," he growls, shuffling nervously in place. He scratches
at the meaty fullness in the front of his underwear. I see that he's gotten
stiff, despite our tumble earlier in the morning. All the moisture drains
from my mouth. The masculine, phantom taste of his cock and balls

ignites on my tongue. Choking down a swallow, I realize I've started
to salivate, like one of Pavlov's dogs anticipating a treat. I reach up,
massage his erection, and work it free from imprisonment. Time for an
encore performance.

"Can't, duty calls. Gotta get to my shift," Tom laments.

He tucks his cock back into cover and zips his pants. The rest of
his uniform goes on, in quick order. The obvious bulge at crotch level
persists, and I know if he doesn't disconnect from me soon and hustle
his butt out to his truck and motor to work, he's going to start leaking
pre-cum. That first time we kissed, his excitement left an obvious and
expanding wet spot at the front of his jeans. I was his first guy. He was
my best.

"Get out of here, Orfino," I yell at him, not in anger but playfully.

Tom fires a salute. A kiss, at this point, is far too dangerous. A
kiss leads to being tardy for his shift. A kiss means pre-cum, flowing
in torrents.

"I'll see you later, Yuri," he growls.

And I steal another glance his way: Tom, six foot three, his neat,
dark athlete's haircut disappearing beneath the black baseball cap
with the gray bill and the police department's insignia; pale blue eyes,
almost gray in color; thin mustache, capable of unleashing supernatural
pleasures over another man's most sensitive flesh; the body of a deity,
toughened by four years in the military and a lifetime of pickup hoops
and summer baseball leagues; strong hands; handsome face; heavenly
distraction.

And then he is gone. I, too, curse time.

❖

I met Tom Orfino in a dark alley outside Ellis Infields, though *met*
is sugarcoating it. At first, I couldn't see much through the blood pouring
into my eyes, and it was hard to hear beyond the ringing in my ears.
One of my two attackers had driven my head into a brick wall. Luckily
for me, I have a thick skull. Even luckier, an off-duty officer from the
Ellis, Massachusetts, police department happened to be strutting past
when he heard my shouts. When later questioned why he was near the

town's only gay bar, Tom calmly answered he was grabbing a pack of smokes at the all-nighter across the street. The only time he ever lit up after I moved in was for the occasional cigar, not cigarettes.

"You're gonna be okay, pal." His voice, deep and reassuring, worked through the exquisite pain.

"But," I interrupted, tasting what felt like a pocket's worth of pennies on my tongue.

"Those two fuckers?" I figured there had to be at least ten. Maybe a baker's dozen. Turns out, Tom had overpowered both of them. "I'm gonna stay with you until more help arrives."

A mechanical symphony punctuated his vow, then—

"Yeah, Officer Tom Orfino, Ellis P.D. I'm calling this in on my cell. I'm in an alley off Daisy Street and need immediate uniform backup and ambulance assistance. I have one victim of an assault, male, twenties if I had to guess, presently conscious, and two assailants, both subdued."

His voice took on a distant, disembodied quality, and I found myself drifting off into darkness more stygian than the shadows of night in the alley. An eclipse engulfed me. The searing heat from my wounds abated, replaced by a layer of ice.

"Hey, stay with me," he said, cutting through the chill.

The darkness retreated a step. Tom gripped my wrist, tethering me to consciousness, to life.

"You with me, pal?"

I was. "Yes."

"Good, now I want you to talk to me until help arrives. Will you promise me that?"

I pledged that I would. I told him that the club hired me to DJ for the night and rambled on about my most excellent collection of CDs and vinyl; extinct music from musicians long departed, and the shame of it all compared to most of the modern crap being played on the radio and pawned off as Top 40. I attempted to make a joke, that maybe the two men who beat the shit out of me hadn't liked my selections.

"You're being kind," Tom said. "They're a pair of degenerate thugs. I'd bet they were lurking around just waiting to jump some poor dude from the club and go a few rounds on him."

Not sure why, I told him I could play the guitar and was fairly competent on the piano, too. And that his deep voice was poetic, musical; an angel's or some other superhuman creature's.

He thanked me and his grip tightened. The night cleared from my eyes and suddenly I could see again. The handsomest face I'd ever beheld hovered over mine, illuminated in the strobing blue light of an approaching police car.

❖

Two surgeries and three weeks later, Tom asked me to move in with him. I didn't know as much about him as people will tell you that you should before making such a huge commitment. He was divorced from what he called "your typical Army marriage" and owned a little house out in North Ellis on the edge of the town's conservation woods. He stayed with me at the hospital right until they wheeled my stretcher up to the O.R., and he was waiting for me in the recovery room.

Sometimes, knowing a little is enough. And sometimes, in those rarest of chances, two people meet and instantly, completely fall in love, like we did.

❖

Tom left for his duty shift and, like so many mornings, I drifted through the house in something of a happy daze. He'd given me the spare room that used to be his "man-cave" for my records and stuff. After almost five months, most of the boxes were unpacked. Tom didn't need a man-cave, he said quite easily, because there were plenty of caves in the forest if he needed someplace dark to escape to. Besides, he was having more fun in the bedroom since I moved in than he was watching sports or jerking off to porn in that same tatty easy chair where he now daily laid out his uniform.

In the kitchen, I brewed a fresh pot of coffee after taking a sip of the gasoline he left on the burner for me. And then, unable to control myself, I wandered into the bathroom, found one of Tom's discarded T-shirts, the same one from that morning's jog through the woods, and raised it to my nose. The piney scent of his sweat made me gasp. Eyes half-closed, I relived the morning's lovemaking.

❖

Tom, dressed in black loose-fitting jogging shorts, the T-shirt, baseball cap, old sneakers, white socks, marched across the backyard, a weedy expanse more meadow than actual lawn. The decision to let it go wild, he'd told me, was equal parts his desire to honor the natural world, and laziness. Tom loved the deep woods beyond the little house. I was starting to.

As I watched, he raised the bottom of his T-shirt to wipe his face, exposing the furry ring of his belly button. His muscles glistened with fresh perspiration. My heart—and other body parts—pulsed.

Tom trotted up the back stairs, entering the kitchen. The heavenly haze of his scent swept in with him, along with the fragrance of the late summer meadows. His face lit with a smile at seeing me.

"Hey babe," he said.

A moment later, his warmth gently engulfed me. I loved his smell, his strength, and the excited thickness of his cock as it stabbed against my thigh. I ogled his swell, which was wet with pre-cum and growing wetter, eased my other hand along a patch of hairy upper thigh and into his shorts. Tom hadn't worn any underwear, which explained the stickiness between my fingers. His balls hung loose and sweaty. I gave them a tug, an action that sent him to the tops of his toes, growling his approval.

"Good morning," I said around kisses.

"Morning *wood*," he grunted.

"So I see…"

I freed his cock, which had stiffened to its hardest state. I loved Tom's cock because I loved Tom. I loved its steely, slightly bent shaft, thickest around the middle, the dense pelt of fur around its root, and the blue vein running along the topside of its shaft. And I showed Tom just how much after sinking to my knees.

In the shower, he moved up behind me. I waited for the initial rush of energy as the condom-covered head of his cock connected with my ass.

"Yes, Tom, *please.*"

His arm around my waist tightened, drawing us even closer together. His cock eased in. We were one.

"I love you," he said.

And then, as I had done in the kitchen, he proved his promise in actions as well as words.

❖

Tom loved to jog through the woods. I preferred a slower pace. The conservation woods behind his house—I can hear Tom's voice, as clear as a bird's song, reminding me that it was *our* house now—ran for over three hundred acres. Guarded at the outer limits by the gnarled trunks of giant sap pines, a trail meandered through stands of towering oaks, hemlocks, and paper-white birch, which always reminded me of skeletons standing guard. The woods were filled with gullies and streams and, beyond the ancient stone ruins of what we assumed were once houses, the river.

Tom told me that during a summer drought years earlier, the river evaporated down to its bed stones and he crossed it to see what was on the other side.

"Caves," he said. "Dark, deep caves. I didn't go in too far because I didn't want to get lost or trip and break my neck."

I teased him about being afraid of a vicious dog with three heads and other mythological monsters and he told me to shut up. His face turned red because he was the man, the dude, and dudes weren't afraid of bogeymen. And then he tackled me onto the bed and we fucked for hours, as I recall. It wasn't the kind of afternoon one is likely to forget.

"I love the woods," he said as we lay together, sweat cooling, listening to the gentle sough of the wind through the trees. "Our woods have their own mythology."

❖

I masturbated, thinking of Tom, sniffing not only his T-shirt but his sweaty socks and sweatier jogging shorts, reliving our latest round of lovemaking while letting the last aborted attempt play out to conclusion the way I would have wanted: me, on my knees, blowing Tom in his Ellis P.D. uniform, a favorite theme of ours. I came once, then resumed and came again. A lazy end-of-summer breeze drifted across my sweaty flesh and I shivered, not unpleasantly, realizing how happy I was.

The call came in early that afternoon. Part of me heard the house phone's outdated ring before it blasted forth, tolling ominous news. I was standing at the sink, staring out at the woods, and a sense of dread worse than what I'd experienced the night of the attack outside the Ellis Infields wrapped its dark wings around me. Reaching the phone, a matter of steps, seemed to take hours. I lifted the receiver from its cradle. It took me two tries to say hello; my voice shorted out on the first attempt.

"Is this Yuri Dissehe?" an officious voice asked.

"Yes," I stammered.

"You're listed as the emergency contact for Officer Tom Orfino."

The phone slipped from my grasp after the cop at the other end of the line told me Tom had been shot, and I needed to get to Ellis General Hospital without delay.

❖

Eyes wide and unblinking, I marched through the sliding glass doors and into a land of limbo sitting beneath the unforgiving white glare of fluorescent lights. The bitter smell of antiseptics and spilled blood burned in my shallow sips of breath.

"Can I help you?" barked the gatekeeper seated behind the reception desk at the nurse's station, her tone more authoritative than kind.

I identified myself, sure that I was going to pass out at any second. "I'm here for Tom Orfino."

The woman's grim expression tightened. "Are you related to him?"

Related by love, I thought. Before I could think too deeply on how I needed to respond, I answered, "Yes."

She guided me toward a row of hard molded-plastic chairs, pale blue beneath the light, a color that reminded me of death, and told me to wait.

Death. Just as soon as I sat, I caught sight of one emergency care room, its curtain hanging open, ripped aside in haste, I imagined. Blood-soaked bandages and the remains of a police uniform cut open for fast access littered the floor. The stretcher in that room was gone; its patient and an entourage of care workers had raced away to the surgical unit three floors directly overhead, I would learn.

My gorge started to rise, putting painful tears in my eyes when I'd been able to stem their flow until that moment. Sourness shuddered up my throat. I jumped out of my seat and started toward the public restroom I spied at a bend in the long succession of rooms filled with pain and suffering.

The image of two men in police uniforms, standing at an open curtain, froze me in place. That exam room, unlike the one where Tom's life had ebbed, still contained its stretcher and the stretcher, its patient. A man was cuffed to the metal safety rail. Though his face was puffed up and bloodied, his lips split and his shirt torn, I had no trouble identifying him.

The man who'd shot Tom, whose face had gone a few rounds after the fact with the fist of the officer who'd wrangled him to the ground and arrested him, was one of the same two who'd attacked me in the alley near the Ellis Infields on that fateful spring night.

❖

I knew they'd made bail. As the trial date loomed, Tom had done his best to protect me, filtering through the most relevant information to allow me to heal and be happy. But he hadn't been able to protect himself after pulling over a beat-up brown muscle car when it ran a red light.

The news was not hopeful.

The husk lying inert in the intensive care unit bed wasn't the Tom

I knew, who sometimes played the air guitar dressed only in his white socks while I plucked at the real thing, only to jump up and grab me and play me like an instrument; who fucked with the enthusiasm of a teenage boy but the body of a man; who was always kind to animals and a hero to anyone in need of rescuing.

And who once admitted in the middle of making love why he really was there, near the gay bar, the night he saved my life: because, he'd revealed, though he always knew he had an attraction to other men, a voice in his head told him he needed to take a right turn, then a left, and another left, as clearly as the shouts he roared while unloading his seed into me. He was compelled to be there when I needed him most.

That man, I was told, was gone and likely wasn't coming back. Officer Tom Orfino lived through the night, hooked up to wires and tubes and monitors. But he wasn't expected to last until the next sunset.

It was easy to remain stone-faced in the waiting room, sitting in a chair that was as miserable as the one downstairs in the emergency department, across from Tom's cop buddies. They barely talked to me, though their grim expressions spoke volumes. I had gotten him shot, after a manner. This was just as much my fault as the scumbag Tom had pulled over on Merrimack Street in South Ellis.

Feeling gross and sore and miserable, the next morning I drove home methodically, stopping at stop signs, looking both ways before making turns, until reaching our little house near the big woods. I set my keys in the pottery bowl on the counter and then the sadness crashed over me, merciless in its intensity. A downpour of tears flooded my eyes and cascaded down my cheeks. The sobs followed, catching in my throat. The only way to dispel their ricocheting voices was to howl, which I did to the limit of my lungs.

The water flooding my vision and the screams tearing through the house created a realm of the rawest emotions. Blinded, I reached for the closest object to me, intending to smash it and probably the next dozen or so things I put my hands on. But the white-hot rage shorted out as my fingers wrapped around the neck of my guitar. A flicker that both chilled and channeled the heat in a positive way pulsed through me in concentric waves. I imagined the release traveling outward, like the surface of a pond overcome by ripples. I grabbed the guitar and held it against me. It pulled me back far enough from the abyss to think.

To hope.

❖

I walked out of the house in something of a daze, not knowing where I would go or what I was going to do once I got there. Holding the guitar, I walked on memory, taking the trail through the tall pines and past the skeletal birch trees. A stand of towering hemlocks rose to my left. I remembered the first time Tom took me there, right at the start of May on a day when the sky had been the color of denim. It was again today, cloudless and blue. I shuffled over to the same trunk where Tom had fucked me standing up and began to play.

I kicked off the performance with that old tune Tom loved, my private cover of "Mr. Dieingly Sad" by the Critters, and sang the lyrics between sobs for breath that refused to come easily. Halfway through, I switched to part of a prayer to Saint Jude, Patron of Lost Causes. I strummed and recited a lullaby. I didn't care which god, goddess, gods, or combination of faiths up there was listening, only that some merciful presence was, so I sang and prayed for Tom's life.

"I know that eventually all of us must say good-bye and exit this world," I said, making up chords and riffs on the spot, my fingers flying gracefully over the strings. "But please, I beg of you in the name of all that is good and caring in this world, don't take the man I love just yet. Don't take Tom from me!"

I began to sob again, and the cries carried up to the distant treetops on a sad melody. Higher yet, I imagined the counterpoint of chords and cries rising beyond the clouds, to the heavens and the very stars themselves.

Among the music, I heard the song of birds in a way I never had before. The wind joined in, ghostly and melancholy. For a brief and startling instant, raindrops spattered my flesh. I gazed up, tasting their saline warmth, to see the sky a cloudless expanse of denim blue. No clouds lurked overhead. Were the gods crying with me?

Before I could ponder an answer, the crunch of footsteps on dead leaves alerted me to another presence near the stand of hemlock trees. Wiping the tears from my eyes, I looked in time to see a man moving along the trail. I blinked, not believing my own eyes, and dropped the guitar as Tom jogged toward me.

❖

That other day, beneath the hemlocks…

He'd gone jogging through the woods, which Tom loved to do. It was a warm May afternoon, in that week of elegant weather between a muddy New England spring and a muggy New England summer, when everything comes alive. Lilacs, tulips, daffodils, and fruit trees blossom and pale lime-colored leaves appear, seemingly overnight, on branches that looked bare the day before.

Seeing him in his shorts and T-shirt, his old baseball cap and sunglasses, his dirty old sneakers and a length of white sock and the image of those incredible legs left me feeling itchy in my own skin. I knew how he would smell, his sweat musky with the unmistakable trace of testosterone. I'd grabbed two beers from the fridge, picked up my guitar, and staked out a place beneath the tallest of the hemlocks, in clear view of the trail. I was strumming on the guitar when Tom jogged up, a wicked smile on his handsome face.

"Come here often?" he asked.

I ceased playing. "That depends."

"On what?"

"On you—and how often you want to make me."

Tom wiped his face on his T-shirt. I felt his eyes tracking me from behind his shades. The lusty smirk above his unshaved chin widened.

"Nasty. And I approve."

"Good."

"So what brings you here?"

I raised one of the sweating longnecks. "Cold beer, hot sex, my tall and hunky friend."

Tom strutted over. The sun caught in the beads of sweat clinging to his leg hair, making his skin glow. I remember thinking how supernaturally attractive he looked, my mind accessing snippets of

Greek mythology; it was as if Tom Orfino was the magnificent byproduct of a tryst between a horny god and a mortal. A son of Apollo, perhaps.

I handed him the bottle of beer. He popped the cap and drank.

"There's the cold beer part," he said, following up the statement with a manly burp. "Now, about that hot sex…"

Matching his smile, I cupped the side of his face and pressed my mouth against his. The beer on his lips, crisp and sweet, added to the sensory rush as Tom's masculine scent filled my next breath. I kissed him, loving the scrape of his stubble, his sweatiness, and all that he was.

My protector placed his free hand on my shoulder and guided me down. I dropped to my knees before him and worked Tom's shorts to his ankles. His cock jumped out, stiff and ready to be worshipped. I took him into my mouth, sucking him down to the musky thatch of curls lining his pubis. I tickled his balls, which were ripe with his powerful smell and hanging heavily beneath the base of his shaft.

"Oh yeah, just like that," he growled.

I glanced up to see him knock down another swig of suds. When he lowered the bottle, there was a telling smile on his face. Tom was happy. Early in this new living arrangement, we both were. Supremely so.

I started to suck on Tom's balls, loving their ripeness, but Tom soon pulled me off them and back to my feet.

"You keep that up and I'm gonna nut," he said.

"I thought that was the point."

Tom's powerful right arm drew me close. He crushed his mouth over mine and we again kissed, this time with his tongue testing my willingness. I opened, accepting his offer.

"The point," he eventually said, stabbing his stiff cock into my thigh.

Then Tom turned me around and unbelted my jeans. He forced down my pants, baring my ass to the sunshine—and that incredible tongue. Tom lowered, spread the two halves of my butt, and feasted on the tight knot at the center.

He fucked me standing up, and we professed our love for one

another around a rosary of expletives, knowing how lucky we were to have found one another, two wandering souls that had crossed paths at precisely the right moment.

❖

In the present, our souls crossed paths again.

Through my tears, I watched as Tom jogged up to the hemlocks, there but not fully, for I could see the skeletal limbs of the birch trees on the other side of the trail through the opaque shadow of his T-shirt. Tom's legs were a ghostly representation of their former self; no beads of sweat captured the sun. His big feet, which I had sniffed and licked so often following his daily jogs, wore their usual well-traveled sneakers. An old T-shirt, black. Baseball cap. Sunglasses.

Tom slowed, dug in his heels, and turned to face me. I caught a ghost of his masculine sweat across the distance, only it entered my nose on a chilly current of air. As I stood trembling, Tom reached up and peeled off his sunglasses. His blue-gray gaze had been replaced by solid whiteness, the eyes of the dead.

"Yuri," he said, his voice sounding a hundred miles away, spoken from a bottomless well.

"No, Tom," I gasped.

Tom stood there for another long second or two before replacing his shades and resuming the jog.

I whispered his name, unable to find the timbre to shout it, begging him to come back.

"Go after him," a voice directly behind me urged, warm and masculine. "Bring him home if you want him to live."

The only living thing behind me was the towering hemlock tree.

I thought of Tom and the night we met and that voice he'd heard telling him to turn right and then left, twice. I pursued.

My pulse galloped. Far ahead of me, I saw a telltale hint of dark color—Tom's T-shirt—turning a bend in the lush sea of undulating leaves. Tom was the jogger, used to moving quickly. Me, I was a walker by nature. But now, urged on by a voice that seemed to originate from the very air whisking past my ears, I took to the path with hasty steps.

"Run," it urged. "Run, if you want to save the life of the man you love!"

I ran.

And ran.

❖

It didn't matter that I fell, slamming face down into the dirt hard enough to taste blood. I picked myself up and raced on, turning deeper into the mysterious realm of conservation woods. I was focused on Tom, but from the periphery I gleaned the area to my right where blackberries grew on thorny bushes, where Tom and I had picked the luscious fruit for hours, swatting at bugs, earlier that summer. Farther up loomed a section of stone farmer's wall. Beyond the lichen-encrusted stones rose the gnarled trunks of a long-forgotten orchard.

I passed beneath the cathedral of giant oaks whose interlaced branches nearly blocked the sun. The effect was like nightfall; I lost sight of Tom's spirit there and began to panic.

"Go to the river," the disembodied voice urged. "Quickly!"

The river. I put on a burst of speed and ran through the tunnel of darkness. The dense canopy overhead thinned, and I emerged into an area of shadows broken by gray light. A chill infused the air, which had been so warm on the other side.

You're in the land of lost souls now, I thought.

Ahead of me, the trail took another turn, to the right. An apparition trotted at the limit of my visibility, vanishing out of sight behind the sweeping green tentacles of a willow tree.

The river.

I ran, my breaths burning in my lungs, and invisible ice lying over my skin.

"Tom," I whispered, but the wind stole my voice and carried it away.

❖

The structures lurked beyond the line of willows, at either side of the path. Time-eroded granite blocks covered in skeins of lichen, we'd assumed they were the remains of foundations. But now, from the cut of my eye, the ruins appeared far older in origin, looking like Doric columns, fallen lintels, and friezes decorated in bas relief, all hewn from marble. Adding to the dreamy vision was the hypnotic perfume of colorful flowers growing wildly among the stones.

I shot a look at the nearest section of blocks, and the illusion broke. Piles of rough granite met my gaze.

The guttural plunking voice of the river reached me through my desperate gasps for breath. My heart galloped. Tom…I was so close to reaching him, I was sure.

I emerged from the ruins to see that apart from me, my side of the riverbank sat empty of both the living and the dead. The water raced past, dark and swift. No Tom. I froze.

But on the other side of the river's bank, a simple wooden rowboat lolled in the current. I glanced up in time to see a shadowy figure cut through the tangle of greenery, moving toward the area of deep forest where the caves were located.

"Hurry," said the ghostly voice, shocking me out of paralysis.

Without thinking, I hastened down to the water and waded out to my waist, fighting current. The river worked to topple me. It failed, but a slippery stone underfoot succeeded, throwing me fully beneath the turgid surface. I reached forward and swept my hand back, paddling madly, and scrambled forward, unsure as to whether or not I was making progress or being carried downstream. On one grab, my hand landed on smooth rock. I'd reached the other side. My waterlogged clothes trying to weigh me down, I jumped back to my feet and ran.

"Tom," I called. *"Tom!"*

The trees pressed in. Shadows engulfed me. The caves rose directly ahead, cavities eaten into the bones of the foothills. The entrance to the underworld.

❖

"Oh my God," I gasped, digging in my heels.

Tom stood just outside the mouth of the cave, in single file behind other figures, already in the shadows. The souls of the recently dead, screamed the voice in my thoughts. I didn't need the one floating through the trees to tell me that if Tom's spirit stepped into the darkness of the hills, he would be lost forever.

"Wait," I shouted across the distance. "Tom Orfino, don't you go in there!"

The flickering specter halted its advance toward the entrance of the cave and hesitated. I approached the wall of its back, still turned my way. The scent of blossoms had soured, smelling like flowers past their prime. The air was noticeably colder. My arms broke in gooseflesh.

"Tom, please turn around and come back with me," I pleaded. "Come home with me, my love."

The apparition turned. His sunglasses hung from the collar of his T-shirt in that jaunty way, such a Tom thing to do. His empty white eyes tracked my voice. "Yuri?" The voice was Tom's, but Tom's voice whispered through a mausoleum wall.

"I'm here, my love. I won't leave you, if you promise to come back with me."

"I can't see you."

"No, he can't," said the disembodied voice. "But he can *hear* you. This is your last chance to save him. Turn now and lead him away from the shadows, into the light. And don't look back—you've already seen more than is usually permitted. If Tom loses the sound of your voice before you're both standing in sunshine, he will exit this mortal coil forever."

The voice shorted out with a crackle, and I knew I wouldn't hear it again. The sprite or angel, the minor god or friendly ghost, had told me what I must do, so I began to sing.

I sang the lyrics to some of Tom's favorite songs, the kind of jock-rock anthems played at stadiums between innings at baseball games. Fighting panic, I boarded the rowboat, waiting for the shift that signaled Tom had entered behind me. When it happened, I reached for the oars, but the rowboat began to move on its own.

By the time we reached the far side of the river, I was singing everything I could remember from my collection of CDs, records, and digital downloads, the best of the old and new. I stepped out of the rowboat, the temptation to turn around for reassurance that Tom's spirit was still there nearly overwhelming me. It took all of my will, but I resisted.

The rowboat came to a stop and I got out. Training my eyes on the trail, I cut through the ruins and the willows and walked into the darkness beneath the cathedral of ancient oaks. Far ahead of me, golden daylight beckoned. I only needed to reach its safety for Tom's soul to rejoin his body. We would be reunited, able to enjoy the rest of our mortal lives together.

Steeling myself, I headed toward the sunlight, walking at a brisk clip.

"You're so mystifyingly glad," I sang. "I'm Mr. Dieingly sad…"

I reached the end of the song and started from the beginning. Tom loved that song. Tom loved me. Oh, how I loved him.

The cathedral loomed overhead, dark and ominous, but the golden glow on the other side grew closer with the seconds. I hastened forward, still singing, desperate to reach the light. Nearer yet…

I stepped out of darkness and into glorious daylight. The sunshine raining down drove the chill from my flesh. I felt whole again, for I knew I had reached the safety of the world of the living.

My first impulse was to turn around, to reach for Tom. I started to revolve, but caught myself, because while I was freshly emerged in the land of light, I guessed that Tom wasn't. I imagined him still standing in the darkness beneath the ancient oaks.

I moved forward another dozen steps before looking behind me. Tom's soul shimmered in the light.

"Yuri?" he asked.

"I'm right here."

Tom smiled, the vacant whites of his ghost's eyes altering. Blue-gray formed at their center.

"I can see you, Yuri."

"Come home to me," I said.

I reached for him, but it was like trying to hold empty air. Tom's soul vanished, leaving me alone on the trail in our woods, wondering if I'd lost him for good for the second time in as many days.

❖

I heard the phone ringing from the edge of the wood line. I grabbed it on the next cycle of bleats.

"Hello?"

Twenty minutes later, I entered the intensive care unit, which sat under a pall of darkness equal to that beneath the cathedral of oaks. A male nurse I recognized from my first visit led me through the huddle of uniformed Ellis cops at the nurse's station and over to the bed.

"He's been asking for you. Demanding to see you," the nurse said. "He's breathing on his own, completely coherent. It's a miracle, I tell you. A fucking miracle."

Tom lay in the bed, his face pale, but there were considerably fewer wires and tubes clamped to his body, and the pattern bouncing across the monitor looked strong, the blip of a healthy heart. A heart in love.

Tom's eyes met mine and a smile broke on his lips. I reached for his hand, taking it the best I could around the intravenous line snaking out of its back, its shunt poking through coils of gauze, and the device clamped to his forefinger.

"Hey, tough guy," I said, tears welling in my eyes.

"Hey."

Our eyes locked and, in that bottled gaze, words passed without the need for voices.

Struggling, he eventually said, "There was music."

"Music?" I parroted.

"Yeah, beautiful music. It guided me home."

I caressed Tom's cheek. "Welcome home, my love."

POPO BAWA
DAVID HOLLY

Goddamn Exploder," Jess swore, kicking the gravel alongside the highway. He was, of course, damning our Ford Explorer, which had broken down just at sunset about two miles up the road from where we were forlornly hiking. He looked over his shoulder. "Somebody's got to come along soon." An ominous crackle greeted his words, and the thunder rolled across us.

I kept quiet since it had been my bright idea to try a shortcut through the hills. There was no reason to mention that the road looked like nobody had driven on it for months. Night was falling quickly, and the approaching storm only made the sky all the darker. I switched on the flashlight I'd brought from our broken-down car.

"We'd better get off the road, Jess. Maybe we can find shelter along those rock formations."

Jess groaned. "Another shortcut, Colton? Oh, fuck it. I've already ruined my tenny-runners. Might as well pile on a nasty case of poison oak." My beloved had a point about the poison oak. We were wearing shorts and thin cotton shirts. I decided not to mention that there were worse possibilities than poison oak. The hills were alive with snakes. I just hoped that all the neighboring serpents had enough sense to go in out of the rain. As the thought crossed my mind, the first cold raindrops began to hit me.

❖

It had been a glorious day right up until the moment the Explorer broke down. That morning, Jess and I drove to the Maryhill Museum of Art near Goldendale, Washington, and spent the day marveling at the museum's wonders.

"Oh, my cock and balls!" Jess kept howling to the annoyance of other museum patrons. "This is Russell's *Buffalo Hunt*. Who'd ever dream of world-class art in this desert dunghill?" A group of conservative-looking women gave us the evil eye, whether because we were sexually free-spirited or because Jess's skin was the shade of ivory and mine jet, who could say.

We ate our picnic lunch in the gardens, surrounded by strolling peacocks. One peacock was such a determined beggar that he kept inserting his head into the crook of Jess's arm as he ate. I laughed so hard that I nearly choked on my croissant.

After leaving the art museum, we visited the Stonehenge-replica monument to the dead of World War I, created by Sam Hill, a Quaker. Solemnly we walked, dwarfed and chilled, among the funereal stones, so cyclopean in their size. "It's eerie, isn't it?" Jess whispered as he read the names of long-dead Klickitat County residents.

"Hill believed that the Druids practiced human sacrifice at Stonehenge," I said softly. "War is needless human sacrifice."

"Not just humans," Jess reminded me. "Think of all the little animals that are killed when the bombs fall. Or they are driven crazy by the terrible sounds."

Jess is like that. Every few minutes he manages to do or say something that reminds me how much I love him. I pulled him close and kissed his lips hard. Although it was a warm summer day, the stones cast long cool shadows. We stood in the chilling shadow of sacrifice and death, and kissed until we were both flushed and aroused.

In the late afternoon, we dropped by the magnificent tasting room of the Maryhill Winery. Standing at the twenty-foot-long bar, we sampled seven wines and ended up putting a strain on my credit card balance with the bottles we bought to take home. "It's worth it, Colton," Jess informed me. "Think of us lolling naked on the carpet while we sip this wine. Besides, after your next book comes out, you can pay off your credit cards."

Leaving the winery, we drove toward the late afternoon sun, Jess at the wheel of the Explorer. We crossed the river, stopped to take a few pictures, and headed east through the Columbia River Gorge. Everything was going fine until we got stuck behind the rock trucks. The third time a flying piece of gravel dinged our windshield, Jess screamed with impatience. "Those butt-fucking bastards are determined not to let us around them." He laid onto the horn, but the trucks loaded with gravel from a quarry continued their rolling roadblock. "They're gonna crack the Exploder's windshield, sure as you're born."

"Take this exit," I yelped, and Jess turned the wheel. More sand and gravel struck the Explorer as we veered off. Sandblasted but free from flying debris, we followed a highway that cut south.

"This road is taking us in the wrong direction," Jess complained. "I don't want to wind up in Utah."

"How about we try that road?" I suggested, pointing toward a two-lane blacktop that seemed to lead in the right direction.

The Explorer's engine coughed once as Jess turned around. We should have heeded the warning sign. We did not pass another vehicle as we drove down the road toward the glowing sunset. The engine caught twice more while we drove eight miles down the road to nowhere. Suddenly the engine caught again and quit, and it would not start again. Jess and I opened the hood and stared with befuddlement at the mass of silent gizmos.

"Goddamn Exploder," Jess said, whipping out his cell phone. I'd already checked mine. No signal.

"Roaming. Roaming to fucking nowhere! And that's exactly where you've landed our asses, Colton. Right in the town square of sparkling downtown Butt Fuck, Nowhere."

"I guess we'd better start walking," I contributed. It was a fateful decision. We should have slept in the car, but how were we to know what waited for us among those dry desert hills?

❖

A lightning bolt blasted a juniper on the pinnacle of a rock formation, nearly blinding us, while the deafening thunder boomed overhead. The rain was falling hard by then, but there was no shelter beyond the strange-smelling sagebrush and the occasional juniper. Desperately, I shined my flashlight around.

"Let's follow the chicken," I suggested.

"Chicken?"

"Yeah, I saw a chicken." I pointed with my flashlight. "It was walking over that way."

"You're seeing things, Colton." Jess shivered as the rain beat down even harder. The lightning was creating purple and green blotches before our eyes, so visual hallucinations were not out of the question, but I knew that I had seen a chicken. I grabbed Jess's hand and pulled him in the direction the chicken had followed.

Along the eroded face of the towering rock formation, the flashlight beam picked up a black place that was blacker than all other black places.

"What the fuck?"

"What do you see, Colton?"

"It's a cave." I shined the light inside. My teeth were chattering from the cold rain and the terrifying lightning. I started inside, but a protesting Jess pulled at my arm.

"You don't know what's in there, Colton. It's dangerous."

"Stay here. I'll take a look inside."

"Fuck that shit. Where you go, I go," Jess said. "You wanna provide dinner for a bear or a cougar, then I'm dessert."

The cave had an odd odor, but it was dry. I shined the light around, but the interior was empty of wildlife. It only extended about fifty feet. The floor of the cave was smooth hard rock, free from animal droppings or gnawed bones. "It looks safe to me," I whispered.

"It *looks* safe," Jess agreed. "I've got a bad feeling. The place gives me the creeps."

"That might be the smell. I've never smelled anything like this. It's not an animal smell. It's something else. You're right about it being creepy, but I don't see what other choice we have."

"You have smelled this odor before, Colton. It smells like cum. Old stinky cum."

I sniffed again. My beloved was right. It smelled just like cum, not my cum or his, but cum that had been gushed, load after load, and left to season. "Maybe this is a happening place during the mating season," I joked. I made a careful inspection with my flashlight, but I found no hidden hidey-holes. In fact, I came to the alarming conclusion that animals avoided the cave. I sensed a lurking presence, but beyond smell, the presence existed at some level that I could not detect. Outside, a sudden burst of hail fell like ice bullets, and the thunder increased. The storm's violence raged. Whatever watching presence lurked, we were stuck in the cave.

"I wonder what happened to the chicken," I said.

"You imagined the chicken. Probably because you're hungry. I'm starved."

"Don't talk about food. Let's try to sleep." I yawned. My eyelids were heavy.

"I couldn't sleep a wink in here," Jess protested as I stretched out on the smooth floor. He yawned and sat down beside me. He shook his head as if to clear it. "That wine must be going to my head." Then he stretched out beside me and promptly dropped off.

This isn't right, I thought. *Why did we get so dopey?* Alarm bells were ringing in my mind, but I couldn't fight the extreme drowsiness. I fought to sit up again, but I was too tired to rise. My will was gone. My resistance faded into nothing.

I do not know how long I lay in the whirling slumber that whispered strange words and evoked odd images. Dream followed dream down the path toward nightmare, but the horror I felt was undefined, unspeakable, unimaginable, and unknown. Sluggishly, my mind climbed out of the pit of lurking dread toward a blissful sensation. Jess was stroking my thighs. He was tweaking my naked nipples between his thumbs and forefingers, both at once. At the same time, one hand was sliding across my bare abdomen, while another hand was caressing my thigh.

As I arose from the misty dreamscape, logic assailed me. That was too many hands. Whatever his qualities, Jess had only two. I tried to rise, but the hands were holding me down. I did turn my head enough to see Jess. Arms had risen from the floor of the cave, seeming to grow live from the hard rock—many arms ending in human-looking hands. Human-looking but far from human, those hands stroked Jess, pinched his nipples, examined his face, played with his ears, caressed his arms, and explored his feet and legs. One was even fondling his cock, which was quite erect.

Jess's clothes lay beside him, a pile of shredded rags. Mine were there too. Even our shoes had been ripped apart. Our shorts and underwear had been reduced to strings and ribbons.

As I looked, the sensations of pleasure grew stronger. The hands caressed me wantonly, doing all the things they were doing to Jess, and even more. Fingers ran along my lips and pushed into my mouth. Simultaneously, two hands explored my buttocks.

The hands turned my head so I could see Jess again. The hands were still playing with him and holding him down, but other shapes had arisen from the rock. Thick projections were slithering over his body. As I watched, one pushed into Jess's mouth. Another touched his face, rubbed along his chin, hardened, and squirted long blasts of slimy fluid onto Jess's face.

If none of this was horrible enough, greater horrors were coming. As I watched, the hands raised Jess's legs, and one of the tentacle shapes squirted the slimy fluid, which had to be demonic cum, directly into the crack of Jess's ass. One of the fingers dipped itself into the spent cum and worked it into Jess's asshole. Jess squirmed and resisted. I knew that he would be screaming if he could, but he could not emit a sound due to the thick projection fucking his mouth.

❖

Jess and I did not do anal. We met in a graduate level class in gay and lesbian authors at Portland State. On our first date, we strolled around downtown Portland, shared a sandwich at Quiznos, watched a horrible old SF movie, The Angry Red Planet, *at a downtown theater, and jerked each other off in Jess's dorm room. On our second date, we jerked and sucked. Then we discussed the things we did not do.*

"I don't take it up the ass," Jess informed me. "I'll never do that."

"Not a problem," I told him. "I don't want anything shoved up my ass either."

"Did something happen to you?" he asked solicitously as he nuzzled my ear.

"When I was eleven, my Sunday school teacher sodomized me. I was screaming with pain, but he shoved it in anyway. Then he promised that I'd go to hell if I told."

"Did you ever tell?"

"Not until now. You're the only one who knows."

"Were you a Catholic, Colton?"

"No, a Baptist. The Baptist Church has plenty of pedophiles and pederasts. They just haven't made the national news yet."

Jess mused over my story before he told his own. "I got bullied in high school. Everybody could tell I was gay, so I got picked on. I got shoved or kicked or punched every time I went into the bathroom or the locker room. Then one day, a bunch of guys held me down and shoved the handle of a toilet brush up my ass."

That conversation echoed through my consciousness as I watched the hands fingering Jess's ass. Jess was wriggling and squirming, but he could not escape the clutching hands and tenacious projections. As Jess struggled vainly, the cock-shaped tentacle that was stretching his jaws wide drove in deeper. Demonic cum began to run out of the sides of Jess's mouth as the thing poured its slimy spunk into his throat.

While Jess struggled to swallow and to breathe, another projection pushed into his asshole, unrelenting.

I did not see what happened next because the hands were prying my mouth open. The long fingers pulled down my chin and pushed between my teeth. As my mouth opened, a tentacle with a tip that closely resembled a hard cock hovered over my face. It quivered before it went into a spasm and spurted a thick splat of cum onto my face. I could taste the cum, which was hotter and thicker than Jess's. Much of my face was covered, and the stuff ran down my cheeks and off my chin. The second spurt hit my eyes. It did not burn like human spunk, but it completely obscured my vision. I did not see the tentacle that pushed into my mouth. I only knew that it was thick, so thick, indeed, that my jaws were forced wide as it drove along my tongue.

Please don't go up my ass, I thought, unable to speak. The tentacle was sliding deep into my mouth, almost to my throat, and pulling back until it barely parted my lips. Then it would press forward again until it hit the back of my tongue, leaving a trail of spent cum along the way. My mouth was alive with the rich taste, and my nostrils were full of the heady aroma. The hands were jerking my dick, and I knew that I was fully erect. *That's it*, I thought, *fuck my mouth. Just don't go up my ass. I couldn't stand it if you invaded my ass.*

Fingers were exploring my buttocks. They caressed the cheeks of my ass. They squeezed my butt. I did not mind the caress, but the exploring fingers did not stop there. My heart thundered as the fingers slid into my ass crack.

Looking back now, I wonder that I did not lose my mind. Neither Jess nor I were particularly superstitious. We had never indicated the slightest belief in the supernatural, not in organized religion, nor in demonology. We did not believe in spiritual events, dualism, gods, devils, demons, or angels. Yet when we felt the full evidence of a supernatural being invading our bodies, we accepted the situation. Certainly, I was terrified that the horror was going to invade my ass, but that was virtually the extent of my horror. The fact that hands and tentacles had grown from the very floor of the cave hardly fazed me.

The demonic being's cum was both pungent and sweet. It stimulated all of the senses, and it provoked erotic fantasy. Myriad thoughts whirled through my mind, including images of sexual perversities I had never even imagined. Sight, sound, taste, smell, and touch were all magnified. The hands jerking my cock sent raptures through me. I was so enthralled that I did not feel fear as the otherworldly hands inexorably lifted my legs and the fingers probing my butt crack drove deeper. Another projection that felt like a wet tongue slipped into my right ear, while another slid up the crack of my ass. It lingered at my asshole, licking, licking. It licked down my crack to my balls and back up. It licked to the top of my crack, washing me thoroughly. Then it stopped again at my asshole, licking around, rimming me, slowly, so slowly, pushing inside.

Delirious sensations swept over me. I found that my ass was opening even as the horror of my previous anal experience faded from my consciousness. A penis-shaped tentacle had already replaced the tongue before I realized what was happening. I kept sucking on the one in my mouth while more hands grew from the floor and shifted me into position. My asshole stretched pleasantly. The hands jerking me kept manipulating my cock, brought me to the verge of ejaculation several times, but they did not bring me over the edge of orgasm, did not let me come.

The tentacle started fucking my ass with regular strokes. It gave me a heavy feeling inside, not unpleasant, but the greater sensation of pleasure was confined to my asshole. Wonderful feelings filled me as it pulled out and pushed back in, all the time growing in me. My ass opened wider and wider, taking the tentacle, accommodating to it, stretching around it so that the pleasure mounted.

Tingles of pure ecstasy swept over me. My skin crawled in a good way. My nipples were crinkling as the fingers twisted them, and waves of pleasure swept up from the head of my cock. A pleasurable buzz grew in my ass. Wonderful sensations filled my midsection while the tentacle cock in my mouth unloaded spurts of sweetish cum that slid down my throat. The tentacle up my ass twitched pleasantly and I felt like I was being filled with a hot wet substance.

Then tornadoes of pleasure touched me, inside and out, and my cock erupted. My orgasm lasted longer than any previous orgasm, millions of tiny pleasure points striking my skin and erupting from the inside out. My asshole was in raptures. I was being filled in every way imaginable; even foreign images were invading my mind. I saw kaleidoscopic figures whirling. I was a dog priest of Baal, chief butt slut in a North African boy brothel, proprietor of an eighteenth-century Molly house, and many other delightfully homosexual men.

I was still myself, though a great weight descended upon me. I was still myself, and so much more. The weight grew heavier as I slipped into a tunnel of pleasure. I felt like I was riding down an endless naked waterslide into eternal wetness.

❖

The walk to our car was long and difficult. The sun beat our naked skin and the rocky road tormented our bare feet. We were carrying our wallets, the car keys, the flashlight, and our cell phones. Nothing else had been worth salvaging. Our shoes were scraps and our clothes nothing but threads.

But strangely enough, we did not feel as miserable as might be expected. In fact, I felt rather buoyant. I certainly wasn't hungry since my stomach and bowels were utterly stuffed with demonic cum, which should have worried me, but didn't.

"Are we going to talk about it, Jess?" I finally asked.

"Talk about what?"

"What happened to us?"

"It was only a dream, Colton. A nightmare."

"You think a nightmare left our clothes in threads? Is a nightmare the reason we're walking buck naked down the road? What kind of nightmare leaves our assholes stretched to the limit? What nightmare fills us with cum?"

"Stop, Colton. Please stop," Jess shrieked. "If I thought it was real, I'd go crazy."

I wasn't crazy. I knew that I was as sane as I ever was, for whatever that's worth, and I *knew* that everything that had happened was real. "Let's try our phones now."

"There's the Exploder," Jess shouted, pointing. Sure enough, our Explorer was sitting right where we left it. Within a few minutes, we had stowed our stuff inside and dug into our emergency bag for some clothes. We had no shoes, socks, or underwear, but we did have a couple of pairs of gym shorts and T-shirts. We dressed hurriedly.

"I'm going to see if it starts," I said.

"It won't start," Jess said. "I felt the motor die last night. We're going to have to call AAA."

I put the key in the ignition. The engine turned over and roared to life.

"Holy shit!" Jess breathed. "I wanted it to be a dream. I wanted it to be nothing but a nightmare."

"Take it easy."

"Demonic forces are at work. Don't you get it? We got stranded because the Exploder was possessed."

"You think a demon fucked us?" I asked. A glance at the sheer revulsion clamping Jess's face made me backpedal: "I'm only asking."

"Goddamn right," Jess wailed. "We sucked off a fucking demon. The spawn of hell popped our anal cherries. Oh, fuck. I must be nuts."

"Relax, Jess. We're the same as we always were. Aren't we?"

"You think so? We're possessed, Colton. Even the goddamn Exploder is possessed. We've got to call in the authorities. We have to call the media."

"The media? What are you going to tell them—that we got fucked by hands and tentacles coming up from the cave floor?"

"We're supposed to tell. A voice inside my head ordered me to tell everyone."

A blistering chill ran through me. I remembered hearing that same voice, a hot dry rustling voice that talked out of my own head, but I wasn't going to admit it to Jess. "We're not possessed, Jess. Everything is okay."

"But we have to publicize this, Colton." He sounded frantic.

I shook my head. "No, we don't. What happened is our secret. We're not going to tell anyone."

❖

Home in Portland that afternoon, we purified our bodies through heavy weight training and cardio at the gym and sweating hours in the sauna and hot tub. Jess and I sacrificed the next day by searching for long lost novels by forgotten mystery writers at Powell's, lunching on pizza at Rocco's, strolling the Classical Chinese Garden, and researching William Johnson Cory in the Central Library.

We left the library at closing time and boarded the streetcar. Disembarking five blocks from home, we strolled hand in hand past pot-smoking diners at sidewalk cafés and dilatory shoppers. As we passed a side street, Jess yipped and squeezed my hand harder than I appreciated.

"Ouch!" I yelped. "What the fuck?"

"I saw a chicken, a goddamn chicken. The hell-bird was giving me the evil eye."

Cold all over, I tried to dismiss the image. "People have chickens in their backyards," I assured him.

"This was no ordinary chicken. This was a fucking demon chicken."

We backed up a few steps, but I saw no sign of movement in the street we'd passed. However, as I stared up the street, strange vibrations rushed through me. My spine tingled and my asshole twitched. Abruptly a feeling of extreme pleasure rippled up my ass, and my asshole contracted and dilated most pleasurably. Gasping, I gripped a lamppost and wiggled my butt.

"Are you all right, Colton?" Jess asked, concern tightening his voice.

"Oh, fine, just a case of the creeps. You scared me with that chicken shit." I did not tell him that I had been overwhelmed by a spontaneous anal orgasm.

Back in our Pearl District condominium, we supped on shrimp fried in a buttery dill sauce, a sweet basil salad, butternut squash stuffed with pork heavy with sage, and a dessert of sherbet with a raspberry cream sauce. We washed these delicacies down with a Willamette Valley Chardonnay and finalized our gastronomical orgy with a herb cordial.

When we climbed between our yellow silk sheets after pushing our chubby cats, Bushyasta the tuxedo and Shax the orange tabby, off the bed, I began to rub Jess's dick. After pulling a bottle of lubricant from our sex drawer, Jess started jerking me off. However, he stopped abruptly.

I had been lolling back with my eyes shut, waiting for Jess's lips to touch mine while he jerked my cock. However, his sturdy rhythm ceased and his hand shook as he tried to tug me. When his hand released my dick, I looked to see what was wrong. "What's the matter?" I asked.

Jess was shaking; however, before I could become alarmed, the tremors ceased. Crouching back, his cock stiffer than before, his lips curled into a wicked sneer, he regarded me with abnormal haughtiness. He did not give me time to speculate. His hands brushed hotly over my chest. Tweaking my nipples, he slid one hand down my back until he was caressing my ass. Then he slowly stroked up my body until he gripped my chin as one finger traced my lips.

Down my body, Jess went again. His hand was slipping into my butt crack as he pulled my face to his. His lips were hard, and he kissed me hard. Out of the blue, Jess had put on a guise of mastery. With his new personality, he drove his tongue into my mouth. His hand played in my butt crack.

My cock had been stiff, but it grew harder. It felt like it would burst. Wild sensations rippled through me as strange pictures flooded my mind. I not only saw, but also felt, the orgies of homosexual cults in prehistory. Sucking orgies and human trains of proto-human butt fuckers banging in dark caves filled my senses. I could hear the grunts as men who were only struggling to become men shot their inhuman cum into asses and mouths, and received the same.

"Oh, what is happening to us, Jess?" I moaned, half-lost in the mist of times beyond history. Jess did not respond. His breath came as a sharp rasping hum, a breath of days lost in time.

Then he spoke in a voice that was not his voice. "Roll over, Colton."

"Huh?"

"Roll over." His voice sounded harsh, quite unlike his normal tone, and his words were odder. "I'm going to fuck your ass."

Ripples of pleasure ran over me. My skin tingled, and a rush of gratification twitched my cock. My asshole palpitated. I felt suddenly wet. Unable to resist, I rolled onto my side. Jess pressed close behind me so that the tip of his splitting erection touched my anal cleft. His fingers traced down my back until they slid into my ass crack. Jess did not speak a word as his lubricated forefinger touched my asshole. After he worked my asshole open, his hand pulled away. Then I heard him opening the lubricant a second time and smearing his fingers.

Eerie sensations rushed through me. The experience was so foreign. Jess and I always talked during sex. We talked about how it felt, and we told each other what we liked. This time we moved in silence. Jess worked his slick finger into me again and my asshole grew slick with the lubricant. He twisted his finger to and fro. He pulled it out and pushed it back in, finger-fucking me. As he opened up my ass, he added more and more of the lubricant. Finally, he pushed in two fingers. My asshole opened readily. He twisted his fingers, dilating me for his cock.

"What has come over you?" I managed, but my words sounded more like a gasp than a question.

Without answering, he finger-fucked my ass. He opened me up, and as he did so, I received him willingly—even eagerly. Two days earlier, I would have been screaming in protest if Jess had tried anything like what he was doing. But, of course, two days earlier he would not have been doing it.

Still without speaking, he opened me all the way. I wondered whether his whole hand was inside me. "Are you fisting me, Jess?" I demanded as little bursts of pleasure ripped every cell. I quivered on the edge of molten ecstasy.

The intense pressure ceased. "On your knees," the Jess who was not Jess demanded. Shakily, I rose to my knees. "Down on your elbows. Stick your ass back toward me."

My ass was offered and taken. Jess entered me slowly, his cock opening me more pleasantly than even his fingers had. I was penetrated, opened widely, and probed. The intense pleasure made me hum. My cock was throbbing and leaking upon our sheets.

I moaned. "My ass is yours, Jess." A dry rustling laugh greeted my offer. The Jess who was not Jess hardly needed urging. He pushed, impaling me to the hilt. His violent thrust made me gasp, but he said nothing as his pubic hairs ground into my spread.

Jess pulled back and thrust his cock deep again. I thought that I would come then. My dick leaked freely. He pulled back and filled me, pulled back and filled me, filled me with his cock. I was close to coming; I could not hold out another minute. The demonic fucking was massaging my prostate fiercely, pumping cum up my shaft. My asshole gripped his dick. Wild tingles throbbed from my anus and into my dick. My orgasm was dark and rich. Breath-stopping waves surged. My dick bucked, trailing a lengthy stream of cum onto our bed. The pleasure was unbearable in its intensity. I thought I would die, and would have gladly died to have it go on without end. Nevertheless, all bliss is fleeting, and my orgasm quieted to a last spasm.

Drawing his spent cock out of my ass, Jess pressed his lips close to my ear. "Do you value the gift I gave the men of Sodom?" Jess's voice was harsh and taunting, quite unlike his natural tone.

"What? Jess, are you all right?"

"I am not Jess," Jess said. "You may call me Popo Bawa."

A frozen feeling climbed through my body. "Jess? What's happening?"

"I am in possession of your beloved's body," Jess said. "His spirit dwells here with me, but I have caught him up in an eternal orgasm so he cannot speak."

"Who are you?"

"I told you. Popo Bawa. You know me by many names: incubus, mare, walrider, trauco, tokolosh, ignis fatuus, will o' the wisp. I am the fiery light that flies at night. I am the groping hands that rise. I am the tentacles that penetrate. I am the unsummoned cock that spews demon seed." His laughter was creepy. "I am the magical chicken."

"You're a chicken?"

Popo Bawa laughed at my stupidity. "Watch what I can do."

"What the fuck!" Jess yelped. "Holy shit!"

I saw at once that the demon had released him. "Jess. Jess, do you know what happened?"

Jess shuddered, but his shudder was not one of horror. "The demon was inside me. I was possessed." Jess paused. "Colton, I felt everything. I know everything that happened." His voice dropped to a whisper. "It was fucking bliss."

As Jess's eyes glowed with recollected ecstasy, ethereal hands the color of yellow silk arose from our yellow silk sheets. Twenty hands stroked him, pulling him down into the bed as they caressed his body. I touched a couple of the hands, which felt silky and warm under my fingers. I hoped that my touch would attract them, but they ignored me. Jess was their select victim, were *victim* the accurate soubriquet.

The tentacles arose, thrashing as they sought Jess's orifices. Rapt, Jess sprawled luxuriously while the hands felt him up. The demonic fingers played him like a saxophone. Monstrous tentacles squirmed over Jess, decorating his body with splatters of cum. One tentacle, thicker than the rest, coated his chin as it sought his lips. Fascinated, I watched as it drenched his lips with cum before it parted them and pushed into his mouth. Jess opened wide to receive it, and it slid along his tongue. Jess swallowed convulsively as the tentacle kept sliding into him.

Other tentacles wrapped around his arms, legs, chest, and stomach. They lifted him from the bed so that he was riding three feet above the sheets. They turned him in the air, and the arms grew longer so the exploring hands could continue their obscene caresses. Then the tentacles twisted Jess into a more vulnerable position. They bent him ass over teacups as the worst monster of them all rose from the sheets. This last tentacle was impossibly thick and had a wicked look. I blanched as it pressed toward Jess's ass crack.

"Don't do that to him, Popo Bawa," I pleaded.

Hot rasping words flickered like heat lighting in my brain. "Will you take it for him, Colton?"

Such was my cowardice I was unable to speak, and during my hesitation, the monster parted Jess's buttocks, lubricated him with its hellish cum, and drove into him. Compelled to masturbate, I grabbed my cock and stroked it. Jess thrashed as much as he could in the bondage of the tentacles. I was certain that he was in agony until something strange happened. Jess appeared to be trying to impale his ass even farther onto the tentacle. He drove his butt back as if he wanted his asshole stretched beyond recognition.

His cock was hard and appeared to be throbbing, locked into a continuous orgasm. As he hunched his ass back, his cock bucked so that he shot a gusher of demonically inspired cum. Soon he was shooting more cum than any human male could possibly produce. Somehow, the demon was giving him cum to shoot. Jerking off, I fantasized that it was blasting out of the monster tentacles in his mouth and ass and shooting directly out of his dick.

Without warning, the hands and tentacles pulled away from my beloved. Sloshing with hell cum, Jess dropped onto our bed. He was so drenched with the odd spunk that he was almost unrecognizable. I touched him as I stroked my cock, and he moaned.

Dry burning words formed in my head. "Tell everybody," the demon commanded. "Spread my fame far and wide. Tell the world so all men may prostate themselves before Popo Bawa." Only then did I reach my masturbatory climax, and my cum joined the demon cum on Jess's naked skin.

❖

The next day, after we recovered from the night's exertions, Jess and I returned to Central Library and researched the Popo Bawa phenomena. It seemed that the Popo Bawa stories came from the villagers and farmers of Zanzibar, though the first recorded attack occurred on the island of Pemba in 1972. Attacks continued thorough the seventies, eighties, and nineties, and into the twenty-first century, the most recent occurring in Dar es Salaam in Tanzania.

"It's a bat wing," Jess exclaimed. "*Bawa* is Swahili for wing, and a *popo* is a bat. Of course it could be a *pepo*, which means spirit."

"In other words, a demon," I said. "It's no more African than you are. It's just a sex demon."

"Maybe it's after you because you are African, Colton."

"I'm an African American," I protested. "Just because my skin is a lovely dark hue does not make me a peasant farmer from Zanzibar."

The reference librarian was young and rather pretty, for a female, but her annoyance had thinned her lips and turned them an unattractive shade of blue. "You gentlemen need to keep your voices down," she hissed. "This is a library."

"It's the reference room, not the reading room," I protested. "We're discussing an important subject."

Jess was somewhat more forthright. "Listen, lady, have you ever been ass-raped for one solid hour, and when I say ass-raped, I do mean butt-fucked by a one-eyed, bat-winged, tiger-clawed monster with a gigantic cock?" he demanded. The librarian shrank back in revulsion. Eying her, Jess went on, "Well, I have. And I gotta tell you, it was the best sex I ever had. It was the orgasm of the millennium. My asshole is still tingling."

Going for the most startling part of his speech, I yelped, "The being that butt banged us has only one eye?"

"That's what this book says," Jess answered as the librarian fled toward the window. Since we were on the fourth floor, her options were limited. I watched to see if she would throw the window open and toss herself into the traffic on Tenth Avenue, but she veered off in time and disappeared into the ladies' room.

"A cyclops with one eye in the middle of its forehead. According to this book, Popo Bawa is a homosexual incubus that attacks sleeping men, pushes their faces to the floor, lifts up their backsides, and sodomizes them. Then Popo Bawa orders its victims to tell everyone exactly what happened to them—in graphic detail, and if they don't spread the word to their friends and neighbors, Popo Bawa returns and subjects the luckless victim to even longer and more brutal ass-fuckings."

"I guess you're in no danger, then, Jess, because you just told the librarian all about it."

"Yeah, but did you tell her that I fucked your ass while I was possessed?"

"Jess, wake up," I said. "The African men who got sodomized are describing something completely different. Our Popo Bawa can take control of our bodies, and it sends up arms and tentacled cocks from our mattress. I don't even believe that it's got only one eye."

"That one eye stuff bothers you, doesn't it? Listen to me, Colton. It did not follow the regular pattern with us for one very good reason."

"What's that?"

"We didn't tell everyone about it."

"So what?"

"It's going to come back to do us again—because by not telling, we're asking for it!"

❖

Popo Bawa came back and did us again. Cozy in our briefest underwear and watching our favorite television show, we both saw the flash of feathers before the magical chicken slipped beneath the couch. A strange change came over Jess. He pulled off his briefs and positioned himself over the back of the couch. When I saw how Jess was offering his ass, the moon curves of his butt spread by his doggie position, my cock hardened. A hot lust swept through me. When I spoke, my voice rustled like the wind off the Mount Hood snowfields. "Your hole needs filling, Jess," I croaked, knowing that I was demonically possessed. The perverted demon was charging every cell in my body with erotic fire. I could feel his ancient evil thoughts mingling with my own, and I wished that I could keep him inside me always.

"Stick it in," Jess howled, proving that Popo Bawa had possessed us both at once. "My ass can take your big boner."

My cock throbbed pleasingly, and a thick fluid dripped from the head. I lubed my cock with the slippery fluid oozing from my piss hole and pressed the head against Jess's asshole. The strange lubricant slicked his ass crack. His asshole was slippery with it. When I pressed my cock harder against his pucker, his asshole dilated and the head of my dick slipped inside. Jess howled obscenities as his hole sucked in my cock. "Give me your fucking woody," he shrieked. "Bang my butt-slut ass." Before I knew it, my lap was slamming his buns and my dick was encased in a hot, grainy shaft that gave better friction than any mouth or hand.

"How about that, Colton?" the demon sharing my body whispered down the flowery boulevards of my psyche. "Now you're the top."

I rammed Jess, unable to manage my lust. His hole scorched my dick, and the friction of his grainy tube set off explosions of joy in my brain. As I fucked him, I gripped his ass swells, thrilling from the feel of his curves. I humped so wildly that I wondered whether my actions were my own or those of the demon within. Ripples of pleasure started in my dickhead. I tried to retard my speed, but the demon was running our bodies. I had no control as I bucked furiously against my beloved's butt cheeks.

The throes of orgasm claimed me. Demonic thoughts whirled through my brain. I had taken man after man down through the long ages. I had prostituted temple boys to Baal; I had anally initiated the young pharoah; I had butt-fucked the men of Zanzibar. All the experiences of the all the men I had fucked from the first men were mine as I shared the demonic orgasm. My body was squirting cum into Jess's ass. I banged him so hard I could hardly hear his howls and wails, even as Popo Bawa told me that I must honor him with recognition. He required that I bark all I had experienced so all the world would hear my howls and bow before the glory of Popo Bawa.

❖

Back in Central Library the next day, we schemed together. "Maybe we could print flyers," Jess suggested.

"Flyers? What are you talking about?"

"Print up flyers describing how Popo Bawa fucked us. Lay out every detail and pass them out. That should get rid of him."

"Why would you want to do that?" I glanced at the librarian, who was eyeing us suspiciously.

"He said that we've got to tell about it. Otherwise he'll come back and keep doing us."

I grinned at my beloved. "So let's not tell anybody."

"Huh? We're supposed to tell."

"So what if we don't?" An evil pleasure flooded me as I contemplated the thought.

"Do you wanna keep getting butt-fucked by this demon forever?"

"Would that be so bad?"

"Colton, are you crazy?"

"I'd be crazy to want him to go away. Jess, we've having the best sex ever."

Jess blanched. "But we're possessed by a demon."

"Not all the time. Besides, possession feels damned good. You throw a mean cock while you're in the grip of the demon, Jess."

Jess stared at me with his mouth agape as new ideas percolated through his head. "It's called *tentacle rape* on the porno sites, Colton. We're not supposed to like getting invaded in every hole."

Ignoring the librarian who was phoning for security, I said, "Who gives a flying fuck what we're *supposed* to like. I *like* being possessed. I *like* demonic sex. I *like* Popo Bawa."

At my words, a chicken ran from the book stacks and disappeared under our table. Jess snickered and his eyes turned green. Pulling down my pants, he threw me over my chair, slicked his cock, and drove it into me. Library patrons ran screaming down the marble staircase, led by the librarian. Security guards arrived while Jess was ejaculating into my ass and I onto the carpet.

Under intense police questioning, we broke down and confessed. Our experience was titillating enough to spread from the local news to the national tabloids. Our scandal-hungry fellow citizens devoured every salacious detail of our demonic sexual escapades, thus fulfilling Popo Bawa's demand for notoriety. Alas, that final fuck was the last we felt of Popo Bawa. Never again did demons invade our bedroom, although Jess and I cast spells, offered up our souls, and engaged in ritual anal sex nightly. Years have passed, and we're still at it, hoping against hope for the night a magic chicken will scurry beneath our bed and eerie hands and pricks will arise from our mattress.

SALVATION
LLOYD MEEKER

The California synod he had traveled to attend had finished on a high and sacred note, but tonight William would dance for the devil. He stared at his reflection with disgust. He looked young, in a blond, Midwest collegiate way, even though he was thirty-one. Fit, slender, just a little too pretty for comfort. Like Dorian Gray—a comely shell housing a deformed soul. He dismissed himself, turning away.

He'd searched the online guide for the place he could get to quickly tonight—must get to. Google Maps had given him the street grid to memorize, and William was ready.

He was going out for a long walk, he'd told his elderly hosts, just to get a better feel for their neighborhood. He'd reassured them he would be perfectly fine on his own, and urged them not to wait up for him since they'd given him a key. Dear Mrs. Griffin had just looked up at him from her crossword and smiled, chirping out her usual good-bye. "Angels watch over you, dear."

He almost jogged to the street corner and over to a thoroughfare, where he flagged down a cab and gave the driver the address. Adrenaline made his limbs taut and ready, his breathing quick, his senses electrified, acute, as if he were a jungle cat hunting its prey.

Hunting for abomination, he admitted without flinching. Phrasing it more nicely didn't matter—he was already lost. His body was starving again for the sin that would send him to hell. He had prayed and struggled, but his flesh had beaten him yet again. There would be plenty of time for remorse later, for the too-familiar self-loathing and anguished repentance. Again. William sat in the cab, trembling, watching the passing streets as if they were breadcrumbs he was leaving behind in a darkening forest.

He felt serene even as his heart hammered in his chest; he had surrendered control to his body. He was a mere observer of his flesh, which like a drug addict was stealing him again to get its fix. He would have a drink or two first, make it easier to bear the shame. Temporarily.

The cab stopped. William paid, got out, and started walking. Herndon Street would be the next intersection. Ten o'clock and the streets still radiated a sensuous warmth from the summer sun. The air was soft with promise, heavy and metallic, intoxicating. Like the taste of the gun barrel, months ago, he realized. This smoggy air had the same ugly sweetness to it.

But William had been a failure in suicide as well as a failure in faith. He'd really wanted to die that winter night back home in Minneapolis, but somehow couldn't bring himself to pull the trigger. He'd paused when he imagined some angel had whispered to him to stop—that his particular road to hell would be paved not with good intentions or even his sins, but with his own brain tissue splattered across the bathroom wall. At the time he'd told himself the voice had been divine wisdom, but he knew deep down it had been mere cowardice—one more weakness to despise in himself. He'd sold the gun at a pawnshop the next day.

Five-sixty-two Herndon Street—he'd arrived. The website listing had promised this place had a dark room downstairs. His gut twisted and coiled. William knew with certainty who and what waited inside, beyond the battered black door only partly lit by the stylized neon phallus above it. The door may as well have been the hellmouth for the morality play he'd produced back in seminary, inscribed with the grim words over its lintel: *Forsake All Hope, Ye Who Enter Here*. Shaking with need and excitement, William entered.

He strode to the bar, quickly downed a Scotch and then ordered a double before turning to check things out. He looked for the dark room. There, that must be it—behind those black strips of vinyl. *Oh!* William stopped breathing. The man standing next to the entrance… damnation had never looked so hot. William suppressed a snort at the perfect irony. He walked over to the curtain, pulled the strips aside, and looked into the abyss. The odor of amyl nitrate and male sex surged up, grabbed him by the throat. He coughed and let go of the plastic as if seared by brimstone.

"It's not as scary as all that," rumbled a voice behind William. "I can show you, if you want." Damnation Man was standing so close that William could feel his body heat pushing through his shirt into his spine. He turned and slowly backed away until he bumped against the wall. Damnation Man advanced, and then there was no escape. But William didn't want escape. He stared at Damnation Man's bearded face. He wore a conqueror's smile—confident, enigmatic, ruthless. William looked down. The man was wearing heavy-soled black work boots, Levi's, and a snug white athletic undershirt. Dark hair curled over its neckline, and a brilliantly colored dragon clawed its way out from behind the cloth, winding across one shoulder. Damnation Man. Dragon Man. Handsome devil.

"Show me?" William swallowed. His voice was strangled, barely audible.

"Sure. I'll show you anything you want to see," the man whispered, raising the back of one hand to brush William's chest, knuckles dragging down to his stomach, landing to hook heavily on his belt and pulling his hips forward. "What *do* you want, boy?"

Need so urgent it was almost nausea blocked William's throat. His tongue flattened, pushed his mouth open, but no sound came out. He shuddered. With a brash honesty all its own, his hand reached out and grasped the denim-covered bulge in Dragon Man's crotch. Oh, that sweet firmness, the mysterious softness, the wild, smoldering promise...

"Yeah, I'm gonna give you what you need, boy," the man muttered, cocking his head toward the dark room. "Let's go." He turned and disappeared behind the curtain without looking back. William lurched to follow, down stairs he could barely see, keeping his eyes on a white athletic undershirt descending into the darkness in front of him. He angled away from the stairs and stopped when the shirt stopped. William could barely make out Dragon Man leaning against the wall, unbuttoning his jeans.

Spellbound, William approached to stand between the man's splayed legs. Again, he reached down to grasp. This time he found the electrifying heat of silken skin, the scrape of pubic hair. William knelt in worship, his reverence ancient as a tribal drum. The scent of Dragon Man's crotch was incense to carry away his devotion. Leaning forward, William filled his mouth with the man's hardening cock, pushing back the soft mystery of foreskin with his lips. He reveled in the veined skin sliding, and the wild salt on his tongue was unspeakably sweet. He steadied himself against the man's thigh and reached to fondle his balls. They rolled heavy and slow in his hand, the most exquisite things on earth. In a frenzy of need, William dove forward, sucked and tongued and tasted and gagged.

"Hey! No teeth!" Dragon Man commanded. He reached down and shoved a bottle against William's nose. "You need to loosen up some, boy. Here."

Stinging fumes broke the spell. Coughing out the man's cock, William let go and stood, terrified. "No! No!" was all he could gasp. William bolted—up the stairs, out the hellmouth, into the street.

Carrying the scent of popcorn, fast food, garbage, and cigarettes, the soft night air curled around him, cooling his slimy lips, banishing the popper fumes. He stood rooted to the cement, panting, unable to think of what to do next. But he had escaped. Angels were indeed looking after him. Finally his feet came free and he began to walk.

A familiar harsh voice shamed him. *What were you doing in a bar like that?* A man of God, caught in the devil's snare, risking everything now and forever for brief and sleazy pleasure. William shuddered, disgusted. He whispered a prayer of thanks and headed for Beach Avenue.

Bright light from behind a wall of glass flooded the palms in planters on the sidewalk ahead of him. Yes—safety, a decent hotel. William pushed through the revolving doors into garish, startling normalcy. So much light, clatter, and chatter. No danger. So many people here, simply being normal. William headed for the bar. He needed something to calm him down and to celebrate his deliverance.

A waiter with extravagant blond-streaked hair passed in front of him and smiled. "Good evening, sir," he said, and moved on. William sighed. The waiter was obviously gay, but William didn't mind. He was safe in this busy brightness. He sat and ordered Scotch.

Oh, God. The handsome guitarist on the tiny stage had winked at him. William knew the wink had been for him because his heart had begun to pound frantically again the moment their eyes had met. That smile meant new danger. Was there no such thing as safety? Transfixed, William sat and drank, hopeful, hopeless. When the set was over, the guitarist came over and sat without asking permission.

"Hi there, I'm Rafe," he said in a voice as strong and gentle as his music had been. "What's your name?"

"Uh, William."

Rafe seemed to think something over for a moment. "Yes, William. Thank you for not lying to me."

William recoiled, afraid and suspicious. "Lying? How could you possibly tell?"

"Oh, I can tell lots of things, William." Rafe grinned like a farm boy whose hog had just won first prize at the county fair. He pushed shoulder-length auburn hair behind one ear. "F'r instance, I can tell you're one hurtin' unit tonight, that's for certain."

"How on earth..." William began in protest, but stopped, held in the beauty of Rafe's gaze.

"What can I say?" Rafe shrugged. "I got the Gift. Bothersome, sometimes, but I came to terms with it long, long ago."

"Long ago? But you're even younger than I am!"

Rafe laughed, a knowing, tender laugh, throwing his head back so the long hair escaped his ears and tumbled around his shoulders. "Well, maybe in some ways." He shook his head. "Not so much in others." He leaned forward, his flowing hair framing high cheekbones and coruscant eyes, eyes that bathed William in kindness. "I can lift your torment from you, if you want."

William's stomach convulsed as if to vomit. "What?" he gasped, swallowing hard. "What do you know about me, about what I'm feeling? You can't possibly make a promise like that!"

Rafe shrugged and leaned back in the chair. "It's part of the Gift. I'm a healer. I know exactly what you're fightin', bro. I can help." He leaned forward again, patted William's hand gently. "But you got to decide. You gotta decide if you really want to be free of that pain, no matter what." Rafe stood, smiling down. "Tell you what—you sit here while I do my last set. If you're still here when I finish in thirty minutes, you and I can go to my place, and I'll heal you. That's a solemn promise, guaranteed."

William sat. Rafe's music washed over him, playful, sweet, enchanting. When the waiter came around, he ordered water. He knew what he wanted, more than anything. He wanted his torment—and its cause—taken away.

Rafe popped the case latches shut on his guitar and came over to sit next to William, draping an arm around his shoulders. "You're a good man, William. I can tell. Brave. Worthy of healing. Let's go."

William stood, tentative, looking for signs of menace in Rafe's face.

"Naw, William. I for sure ain't gonna hurt you. You have my solemn word on that."

Blushing, William nodded, still unable to speak, and followed Rafe into the sultry night.

They walked in silence for blocks. With alarm William realized he had lost his way, that the street grid he had carefully memorized was now useless. "Is it far? I mean, your place. Is it near?"

"Yup, we're here," Rafe chuckled, pointing ahead at a modest apartment block—white stucco, red tile, and wrought iron, one of countless others like it, decently lit. They climbed stairs to the third floor, past big pots of bougainvillea, jasmine, and bird of paradise. Rafe unlocked his door. "C'mon in, William. This is it."

Inside the apartment, Rafe put down his case, took off his jacket, and kicked off his shoes with a sigh. William stood just inside the door, mute, tense, ready to flee.

"I'm sorry, Will. My manners are plumb terrible. Don't get enough visitors, I guess, to keep me in practice." Rafe waved to the sparsely furnished living room. "Make yourself comfy! Would you like a glass of water? I don't think I'm gonna offer you any booze. I want you clearheaded for the healing."

"Water would be perfect, thanks." William sat on the edge of the couch and looked around, pretending his heart wasn't beating like a madman's drum.

"So tell me," Rafe's voice floated over from the open fridge, "when did you first have sex with a man?"

William jumped up from the couch, panicked. "What did you say?"

"Now you just set yourself back down, Will." Rafe's voice was friendly and firm—patient, as if explaining something to a child. "I told you I knew, didn't I?" He came out of the kitchen, two tumblers of ice water in hand. "It's all good—but I heal folks only when they want healing." He shook his head in sad disbelief. "You'd be amazed how many people don't really want healing, though. Most just want fixin', and I surely ain't no mechanic."

William sat. He liked being called Will. Nobody ever had, until now. It sounded right to him. Real.

"So when was your first time?" Rafe asked, more gently this time, handing him one of the glasses.

"In seminary. Eleven years ago, now. One of my teachers."

"Seminary, huh? Those people—sometimes I just..." Rafe shook his head and looked away, swallowing hard. He turned back to William. "The sex, though. You liked it?"

"They were the most wonderful, magical moments of my life. Even though I knew it was a sin."

"You loved him?"

"I adored him."

"And then it got complicated."

The burn of shame made his throat constrict. "Yes. Very."

"And then he told you that it had to stop."

"How did you know?" William stared at Rafe and took a long drink of ice water. "Yes." He put down the empty glass, feeling lost. "He said that it was wrong and we had to stop seeing each other."

"You were betrayed, bro." Rafe sat beside William, holding his eyes with a fierce stare. "Do you want that wonderful magic back again? Without the pain?"

William's answer caught in his throat. Sobbing, he dropped to his knees in front of Rafe. "Oh, Rafe—can you really make me normal? I've hoped and prayed so hard, wept, begged to be made whole! Can you really take this awful sickness from me?"

Rafe eased William off his lap, stood, then drew him up to face him. "Now, listen to me, Will. This is real important. I said I could lift the torment from you. But the Good Lord made you the way you are. I'm surely not gonna try to undo what God has done—that's plumb against my nature. Besides, you're already just right the way you are. What you got in mind is gettin' fixed accordin' to some goofy ideas that just ain't true. What I'm offerin' you is true healing. The real McCoy."

A freezing darkness seized William's guts. "I knew you were too good to be true! You're just another Dragon Man!" A vision of his barren future unfolded behind his eyes, a pathetic and lonely man lurching from one shameful, uncontrollable humiliation to another until... William pushed away, angry and hopeless, blind from tears, but Rafe's arms were warm bands of steel, holding him tight. William moaned, struggling against his captor's grasp, and finally failed, collapsing against Rafe's chest and sobbing in his shame and helplessness.

Rafe's arms still wouldn't let go. "Naw, Will, huh-uh. I ain't no servant of Satan," he crooned. "Not by a long shot. I'm here to deliver you, and if you let me, I will." He kissed the top of Will's head. "What's more, you ain't goin' to hell. Shucks, you're already there. I'm here to lead you outta that hell, into the good world God intended for you. You want that?"

"Oh, I don't know!" William's head spun as if he'd been drinking all night. He gave up. His hands unclenched, dropped away from Rafe's chest, and wrapped him in a tight hug of his own. "Yes, I want that." William breathed into Rafe's shoulder. "I'm so tired. Tired of fighting, of hating myself. If you can take it away, I don't care anymore how you do it. In God's name, heal me, please!"

"Yeah, that's right, Will—in God's name," Rafe repeated gently. "God wired you up to love men, and I'm gonna heal you so you really can. C'mon, let's go into the bedroom. That's where I do my healing."

The bed was set in the middle of a remarkably warm room, with several small tables placed around it, each with clusters of candles. Rafe closed the bedroom door behind them and lit the candles, humming something happy under his breath. Will thought he should recognize the tune but couldn't place it. The room filled with the scent of the beeswax and spices.

"My healing has to be done without clothes on, Will. We gotta be just as nekkid as God first made us." Rafe pulled his shirt over his head, exposing an exquisite torso covered with the tattoo of a magnificent sun centered below the sternum, blazing out to his shoulders, down past his navel. Will stood frozen. Rafe peeled off his slacks and shorts, socks, and then he was naked, erect, incandescently beautiful. He plopped on the bed and leaned back against the cushions along the headboard. "Your turn, bro." Laughing, he made a little drum roll and cymbal crash against his thigh. "Take it all off!"

Mechanically, Will obeyed—down to his briefs. Then he stopped, blushing.

"Them, too, Will. C'mon, now, don't be afraid."

Will tugged them down, and his trapped hard-on sprang free.

"Well, well!" Rafe laughed. "I'm mighty glad to see you, too!" He smiled and patted the bed beside him. "C'mere, babe. Time for healing."

Will sat, then stretched out next to Rafe and lunged to take a nipple into his mouth.

"Now hold on, hold on," Rafe murmured, happy and sweet. "That's way too fast. We gotta do this healing right, or it won't take, and we don't want that, do we? Nosiree, we don't. We want this to last your whole life, and longer. So you gotta follow my directions."

Rafe stroked Will's head, calming him. "First, we gotta lie here in each other's arms until everything is real peaceful. You can hold on to me anywhere but my dick or balls, and I'm gonna just hold you till you're plumb full of peace. Along the way you might cry, or scream, and that's fine. You just let all that old pain come right on out while I hold you safe. Then I'm gonna heal you when you're peaceful and ready."

Will burrowed into Rafe's lithe body and rested his head on the sun. He listened to the steady, serene heartbeat below his ear. Sure enough, waves of grief and fear and shame boiled up, erupting from somewhere deep, making him weep and drool and sob and cling to

Rafe with the desperation of a man fighting for breath. In wave after wave sorrow, shame, fragments of memories, years of despair surged up, escaping through his moans and wailing, until finally all the anguish faded away.

When it had, he knew with a strange certainty it was really gone. There was a new, sparkling calm inside his chest. It was beautiful. He was beautiful.

Eventually, in spite of being afraid he might disrupt this new beauty, he opened his eyes and focused on one of the candles burning beside the bed. He lifted his head, and Rafe's gaze, luminous with patient fire, enveloped him. He opened his mouth to speak, but Rafe bent and kissed him into silence.

"Naw, Will, don't say nothin' just yet. Leastwise, not till you answer a question I've got to ask you." Rafe propped himself up on one elbow and gazed down. "Now, this is real important. If I heal you, you got to promise me something."

The old terror tried to retake Will's gut, but it couldn't. "What do you want from me?"

"One day, you're gonna see a man who's suffering just like you've been. You'll know in a second—know so clearly you'll be plumb amazed. You got to promise me that you'll heal him like I'm gonna heal you. Doesn't matter if he's old, young, pretty or ugly. If he's willing, that is. Like I said, you'd be surprised how many ain't really willing to let go of their suffering. But if he's willing, you gotta do it, just like I'm gonna do it for you. After I heal you, you're gonna have the power, too. You'll see—it's real natural. So do you promise me that?" Rafe's smile was gentle, solemn, as if from very far away. "You can be sure I'm gonna hold you to it, so think real careful, and then answer me true."

Will stared into the sun tattooed on Rafe's chest. It seemed to pulsate as if it were real. He followed one of its rays up to the throat, then up again until his eyes locked with Rafe's. "If you can heal me and give me the power to heal others like me, I promise."

Rafe beamed. "Good man, Will—promise recorded. Now we do the healing." A fierce golden fire came up in his eyes like none Will had ever seen. His body drank it in, sang in the power of it.

There was soundless motion all around them, and Will looked

up to see. In soft procession, the room filled with a throng of semi-visible spirits, laughing and conversing silently like old friends coming together. They encircled the bed and held out their arms, so full of love that nothing could withstand their blessing. Will could feel their circle fill with something palpable, exquisite. It made him laugh, giddy with something he didn't recognize at first. Innocence. He began to cry.

And then Rafe covered him, clamped his mouth over Will's and filled his lungs with his breath, rich and sweet as crushed apples. Will wrapped his arms and legs around him, pulling the heat of the sun against his skin, igniting with it. Rafe lifted, caressed, bit, sucked, kissed, took Will from within and without, twisting, opening, bucking, filling, and Will lost sense of everything but the glory of their bodies sliding together—a psalm of tastes, sounds, textures, sight, and smells played on the strings of their loving.

Once, when they were resting, Rafe lifted up on an elbow and bent over Will, his long hair falling forward to make a secret cave for their faces. "Welcome to Paradise, Will. This is what it feels like," he whispered, licking Will's nose. "This is what salvation feels like." Rafe nibbled on his chin. "Worship God with your deepest, finest love, just like you was made to do. You remember this, now—you call on this feeling when you open heaven's doors for others." And then again they rolled together—playful, sacred, fierce.

At sunrise Will woke to find Rafe wasn't in the bed. In fact, Rafe was nowhere in the apartment. His guitar was gone, too. There was coffee in the kitchen, though, still fresh, and a note beside a single waiting mug.

> *Hey, Will—I had a great time last night, thank you. You're a good man and a terrific lover. We won't see each other again until we meet on the other side, when you're done with this life. Remember your promise to me, though—that promise counts forever. You have the power to heal others like you now. You'll be able to tell who and when and how. It'll be different every time, but like I said, it's real natural, direct from heaven. That's what makes it so powerful.*
>
> *So have a cup of coffee, shower up, and go meet your*

new life. It won't always be easy, but it'll be wonderful and creative and strong and true, I promise you that. More than anything else, it will be true. And all the while, I'll be watching over you, cheering you on.

Remember, I'm a part of you always now—closer than breathing, nearer than hands or feet.

Your loving friend,

Raphael, Arch.

Slowly, Will folded the note and put it in his pocket. Then he poured himself a cup of coffee and walked over to the window for a first look at his new world. Early sun slanted onto the palm-lined street below, light and shadow playing in a clarity he found startling. In a rush of tenderness he thought of his friends, his family, colleagues and obligations. There were so many new unknowns now, and he had no idea how to handle any of them. Surprised, he realized he was also at peace with all of them, regardless of what might happen. Maybe he had no idea of what his new life might become, but he knew one thing. He knew he liked feeling true. He'd stick with that and find out where it took him.

GORDY AND THE VAMPIRE
ERIC ARVIN

A blow job in the locker room was always hot. Max had no problem letting another fella suck him off. He wasn't gay, but a mouth is a mouth, and a good BJ was hard to find. Guys sucked better than girls. That was just a fact. Why wouldn't they? They had the same equipment, after all. They knew exactly what flick of the tongue felt the best.

And man, could this guy suck!

He was new to the college, the guy on his knees. Max hadn't seen him until this year. But he could pack on muscle faster than anyone Max knew. Well, anyone but Gordy. But then, Gordy was some kind of genetic freak, wasn't he? A nice guy, but a freak nonetheless. A freak with bigger tits than any girl on campus and an ass that just screamed *Fuck me!* Max and the other gym rats had to use the 'mones if they ever wanted to even dream of Gordy's size. The fantasy of pumping Gordy's perfect pumpkin patch ass got Max even harder. He clutched the large traps of the guy on his knees, digging in his fingers.

"Suck it, bitch!" he growled. "Suck my cock."

Still, as far as size went, Max was pretty big. He liked it when this fella—when *any* fella—ran his hands over his abs and chest as he sucked away. No girl knew to do that.

Damn, he could suck! Was this guy getting lessons from a vacuum cleaner?

He liked how he—what was his name? Graham? Gary?—grabbed his ass cheeks and kneaded them. Definitely gay. No straight guy would do that. Max wondered if he would be allowed to come in the fella's mouth. That would be hot. Bobby let Max come in his mouth once, but Bobby wasn't nearly as good as this guy. Bobby gagged afterward. Bobby was used to being the fellated muscle boy, but Max had convinced him just once to blow him here in the locker room. Bobby freaked out that he had swallowed some Max juice.

Strange, what had happened to Bobby last week. He was found behind a Dumpster in the rear of the dining hall. Max had heard he was basically skin hanging off bones, but still alive. At the time he was told this he thought that someone was pulling his leg. Then he and some gym and frat buddies went to visit Bobby at the hospital, and what they saw was horrifying: Bobby was just as he had been described. It was no urban legend. Just that morning Max had been admiring Bobby's muscular back in the shower, wondering if he could get some workout tips, and now the dude was a skin bag in a coma.

Shit! Max was going to come any moment. It surged in him like hot lava swelling from beneath. It was right there, at the tipping point, but the guy wasn't pulling off. He was gonna let Max dump in his mouth. *Hot!*

In a blinding flash of pleasure, Max came. But this was no ordinary climax. This guy had some superhuman suction powers or something, like he was sucking it all out of him. Max had the strangest sensation that he was being drained. He found it difficult to do anything through the pleasure. The orgasm went on far longer than any Max had ever experienced. He was weak in the knees, then suddenly weak all over. There was a tightness in his groin area, and his fingers relayed to him that his balls had shrunk to the size of grapes. He fell to the ground, but the guy was still attached to his dick, sucking with more ferocity than ever. Even as Max fought against the horrific ecstatic haze, he noticed that the guy now seemed to be much bigger, fuller. Or was it Max who seemed smaller? Yes! His own thighs looked much thinner.

The guy looked into Max's eyes with a devious glare.

Oh shit! This is what happened to Bobby! No! No!

He tried to kick the guy off him, but it was no use. His legs were easily subdued. Max's eyes rolled back in his head as the dangerous ecstasy sent him into a comatose state.

❖

Gordy woke in his room in Buxom Hall, his head comfortably on his roommate Bubbles's round, firm ass. They weren't lovers. They had tried that, but found each other's bodies too thick and cumbersome to navigate. But they did find each other more comfortable to sleep on than their dorm room beds and pillows. If either was late for class, they could both probably be found oversleeping in nude bliss, one serving as a big, cushy mattress to the other. After sleeping like this for four years they had gotten used to the nightly "pillow fluffings." A smack on the ass or a knead of the cheek rarely woke either of them up anymore. Gordy had the biggest ass, but Bubbles wasn't called "Bubbles" because he liked to chew gum.

Gordy yawned and stretched and heard the commotion outside. He looked out the window toward the gym to see a stretcher being loaded into an ambulance. He wiped his eyes.

"What you suppose happened thar?" Bubbles asked. He sat up, shoulder to shoulder with Gordy, as they peered out the window. Their buff torsos filled the frame.

"I dunno. Do you suppose it's one of those muscle-shrinking accidents again?"

Gordy and Bubbles had heard the strange news: three young men found drained of fluids and emaciated. Drained to the point that their ribs showed, in fact. These were big guys, too. He knew them from his many hours working out in the college weight room. They all belonged to fraternities on campus. Gordy had really never got into the whole frat thing. They had tried to rush him. Having Gordy in a fraternity would have been a coup for any house. He could count as *three* pledges. But even if he had been interested, he couldn't have gotten into one. Though his body went far above Greek criteria, poor Gordy's grades were not up to its standards. How he had even gotten into college was a mystery to all but himself and a very satisfied dean of students.

"Gee whiz, I hope not!" Bubbles shivered. "I'd just hate that to happen to me. What do ya think is causing that anyways, Gordy? D'ya think it's a cold or somethin'?"

Gordy scratched his head. "Maybe bad 'roids?"

"That makes sense."

"It docs?"

"Maybe?"

"Hey, fellas!" a chipper voice called from the doorway. Bubbles and Gordy had a habit of forgetting to shut the door when they slept. They were used to admirers watching them at all hours and didn't mind the constant stream of audience.

The two muscle beauties fumbled around one another to see who it was. "Hey, Bram!" Gordy smiled enthusiastically. Bubbles did not.

Bram was new to the school. He had become a regular at the gym and seemed to pack on muscle quite easily. Why, he looked bigger every day! Gordy was impressed with him. And Bram seemed to really like Gordy, and Bubbles, too, to a lesser extent. He was very attentive to them. *What a swell guy that Bram was!*

"D'ya know what's going on over at the gym, Bram?" asked Bubbles. He stood, letting things flop where they may. Gordy tried to stand as well, but tripped over Bubbles and fell to the floor with a resounding clamor. His big booty clenched at the fall.

"I'm fine!" he said, jumping up before anyone could ask if he was hurt.

"It's Max!" Bram said in reply to Bubbles's question. "He was sucked dry, just like the others."

"Not Max!" Bubbles cried. Bubbles had a bit of a crush on Max even though Max had a habit of overloading on protein. (One of the pitfalls to looking good can be smelling bad. Such was the case with Max.)

"Yep. They just reopened the gym. It was closed for a bit. Or so I heard. You guys want to go get a workout in?"

"Poor Max." Bubbles continued to mourn, flopping down on the bed, unaware he was pulling on his balls. (Such was his habit when thinking.)

"I'll go," Gordy said. He bounded across the room to his closet of gym gear. Buxom Hall shook. Gordy's overfed muscles put on a show as he dressed, causing Bram to lick his lips. He tried to hide his lust when Gordy caught him looking.

"Look all you want!" Gordy teased. He bent over and shook his big hairless moon at Bram in the doorway. Bram had some self-control, but there were a couple of passing hall mates behind him who fell to the ground in sight-induced orgasm. Those massive, perfectly symmetrical cheeks were enough to drive a crazy man sane. (What happens in Buxom Hall, stays in Buxom Hall!) Bram heard their seizing behind him, but was busy trying to keep his mind occupied by other thoughts.

"You gonna be okay, Bubbles?" Gordy asked before he and Bram left to work out.

"Yeah. I'll be fine. I'll catch a workout later." Tug, tug, tug.

Poor Bubbles, in his crushed state, didn't realize his mistake by not going to work out with Gordy as he usually did. It soon became clear, however, that Bram was weaseling Bubbles out of the best workout partner on campus. Instead of Bubbles spotting the big guy as straight football players came in their shorts around them, it was Bram. Instead of Bubbles posing alongside Gordy in the mirrors, it was Bram. This went on for a few days. Bubbles would wake up and Gordy was already at the gym with the interloper. Bubbles tried to sleep on Gordy's ass as much as he could, but the big guy always managed to leave without waking him. Bubbles was beginning to resent Bram, who was now eating with them at the dining hall. It was nothing more than jealousy at first. But that began to change.

There was one late-morning workout in particular that made Bubbles suspicious that something was not quite right with Bram.

Bubbles arrived late. Gordy was cheerfully lifting a ton, smiling as if it was the easiest thing in the world. His tight workout shorts had begun to rip and fall off his massive thighs but he paid no heed. Muscles danced beneath the battered fabric. The other jocks in the weight room immediately sat on the nearest bench like crowded muscle dolls on a shelf; they knew what was coming. As soon as Gordy bent over to do his straight-legged deadlifts, the fabric ripped all to hell and the shorts fell in tatters, revealing the most gorgeous badonkadonk any of the young collegiates had ever seen. None could keep their minds from wondering what lay deep in the canyon between those two mighty glutes. Their dicks swelled like whack-a-moles at a county fair. There was considerable determination on the jocks' faces to not come in their shorts, but in the end the power of Gordy's glutes was too much and the dumbbell area was a thriving, moaning mess.

Bubbles didn't see Bram anywhere. That was a bit of a relief. He took the ingredients for his protein shake and went into the changing room to mix it together. As he was preparing his breakfast he heard moaning in the shower area and went to investigate who was getting their rocks off. There he saw Bram sucking one of the larger jocks into a frenzy. If the guy screamed any louder he would attract outside attention. He shook in what was clearly the throes of the best BJ he had ever experienced, though Bram's face was frightening, rather than ecstatic, as he serviced the guy. His cheeks were caved in as if he were sucking a frozen milk shake through a straw. The jock continued to seize and shout. Bubbles backed away, not wanting to feel like a voyeur, and, having made his shake, went back out into the weight room.

"Hey, Bubbles!" Gordy said. He was patching together his green shorts with bobby pins. "Sorry I didn't wake you this morning, but Bram came by again and…"

"Yeah." Bubbles tried to act like he wasn't hurt. "Good workout?"

"So far, it's great! I've already ripped through these shorts twice. I wonder what's taking Bram so long in the locker room."

"I saw him. He's… There's something about that guy, Gordy. I don't trust him."

"Bubbles." Big meaty hand on big meaty shoulder. The jocks watching were wondering if they might soon see some muscleman on muscleman action. Pop went the weasels again. "You're still my best bud. Don't worry."

"That's not it. I—"

Just then, the locker room door opened and out walked Bram, looking bigger and more cut than ever. He wiped his mouth with satisfaction and gave Bubbles a strange stare. "Ready to git her on?" he asked Gordy.

"You bet! Are you okay to work out by yourself today?" Gordy asked Bubbles.

Bubbles smiled politely and watched as the pair walked over to the deadlift, leaving him behind. There was no way those pins were going to keep the torn fabric on Gordy's ass. Positioning his legs shoulder-width apart, Gordy bent over to pick up the ungodly rack of weights, his obscenely large bum jutting at a lusty angle into the air (the jocks couldn't take it and ran like a frightened herd into the locker room). Bram took hold of Gordy's barely covered hips, digging his fingers into the muscle, and yelled some encouragement. He licked his lips and shot a glare at Bubbles.

It was at that moment one of the jocks yelled from the locker room: "Holy shit! It's happened again!" People raced to see who it was *this* time.

Bubbles was not concerned with the commotion behind him, however. His attention was on his best friend and this new guy. "Something ain't right about that fella," Bubbles grumbled under his breath as Bram continued to grab Gordy's glutes and growl his angry encouragements as he stared at Bubbles. He moved his hips up and back in a semblance of sex. Bubbles knew *that* when he saw it. The reflection in the mirror made it seem as if Bram was sprouting right out of a watermelon patch. He wasn't a good guy, after all! Why, he was making sport of Gordy literally right behind his back!

❖

Gordy didn't pay much attention to Bubbles's warnings about Bram. "I'm tellin' ya, Gordy, there's something off about him."

"Naw. He's a good feller." Then he'd always give Bubbles a big hug, thinking it was jealousy that caused him to bash Bram so. Gordy made sure that he hung out with Bubbles more after that.

It was a few days later, however, after yet another super jock was found emaciated and gasping, that it occurred to Gordy that maybe there was something to Bubbles's warnings after all. Gordy was toweling off after a swim in the gym pool. The towel barely fulfilled its purpose. Gordy noticed Bram at the side of the pool watching him. But that wasn't abnormal. Most people watched him swim. What else could they do? The pool area was a lifeguard's dream when Gordy was in the water. There was a frenetic splashing to get out of the pool whenever Gordy walked in. Nobody wanted to be the guy who nearly drowned by orgasm. Guys took seats and crossed their legs, hoping their trunks would hold. When Gordy's tiny green bikini snapped off (which it always did), nobody wanted to be the first to cream in their

AussieBums. This day the snap happened just as Gordy climbed out of the pool. That big ass rising from the water fixed itself in slo-mo in the minds of the other swimmers. His glutes flexed as he pulled himself up by the rails, and the bikini gave. The material was so slight, however, that instead of flying into the water, it disappeared into his ample ass like floss, pulled in between the cheeks. His bum moved in a welcoming rhythm as he made his way cheerfully to the locker room, saying hello to anyone he passed.

Gordy's massive movie-screen back was what Bram came upon when he rounded the lockers. He could get away with it easily here. Gordy always chose the lockers that lay the deepest in the shower room. This way he could dress without any apparent peeking (though there was *always* some peeking). Bram dug into Gordy's ass and pulled out the smothered swimsuit. The sensation sent a nice chill through the big guy, making his dick spring immediately to life. Bram dangled the green cloth in front of Gordy. "It was about to be eaten up," he said.

Gordy blushed and smiled. "I lose a lot of them that way."

Bram's free hand began to caress Gordy's stiff dick as if it were a doorknob. In truth, the bulbous head was big enough. Bram playfully turned it as if turning the knob might open the back door.

"Er…" Gordy looked around uncomfortably.

Bram hushed him and went to his knees.The flick of tongue on Gordy's bulbous glans gave him the inner fortitude he needed. Gordy liked a good blow job as much as the next guy, but he didn't care for locker room sex. It seemed tacky. And the look in Bram's eyes was a bit…well, somewhat cannibalistic. As if Bram truly *did* want to eat Gordy's meat.

Before Bram could wrap his unbreakable oral hold around the big guy's member, Gordy pushed him away. One gentle shove on the forehead (gentle for Gordy anyway) and Bram fell backward, his dick painfully stiff and a look of unsatisfied need on his face. "What's wrong?" he asked, his hunger coming close to madness.

"I don't want this. Not here."

"Yes, you do. I give the best blow jobs on campus. They're draining." Bram seemed to crawl, almost slither, near to Gordy again.

"No thanks, buddy. Maybe later." Gordy grabbed a towel and wrapped it as far as it would stretch around his waist.

Bram grabbed at the towel in a sort of greedy hysteria, but Gordy stepped away in time. He swung instinctively and knocked Bram down once more. This time he stayed down, leering up at the muscle king with something close to hate. Gordy took his gym bag and quickly left.

❖

Bubbles wasn't paying too much attention to the pounding his ass was taking. Normally he enjoyed bottoming. It got his mind off school. He had thought a good ass plowing would get his mind off Gordy and Bram, too, but it hadn't. Instead, as he sat in Roger Bigstone's lap, his buns bouncing in vicious rhythm and his pecs being sucked sore, he could think of nothing but Gordy. Roger, however, was a man lost in mounds of flesh. He squeezed Bubbles's ass red, white, and blue as he pounded in and out, screaming and wailing like a boy in a fit. There was an audience outside the room, but Roger didn't care. He had been trying to get inside of Gordy or Bubbles since school started, and this was his dream come true. Bubbles's ass was an even better fuck than his girlfriend's, and she had a big ass. Bubbles had bigger tits, too. Roger was certain he was rocking Bubbles's world even as Bubbles glanced around the dorm room, bored. Roger was hoping that if Bubbles got off on this fuck, he'd come back for more and maybe even bring Gordy with him. The thought of both muscle gods together, well, that sent Roger right over the edge. He withdrew his dick from its burrow and shot a stream of man goo so high into the air that it stained the ceiling.

There was nothing from Bubbles, though. In fact, his dick was still flaccid. He climbed off his much smaller hall mate and began to dress. Roger immediately freaked.

"I can do better!" he pleaded. "Let me try again."

"I'm not into it. Got somethin' on my brains. Sorry."

Feeling that he had somehow screwed himself out of his chance for another mind-blowing fuck session, he ran after Bubbles as the fuckee opened the dorm room door to leave. "Please! Gimme another chance."

The crowd gathered outside was enrapt.

"I'll see ya," Bubbles said as he walked away. Roger fell to his knees in tears, naked and defeated.

"You're breakin' my heart!"

"Jeez, dude!" one of his hall mates could be heard to say. "Pull yourself together. It's just sex."

But they all knew that wasn't true. Bubbles and Gordy were more than *just* anything. They were the best man-pussy on campus.

Bubbles decided a workout was what he needed. Not sex. He gussied down in his most pec-exposing tank top and his shortest shorts and was gone before Gordy returned to Buxom Hall. Their paths did not cross. If they had, the following near disaster might not have occurred.

"Bubbles!" Gordy swore as he burst into the dorm room and flung the towel aside. "I think you may be right about Bram." But there was no Bubbles to be seen. Gordy assumed correctly that his friend was probably getting his workout on.

"Wait a minute!" Gordy shouted in an instant of clear thought. "Bubbles is going to the gym; Bram is at the gym; the gym is where a bunch of those fellers got all sucked-out looking; Bram tried to give me a blow job, and what was it he said? Something about sucking dry?"

To the casual listener it might have seemed that Gordy was deducing something important, that he was coming to an answer or piecing together a puzzle. Unfortunately, however, two and three made seventeen and Gordy missed his own point. He shrugged, his moment of clarity past, and plopped his big naked bum at his desk to do a bit of homework. He had to keep his D- average, after all, or he'd have to go see the dean again.

Bubbles was right about the workout. It *was* helping him get his mind off things. He was ripping the bicep curls out like the weights were made of air today. His veins popped from his arms, legs, and throat like 3-D road maps. Bubbles didn't have the same orgasmic effect on the other guys in the gym as Gordy, but that didn't keep them from popping boners at the sight of him. There was just so much of him, poured into his tiny workout shorts. The room was thick with want and testosterone.

Bubbles caught sight of Bram watching him from the just beside the entrance to the locker room. His face seemed a bit meaner, a bit uglier than before. He smirked and then disappeared into the locker room. *Well, that's it!* Bubbles put down the dumbbells and charged after the villain, ready for some ass pounding—and not in the good way!

He burst into the changing room, catching a glimpse of Bram as he slid behind the lockers in the back. There were other guys in the room, but they only nodded at Bubbles as he passed. His expression made it apparent he was in no mood to stop for a muscle worship session. He cornered Bram in the very last section of lockers, the same section where Bram had propositioned Gordy earlier. Bram was standing nonchalantly, leaning back against a locker, as if waiting, a strange look on his face. Bubbles cocked his head and gave it a scratch, and in that moment of indecision Bram tackled him. He took him down with a pounce to the midsection, simultaneously tearing off Bubbles's shorts. Bubbles felt a powerful, though not unpleasant, suction around his pecker...

❖

After about ten minutes of staring at a blank computer screen, Gordy gave up on studying. He needed Bubbles for that anyway. Together, they had half a brain. He decided to get dressed and head over to the gym for the second time that day. It was getting on in the evening. He would wait for Bubbles to finish his workout, and then they could talk about Bram. But as he walked down the hall past open dorm room doors, he was stopped by Boo. Boo was a skinny thing with a lot of determination. There was no way he'd ever get as big as Gordy, or even Bubbles, but darn it if he didn't try anyway. He was the hardest-working lost cause on campus.

"Hey, Gordy!" Boo shouted as he strained and kicked out a pull-up on his door frame. "Can you spot me?"

Well, hell yeah, I can spot him! That's what Gordy did best. So he put down his backpack and stood directly in front of Boo. Gordy held the tips of his index fingers on each of Boo's puny biceps. This seemed to help the little guy out quite a bit. There was only one problem: Gordy's chest was so huge, and he was so very near Boo's crotch, that an accidental titty fuck commenced. Gordy supposed the big smile on Boo's face was surprise and satisfaction at a job being well done, each rep a victory. But those watching and drooling knew different. Boo's hard-on grew with each pull-up. Gordy's chest unintentionally flexed and squeezed his hall mate's meat. Of course, he felt the thickening dong sprouting in his cleavage, but an erection during a workout was a common thing. All that testosterone flowing through the body makes things come alive.

Boo got caught on "ten." Or rather, he knew that if he completed the pull-up, he would splooge all over his shorts and maybe all over Gordy. But his spot wasn't having any wimpery. Not on his watch! He encouraged Boo vocally, and when that didn't seem to work, he helped with a slight push up on Boo's triceps.

That did it. Boo's gym short-wrapped dickhead popped out from between the two massive pecs and spewed jizz. Boo let go of the door frame and Gordy stepped back in surprise as the Boo goo gushed out of the thin material and all over Gordy's face. Boo did not fall to the ground, however. Oh, no. Gordy's massive pecs held tight to the thin boy's penis as Boo spasmed high in the air. By this point, the hall watchers were wiping up their own accidents. Gordy eventually realized he needed to relax his chest if he wanted to detach little Boo from his being. Having done so, Boo slid exhausted and happy to the floor.

"Dude!" Gordy said as he made his way to the bathroom to wash his face. "This always happens. I try to be a nice guy, and I get a face full of goo."

❖

When the gym bunnies of various size and shape saw the Great Gordy approaching, naturally they assumed he was there to work out. He walked in wearing a pair of stretched-to-the-extreme Spandex shorts that displayed the overabundant fruits gifted him by an inebriated god. It wasn't his package that turned the jocks on, however. It was Gordy's tits and ass. They were *straight* boys—at least, that's what they would convince themselves of after jizzing to Gordy's spectacular sets. They would then hurry off to their girlfriends to convince themselves again, in frenzied fuckings, of their heterosexuality.

As was usually the case when Gordy entered the gym, there was a mass exodus out the door. Who wanted to be compared to *that*? A few of the hardcore jocks stayed, as well as the newer students who didn't know better, and the workout always ended in transformation for someone. Without knowing it, Gordy had actually helped many a closeted athlete come out.

On this day, however, Gordy had not come to work out. He looked around the weight room, and, not seeing Bubbles amongst the muscle and steel, headed for the locker room. He went in deep, and as he passed the lockers and the leers of confused muscleheads, he began to hear moaning that was all too familiar. Someone was getting his rocks pulled right off. Gordy recognized the voice of pleasure this time. He peeked around the corner, and there, to his shock and horror, was Bubbles, or rather, a somewhat deflated version of him, being fellated with angry vehemence by Bram. Bubbles's cheeks were already beginning to cave in—both sets of them—as Gordy, realizing something was terribly wrong, snuck up behind the vampiric dicksucker. Bram was too blissed out ravishing Bubbles to sense Gordy's looming shadow. The King of the Weight Room smacked the side of Bram's head, and the villain gasped, allowing Bubbles, with what strength he had left, to free himself from the suction and crawl to safety.

Bram was in a daze. Gordy wasted no time. He took a jump rope from a nearby locker and tied the cum-pire's hands and feet together.

Bram, strong even in his knocked-about and dazed state, writhed against the binds, mighty muscles flexing, hissing with an unflattering scowl set across his face.

Gordy went to his friend's side. "Bubbles! I'm so sorry! I should have listened. Lord knows, you're smarter than me. What did the snake do to ya?"

Bubbles struggled to speak. "He nearly sucked the life outta me, Gordy. My well's gone dry. My…" He faded into incomprehensible moans.

Gordy thought hard about what he should do next. If he went for help, Bubbles would end up like all the others: in a coma in the hospital. And, anyway, who would believe that Bram had the power to drain a fella of his fella-ness. In an all too rare moment of lucidity, Gordy realized that the only way to get Bubbles back to normal was to take back what had been stolen from him.

Gordy looked at Bram, still scowling and hissing and struggling against his bonds. "Now, you just calm down, you hear?" he said.

The big guy searched through the lockers and found a plastic water bottle of sufficient size for his plan. Bram realized what was about to happen and banged against the lockers, yelling for help. His voice was shrill and panicked. The gym was emptying out at that time of night, but Gordy stuffed a jockstrap in Bram's mouth.

"I hate to do this," Gordy said as he squatted at Bram's crotch. "But, well…you just can't go around taking what's not yours."

Bram raged as Gordy milked the cum-pire's balls. Soon Bram spasmed, unloading a torrent of cum into the water bottle, a significant amount. Gordy continued to stroke Bram's shaft with a gentle grip as he pulled on the bodybuilder's balls and scrotum. He probably had enough of the stuff for Bubbles, but what about the other poor muscleheads in the hospital? They had been stolen from as well.

He tugged and milked and yanked, Bram moaning and spasming, his muscle mass deflating all the while, as if air were being let out of a balloon. But there was so much air! How long had this guy been at it? How many guys had he sucked dry?

With one great final hip thrust, the bottle was filled and a shrunken

Bram sat back against a locker. Gordy hurried over to Bubbles and lifted his best bud's chin, feeding him the goo shake. At once Bubble's eyes shot open. He slurped at the cum in extreme hunger, but Gordy knew when to pull the bottle away.

He waited for a moment, and nothing happened. Then Bubbles's muscle began to balloon. Even his tiny dick (Bubbles was not as blessed as Gordy in that area) sprung to life. The sudden transformation made Gordy feel giggly in his naughty parts, and he rubbed at them soothingly.

Gordy's joy, however, was cut short as he heard a rustle from behind. Bram had freed himself from the jump rope and jockstrap. He was on Gordy faster than the big guy could react. Bram was no longer the gorgeous muscle stud he had become, but now resembled a batlike being with emaciated arms and legs. Gordy's sudden shock stunned him. Bram's strength had not waned with the milking. Bubbles, on the other hand, while returned to glorious muscular form, could not yet stand. He could only watch in horror as Gordy struggled against the strength of the creature crushing his bod—an eerie, savage wrestling match. Bram's head was near Gordy's dick as his own rather crooked and sickly penis wagged in the muscle hero's face. Gordy did what he could to keep the super-suctioning mouth from his prick, but the fucker was strong. Gordy's shorts were torn from his body with ease. Bram was able to lick Gordy's exposed cock once before Gordy threw him into the wall.

But the monster was not deterred—he lunged for Gordy's massive ass, grabbing his butt cheeks and sinking in his long fingernails. Bram began flicking his snakelike tongue into muscleman's asshole. Musclebound Gordy was neither as nimble nor as flexible as the voracious beast probing his butt. With his nails still embedded in Gordy's glutes, Bram raised himself in an impressive acrobatic manner, pulling a writhing Gordy's muscular ass mounds painfully apart until his long cock found access and he began to pound the muscle stud's anus. Gordy fell to all fours as the monster entered him again and again, squealing in wicked delight.

Gordy sensed something essential being suctioned out of him as

Bram fucked him, as if Bram's dick were a sort of vacuum. Gordy reached deep inside for the second wind he needed. He was not about to give all of his hard-earned brawn to this creature.

With all his strength, Gordy flexed his glutes harder and quicker than he had ever done in any bodybuilding competition. Bram howled as his long fingers were forced out of their hold and his dick was crushed between two muscular walls. Taking advantage, Gordy abruptly sat back on the floor, smashing the monster's thighs and breaking its pathetic prober right off. The penis fell to the floor and wriggled wormlike. When Gordy stood, the miserable wretch that was Bram hissed, curling about like an injured serpent as it reached for its dismembered member. Gordy ran to Bubbles's side, and the two stared in absolute terror as Bram slithered into the shower and worked his way down the drain, bones cracking as it went.

Silence.

"Holy shit!" cried Bubbles.

❖

The water bottle of stolen jizz was taken to the hospital, where, under the guise of visiting friends, Gordy and Bubbles administered healthy doses of the elixir to the comatose patients. By all the doctors' accounts, it was a medical miracle. Max, Bobby, and the others made remarkable recoveries.

So very grateful were Bubbles and the other muscle studs to Gordy that they decided to throw him a private party, for members of the club only—fellas who had been deflated by a cum-sucking, muscle-fucking vampire.

Gordy arrived late to his own party. Bubbles had no idea what the holdup was. While they waited, the guys told tales of astounding feats on the bench press and the squat rack, each trying to outdo the other, reveling in the muscles thay had regained. They all wore their tightest-fitting gym clothes, pleased once again to have the bodies to pull said outfits off. They also knew to wear extra padding in their crotches, since Gordy would most likely be wearing something not only tight, but unintentionally obscene as well.

Sure enough, when Gordy strolled in with his big smile, the green shorts had almost become a thong, the material working its way up his massive thighs with each friction-inducing step. He had just come from a workout. He held the very water bottle that had given his fellow meatheads back their pride. "Sorry I'm late, fellas. There was a mess in the gym."

"With you, there always is, Gordy," Max said. "I gotta say, you're looking extra pumped today."

"Yeah. I don't know why, but I'm more swollen than usual." He took a swig from the water bottle, and then another to empty the container—and then it happened. The seams gave and Gordy's clothes were shredded by a ridiculous ballooning of muscle. Gordy's dick roared from his shorts, pumping a load all over the guys. And, strangely enough, his nipples, hard as rocks, lactated, shooting streams through the air. He fell to the floor in shocked ecstasy. The guys in the club grabbed their own crotches to encourage their dicks along.

"What just happened?" Gordy asked. He was now a man of cartoonish size. The kind of character perverted erotic writers lust over.

Bubbles held up the water bottle upside down and grinned. The guys looked at one another. "Gordy," said Max. "Did you happen to wash that bottle out yet?"

"Oops. No. I forgot. Why?"

The room filled with laughter, and Gordy, the world's sweetest gym bunny, smiled sheepishly.

Meet Martin
Davem Verne

In December, I traveled to New Haven on the chance that an old classmate still lived there. At Yale, Martin Doherty was a political science major while I studied economics. Like many kids our age, we became friends through our mutual love of movies. Neither of us cared for our practical choice of concentration, but we dreamed of one day making a movie filled with enough paranormal suspense to please an audience.

After college, we got caught in the old loop called reality. Martin took a job with an overnight postal service in Connecticut and I returned to New York to become a banker. Time tricks the dreamer, and suddenly he finds that many winters have passed and the big hopes he once entertained have all faded. Now I found myself driving back to New Haven to reclaim lost time and see if Martin still remembered me after ten years.

Martin doesn't know this, but there's a good reason why we became best friends during college. You can say that, apart from being film geeks, I actively sought his company. I stationed myself beside him in class and never budged. Through my excellent note taking, I made him think I was indispensable. I even scheduled my sections to coincide with his so we could walk back to the dorm together. The truth is I harbored a fantastic crush on him.

The first time I met Martin during freshman registration, my blood began to boil. Not because of the price of tuition—that, too! Rather, because of the vision standing ahead of me in line. Could this be the sum of all manhood at Yale? He was exceptionally tall and wore his jeans tight. His frame was outstanding, with a well-formed chin, large hands, and lean thighs. Most appealing of all, he had copper-colored hair, rusty and burning like a desert at dusk. The varied tints of orange and red spoke of a wildfire of hormones surging within. And after our first greeting, I told myself this guy had to be *my* friend.

Life sometimes does that to you: amidst all the freedom and revelry of a new day, a new school, or a new job, something truly wonderful happens, a friend comes along or lover that might be once in a lifetime. In an instant, the encounter cleans the slate of whoever has come before, leaving you empty and teetering on absolute nothingness but with your sights set on a new horizon that is racing forward to meet you.

Martin Doherty was that new horizon, copper tint and all.

I hadn't had a similar encounter before. I didn't know the kind of guy I liked. Maybe he was young or old, maybe pretty or bold; I hadn't a clue. But Martin, like his Irish ancestry, was deliberately good-natured and quickly pulled me under his spell. He loved to talk, laugh, and tease. He could play pranks when you were being serious. Once, he made me wear jeans and nothing else to a frat party just so he could tell everyone there that I came in my pants. He was completely loyal, however; I never suffered too long under his spells, and he professed endless apologies if he saw that I was sincerely annoyed.

In this way, with my soul newly taken, I had hoped we'd be friends forever, the odd couple perhaps, one hesitant and the other rambunctious. I never heard him complain when I faked homesickness and followed him to his dorm. We spent hours curled up in his bed, yapping about food and cinema, devising elaborate ways to pass exams, or just giggling like boys. Though we never explored the full-grown bodies we actually had, side by side and snug in his sheets, we slept as one—our dicks conspicuously tucked away.

Martin was especially friendly as compensation for the five evil brothers he had, all of whom were older than and as redheaded as he. Outside of being police officers with the NHPD, they were all amateur wrestlers. Poor Martin was the perpetual cadet, the *Cinderfella*, who was a swimmer and pretty while the older Dohertys were impressively huge like their father. His brothers exercised their vanity by heaving their muscular frames all over the wrestling mats of America. In amateur celebrity matches, they challenged the Hulk and took on John Henry. Whenever I saw the family portrait of father and sons, I jokingly called them the Devil's Brood because of their dominating builds and fiery red hair.

Once I saw the eldest wrestle at the police academy, and I have to say that from a distance he, too, arrested me. The glaze on his face and the width of his back were almost machinelike. Hugh Doherty commanded the mat like he was at war in Hades, alarming his opponent into rapid submissions. And in fits of undisciplined rage, he purposely exposed his cock: a thick rope protruding between teeming thighs. With it, he cajoled the audience and baited his combatant into collective humiliation. Pursuing Hugh in the same puppylike manner I pursued Martin was not practical. Martin was exquisite, dreamy, and quick-witted, the perfect Ivy League friend, while Hugh Doherty grabbed what he wanted, fucked what he wanted, and did not retreat until he got more.

❖

New Haven was overcast when I arrived, gray and brooding in December. My excuse for traveling to Connecticut was to meet Martin and offer him an executive role in producing an independent film. A group of downtown investors had agreed to finance a short story I had scripted about soul possession. I could make it for under two thousand if we shot on location. But what I really wanted was to see Martin again. Okay, I admit I was about to trick him into thinking we could be producing partners, a well-intentioned fib coming from someone who *came in his pants*. But I just couldn't rest another day in New York knowing that my college playmate was trapped in overnight postal purgatory without me by his side.

The Dohertys lived in a housing project in a low-income section of New Haven. I was reminded of the midtown neighborhood where I grew up, Hell's Kitchen. We often wondered how two kids from urban homes ever got into Yale. As I entered, there was loud noise everywhere: in the lobby, in the elevator, down the halls. People were screaming and pounding on the walls. I searched the sixth floor for his apartment, 6D. As I walked, the letters jumped out at me, 6A to 6C; and continued, 6E to 6G; but no 6D.

Then, at the far end, I saw a large steel door conspicuously unmarked. The door had bars on it and a double lock, and the door frame bled of rust. By the red streaks around the hinges, my intuition told me that this secret passage led into the Doherty lair.

Courageously, I knocked.

Someone was inside. I could smell meat frying and a kitchen utensil scraping. My imagination joked, *Could it be a sacrifice?* Maybe Martin was out. Or maybe he no longer lived here. That was a splendid idea. As I turned to go, the door pried open and a large hand reached out.

"Wait, you!"

Quickly, someone unbolted and opened the steel door. A middle-aged man, around forty-five, stepped out wearing a kitchen apron. I immediately knew who it was from the photographs in Martin's dorm. In the dark of the hallway, Mr. Doherty's hide was fully exposed: patches of rusty hair sprouted from his chest, meaty biceps clung to his arms, and a massive neck anchored a little chin as he breathed heavily. Mr. Doherty was steaming from the kitchen, a hulking Irishman in an apron, which he had tied around his waist to act as both cooking agent and today's clothes.

"You're Marty's *friend*!" he blared at me.

His voice encouraged fear, while his eyes spied, hunted, and trapped me.

"Marty's not here!" he growled. "Those losers took him away this morning. But if you want to come inside, I'll let you lick my *fork*."

Pretty, I thought. But truthfully, I didn't know what he meant. Was he trying a new recipe that he was particularly proud of? Behind him, smoke engulfed the apartment, blurring light with shadow. I peered over his shoulder for a sign of my dear friend, but Mr. Doherty's steel neck prevented the room from arresting into form. I wondered who actually tended this murky lair and if that person—Mrs. Doherty—really knew what the men were up to.

"Where's Martin?" I asked out loud.

He rolled his eyes and scratched a long cooking fork down his back.

"Didn't you hear me, knucklehead? I said he's not here! They took him away this morning. Do you want to lick my fork or what?"

I looked down at his fist and grew alarmed by the proximity of the cooking fork as it slowly scratched a bulge beneath his apron. I was afraid the apron was all he was wearing and if he turned around I would see the full power of his physique: two naked haunches besieged by copper hair, thighs like steam locomotives, and a pair of iron-plated balls ready for inspection. Just then, someone stepped out into the hall and witnessed our performance; he frowned and nodded, thinking the worst about both of us.

"Let me in!" I said.

The door closed behind me. Inside, the scent of roasted lamb hovered in the air.

"Dinner's burning!" Mr. Doherty squealed and ran into the kitchen.

I was right! He was fully exposed in the rear. Hair engulfed his ass and swept into his crack. More thick patches crawled down his legs. From behind he looked like an orangutan in an apron swinging across the room, but more muscular and with human speech.

"You're the only *friend* who's ever come by!" Mr. Doherty yelled.

No need to shout, I thought. *I can hear you in your cage.*

Mr. Doherty returned, sprayed in juices.

"That's why I let you in. Otherwise you'd be waiting outside with the rest of the garbage: the bill collectors, the drug squad, the Mormons. Can't lick the fork if you're waiting outside, huh?"

Martin's father collapsed on the sofa. His fists squeezed the cushions beside him while he spread his legs. He deliberately exposed his cock from under the apron and waited for my response. It was swollen, polished, and brooding. Outside of the Yale locker room, I hadn't seen one like it. It was practically radiant for a man his age. Confined to this urban crib, Mr. Doherty lived in a perpetual state of arousal, like a satyr ready to get chewed and serviced by any mortal who accidentally dropped by.

"Where is *Mrs*. Doherty?" I asked, throwing some of his own fear back at him.

Mr. Doherty didn't respond. He fussed with the hem of his apron.

"Ha!" I laughed. "I guess that little scene at the door and now this one inside means that you wear your most revealing apron in the hopes of attracting some sap to sit on your lap! But you won't fool me. I went to Yale. I can see what an uneducated, mean-spirited man you are," I wanted to say but didn't. I continued staring at his great cock.

"I like you already," he said, catching my eye.

"Where is...?" I hesitated. "Where are your other sons?"

"You mean Hugh and those losers? They're losing!" he said bitterly. "This weekend it's Minnesota, third wrestling meet this month. Those bastards are always halfway to nowhere. Naturally, they took Marty with them. The thieves. Stealing him away from their poor dad. Don't they know he's gotta work on Sunday?"

Greasy smoke floated from the kitchen and into living room. The fumes surrounded me like the arms of an octopus. Its poisonous ink greased my face and neck. And I was getting hungry, real hungry.

Mr. Doherty spread his legs so that his leaking prick slathered on the sofa. He stared at me some more. His left eye was seething with desire while the other was flushed with a tear.

"She left me—did Marty tell you? Three months ago she took my credit cards and emptied my savings. Then she flew to Tahiti, leaving Marty and the boys with me. It was a curse—and a blessing. Because she was gone and Marty was here. Blessed Marty, beautiful Marty, my namesake child, my favorite son..."

Mr. Doherty wiped his eye and sniffled.

I wanted to throw up. Martin, *Sr.*? How dare he be named after my only friend!

"I prayed she wouldn't come back. And she didn't. But do you know what she shipped back just to spite me? As payment for all those years I suffered as a beat cop in order to feed her? There—that thing."

He didn't move but his prick pointed to the widescreen TV. In the chafing curtains of smoke I saw a small statue, about six inches tall, poised on top of the TV. It was burnt like the earth with big red eyes and a scheming grin. Its ears were like a rabbit's but its body was that of a stout man with a bulbous cock protruding from its waist. Obscene in every way, it searched the room and caught our voices.

"Marty says it's a god," Mr. Doherty smirked, "the god of male beauty and fertility. Have you heard of such a thing? That kid's always making up stories and playing pranks on his lonely dad. He said if you have one of those in your home, then all your semen will come true—or did he say *dreaming*—or something. You catch my drift."

I looked at the large phallus on the idol.

"When you chant its name—*Oh, great Mara god*—it borrows someone's soul for a while. Then you can request anything you want and it's yours: a pussy to fuck, an ass to screw, a mouth to drill, even a wrestling match to win. A few hours later, the soul is free to return to the body, your wish fulfilled. Hugh and the boys worship the little woody all day long, but they still come back losers."

Looking back to his sweating face, I compared Mr. Doherty's teary eye against his drier eye. Was he being frank or pulling his own prank?

"Who…?" I began, but my head grew dizzy. "Whose soul does it use?"

"You knucklehead! Marty's!" he exclaimed, drawing his beefy face into a grin.

He started laughing loudly. His laugh grew into a chortle. Then I started laughing, too, because my thoughts got dizzy and my crotch got jizzy. Mr. Doherty slapped his knee and blared like a canon in the fog. His gaiety thundered in my ear. Then he reached beneath his apron and groped his dick like he was yanking on a bell. *Clang-clang!* He pulled it out. He stroked it from balls to head until it got harder and longer and vibrated with each chortle. As his breathing grew heavy and his face simmered in fire, he tightened the grip around his dick and glared at me.

"Now lick my fork, you knucklehead!"

❖

A little while later, after fucking, Mr. Doherty let me prowl on my own through his home. "Third door to the right" were his only instructions. I was afraid once I found Marty's room he'd lock the door and keep me as his slave. That bullshit about the Mara god had somehow come true for him. I still tasted his cum in my mouth. Off-duty police jizz is some of the best—so I've heard. As I exited the living room, wiping the hairs from my lips, I noticed the way he watched me while consuming a lamb chop. He liked what I did with my mouth, no doubt, and was thinking about doing the same to me.

The hallway in 6D was congested with junk. Mrs. Doherty had been a packrat and her sons were the same. Over three decades their apartment had swallowed an array of rubbish. Fitness magazines were piled on top of free weights, gym shorts collected in massive piles, and posters of professional athletes plastered every inch of hall space. The smell of sweat and jizz clung to every door frame, startling my breath. Each passing door revealed a more menacing portrait of the Doherty clan, with one room in particular overwhelming me in its magnificent aroma. I almost fell unconscious into its manly chaos—no doubt Hugh Doherty's.

At the third door, I hesitated.

Gently, I pushed it open to reveal the world of Martin Doherty. The Martin I knew from college had been fastidious, and to this cause he had remained. It was like I entered an adjacent apartment that was neat and tidy. The bed was made, the shelves were in order, the desk laid out in anticipation of future studies. Only the closet door remained open, an act of rebellion perhaps, though the clothes hung respectfully on hangers.

This is how I remembered Martin from Yale; this is how I dreamt of him today.

I paused, wondering if I should leave a note on his desk telling him that his best friend from college had swung by, met his appetizing father, and here's a number to call.

No, I decided. Better leave his room in order. I'd catch him outside.

As I turned to go, I saw something peek out from the corner. Not a thing, but a bush, a mane of curly red hair. It was hiding behind the door but could not be camouflaged.

"Martin?"

The closet door was propped against the bureau, concealing a triangle of space from view. At the triangle's edge reclined a feast of copper hair.

It was Martin! My Martin! But why was he hiding in his own room?

I closed the bedroom door and hurried to my friend. The closet door swung away to reveal Martin poised in the nude.

"Martin, what are you doing back here?"

Martin was standing still, his bare body pressed against the corner. His eyes were open but barren, placidly staring into nothingness. He did not appear haunted or tormented or the victim of a crime. As in so many classes, he appeared dazed and absent, as if contemplating a distant place or more playful activity.

I took in his pink torso and the tucked abs that led down to his pubes. The hair down there was rich and furry. And beneath his pubes hung his cock, dangling stiffly on top of two weighty balls. The balls looked familiar—Oh wait, they were Mr. Doherty's—large and heavy, too. I could see that Martin had gained a little weight. Now his legs were full and his thighs appeared stronger, urging his meat forward. I wanted to yank his cock, tug it like the family bellpull, and make some noise in order to wake him up. But I was cautious about acting too alarmed. He might be sleepwalking—or this might be some kind of practical joke.

"Martin, are you *okay*?"

He didn't respond.

"Martin, can you hear me?"

He gazed pleasantly.

I suddenly realized that if he was home the whole time, he probably heard his father and me in the living room. He heard that nonsense about a Mara god. And he heard me simper and moan as I drank Mr. Doherty's jizz…

"Martin, answer me!"

Nothing in Martin's beautiful expression indicated that he was at all aware of me, standing only a breath or two away. While his body stood full and exquisite, shoulders straight and pecs apart, his spirit was elsewhere, obeying the will of some energy, some force. Was he under the spell of his brute brothers? Was he performing who knows what enchantment to satisfy their desperate needs?

But I needed Martin, too. That's why I had come all this way. And I didn't use idols or spells to get here. I was an economics major. I believed in numbers. Practical statistics. How many miles does it take to drive to New Haven? How much gas is necessary to fill the car? How much courage will I need to walk in Martin's room?

My left hand squeezed Martin's shoulder. The warmth of his skin reminded me of our mock-wrestling matches when we pretended to be brothers. And after all these years, he still smelled of baby powder. Martin bathed in baby powder: after showering, after shaving, after masturbating, making his skin soft and so filled with Martin!

"I love you, Martin!" I let it pour out.

His empty stare neglected me.

I hugged my handsome classmate just then, wishing him to come back to me, to New Haven or New York, and be my forever friend. I rubbed his chest and massaged his neck. I pinched his nipples and tickled the dimple in his chin. These tender gestures were small in comparison to what I really wanted to do—and more sincere than the blow job I had recently given.

But he did not awaken. It was clear that Martin was being deceived. Through forces unknown, his soul had been tricked and borrowed for diabolical doings. I might never see him again in the same bright-eyed state as in college. Hiding naked in the corner of his room might be the last opportunity I'd ever have to get to know my friend.

Should I kiss him? Should I touch him? Should I recklessly enjoy his body standing silently like an instrument from God? And was it morally right to make love to a beautiful body that, at least temporarily, had no soul?

I didn't have the answers to these questions; I only had Martin.

I lowered my hand down his torso and combed his pubic hairs with my fingers. The copper bristles were thick, bunched in uneven clumps, but as soft as silk. They protected his cock from the world of pain, from his brothers, from women. My hand found his penis and squeezed it gently. No small tidbit there. Martin felt hot and swelled in my grip. His balls were warm, too, and filled with juice.

I squeezed his testicles and produced a small drop of pre-cum from his dick. Martin made no gesture and uttered no complaint; he saw no demons in my actions. I kissed his neck, his pecs, his stomach. I got on my knees and stared at his penis. I had once envisioned his cock wrestling against my collegiate ass, rubbing its length between my crack, and finally entering me to pump a semester-sized cumload. So thick and obedient; so red and steady. His dick swung to one side and stayed there—how cute!

I kissed the soft head, the long limb, the powdered balls, and then boldly swallowed him in my mouth. He tasted clean and pure, unspoiled like a virgin—not well-beaten like his father. And to his credit, the sensation of a blow job excited Martin. His cock grew hard as I took him all the way in.

Fully erect, Martin was enormous, bigger than captivity in my mouth. I gagged trying to make him fit. His balls met my chin as I sucked him. His thighs were solid and supported his balls as they swayed back and forth. I held on to his hips and shoved them against me, blowing him quickly. Martin tightened his crotch and shot a welcoming squirt in my mouth. Another small squirt became thicker as he grew harder.

His thin physique collapsed against the wall and he began fucking my mouth. I continued sucking him off, hoping a blow job might bring his soul back. Bring Martin back! *Bring back my god!*

I imagined he was screwing an invisible pussy at my lips. His balls shifted. His dick extended. I sucked him harder, finally tasting the reality of Martin in my mouth. The longings I had repressed for ten years jumped out of me. I was willing to swallow his semen if he only came now!

Martin muttered something. His hands were uncoordinated but they found my head attached to his groin. I kept sucking and sucking, imagining that I was drawing his soul back to New Haven and apartment 6D. His fingers dug into my hair and propelled his cock in my face, burrowing a hole large enough to fill with his load.

If he hadn't a soul before, it came rushing back now!

Martin captured my temples and greedily humped me. His thighs thrust. His stomach contorted. Beat upon beat, he groaned, he growled, the same animal sounds he made in his dorm, pretending we were camping in the jungle, pretending he was hunting me like a tiger. Maybe he was serious then, when he captured me and bit my ear for his meal. I don't know. But he was serious now, aware and awake and in my face. Like his father, he turned fire engine red as he anxiously moaned.

"Suck it! I wanna come! Make me come!"

"I am. I am!"

I let him come. His copper hair burned in my face. The hot semen burst from his dick in a turbulent expulsion. The first load scorched my throat, clearing the way for a second and then a third. I swallowed him and beat his hips for more. My fists grabbed each ball and wrestled the ooze out. His chest heaved; his head banged; he pumped for more. I took his rhapsody for real as one more cum shot burst from the copper mine. The Cumstock Load was more than I dreamed! I swallowed it and welcomed him back by licking him dry.

Martin tossed his arms around several times as his soul returned home. I sat between his knees with his hot dick in my mouth and waited. Red pubes clung to my chin and his semen dribbled out. I was a fine portrait of a college grad. I wiped my lips, found a robe, and threw it on him just as his eyes brightened.

"Hey, buddy!" I said, swallowing.

Martin stumbled forward. His knees were wobbly. When he noticed me, realizing his robe was half-open and he was exposing his meat, his face flushed. Martin tucked his dick away and stammered.

"Your dad told me to wake you," I said. "I hope you don't mind. Were you sleepwalking? Hey, look who's here. Martin, it's me!"

"Hey," Martin said, sleepily.

I looked him up and down as if for the first time.

"You haven't changed much," I said, gratefully. "Listen, I know you were taking a nap, but I got something I'd like to talk to you about."

"Yeah?" he asked.

I helped him to the corner of his bed, where we sat.

"I've got an idea for a movie. About a guy who has his soul snatched. Funny, but it kind of mirrors life. I've got the capital and I want to shoot it on location, maybe in your crib, with a handheld camera like it was shot by an amateur, and scare the audience to pieces. You interested?"

"Yeah," Martin said, still groggy.

Martin looked around the bedroom as if for the first time, then saw the clock.

"Doesn't this feel like college?" I asked, leaning my head on his shoulder.

"Listen," he said, half-mumbling. "I've got something else going on here. I've got a job—and a girl. We'll probably get married this summer. In fact, I gotta get a move on. She's expecting me at her place."

Martin shook the cobwebs from his head.

"I don't know why I keep falling asleep. I'm always tired. It must be December. Say, thanks for coming. I really mean it. It was nice to see you. You brought back some good memories. Good luck on your film."

Martin stood and started to dress. He put his boxers on, then his jeans, and finally a shirt. He still dressed like he was in college, but he wasn't dressing for me.

"My dad's cooking supper if you want to eat something before you go," Martin said, half-graciously. "I won't be home until later." Then a long pause. "So—I guess I'll see you around."

Martin exited the bedroom, his copper hair burning a trail down the hall.

I sat dumbfounded. Did I say something? What just happened?

Like a lost lamb chop, I followed him into the living room, but he was already out the door. His father was watering a plant and saw his son pass. They exchanged a few words, which I couldn't hear, and then Mr. Doherty laughed. Martin laughed, too, the same laugh like he always had, not groggy or sleepy, but filled with mirth and foolery and with that extra chortle he had inherited from his father. Then he nodded to Mr. Doherty, who slapped him on the back, and Martin was out the door.

I stood in the living room with my mouth ajar.

Whistling, Mr. Doherty continued watering in his apron.

At first I thought of chasing Martin down and wrestling him in the elevator, tell him how he had been tricked by a Tahitian god and how it took his only friend from college to bring him back.

But it was *I* who had been tricked.

I had been fooled.

By the Devil's own brood!

I stared at Satan—that is, Mr. Doherty—as I walked to the front door and opened it. He stood over the azaleas, bathing them tenderly. The watering can was bent at his waist so as to make it look like he was pissing. His aroused cock still swung beneath his apron and I could tell he was ready to piss some more—piss some semen in my mouth just like he had done. Just like Martin had done. Into my dumb, naïve, knuckleheaded mouth!

I was about to say something rude, call him on his prank, when Mr. Doherty turned around.

"Oh, are you still here? What a nice *friend* you are. Coming all the way from New York to check up on Marty. Any time you want to lick a fork, you come by New Haven. There's plenty of forks here. There's me. Marty. Hugh. Tommy. Bobby. DJ…"

"Fuck you! I'm going to call the New Haven Board of Police Commissioners and—and—and—make you turn in your gold badge— and—and—go back to patrolling the streets with the pimps and hustlers like you!" And I slammed the door.

Something weird was going on. Something terrible was at work. Little policemen were beating inside my head, touting their sticks, calling their chiefs, but there was no criminal to be found but for me. As fortified as I was when I drove to New Haven, I left a mess, the repeat offender of a sexual prank.

Had I taken them all too seriously? I wanted to go back and break that wooden doll. I wanted to yell at Sgt. Doherty, stab him with his own fork, and scream at Martin, who had taken advantage of a true Yale friendship. Under the disguise of soul possession, he had spruced and serviced his dick in my loyal mouth!

I drove recklessly down Grand Avenue, angry and crying, sorry I had ever taken the trouble to know Marty, to listen to his jokes, to do his laundry, to take his exams, to make his bed, knowing how he would deceive me one day.

But wait!

Wait, wait, wait!

I stopped the car and looked down.

That little shit. That five-minute lip-fucker. I had been fooled, yes! Betrayed by beauty, yes! But that gorgeous creature of fire and delicacy, who had wrapped me in his spell and tricked me into wearing nothing but jeans to a dinner party, now tricked me again just so I would jizz in my pants—in my pants!

"Martin!" I shouted, wet and beating the steering wheel. "I hate you, Martin!!"

I stepped on the gas and swore never to go back to New Haven. *I'll never pursue a beautiful face. And I'll never pine for love in all its transparent, malignant forms.* It wasn't until I crossed the turnpike into New York that I realized who had *actually* made me jizz.

That brute. Martin, *Sr.*

THE HORROR IN DUNWICH HALL
JOHNNY MURDOC

There was a naked jock on my bed and a thing with tentacles coming out of my toilet. One of these things did not belong, and if you tell me that it was the naked jock, you shouldn't be reading this story. The jock, Brian, was asleep. At least he was when I first turned on the light, because shortly after that I screamed loud enough to wake him up. I couldn't scream at first. I was too stunned.

The thing with the tentacles in my toilet was just that: a thing. I can't say it was an octopus or squid—it had more than eight tentacles— but it was definitely cephalopod-ish. It was making all kind of slurp-ish and splashy noises. I don't know if it was making them before; I was making all kinds of slurp-ish noises myself. It definitely wasn't making them when I walked to the bathroom because I probably wouldn't have gone in alone. Maybe I startled it when I turned on the light.

Regardless, it was definitely going spastic. Tentacles slapped the cold porcelain and slid along the commode, the very definition of writhing. I couldn't do much but stare. I stood in the doorway, butt naked with a condom still hanging on my dick and a fucking monster coming out of my toilet. Its tentacles were flopping and writhing, but I could see enough to tell they were still coming up and out of the toilet. Whatever it was, it didn't fit in the toilet bowl.

Finally, I had the good sense to back slowly away, and that's when it made its move. And it moved fast, fucking lunged. A single tentacle, much longer than the rest, shot out at me and wrapped around my dick.

I screamed.

❖

Wait, maybe I should start at the beginning. At least then you get to hear the hot story of how I just buried my dick deep into a hockey player's ass, right? Then we'll get back to the monster. Don't say I didn't warn you. There's a monster at the end of this story and it is not Grover. So if you're going to jerk off to my little tale, you'll want to make sure you shoot your wad before the part when I get out of bed and turn on the bathroom light. Because, again, monster.

So the night started after a day of shitty classes, the only kind of classes when you're as educationally inept as I am. Don't get me wrong. I'm a smart guy, maybe a little too clever for my own good, but I just don't do well in the educational setting. I can spend hours reading a book, but listening to some of these professors makes me want to kill someone. Not really, but you get my drift, right?

After a long day of contemplating professor-icide and looking forward to the weekend, I was pretty excited to get the call from Henry asking if I wanted to go to the hockey game that night. Now, I'm not much of a hockey buff, but I had a secret interest in going due to the presence of one Brian Johnston, hockey jock extraordinaire. Henry didn't know about my thing for Brian, or the fact that Brian had drunkenly come on to me at a party the weekend before. He just thought I had taken a sudden interest in hockey for a completely innocent reason. I was a guy, after all, and it was a hockey town, and blah blah blah.

We went out to dinner and then headed over to the arena. Henry was on the junior varsity team and worked part-time as a janitor for the athletic center. We got in for free and had pretty good seats on top of that. We were right behind the home team's box, where everyone on the team crowded together between rounds, which gave me plenty of time to watch Brian. The rest of the team was filled with hot guys, too, but hockey uniforms leave entirely too much up to the imagination and everyone wore their helmets most of the time, so it was hard to get a good look at anyone. I had to ask Henry which one Brian Johnston was, and he pointed to the player with a huge number 10 on his back, the name *Johnston* written in blocky collegiate text over the number.

Henry was in the middle of telling me about his roommate Max and how he'd almost gotten busted for dropping a cherry bomb in a trash can. I cut him off and reminded him I was now the proud owner of a box of cherry bombs, hiding them out on Max's behalf until the heat died down.

"Wait," Henry interrupted. "Why do you care who Brian Johnston is?"

"Um…" Because the school paper writes about him all of the time, and that's the only reason I knew who he was before he tried to pick me up last weekend. I would have gone for it, too, except he was so damned drunk that he passed out halfway through his pickup line. "I don't know, that's just the only name I remember from the paper," I said.

The game was completely thrilling. While I don't really have the words to describe what happened, due to having never cared about hockey at all before last weekend, it was easy to get caught up in the crowd's excitement and even the school spirit as students cheered for our team and insulted the other. The sound in the arena was deafening when Brian got in the winning shot right before the final buzzer. Through all of the noise, I thought I could hear Brian tear out into a victory yell, his arms thrust into the air, his stick over his head, and I got hard just watching him.

"Dude, that was fucking awesome," Henry said.

"Yeah," I said, checking my cell phone for messages. I'd gotten a text from Max, asking if we'd like to go out for drinks tonight. I pitched it to Henry.

"Sure, but let's go congratulate the team. I can totally get us in to the locker room."

I could have kissed Henry for that. I'd been in the locker room dozens of times in the past two years, but it never got old. On top of that, I'd never been in there with an entire hockey team, and I started daydreaming about hot naked jocks slapping each other on the butt. "Won't it be weird?" I asked.

"Whatever, dude. I know I just made your gayest wet dream a possibility," he said.

"Yeah, but do they usually let just anyone come in after a game?"

Henry led the way through the corridors that led down toward the locker room. "We gotta wait until they have a post-game, but then they'll let some people in, like reporters for the local news and stuff. Just don't gawk, and look like you're supposed to be there."

Easier said than done. Inside the locker room, it was like a gay utopia. We went in right after Coach Henson finished up his congratulatory speech. As the guys got up to strip off their uniforms, they really did slap each other on the asses and on the shoulders and anywhere else they could. The slapping didn't slow down as their layers disappeared, either, so the impact sounds mutated from hand on plastic to hand on flesh. No one seemed to care that we were there, and no one even bothered to cover up when the news guys showed up, even though one of them had a video camera.

So much naked flesh.

I recognized a couple of other guys from the school paper and from around campus. One hockey player, Tommy Hayes, was in my Advertising 203 class. I had never even known he was on the team. He was a good-looking guy, maybe a little too blond, but watching him strip down his jockstrap totally changed my view of the guy. He had a huge dick that tumbled out of the pouch of his jock and swung back and forth as he straightened up and a thick patch of too-blond pubic hair. Tommy had always struck me as kind of gay, and if it weren't for the fact that Brian Johnston was stripping down just two lockers down, I might have tried to strike up a conversation. Maybe another day.

It wasn't just that Johnston had made a move on me that made him special. He really was fucking hot, and he had a spectacular body. From the moment he pulled his jersey over his protective gear, my eyes were for him only. The hockey uniform seemed to be made of an infinite number of pieces, and watching him disrobe was like watching a strip show.

He obviously worked out, and his time on the ice had made thighs and calf muscles impossibly thick. His arms, legs, and ass were covered in dusty blond hairs, and a small patch rested between his nipples as well. His hair was darker than usual, soaked with sweat and plastered to his head and against his body. He was smiling, a huge heartwarming small-town smile, obviously proud of the team's win and his own score. It seemed like everyone wanted to pat him on the back, love-punch him in the arm, or grab at his ass. I could more than understand the need to touch him, to feel him. Brian was loving every minute of it, too.

Guys were making their way over to the showers, and it was getting harder to watch Brian from my vantage point. A big brick wall of a dude, presumably the goalie, walked right in front of me as Brian ditched his jockstrap, and by the time my view was clear again Brian had turned his back to me, robbing me of seeing his dick. Brian headed off to the showers, and while I could have spent the night watching his beautiful ass move back and forth, each cheek gliding up and down like a perfectly smooth machine, I lamented missing his dick, and I didn't think my presence in the showers would be quite so acceptable as my presence in the locker room.

There was plenty of other eye candy, though. Dudes big and tall, large and small. One guy, a redhead with piercing green eyes, had freckles all over his body and a cute, uncut dick that seemed to point perpetually outward even though it was soft. Another guy—

"Chris," Henry said. I looked over at him. He was talking to a near-naked black guy. "This is Dwayne. He's my chem tutor. Dude's a walking-talking chemistry lab on top of being an awesome forward."

I shook hands with Dwayne and he smiled, his teeth bright white like his jockstrap. I couldn't help but examine his bulge, his thick dick clearly visible against the white cotton mesh, enough to know he was cut. "Nice to meet you," I said.

"You enjoy the game?" Dwayne asked.

"Hell yeah. It was a good show."

"Henry here tells me you're new to the sport."

"Consider me a convert."

"Good to hear. Look, excuse me, but I don't want to miss my chance to be on the ten o'clock news." With that, he stripped off his jockstrap, gave a cheeky grin, and walked off, his path taking him right behind where Coach Henson was being interviewed by the newsman.

Henry let out a laugh.

"What just happened?" I asked.

"Dwayne was telling me how the guys all try to get their wangs on the evening news by walking in front of the camera any chance they get."

"Nice," I said, thinking about how I was going to have to start watching the sports coverage on the news.

It got kind of boring after the last guy filtered into the showers, and while I could have all kinds of fun imagining what was taking place under the spigots, it wasn't nearly as much fun as being surrounded by naked guys. Henry had gone off to chat with Coach Henson. I sat down on one of the benches and stared at my feet.

After a few minutes, I thought *fuck it* and stood, intent on wandering around. Who knows where I might intentionally unintentionally end up. While I knew full well that Henson's office, where he and Henry were off chatting, was off to the left, I decided to pretend that it was to the right. I couldn't have planned it better if I had tried. As I rounded the corner, I ran right into Brian Johnston. He was toweling his hair dry and looking at the floor, so he didn't see me in enough time to stop. His wet, naked, beautiful body pressed against mine and then he stumbled back. I could already feel his shower water soak through my T-shirt by the time he said, "Oof!"

"Sorry," I said. It was a dirty trick, but it got the intended result. Brian looked me right in the eye and then blushed.

"Oh, hey," he said. "Chris, right?"

He remembered my name! Christopher King for the win!

"Yeah," I said. "Good game, tonight."

"Oh, thank you. You were there?"

"Yeah," I said and then decided to take a gamble. "I thought I'd come see you in action." I was horny and bold. At that point the rest of the team had started making their way from the showers, and Brian and I were surrounded by wet naked jocks. My khakis and briefs were barely enough to keep my erection tamed.

"So, what are you doing after this?" Brian asked.

"Dunno. Couple of ideas, but I haven't committed to any."

"Right on."

"What about you, big celebration?"

Brian leaned in close until his lips were near my ears. "That depends on how much you're up for getting laid."

"That's a little blunt, don't you think?"

"Yeah, well, I wanted to say it before I passed out, again."

"Are you planning on passing out tonight?"

"That depends on whether or not I'm going home with you."

❖

Dunwich Hall, where my dorm was located, was a good mile or so from the arena. Neither of us had a car, so Brian and I found ourselves walking across campus. The air was unseasonably warm for late October and it felt downright ridiculous considering we'd just come out of a freezing hockey rink. Brian was carrying his duffel bag with his uniform and equipment in it, his hockey stick tucked into the bag's straps. I have to say that I felt a little cooler than usual (reputation-wise, that is) walking with Brian, like some of his jock studliness might rub off on me.

We made a little small talk, but mostly we walked in silence. What do two people on their way to fuck talk about, anyway? I knew next to nothing about Brian, frankly. I didn't even know if Brian was openly gay, although his directness in the locker room suggested that he was hardly hiding.

Just when it was getting almost too awkward, we ran into my friend Max, the infamous cherry-bomber.

"Hey, Chris," he said.

"Hey."

"You guys catch the crazy dude over at the library?"

"What? No."

"Oh, shit. You have to go check him out. Some dude in, like, a cloak and hood and shit is pulling a street preacher routine. Only, he's making shit up as he goes along, it sounds like." Max's eyes shifted from me to Brian, and then back to me. "Is that Brian Johnston?"

"I am," Brian said, sticking his hand out. Max shook it tentatively and then shot me a look, the kind most known for its tented eyebrows and wrinkled forehead. The kind that said, basically, "What the fuck?"

"Weren't you hanging out with Henry tonight?"

"I was. I did. Now I'm…hanging out with Brian?"

"So, yeah, you know you're going to have to explain this tomorrow, right?"

Brian laughed.

"Yes, Max. I will see you tomorrow."

Max smiled and gave Brian a curt nod.

"Friend of yours?" Brian asked.

"Don't forget to check out the creepy-assed street preacher!" Max yelled back.

The creepy-assed street preacher he was referring to was holding court on the library steps. He was dressed exactly as Max had described him, in a cloak with a heavy hood that covered his face. His arms were outstretched and raised slightly, and he was shouting:

"It must be allowed, that these blasphemies of an infernal train of demons are matters of too common knowledge to be denied; the cursed voices of Azazel and Buzrael, of Beelzebub and Belial, being heard now from underground by above a score of credible witnesses now living."

"Holy shit," Brian said. I hadn't ever seen anything quite like this on campus, but I had seen some weird shit, mostly perpetrated by the frats. It wasn't Rush Week, or anything, though, and this was pretty fucking weird.

"I myself did not more than a fortnight ago catch a very plain discourse of evil powers in the Hill behind my house; wherein there were a rattling and rolling, groaning, screeching, and hissing, such as no things of this Earth could raise up, and which must needs have come from those caves that only black magick can discover, and only the Devil unlock." Drama department, definitely.

"Okay," Brian said, stretching out the *O*. "Time to go."

"This is kind of entertaining, actually."

Brian leaned in close. "Maybe, but my dick is way more entertaining."

❖

Brian barely waited for the door to close before he was pulling off my shirt. He was a strong kisser. Fuck, he was a strong everything. When he wrapped his arms around me and pressed his lips against mine, I could have gone slack and he would have held me up without a problem. If only I were the swooning type. Instead, I was just as eager as he was.

I helped him pull his shirt off and then I planted my mouth on one of his nipples, wide and perky and perched on his fantastic pectoral muscles. His chest was well defined, the result of years of firing hockey pucks at goalies. He moaned when I nibbled on his tit. I cupped his junk through his jeans and gave his balls a squeeze. His dick was already hard, I could feel it under denim, pointing at 10:00. I continued to work his nipple as I unbuttoned his jeans, but I pulled back as his pants dropped so that I could see his hard dick encased in his boxer briefs. I had seen it back in the locker room, but it was a different beast hard. His underwear kept it pressed tight to his upper thigh, pointing toward his hipbone.

"You gonna stare at it or are you gonna suck it?" he asked.

"You tell me," I said.

"Get on your knees."

I did as I was told and Brian stepped in front of me, his dick inches from my face. I started to press my face into it but Brian planted a hand on my forehead and kept me back. He wrapped his other hand around his shaft and started stroking. "This what you want?"

"Yeah."

"That turn you on? Big jock dick waiting for your mouth?" It sounds kind of ridiculous now, but at the time there was nothing hotter than his dirty talk.

"Yeah."

"You want this hockey dick?"

"Yes sir," I said and Brian's mouth broke out into a wicked grin.

"That's what I wanted to hear," he said. He pulled my face into his crotch, his hard dick smashing against my cheek and nose. I kissed, licked, and sucked at his cotton-wrapped erection. Tried to engulf his balls and lick his taint. Through it all, I kept eye contact with him as he looked down in approval. I wrapped my hands around his beefy thighs and rubbed my fingers through the hair on his legs.

I could have serviced him all night, but Brian had other ideas. "Get up."

I stood and Brian embraced me again, kissing me. He slid a hand into the back of my pants and gripped my ass, pushing his crotch against mine. I thought that was sexy enough, until he gripped my ass harder and then picked me up, walked over to the bed, and threw me down. The full weight of his muscular body felt amazing to me. He buried his face into my neck and sucked and licked at my skin, causing my hairs to stand up on end. He ground his crotch against mine like he was trying to hump me into the bed.

Brian swung his leg off me and I started to sit up so that I could regain some control, but he pushed me back down with the palm of his hand. He swung a leg over my head and turned until his crotch was poised above my head and then he sat back, burying my face in the taint of his underwear. I had a momentary panic where I considered that I probably couldn't wrestle him off me if I tried. Then I realized that I had Brian-fucking-Johnston's underwear-clad scent pressed against my face—my fucking nose was buried in the cleft of his ass—and wondered why I would ever want to wrestle him off.

Brian started tugging at my belt and eventually managed to slide down my pants and underwear in one swift push. My dick slapped against my stomach with a satisfying thud that I couldn't hear, but felt. Brian didn't waste any time grabbing it and only gave it a couple of strokes before he leaned forward and engulfed it in his mouth. His hips shifted over my face, dragging his nuts and then his erection over my face. I groaned against his thick cock as he gave me top-notch head. His whole body rocked against me as he stroked and sucked my dick.

I grabbed the waistband of Brian's underwear and tugged at it, trying to hint that I'd like him to remove them.

"You want that dick?"

"Fuck yeah, I want your dick."

He reached one hand down and pushed the waistband under his nuts, exposing his hard dick. He pressed down on it until it was pointing toward my mouth, so I wrapped my lips around it. I thought for a moment that he might try to bury his entire cock in my throat right away, but he was good, cautious, and slow, gently pushing the head of his dick against my tongue. He took his mouth off my dick, continued to stroke it with his hand.

I pushed at him until he rolled onto his side and I took the opportunity to push his briefs completely down his legs. Still face-to-crotch, his cock was there in front of my face in all of its hard glory, exposed for this first time. It was easily eight inches long and looked longer for his heavy nuts sagging in his nutsack.

There was a moment where I couldn't decide what to do first, but his nuts were so damn appealing. I pulled one into my mouth and Brian laughed, almost a giggle. He swallowed my cock again as I reached around to cup his bare ass. The skin of his nutsack was soft and his ball rolled freely around in my mouth. I wanted to bury my face between his ass cheeks, but he was tall enough that the angle was all wrong, and I wasn't about to pull my dick out of his mouth.

We lay there for what felt like a happy eternity, swapping blow jobs and sucking on nuts. I pushed his dick to the side and buried my face in his pubic hair, a feature I was pleased to see that he had. So many gay men were in the habit of trimming it or shaving it down, but Brian's was full and beautiful and warm. The hair curled around his dick and traced onto his nutsack.

Finally, I broke free. "We have to change positions."

"Why?" Brian asked.

"Because I want to eat your ass."

"Oh." He quickly crawled onto all fours, and I positioned myself behind him. Seeing his ass like that, angled up like he was displaying it for me, made me think about fucking him. Something told me that, as aggressive as he was, if there was fucking to be done it was going to be done by him, not to him. Still, he offered his ass to me like a present and I wasn't going to waste the opportunity.

The dense hair on his ass slid down into his crack to make a furry canyon. I spread his cheeks apart and was happy to see his pink pucker staring back at me. I've always been a teaser when it comes to rimming, so I kissed the mounds of his ass cheeks and licked up and down his crack without ever touching his hole. Brian responded enthusiastically, pushing back into my face. His crack was sweaty, already, but clean. It tasted like a more intense version of him.

"Oh God," he said, "will you lick my fucking hole already?" My teasing had taken the assertiveness out of his voice, turned him into a beggar. I obliged, pushing the tip of my tongue right against his wrinkled pucker. I drilled against his hole until it relaxed and my tongue slid inside him.

"Oh, fuck yeah," he groaned into the mattress. I wanted to stick my tongue as far into him as I could, make him come just from the pleasure I could give his asshole. I reached a hand between his legs and tugged on his cock, pulling it back between his legs and stroking it. I could see everything at one time, his begging hole, his hefty nuts, and his thick cock. I dug back in, teasing his hole, kissing it, licking it. Brian was going nuts, and I could feel his nuts tightening.

"I want you to fuck me," he said.

"What?"

"Fucking fuck me!"

Usually you don't have to tell me twice, but I wasn't expecting him to go there. I hopped off the bed and dug into my nightstand for condoms and lube. Brian reached a hand between his legs and was fingering himself, his middle two fingers sliding into his hole. Holy shit, I could have watched him do that all night.

I rolled a condom onto my dick and lubed it up. I crawled onto the bed behind Brian and he slid his fingers out of his ass. His hole flexed, puckering and then relaxing. I poured lube into his crack and rubbed it against his hole. Brian moaned.

I scooted closer until the tip of my dick was butting up against his hole. I pushed against it until Brian relaxed and let the head in. I didn't push in any farther; I wanted Brian to be ready for it. His hands were gripping my sheets, his head turned sideways and pushed against the mattress, his eyes closed. He nodded and I pushed in a little more. Brian groaned and I pushed my dick completely inside him. His groan escalated. "Oh yeah, that's it."

His hole was warm and tight and his sphincter gripped the base of my cock. I hadn't touched my dick since I had started rimming him, except to slide the condom on, and the feeling of his ass wrapped around my length was almost too good. I pulled out slowly and Brian bit his lower lip. I took my time pushing it back in, then pulling out, and pushing back in, like I was taking practice strokes.

"You gonna play around, or you gonna fuck me?" Brian asked. So much for begging—he was still completely in control even though my dick was buried in his ass.

I smacked him on the ass, hard, and he smiled. I pulled my dick out almost as far as it would come without slipping out completely and then rammed it back inside him. His ass cheeks slapped against my pelvis and I wrapped my hands around his hips. I fucked him as well and as hard as I could, my balls slapping his taint with every thrust. Brian reached one hand between his legs, I guess to stroke himself.

"That's right," he said. "That's how you fucking do it."

I pounded him for what I was worth. Not many of the guys I'd fucked had begged for it this much, had proven that they could take a hard fuck. Brian, on the other hand, was begging for it, and he was pure muscle. Pure man. I slapped him on the ass a few more times, and once on the back. He grunted with each hit. I started thinking about all of the other things I could try if we ever had sex again. Like, I wondered if he'd be up for getting punched in the chest. Maybe even in the face. Rough, I know, but the thought of it was enough to push me over the edge.

"I'm going to—" Brian's ass gripped tightly against my cock and he let out a long moan and I lost it, pumping my cum into the condom. I pushed in as far as I could go and held my dick there, my head flaring in the condom and filling the tip with my spunk. Brian let out a victory yell that I'm sure could be heard up and down the hall, like one the one he'd let out on the ice tonight when he hit the winning shot. I collapsed on top of him, my body raising and lowering as he breathed heavily, moaning with each exhale. Finally he relaxed, and we both hit the mattress.

We lay there for a while, breathing in unison. Brian's skin was covered in sweat and I traced lines on his skin with my fingertips.

"That was awesome," I said.

No response. I lifted my head up and looked down at him. He was sound asleep and my dick was still buried in his ass. I pulled it out slowly and then climbed off the bed. My legs were weak and I took a moment to steady myself. I looked down at Brian. There was a huge wet spot on my sheets where he had ejaculated. When he first collapsed onto the mattress it was right onto the wet spot, and his softening dick and balls were covered in his spunk.

I decided to go clean up.

❖

Let me take a moment and tell you that there's nothing more horrifying than seeing a tentacle wrapped around your dick. I get that there's an entire genre of porn dedicated to tentacles wrapping around things and penetrating them. Whatever gets your rocks off, right? But a real-life tentacle, with suckers and everything, wrapped around your real-life dick? Horrifying.

It was the condom that saved my life—Safer Sex, kids!—or at least my dick. I stumbled backward and the condom slid right off, the tentacle still gripping it tightly. The thick, suckery muscle flopped to the ground and curled up around the latex tube, pulling it back into the toilet bowl. There was a sucking noise and then the condom disappeared completely.

I backed up into Brian, startled awake by my scream, and he put his arms around me protectively. It would have been sweet and romantic except I didn't want to stop, I wanted to get as far as fucking possible away from baby Cthulhu as I could. I pushed an elbow back into Brian's ribs and he loosened his grip, letting me go.

"What the fuck is that?" he said. I would have come back with a snarky answer, except I didn't have one. I didn't have any answers. And the thing, whatever it was, was still coming out of the toilet. Its tentacles were draped across the bathroom floor now and seemed to keep coming. That bathroom was small, really small. Toilet, sink, and a stand-up shower, with standing room for one at a time. I was lucky to have a private bathroom at all, though, living in the dorms. Most dorms have communal bathrooms. Of course, luck is subjective and mine seemed to have just gone AWOL.

Two of the tentacles had managed to make it out of the doorway, and Brian and I had backed up against a far wall. The tentacles were probing, feeling about like a blind man with a wet, floppy cane. I stumbled over something and looked down to see Brian's duffel bag. He had brought his equipment with him after the game. Equipment... game...hockey! Hockey stick! His hockey stick was leaning against the wall next to me! I grabbed it and pushed it in his direction.

"What do you want me to do?" he asked. So much for being big and strong and proactive.

"I want you to hit it."

"Oh," he said. He took the stick from me and spread his legs like he was bracing himself. Classic hockey stance except the only thing hockey about him right then was the stick. Otherwise he was still completely naked. As one of the tentacles came close to his foot, he chopped down with the hockey stick. A howl came from...somewhere. It vibrated the walls, resonated the pipes in the floor, and rattled the toilet. The tentacles shuddered, and the one that Brian had hit coiled up on itself. Another tentacle (how do you identify tentacles when telling a story? Tentacle #1? Tentacle #2?) lashed out and wrapped around the stick. Brian put up a valiant fight and played tug-o-war, but the Cthulhu-thing had a major advantage: it was made of pure muscle and had suckers. Brian had a lot of muscles, and if I were speaking metaphorically I would say he was all muscle, but when compared to the Cthulhu-thing, he had too many bones and guts and things taking up room in his body. And no suckers. The tentacle won the tug-o-war and yanked the hockey stick from Brian's hands.

While I was watching this I had failed to notice another tentacle (tentacle #3?) slither its way to my foot. I caught it only in time to feel it slap against my skin, its suckers making tiny sucking pulses against my skin as it coiled up my naked calf muscle. I squealed. This wasn't one of my prouder moments, I must say. I did a little dance, trying to shake it off me. The suckers sucked harder. When that didn't work I did my best to stomp on it with my free foot. I finally connected with the tentacle but it was too thick and slippery and I went down, falling on my bare ass. The tentacle curled up on itself and pulled me closer to the bathroom. I twisted around and tried to crawl away from it but I couldn't find anything to grab. Brian had walked farther away along the wall. I called out to him. He fell to his knees and reached for my hand without hesitation. I'll give him that. We managed to lock arms, his hand on my wrist, my hand on his, and he pulled. I could only think of the hockey stick. Brian wasn't going to win this tug-o-war, either. I did my best to crawl toward him, but I only succeeded in giving myself rug burn. There was nothing for me to grab onto other than Brian, and the tentacle was so strong. I could feel it squeezing my leg and I was worried that my bone would snap. At the same time it was crawling up my leg, getting a better grip.

I tried to think of anything in the dorm room that we could use for a weapon. The hockey stick was gone, pulled into the bathroom and enveloped in the cephalopod's grip. I didn't have a knife, or a gun, or… I had a cherry bomb!

"Brian! The cherry bombs!"

"What?"

"The box, in my underwear drawer! Max's fucking cherry bombs!"

Brian let go of my wrist and stumbled toward my dresser. When he did, I slid another two feet closer to the bathroom. I kicked my free leg out to brace myself against the door frame.

Brian had to leap over some tentacles to get there. He yanked open the drawer and started digging through my underwear—I had a lot—until he found the box. He pulled it out and tossed the lid to the side. In the box, twelve little cherry bombs sat in a plastic tray like angry red eggs with wicks.

"Why do you have cherry bombs?" he asked.

The pain in my leg got to be too much, so I let the tentacles pull me into the bathroom. The cold tiles felt good against my raw skin. I braced my leg against the toilet and the force from the tentacles pulled me upright. To an outsider, I might have looked like I was doing my damnedest to pull a long, fleshy rope from the toilet. Instead, I was trying my damnedest to keep a long, fleshy rope from pulling me into the toilet.

"Hurry up!" I said.

"I need a fucking lighter!" Shit.

"Look in the junk bowl!" The junk bowl was a glass fishbowl I kept on the dresser, where I dumped change and anything else small that got shoved into my pockets. I didn't remember having a lighter, but if I did, it would probably be there. I tried to peer out of the bathroom to see what Brian was doing, but the tentacle was so strong I couldn't lean back far enough. My foot was starting to bruise against the base of the toilet.

"Got it!" Brian said as he appeared in the doorway. He was holding the box of cherry bombs like a waiter holds a tray. His hands were shaking, and the tiny red bombs were rattling in the plastic.

"Set it on the sink," I said. "Hurry!"

Brian set the tray down and took a bomb out. He flicked at the lighter but it wouldn't light, only spark. "Motherfuck," he said, biting his lower lip. He did the same thing when he was about to come. I'm not sure what correlation you can find there, but you notice odd things in odd situations. Finally the lighter lit and the cherry bomb's wick caught immediately. Brian threw it into the toilet.

And the wick sizzled out in the water.

"Fucking hell," I said. "Do it again. But wait until it's about to blow this time!"

"I'm trying!"

He reached for another bomb but he caught the corner of the tray instead. It tumbled to the floor, eleven little red balls hitting the ground and scattering among the tentacles. Brian dropped to his hands and knees and reached frantically around. A tentacle lashed around his wrist and he screamed. He hammered at the tentacle with his free hand and finally it let go of him. Again, the Cthulhu-thing moaned and the floor vibrated. I wondered why no one had stopped in. Surely this was all loud enough to catch someone's attention.

Brian reached for a cherry bomb and stood up. The lighter lit on the first try this time, and the wick caught.

"Wait for it," I said.

"I am, I am!"

Another tentacle shot up and tried to catch Brian's arm, but he managed to evade it. The wick was burning so fucking slowly. The toilet bowl was starting to groan beneath my foot. Brian had to dance backward out of the bathroom to keep the tentacles from grabbing him, and I was getting worried that the bomb was going to blow in his hands.

I shouldn't have worried. If there was anything Brian could do, it was score a goal. I watched as the cherry bomb and its now barely existent wick soared through the air, right next to my head, and landed in the toilet. It exploded on impact.

I felt the explosion mostly in my balls, and only then did I think about the repercussions of exploding a cherry bomb mere inches away from my naked body. The blast felt like I had been kicked in the nuts. The tentacle let go almost immediately, though, and I fell backward. The toilet bowl cracked and then exploded and water splashed out over the bathroom.

If the Cthulhu-thing had howled earlier, it screamed now. There was no way no one else heard it, the whole fucking building vibrated. I could see we'd hurt it. There were tentacle bits and pieces flopping about on the wet floor, some of them nearly full-length. The ones that weren't dismembered quivered and then started to pull back into the toilet. In seconds, it was gone. The pipes rattled loudly in the wall and then stopped. If it weren't for the exploded toilet bowl, the water flowing onto the floor, and the calamari chunks, you would have never known it was there.

"What the hell was that?" Brian asked. I couldn't help but wonder if this hurt my chances of getting him to come over again. Then I remembered that a giant fucking monster had just tried to eat me in my bathroom, and I realized that *I* didn't want to come over again, and it was my fucking dorm room.

The words of the so-called street preacher came back to me: "I myself did not more than a fortnight ago catch a very plain discourse of evil powers in the Hill behind my house; wherein there were a rattling and rolling, groaning, screeching, and hissing, such as no things of this Earth could raise up, and which must needs have come from those caves that only black magick can discover, and only the Devil unlock."

Fucking hell.

"Gorgons, and Hydras, and Chimaeras—dire stories of Celaeno and the Harpies—may reproduce themselves in the brain of superstition—but they were there before. They are transcripts, types—the archetypes are in us, and eternal. How else should the recital of that which we know in a waking sense to be false come to affect us at all? Is it that we naturally conceive terror from such objects, considered in their capacity of being able to inflict upon us bodily injury? O, least of all! These terrors are of older standing. They date beyond body—or without the body, they would have been the same. ....That the kind of fear here treated is purely spiritual— that it is strong in proportion as it is objectless on earth, that it predominates in the period of our sinless infancy—are difficulties the solution of which might afford some probable insight into our ante-mundane condition, and a peep at least into the shadowland of pre-existence."
—Charles Lamb, "Witches and Other Night-Fears"

CONTRIBUTORS

ERIC ARVIN lives in the same sleepy Indiana river town where he grew up. He graduated from Hanover College with a BA in history and has lived, for brief periods, in Italy and Australia. He has survived brain surgery and his own loud-mouthed personal demons. Eric is the author of *Woke Up in a Strange Place*, *Subsurdity*, *Another Enchanted April*, *Simple Men*, and various other sundry and not-so-sundry writings. He intends to live the rest of his days with tongue in cheek and eyes set to roam.

JONATHAN ASCHE's work has appeared in numerous anthologies, including *Best Gay Erotica 2011*, *Brief Encounters*, and *Afternoon Pleasures*. He is also the author of the erotic novels *Mindjacker* and *Moneyshots*, and the short story collection *Kept Men*. He lives in Atlanta with his husband Tomé.

'NATHAN BURGOINE lives in Ottawa with his husband. His previous fiction appears in *Fool for Love*, *I Do Two*, and *Tented*. His nonfiction appears in *I Like It Like That* and *5x5 Literary Magazine*. The Triad make their first appearance in *Blood Sacraments* (Bold Strokes Books). He's online at n8an.livejournal.com.

DALE CHASE has been writing male erotica for more than a decade with numerous stories in magazines and anthologies. She has two story collections in print: *If The Spirit Moves You: Ghostly Gay Erotica*, from Lethe Press, and *The Company He Keeps: Victorian Gentlemen's Erotica*, from Bold Strokes Books. Check Dale out at dalechasestrokes.com.

Jamie Freeman (jamiefreeman.net) lives in a small Florida town. He has published a mix of horror, romance, and erotica. He recently published the romantic novellas *The Marriage of True Minds* and *66 Hours in the Devil's House*. His stories are included in *Blood Fruit*, *Video Boys*, and *Beautiful Boys*.

Evan Gilbert is a Southern boy who writes policy and training manuals for various corporations. He spends his free time watching movies, reading fiction of every kind, and writing erotica.

David Holly lives in Portland, Oregon. His books include *Delicious Darkness*, a darkly erotic collection of over-the-top gay fantasy stories. His stories have appeared in *Best Gay Romance*, *Best Gay Erotica*, *Boy Crazy*, and many other publications. Find David Holly at facebook.com/david.holly2 and gaywriter.org.

Jeff Mann has published three poetry chapbooks, three books of poetry, two collections of personal essays, a collection of memoir and poetry, and a volume of short fiction. He teaches creative writing at Virginia Tech in Blacksburg, Virginia.

Anthony McDonald lives in England. His stories have appeared in many anthologies, and he is the author of the novels *Adam* and *Orange Bitter, Orange Sweet*, both originally published by Gay Men's Press, and *Blue Sky Adam* and *Getting Orlando*, both from BigFib Books.

Lloyd Meeker, raised in a religious commune in the mountain West, began his formal trained as an energy healer at age ten. As an adult, he served as a minister and teacher in the community before striking out on an individual path of mystical discovery. His most recent work is the novel *Traveling Light* (MLR Press, 2011).

Johnny Murdoc (johnnymurdoc.com) is thirty and lives in St. Louis, Missouri, with his partner of nine years. He is a co-founder of Sex Positive St. Louis (sexstl.com), likes bike rides and sci-fi movies, and is most recent collection of erotic fiction, essays, and photography is *Blowjob 3*.

GREGORY L. NORRIS is a full-time professional writer with work published in numerous national magazines and fiction anthologies. He once worked as a screenwriter on two episodes of Paramount's *Star Trek: Voyager* and is a former writer for *Sci Fi*, the official magazine of the Syfy Channel. Norris lives and writes at the outer limits of New Hampshire.

DAVEM VERNE, who has been thinking about love and writing about sex since 1995, is devoted to erotic literature and the revelation of sexual desire on paper. While his early stories lent themselves to fanciful journeys around the world, his new millennium work, including "Meet Martin," focus on *l'eros extraordinaire* and sex that is supernatural. A longtime resident of New England, Verne has contributed stories to numerous anthologies, including *Frat Sex*, *Dorm Porn*, and *Blood Sacraments*. "As with *The Story of O*, I believe the literary canon will eventually embrace the erotic genre and I hope to be present when it happens."

MARK WILDYR's short stories and novellas, more than fifty and counting and exploring developing sexual awareness and intercultural relationships, have appeared in the magazines *Freshmen* and *Men* and in anthologies from assorted publishers, among them Alyson, Arsenal Pulp, Cleis, Companion, Green Candy, Haworth, and STARbooks. *Cut Hand,* his full-length historical novel, was published in 2010. His website is markwildyr.com.

About the Editor

RICHARD LABONTÉ (tattyhill@gmail.com), when he's not skimming dozens of anthology submissions a month, or reviewing one hundred or so books a year for Q Syndicate, or turning turgid bureaucratic prose into comprehensible English for the Inter-American Development Bank or the Reeves of Renfrew County, Ontario, or coordinating the judging of the Lambda Literary Awards, or crafting the best croutons ever at his weekend work in a Bowen Island recovery center kitchen, likes to startle deer as he walks terrier/schnauzer Zak, accompanied by his husband, Asa, through the island's temperate rainforest, where he has lived for several years, after managing gay bookstores in LA, SF, and NY from 1979 to 2000. In season, he fills pails with salmonberries, blackberries, and huckleberries. Yum. Since 1997, he has edited almost forty erotic anthologies, though "pornographer" was not an original career goal.

Books Available From Bold Strokes Books

Three Days by L.T. Marie. In a town like Vegas where anything can happen, Shawn and Dakota find that the stakes are love at all costs, and it's a gamble neither can afford to lose. (978-1-60282-569-7)

Swimming to Chicago by David-Matthew Barnes. As the lives of the adults around them unravel, high school students Alex and Robby form an unbreakable bond, vowing to do anything to stay together—even if it means leaving everything behind.(978-1-60282-572-7)

Hostage Moon by AJ Quinn. Hunter Roswell thought she had left her past behind, until a serial killer begins stalking her. Can FBI profiler Sara Wilder help her find her connection to the killer before he strikes on blood moon? (978-1-60282-568-0)

Erotica Exotica: Tales of Magic, Sex, and the Supernatural, edited by Richard Labonté. Today's top gay erotica authors offer sexual thrills and perverse arousal, spooky chills, and magical orgasms in these stories exploring arcane mystery, supernatural seduction, and sex that haunts in a manner both weird and wondrous. (978-1-60282-570-3)

Blue by Russ Gregory. Matt and Thatcher find themselves in the crosshairs of a psychotic killer stalking gay men in the streets of Austin, and only a 103-year-old nursing home resident holds the key to solving the murders—but can she give up her secrets in time to save them? (978-1-60282-571-0)

Balance of Forces: Toujours Ici by Ali Vali. Immortal Kendal Richoux's life began during the reign of Egypt's only female pharaoh, and history has taught her the dangers of getting too close to anyone who hasn't harnessed the power of time, but as she prepares for the most important battle of her long life, can she resist her attraction to Piper Marmande? (978-1-60282-567-3)

Contemporary Gay Romances by Felice Picano. This collection of short fiction from legendary novelist and memoirist Felice Picano are as different from any standard "romances" as you can get, but they will linger in the mind and memory. (978-1-60282-639-7)